About tl

Clive Hart lives in the middle of England, where he spends as much time as he can fighting in armour on horseback. He is a small part of an international community dedicated to recreating medieval mounted combat as close as it originally was.

The two knights in the cover picture are the author and Steven Lawton. The horse that Clive is riding is the mighty Charlie, who belongs to Historic Equitation.

For information on other books: www.clivehart.net

By Clive Hart
The Rise and Fall of the Mounted Knight

The Legend of Richard Keynes series:
Book One: Golden Spurs
Book Two: Brothers in Arms
Book Three: Dogs of War
Book Four: Knight Errant *Out soon

Contents

A LANDED KNIGHT

Normandy, Late Summer, 1166

Yvetot was still just as run-down as it had been on Richard's last visit. This time though, as he entered he rode beside his new lord, Roger de Cailly. He rode under his blue, green and yellow banner too, as the column of armoured knights turned off the main road and into the village.

'I always think,' de Cailly said, 'that Yvetot is neglected because no one knows it even lies off this road at all.'

Richard nodded and wondered if de Cailly knew just how far its fortunes had fallen.

'The apples are starting to look good,' he heard from behind him, and Richard recognised the extensive orchards that grew on both side of Yvetot's entry road. The sun rose high in the summer sky and he looked forward to washing the road's dust off his face once he'd got to the castle's well.

Ahead of them rode Lord Tancarville on his fine and high stepping Spanish horse. The red Tancarville banner dangled lifelessly from the pole held by his bannerman, and irritated the horse's white ears. His son rode on his left and pointed to their front. 'Trust me, father, the whole place is about to be reclaimed by the wilds of nature,' he said.

'Quiet, boy,' Tancarville said, 'remember that this is still my land above all others.'

'Apart from the king,' the Little Lord said.

Tancarville shot his son an angered glance. 'Watch yourself, boy. Fighting one battle and capturing one knight does not make you a man.'

'You did make me a knight though, father, so I am a man. I

need land too, you should grant me Yvetot.'

'Yvetot? I thought this place was about to be reclaimed by nature?' Tancarville laughed.

The Little Lord frowned and looked away.

Richard glanced over at de Cailly and asked in a low voice, 'could they take Yvetot away from me?'

'Yes, but worry not, it is too poor to be worth the trouble of fighting me for it.'

The head of the column separated from the body of the Norman army, the main body of which continued on to lodge in the town to the west. Some of Tancarville's other knights followed him towards Yvetot for the night, most of whom probably expected better lodgings than they were going to get. The village came into view after the orchard, a set of wooden houses surrounding a large pond.

'It has gone to ruin,' de Cailly said with saddened eyes.

'The castle is worse,' Richard said, 'at least people still live in the village, the ones Sir Thomas didn't kill before, anyway. The castle only had Lady Sophie and some servants in it last time we were here.'

'That was only a week or two ago, my boy,' De Cailly looked over to the church that sat on the southern edge of the pond. Its graveyard had a dozen graves with fresher mounds of earth over them. One had a large wooden cross and flowers heaped up at its base.

'Sir Arthur's grave,' Richard said.

'They did love him,' de Cailly said, 'I still cannot believe the Little Lord could kill the old man by accident. Even so, that did not justify their revolt.'

'Sir Thomas didn't think so either,' Richard said.

The senior knight shook his head. 'Such heavy handedness will not end well. I fear your reception will be cold, especially as Sir Thomas is with us,' he said.

'They won't remember me from before, but they will remember Sir Thomas putting down their attack. They won't forget the Little Lord darkening his sword with their fathers and sons blood either,' Richard said.

De Cailly looked at his new vassal. 'My boy, you sound almost like a man,' he said. The knight grimaced at the clogged ditches that ran from the pond and out into the common land beyond the houses. 'The water cannot reach the commons, let alone the fields,' he said.

'Will they accept me as their lord?' Richard asked.

'Their place is to serve their lord, not worry about who he is,' de Cailly said. He scratched his black hair and straightened his posture up so his hunchback almost went away.

'But I don't know what I'm doing,' Richard said, his eyes darted around the land which was now his.

'I knighted you at Neufchâtel because I thought you were ready. You can fight, ride, and have a mind to you. You will work it out. These people will see a knight, young for sure, but a real knight. They will respect your golden spurs,' de Cailly said.

Richard began to feel the weight of his new spurs on his heels and looked closer at the village. 'Where are they all though?' he asked.

De Cailly studied the houses and looked over at the common land in the distance. Three pigs and a handful of cattle grazed on it, but no human life could be seen.

'Something is not right,' the elder knight said.

Tancarville and his son were quiet in front too, their heads searching their surroundings. A hush also fell over the riders behind, who were Tancarville's remaining knights, Sir Thomas and his squires, and Richard's three companions.

'The village fields are empty,' Richard pointed to the fields that stretched out in long strips on the left of the track.

The hedges along the track were growing well, too well, and de Cailly sighed. 'If they have all fled, then I shall find new tenants for you,' he said, 'it will cost me much.'

'Look,' the Little Lord shouted. He pointed to the wooden palisade of the castle that appeared around the hedges at the end of the track.

'The gate is open,' Richard said.

'The walls are breached,' de Cailly said.

'That happened when we were last here, but I'm sure Sir Thomas's men had repaired them,' Richard said slowly.

'Then they have been broken down again,' de Cailly said.

'But why?' Richard asked.

'Lady Sophie,' de Cailly said as Tancarville led the knights

5

through the gate and into the yard of the castle's outer bailey.

Richard's mouth dropped open. The whole village of Yvetot was in the bailey, trampling the overly long grass, exploring the ramshackle stable block, and to everyone's astonishment, placing a ladder against the stone wall of the inner bailey. On the walls a lonely figure darted back and forth, in a red dress with long blonde hair. The figure threw a rock down onto the ladder and the top two rungs cracked and splintered.

'God's teeth,' Tancarville shouted, 'what is the meaning of this?'

His roar froze everyone. The woman in the red dress straightened herself up and looked over.

'Lady Sophie?' Richard's face reddened.

De Cailly looked at him. 'She won't bite,' he smiled.

'Do you know who I am?' Tancarville roared. He wore his mail armour and his red painted helm, and his shield was slung over his back. To the villagers, he was terrifying. Some of them ran into the stables to hide, but most realised they had nowhere to go. For a moment the only movement was from the flag of red with a sheaf of golden wheat on the top of the castle's tower. The four men holding the ladder exchanged glances, then put it down and tried to mingle in with their fellows.

'You,' Tancarville shouted, 'you are their priest, what in God's name are you doing with them?'

A tall man in brown robes stepped forwards with his head down. 'My lord, I was trying to calm them,' he said.

The villagers howled out in protest, one ran over and pointed at him.

'He told us that it was unnatural to be ruled by a woman,' the man cried.

'Quiet, Reeve,' the Priest spun around.

'Stop bickering,' Tancarville said and drew his sword.

The Reeve and the villagers flinched, but the Priest stood his ground.

'You, you are the Reeve of Yvetot?' Tancarville asked.

'Yes, my lord,' the Reeve replied. He was the fattest of the villagers in the inner bailey, dark hair framed an oval face with big brown eyes. His tunic was free from patches.

Tancarville walked his horse up to him and peered down.

'The Reeve serves his lord, he is his brain in the village. What should we do with such a disloyal Reeve?'

The Reeve kept quiet and his eyes dropped down to the floor.

'I suppose you will claim to have been calming the mob, too?'

'Yes, my lord,' the Reeve muttered.

The Priest snorted.

'Pathetic,' Tancarville sighed, 'both of you.'

'I told you, father, you should waste the village and be done with them,' the Little Lord said.

'Someone please tell me why you are trying to storm the walls of one of my castles before I set Sir Thomas on to you again,' Tancarville said, ignoring his son.

The villagers in the stables made a run for it. A dozen of them reached the wooden palisade and started to make a human ladder out of themselves in an effort to get out.

Tancarville spurred his horse on and the Spanish stallion leapt towards them. It covered the ground in a moment. 'Cease this madness or we shall run you all down,' he shouted, his sword pointed at the human ladder.

The peasants scrambled away from the wall and dropped to the floor in supplication.

'God's legs,' Tancarville said and wheeled his horse around, 'Reeve, explain.'

The Reeve looked up as Tancarville approached. His horse snorted in the Reeve's face and he recoiled away from it.

'They will not serve a woman,' he said.

'I hardly blame them,' Tancarville said and sheathed his sword.

'They'd serve me,' the Little Lord said.

'Quiet, boy,' Tancarville said, 'you killed their lord, they would rip you apart. I have no interest in this. Roger.'

'Yes?' de Cailly said. The knight looked at Richard, 'come with me, let's get this done with.'

Richard nodded and spoke softly to his horse, 'Come on, Soli.'

'Roger, this is your castle, as you are so fond of telling me. You sort this mess out, I am going inside to see if this godforsaken place has any food,' Tancarville said.

The Norman lord nodded at his son and rode up to the gate of the stone wall. It opened and Sophie's blonde head peered out into the yard. Tancarville entered along with his knights, leaving Richard alone with his new lord and only his friends for support. Sir Thomas and his squires remained by the palisade's gate to ensure the villagers stayed put.

'Do you know who I am?' De Cailly asked the Reeve.

'Of course, my lord, you are Sir Roger. The lord of Yvetot is your man, as you are Lord Tancarville's man.'

De Cailly snorted. 'I am your lord indeed, and I have appointed a new lord of Yvetot. You no longer need to concern yourself with questions over the right of women to rule.'

'Praise the lord,' the Priest said, 'peace shall be upon us. That Englishwoman was clearly possessed by the Devil, what woman hurls rocks at men from battlements? She is an affront to God's nature.'

'Lady Sophie is not going anywhere,' de Cailly said, 'she is the legitimate ruler, and she will marry your new lord.'

The Priest frowned. 'But she's English.'

'I'm English myself, or have you forgotten? You will have to reconcile yourself to the idea,' de Cailly said.

'Of course, my lord.'

'People of Yvetot,' de Cailly raised his voice.

Skittish eyes settled on him from around the yard.

'Your new lord will marry Lady Sophie and all shall return to normal,' de Cailly said loudly.

The crowd cheered and the Priest made the sign of the cross.

De Cailly raised his hand up to show them Richard. 'Sir Richard.'

Richard had never been announced as a Sir before, but then, he'd only been a Sir for a few days.

The crowd's cheers faded into whispers.

'He is just a boy,' the Reeve said. His brown eyes searched Richard and made him uncomfortable.

'He is a knight, blooded in battle,' de Cailly said, 'and he is your new lord whether you think he is old enough or not.'

The Reeve held his tongue and silence fell over the bailey.

'Well,' de Cailly said.

'What?' Richard asked.

The older knight's dark eyes twinkled. 'You have to talk to your people.'

'Me?'

'You are their lord, they should know your voice.'

Richard gulped. His hands, only recently free from bandages, sweated.

'Hurry up, my boy, you are showing weakness,' de Cailly said.

Richard felt a cold stabbing pain in his stomach. In a fight he could trust his riding at least, but here, he had never raised his voice enough to know if he even could. He tried to remember how his father had spoken to his people at his old home at Keynes, but the memory was ragged and he knew he was wasting time. Richard took a deep breath and pushed Solis on towards the villagers.

'I am Richard, a knight of Sir Roger. I am your new lord and I will do everything in my power to improve your lives.'

'That's brave,' a voice came from behind de Cailly.

Richard knew it was Bowman's so he ignored it.

'Sir Roger,' the Priest said.

'Yes?'

'Do my ears deceive me, or is Sir Richard English?'

'He is,' de Cailly said.

The villagers groaned as one.

'I don't suppose, if God could see fit to guide you, you could possibly find a good Norman to run Yvetot?' the Priest said.

'You had a good Norman,' Richard said loudly, a sudden anger fuelled his voice, 'and look where that got you. Your houses have fallen down, your crops are failing, and your castle is a disgrace.'

De Cailly cocked an eyebrow at his new knight.

'That's more like it,' Bowman said from the background.

'Who are you to care if I'm English once your fields are full and your houses can keep the rain out again?' Richard continued.

Villagers spoke amongst themselves.

'The problem is,' the Reeve said, 'speaking for the others of course, that you are still English.'

Richard sighed. Maybe being a landed knight wasn't quite as good a thing as he'd thought.

'Bloody Normans,' Bowman complained.

'Quiet,' de Cailly said to him, then turned to Richard, 'they will come around, and if not, who cares. You are young enough to impose yourself.'

'The people will not stand for two Englishmen ruling them,' the Priest said, 'Normans should rule in Normandy.'

'We want a Norman,' a voice shouted from a group of villagers.

'A Norman,' another voice cried.

Richard heard the hoof beats of Sir Thomas and his squires, and turned to see them approach. Sir Thomas, a dour knight at the best of times, scowled. He drew his sword and the villagers bunched together behind the Reeve and Priest.

'The villagers,' the Reeve stammered with his eyes glued to Sir Thomas, 'I will keep the villagers in line, of course.'

'Of course,' de Cailly said, 'now go, all of you go before you anger me further, or Sir Thomas loses his patience.'

Sir Thomas and his men slammed to a halt behind Richard, their point well made.

'Yes, my lord,' the Reeve said, and rushed out of the castle. The villagers followed, leaving behind their broken ladder.

Bowman rode up to Richard as they left. He swept back his blonde hair and grinned. 'I think that went well.'

'Shut up,' Richard said.

'We need to go inside,' de Cailly said, 'you need to speak to your future wife.'

'Bowman, can you see to the horses?' Richard asked.

'I'm not your squire, remember, young lord,' Bowman raised his eyebrows, 'but I'd rather stay out here away from those Tancarville vipers, so I will.'

The tall man dismounted gingerly and stretched one leg out once he was on the ground. 'Come on, Sarjeant, let us be our young lord's servants today,' Bowman said.

Sarjeant dismounted his own horse as his blue eyes darted around the yard. 'I did not like it here last time,' he said.

De Cailly dismounted and handed his reins to Sarjeant as Richard got down from Solis and patted him on the neck. The palomino horse nuzzled his side before Richard gave him to Bowman.

'How is the leg?' Richard asked.

'Still attached,' Bowman replied and took Solis away with a

mild limp.

Richard's third companion watched Bowman and Sarjeant go. 'Is anyone going to take my horse?' he asked.

'You can lodge your own horse, Sir Wobble,' de Cailly said, 'it would be best if you did not enter the tower while Lord Tancarville is there.'

Sir Wobble glanced over at the tower. His brown eyes scanned the white tower and the banner at its top. 'I think I would rather go and harvest some of those apples, anyway,' he said.

'Good idea, the last thing we need is you badgering Lord Tancarville for a new horse again,' Richard said.

Sir Wobble looked at Richard and seemed about to argue, but then shrugged and turned his horse away.

'Sir Wobble, I want that horse you are on back, remember,' de Cailly said, 'I am not giving it to you.'

'Of course,' Sir Wobble said as he left the castle.

'You should give it to him,' Richard said to his new lord, 'he has his golden spurs, and with a horse that would mean there would be two of us knights here once you have left instead of just me.'

'Are you scared of the villagers?' de Cailly smiled.

'Shouldn't I be?'

'Probably,' de Cailly said, 'but we need to go and get to Lady Sophie before the Little Lord tries to win her over in that way of his.'

Richard frowned and followed the knight through the gate in the stone wall. It felt good to stretch his legs out after the long ride, and the cool of the tower would be welcome, but Sophie scared him more than the villagers. At least they would run from his sword.

They ascended the wooden steps that led to the first-floor door into the white tower. His white tower. Inside the castle's small hall, Tancarville was looking down at the empty lord's chair. On one of its wooden arms there were dark blotches that stained the otherwise bright wood.

'Is that where he died?' Tancarville asked.

The Little Lord looked away. 'Yes, father.'

Tancarville kicked the chair away and looked around. 'This

hall is smaller than I remember, and the fire isn't even lit. By all that is holy, the food on the table is rotten.'

Richard realised that the table and room was still set out from their last visit. The logs they'd brought in to sit on still littered the floorboards, and bowls of half-eaten pottage lingered on the tables of uneven height. Flies buzzed around the spoiled food.

The Little Lord looked up and saw him staring at the pottage bowls. He scowled.

Richard thought of making a comment but held himself back.

'Did anyone else notice the stables?' Tancarville asked.

'Not fit for a horse,' de Cailly said.

'I'm not putting my horse in there,' Tancarville said, 'we are going to the town. I don't approve of this scheme of yours anyway, Roger, you are getting above your station.'

De Cailly's face remained unreadable.

'I will leave Sir Thomas with you for tonight, just to give the impression that I care,' Tancarville said.

That was good, Richard thought, Sir Thomas was the ward of Eustace Martel, who Richard needed to question before he was ransomed away.

'Come on, boy,' Tancarville said to his son, 'unless you want to see Lady Sophie?'

The Little Lord's eyes bulged and his red head shook. 'No, father.'

Richard felt a chasm open up in his stomach as he remembered what Sophie had done to the Little Lord. He almost felt sympathy for the young man. Almost.

'You can tell Sir Wobble,' Tancarville said, 'that he can stay here for all I care. Out of respect for his parents I will not dismiss him, but my life would be simpler if he did not return to Castle Tancarville.'

'Very well,' de Cailly said.

Tancarville took one last look at the hall, snorted, and stomped out of the room, his mail shirt clinked as he went.

Richard realised he'd been holding his breath, and let it all out once both Tancarvilles had gone.

'I was worried he'd stay,' de Cailly said.

Richard nodded. 'I didn't know how we'd all fit in here to sleep,' he said.

'The Little Lord's reaction to the mention of Lady Sophie was curious.'

Richard's eyes unintentionally flickered to the doorway.

'No matter, I presume she fled upstairs when our glorious leader entered. Come, it is time for you to meet your future wife,' de Cailly said.

Richard wasn't sure he was quite ready for that, but de Cailly led the way so he followed. They ascended the staircase to the chamber above and de Cailly gently pushed the door open.

The chamber was as Richard remembered it. A four posted bed, curtained with faded fabrics, stood as the centrepiece of the room on the back wall. Linen drapes hung down around the bed. The bedding was not on the bed however, it was crumpled in a pile in the opposite corner of the room. Red fabric poked out from under it.

'Lady Sophie,' de Cailly said.

A face with wide red eyes protruded out from under the pile of bedding. Her hair was matted and tears had left streaks down her face. She sniffed. 'Are you here to kill me or save me?'

'Marry you,' de Cailly smiled.

Sophie groaned and pulled a blanket back over her head. She lay there a moment before the covers were thrown aside. 'Death would be better,' she said in a quiet but hard tone. Her eyes met Richard's. 'What is he doing here?'

De Cailly smiled

'Oh. You're serious? Him?' she said and pushed herself to her feet. She smoothed down her red dress. 'He is not old enough to protect me from those wild beasts outside. They were going to burn me, you know. It only took them two days to come here and demand that I leave.'

'My dear, I am sorry for whatever has happened, and I deeply regret the manner of your husband's death,' de Cailly said.

'Sir Arthur? I don't care about that,' Sophie said, 'I care that I was only a day away from being torn apart by a mob. Even if they hadn't, I only have one servant who stayed loyal, and we are out of food. I was going to starve to death, the daughter of the Earl of Leicester.'

De Cailly's eyes stared flatly at her. 'We both know you aren't the daughter of the Earl of Leicester. Leave that fiction for the villagers and guests. Richard knows it too,' he said.

'He is not going to save me, is he? Does he have the first idea how to run a village?'

'No,' de Cailly smiled, 'that is why I am keeping you here. Because you do.'

'You want me to be the lord and have this boy hide behind my skirts?'

'That is not how I would phrase it,' de Cailly said.

Richard frowned.

'He learns quickly,' de Cailly said, 'and that stain on the chair downstairs will serve to remind him of the price of failure.'

'I want that chair gone,' Sophie said.

'The chair stays,' de Cailly said.

Sophie frowned. 'Do I really have to trust my safety to this boy?'

De Cailly sighed and walked over to the window that looked out over the baileys. 'He will grow into his new lordship, and you will grow to work with him.'

'That is not what I'm worried about, I'm quite sure he will do as I ask,' Sophie looked at Richard.

Richard made an effort to remain as still as possible, but it didn't fool de Cailly who stared at him quizzically.

'I don't know what went on here,' the senior knight said, 'but you will make it work.'

'How do I know he won't run away,' Sophie said.

'It is my duty,' Richard said confidently, then paused. He glanced over to de Cailly and swallowed. 'Although my sister is in distress in England and I do need to rescue her.'

'Oh, that,' de Cailly said, 'in time Richard will need to see to his family problems, but I expect him to stabilise Yvetot first.'

'Family problems?' Sophie asked.

'My uncle and the prisoner with Sir Thomas killed my mother and stole my manor in England. The prisoner, Eustace Martel, took my sister for fun and left her in a nunnery. I need to move her from there before Eustace goes back for her,' Richard said.

'But you can't leave me here alone,' Sophie frowned, 'not with these monsters at my gates.'

'Once an heir is on the way you will be secure. Your heir will be born here so the villagers will see him as Norman. Once you are with child, Richard has my permission to cross the sea,' de Cailly said.

Sophie's eyes met Richards. Richard was well aware that Sophie was probably already with child, except that it wasn't going to be his. His eyes lowered to her belly and instinctively her hands went to it.

De Cailly noticed. He thought for a moment but Sophie turned away and went to the north window.

'I see it all,' de Cailly laughed, 'Richard my boy, I didn't know you had it in you.'

'Had what in me?'

'Before her husband was even cold in the ground? I don't know if I'm shocked or impressed,' the knight laughed.

'I didn't do anything,' Richard said.

'Quiet,' Sophie spun round.

Richard's eyes darted between the two of them.

De Cailly's smile faded. 'Do we have a problem? If you have already made a child in her, then your problems here should be short lived.'

Sophie remained tight lipped and Richard felt his cheeks glow.

'The behaviour of both of you tells me she is pregnant already, but your coyness tells me I have something to worry about,' de Cailly said.

'Something happened,' Richard said.

'No, don't,' Sophie said, 'not if you wish to marry me.'

'Don't try to blackmail your husband before you are even married,' de Cailly said, 'Richard, speak.'

Richard licked his lips. The glare from Sophie made him shrink back, but he knew loyalty to one's lord was superior to all others, including wives. 'Sir Arthur left no heir with Lady Sophie, and when he was killed, she feared for her future without an heir.'

'Rightly, as it turned out,' de Cailly said.

'So she used someone to make an heir,' Richard said.

'But not you?'

'No, someone powerful enough to protect her.'

'Richard, stop,' Sophie's eyes welled up, 'I can't hear it said out loud. I have not slept on that bed since that night, I have slept on the cold floor. I can't look at it. My fate will be to burn in hell for what I did.'

'What did you do?'

Sophie started to cry and turned to look out of the window again.

'The Little Lord was very drunk,' Richard said.

'Him? You chose him? On purpose?' De Cailly roared with laughter.

Sophie wailed and de Cailly stopped laughing, a sheepish look spread across his face. He scratched his neck. 'I am sorry, my lady, I meant no offence.'

'What do we do?' Richard asked.

'Who else knows?'

'No one, apart from the Little Lord, although I don't know if he is even sure what happened,' Richard said.

'Good,' de Cailly said, 'then we shall be fine.'

'Fine?' Sophie sobbed, 'how can this be fine?'

'As long as the baby doesn't come out with red hair, then the baby is Richard's,' de Cailly said.

Sophie stopped crying and sniffed. 'But if it is a boy, then Richard's line will not inherit Yvetot.'

'That is not my concern,' de Cailly said, 'and it is better than being hung by the villagers. Besides, it might come out a girl. I think there are certain charms you can wear to ensure a girl.'

'Yes, I will find some,' Sophie said.

'What if Lord Tancarville finds out?' Richard asked.

'Then he will come here, kill you, and marry Lady Sophie to his son. Or just kill both of you and take the bastard child back to Castle Tancarville. So he best not find out,' de Cailly said.

'Aren't you his man, Sir Roger, do you not have a duty to Lord Tancarville?' Sophie asked.

'I might be Tancarville's man, but that doesn't mean I like it,' de Cailly said. The knight went back to the window where the evening light had started to fade. A dim shadow began to form over the bed.

'We need to rush the marriage,' de Cailly said.

Sophie wiped her face and nodded.

'I assume we have your consent to marry?' de Cailly asked. 'You do. But only because it is better than being torn apart by common people or being sent home in disgrace,' she said.

'I will conduct the ceremonies tomorrow,' de Cailly said.

'What about the bed?' Richard asked. He only knew of marriage ceremonies from his book Eric and Enid, and that told of holy water being sprinkled over the couple in their bed.

Sophie glanced at it, a thin layer of dust caked the empty and twisted sheets. 'That will have to be my first sacrifice,' she said.

Richard saw steel behind her eyes, and wondered if he was really going to rule over Yvetot himself at all.

'Good,' de Cailly walked over to Sophie, 'you have my word that I will try to protect you from the Little Lord. He came within a hair's breadth from despoiling my own daughter, and I have no love for his family. Lord Tancarville may be the Chamberlain of Normandy, but I serve him reluctantly.'

She nodded and tried to smile. 'Thank you.'

'As for you,' de Cailly said to Richard, 'do not make me regret giving you my own golden spurs. Your iron spurs around my heels now will be a constant reminder of you. I will remove you if you so much as look like failing. Trouble follows you, Richard of Yvetot, I want you to make sure that it no longer finds you.'

'Yes, my lord,' Richard said.

'Fine. Though it is not a Sunday, tomorrow you must be wed and become a landed knight.'

The next morning, Richard walked to the church with Bowman and Sir Wobble.

'Does he really have to be at my wedding?' Richard asked. He was wearing a fine blue tunic that de Cailly had given him, but ahead of him walked Sir Thomas and Eustace Martel.

'Martel or not, he is second here behind Sir Roger in terms of rank,' Sir Wobble said, 'and custom is custom.'

'If only he would try to escape, then we could kill him,' Bowman smiled.

'Only once I've spoken to him about my father and Adela,' Richard said, 'and that should not be on my wedding day.'

'How are you feeling about that?' Bowman asked.

'Petrified,' Richard said, 'she's older than me.'

'Oh, spare me your pity,' Sir Wobble said, 'you are about to own land. Have your own livery on a flag. People will think I'm your knight, they will envy you for that.'

'Will they really,' Richard replied flatly.

'They will once my shoulder has healed,' Sir Wobble flexed it and only slightly winced.

'Can you stop going on about that?' Richard said.

'Why should I? It still hurts and my mail is still torn open over it. I was knighted before you and have nothing to show for it.'

'You were only knighted one day before me,' Richard said.

'That's not the point,' Sir Wobble groaned.

To get to the church they had to walk around the pond and through the village.

'I wish my father was here,' Richard said as he looked across the water. He thought of his mother too, but the image of Uncle Luke knocking her down and killing her was too painful to dwell on.

'Don't fret, young lord,' Bowman said, 'he would be proud, and we'll find out what happened to him.'

Richard nodded and then grimaced because he saw Eustace Martel with Sir Thomas waiting for them by the church. Sir Thomas wore a yellow tunic for the occasion, but it was the same oil stained tunic that he wore under his armour. He watched impassively as Richard approached.

'This village of yours is a sorry prize,' Eustace said, the corners of his mouth turned down. The captive knight was intimidating even without armour, and he sneered as Richard tried to ignore him.

'I thought you wanted to talk to me?' he said.

Richard walked by. 'Not today. Tomorrow you will tell me what happened in the Holy Land.'

'Your father died a slow death,' Eustace said loudly. Heads turned from those gathered by the front of the church.

'Quiet,' Sir Thomas said to the prisoner, who held his hands up in mock terror.

Knights and squires outnumbered the villagers by the church, many of whom had apparently decided to ignore their duty and stay away. The Reeve stood next to de Cailly and watched Richard carefully.

'Where is the Priest?' Richard asked.

'He has made himself scarce,' de Cailly said, 'which is no matter. The bishops prefer a priest is present for the blessing of the bed chamber, but the ceremony of the church door has no need for one. I shall perform both duties for you as your lord.'

Richard nodded. 'Thank you.'

'Very well, haste is key today. Bring out the bride,' de Cailly said.

The wooden door to the church opened and Sophie walked out in her red dress. Richard suspected she didn't have another good dress, but she had at least brushed her hair.

The Reeve rushed to close the door behind her and stood on her dress. Sophie almost tripped and gave him an angry look. The Reeve retreated into the crowd as Sophie stood by de Cailly.

'Lady Sophie, have you fasted for two days before this ceremony?'

'I have.'

'Richard,' de Cailly paused and realised that Richard couldn't say yes to the same question, 'did you fast yesterday?'

'I have,' Richard said.

'Good,' de Cailly said, 'have you prepared the gold or silver for the bride on a shield or a book?'

'A book,' Richard waved Sir Wobble forwards.

The young knight approached the party with Richard's copy of Eric and Enid in his hands, a small pile of silver coins atop it.

'Is that it?' Eustace said from the back of the crowd.

'Pass it to Lady Sophie,' de Cailly said.

Sir Wobble tipped the silver into her hands and retreated with the book.

'A book too, what sort of knight picks the book?' Eustace added.

'Don't let me hear from you again, or we shall double your ransom,' de Cailly shouted.

Richard was glad the Martel man seemed to listen, but he started to boil inside at his rudeness.

Bowman produced a pair of wooden rings, still roughly carved, and gave them out. De Cailly glared at Eustace before the big man could say anything.

Standing under the archway of the church door, de Cailly motioned for Richard and Sophie to swap rings.

'Pronounce that you intent to marry each other, and the act will come into law,' de Cailly said.

Richard and Sophie both said it, but Richard could see she was choking down tears. He knew his face was red, but hers glowed and he fought to look her in the eyes.

There was a crack from the stone archway. Richard looked up and some stone dust landed in his eye.

'Richard,' Bowman shouted.

Richard pushed Sophie out of the doorway as another crack tore through the stonework and a piece of masonry detached from the building. Sophie screamed and nearly fell over from his push as the lump of stone the size of a large dog dropped to where she'd been standing a moment before.

De Cailly watched it fall from beside her but stayed still. The stone landed an inch from his foot and he looked down on it with disgust. A layer of yellowish dust settled on him and Richard found that he was holding Sophie tightly. To his surprise she held him back.

'Well, that's this wedding cursed,' Eustace said and turned to walk away.

'We knew you shouldn't have done this on a Friday,' a villager shouted.

'Should have been a Sunday,' another added.

'Enough,' de Cailly shouted, which disturbed the dust on his face and sent a cloud of it back up into the air.

'Are you unhurt?' Richard asked Sophie.

She pushed him back and nodded. 'It is done, let us do the rest quickly,' she said, 'before anything else goes wrong.'

Richard led Sophie up the stone stairs that led from the castle's hall into what was now his bedchamber. The bed had been remade and fresh flowers had been placed on the blankets. Lady Sophie's only remaining servant, the man with a large mole on his face, stood proudly in the corner of the chamber.

'What do I have to do?' Richard asked.

'Get in bed,' De Cailly said.

The Reeve was one of only two villagers to bother attending the blessing of the bedchamber, the other was the Miller. Bowman looked out of one of the windows, but Sir Wobble had been waylaid by arrangements for the feast that would follow the blessing.

Richard climbed into bed and held the blankets aside for Sophie. She looked down at her new husband but didn't move.

'The quicker you get in, the quicker we can leave the chamber,' de Cailly said.

Sophie swallowed and rushed into the bed next to Richard. He noticed that she didn't touch him.

'As the Priest wishes to have no part in this wedding, I shall bless the bed,' de Cailly said, 'although a blessing from someone of my position means a lot more than a village priest anyway.'

De Cailly put his hand into a pottery bowl and lifted it up. Droplets of water fell from his hands and he threw them over the couple. Richard blinked as one landed in his eye, and Sophie wiped away water that landed on her nose. It mingled with tears. De Cailly kept throwing water at them until the bowl was empty.

'The bedchamber has been blessed,' he announced.

'It was an honour to witness it,' the Reeve said as his eyes flickered between his new lord and de Cailly. The Miller was the only villager fatter than the Reeve, and he nodded away in agreement.

Richard could see more tears roll down his wife's cheeks so he looked at de Cailly. 'Is there anything else?'

'Just the feast, you have to come into the bailey now for that. Then everything is done, but you are now joined under God and the law of Normandy.'

Sophie threw the sheets off her and walked out of the chamber. Richard looked at de Cailly for help, but the older knight just shrugged. 'Do not try to understand her,' he said.

'I think I will try to,' Richard said.

Bowman snorted. 'I actually think you will, young lord, but let us see what drink this village has dug out for its big day.'

Richard sighed but followed him downstairs and out into the lower bailey.

'The real point of a wedding,' Bowman said as he slapped an

arm around Richard's shoulders, 'is to eat a lot, and drink even more.'

'I could do with some drink,' Richard said.

De Cailly's squires had found every table in the village and were busy stacking everything they'd found to eat or drink onto them.

'Not a promising haul,' Sarjeant said as he walked up from the tables.

'Any wine?' Bowman asked.

'No, and I really looked,' Sarjeant said.

'I bet you did,' Bowman laughed.

'There is only some red water that we found in the church, and some bread and apples,' Sarjeant said.

'Is that all?' Richard asked.

'I'm afraid so, but at least a few of the villagers have turned up,' Sarjeant added, although it wasn't all of them. Eustace walked along the tables, shook his head and walked off towards the stables. De Cailly was already there, and led out a black horse towards Richard.

'This is your wedding gift from me as your lord,' he said.

'He is beautiful,' Richard said.

'He is a palfrey, and as you keep riding your warhorse everywhere I thought I would give you an every-day riding horse. It isn't becoming for a landed knight to ride his warhorse around the countryside,' de Cailly said.

The horse sniffed Richard, who thought it had kind eyes. Back in the stable block, Solis kicked his door and tossed his yellow mane from side to side.

'He's going to be jealous,' Richard said.

'He's just a horse, he'll get over it,' de Cailly patted the black palfrey.

'I'm not sure he will, he's never seen me ride another horse,' Richard said as he put a foot in the stirrup of his new horse. Richard hauled himself up. The palfrey was wider than Solis and slightly shorter. He smelt different too.

Solis kicked the stable door again and a fragment of wood fell out from it. He shouted and bellowed with all his might and Richard sighed.

'I will have to ride him later, when Soli isn't looking,' he said.

'If even your horse can order you around, I am not sure what good you are going to do here,' de Cailly laughed. He called one of his squires to put the horse back and Solis immediately quietened down and went off to eat some hay.

'I'm not sure how this wedding could be any worse,' Richard said to Bowman as he watched the horse go.

'Don't go saying something like that,' Bowman said, 'not until the day is over.'

Richard didn't get time to think about it, because a cry rose from the gateway in the palisade. Eustace vaulted onto the horse of one of Sir Thomas's squires, and started to canter out of the gate.

'Stop him,' Sir Thomas cried, but it was too late. The villager who had called the alarm stood in the middle of the gate holding his hands out. Eustace ignored him, and unfortunately so did the warhorse, which cantered right over the top of him. The man's body was batted aside as if it were nothing. Eustace disappeared out of sight.

'That's your fault, you shouldn't have said anything,' Bowman said.

'This really isn't the time for that, we have to go after him,' Richard started to run towards Solis.

'My men, we ride after him now,' Sir Thomas shouted and his squires ran for their horses.

'You must stay here, Richard,' de Cailly said, 'Sir Thomas can chase him.'

The villagers had come together and the Reeve came over. 'My lord,' he said to Richard, which made him feel strange, 'this is a very bad omen indeed for your wedding.'

'I know,' said Richard.

'If a man dies during a wedding, then the marriage is doomed,' the Reeve added.

'I hope he doesn't die, then,' Richard said hopefully, as over in the gateway, the trampled man's heart gave up and the life drained from his body.

THE FLYING MONK

Richard watched with mixed feelings as de Cailly and his knights rode out of Yvetot. Their horses kicked up dust as they hit the track outside the castle, and their hooves caused the ground to rumble. Soon both the dust and rumble faded away and the castle became silent and still.

'Right then, my young lord, what now?' Bowman asked.

'I don't know,' Richard said from next to him up on the stone walls.

'Knowing what to do is your job now. If you don't know what to do, do you know what you want to do?' Bowman asked.

'I want to go to England, Adela needs to be rescued from her nunnery, and my uncle needs removing from Keynes.'

'Well, then. Sounds like you know what you need to do.'

'I can't go yet, I have to make it safe here for Lady Sophie first.'

Richard looked over to the stables where Sir Wobble was assessing the new black palfrey. He tried to imagine what his father would do. Nothing really came to mind and Richard wondered if he should be the lord of Yvetot at all.

'I think that we must do whatever we need to in order to cross the sea,' Richard eventually said.

'Sounds like half an answer to me,' Bowman grinned.

'Saddle my horse for me, I will ask my wife to show me this village properly. Then I can see what we need to do.'

'Saddle your horse? Do we have to have this conversation once a day?' Bowman said.

Richard raised his eyebrows. 'Please?'

'Oh, you said please, so of course I will, I would love to tack up your horse for you,' Bowman smiled and walked off towards Solis. Richard leant on the stone battlements for a moment, but before he went to find Sophie, she found him.

'I wish Sir Roger would have left us more of his men,' she said. Her red dress looked faded still from the yellow dust from the church masonry.

'They are plenty, we almost outnumber the villagers,' Richard smiled.

'But Sir Roger has only loaned them until the spring.'

'Then we should put them to use while we have them, they can repair the castle palisade so we can be safe,' Richard said.

'You men only ever think of your castles and wars,' Sophie said, 'there is much more to this village then its ability to fund your knighthood. Those men can do a great deal more than mend fortifications. They can do things that will make us far safer than building walls between us and the common people.'

'Really, what can make us safer than strong walls?'

'Maybe you should think less about protecting yourself, and more about stopping the villagers from wanting to kill us in the first place?' Sophie asked.

'They hate us, I can't change the fact that we're both English,' Richard said, 'the Priest and Reeve were both very clear about that.'

Sophie put a hand on Richard's. It was warm in contrast to the cold stone under it.

'A landed knight must learn about his land and he must care for his land. His people are also his to look after, consider what you can do to improve how those people think.'

'I can't change how they think,' Richard said.

'You can't, no,' Sophie said, 'but you can influence those that can, and there are things you can do in Yvetot to make them less inclined to hate you.'

'Show me,' Richard said.

Sophie smiled.

The new black palfrey rode well as a riding horse, but not with Richard as his rider.

'You can have him, consider it a wedding present,' Richard said.

'Are you sure, I haven't had a horse of my own for years,' Sophie smiled.

Richard was sure that she was nearly happy at that moment. 'The horse is the least I can do, the wedding silver wasn't mine to give as it should have been. I'm just sorry we don't have a proper lady's saddle for you.'

'I can ride astride just fine, Richard, thank you for the horse.'

'It's not like I can ride it anyway,' Richard patted Solis on his neck. The stallion snaked his neck at the palfrey with his ears pinned back. The palfrey took a sharp step to the side to stay out of the reach of his teeth. Richard noticed that Sophie stayed solidly in the saddle.

'He's not over it yet, is he?' she said as they turned left out of the castle and rode away from the village. A large wood to their right stretched out beyond the farmland of Richard's own.

'Your demesne land,' Sophie frowned at the farmland. The land looked like the villager's own farmland, but part of their duty to the lord of Yvetot was to farm it for him.

'It's overgrown with weeds, there are no crops here,' Richard said.

'No, they stopped working this land when Sir Arthur stopped leaving the castle to check on them. He was too old to notice and too weak to correct things. You must get them back to work, for without our demesne land, we have nothing to eat. Nothing to sell.'

'I see,' Richard said.

They rode further north and Richard could hear rushing water from over a small hill. Once they'd crested it, only the flag above the castle tower was visible behind them as the mill came into view ahead.

'Like all lords, the mill belongs to you,' Sophie said, 'and the Miller owes you a fee from his work.'

'Has he been paying his fee?'

'Ask the Reeve, collecting the fees and keeping the accounts is his job,' Sophie said.

Richard's face dropped. 'I don't like him, he reminds me of a weasel. A fat weasel.'

Sophie's mouth cracked a faint smile. 'We shall get to him, but the Miller needs to know he has to pay, so that is your first task. Once you have some money, you can hire wage-men to work our land or mend things.'

The mill sat by the riverside, attached to a wooden wheel that turned in the river. It was only missing a few planks. The river was narrow enough that Richard thought he'd be able to ride through it, the banks were low and lined with lush vegetation.

'At least the mill still works,' Richard watched it turn slowly. It creaked and the sound of the water pushing the wooden paddles was both loud and hypnotic.

He pulled his attention from the wheel and dismounted. He tied Solis to the Miller's fence. The horse tugged at it, decided it wouldn't break, then sighed and his eyelids began to close.

'I'll stay outside,' Sophie said, 'this needs to come from you.'

Richard didn't want to do anything on his own but he knew she was right. The mill building was two storeys high, the only such building in Yvetot, and it was also the only one in decent condition. He pushed his way into the house and found the Miller at his table with a sizeable breakfast spread before him.

'I didn't see any of this at my wedding feast,' Richard folded his arms, which acted to make the sword hanging by his side more obvious.

The Miller's blue eyes were drawn to the gleaming metal. 'My lord, I didn't know you were coming,' he said.

'Obviously not, had you known, you would have hidden your hoard in good time. Tell me, Miller, how is it that you are so rich in food, when the villagers barely survive, and my wife actually is starved?'

The Miller peeled his eyes away from the sword and down to the vegetables and cheese in front of him. 'My lord, I am but a weak man, the sin of gluttony is my undoing, I can not help myself.'

'Blaming a sin is no excuse, I will not tolerate dishonesty in my village. Does the Reeve not come to collect your fees?'

The Miller raised his head and Richard noticed that one side of his mouth had a twist to it, as if he'd been kicked by a horse. Without it, the man may have been considered handsome. 'I pay the Reeve enough to leave me alone,' he said.

'But you still collect the milling fee from the villagers?'

'Of course, that is my job,' the Miller said.

Richard unfolded his arms and sighed. 'You can't hear yourself, can you?' He moved his right hand down onto the

27

pommel of his sword and rested it there. 'You will pay the Reeve the correct amount from now on, is that clear?'

The Miller's eyes trained on the hilt of the blade. He nodded.

'I'm not asking more than is your due, and I won't punish you for what went on before,' Richard said. He hoped that would be enough to ease the Miller back into doing the right thing.

'Of course, my lord,' the Miller's fingers fidgeted on the table.

Richard didn't think he looked very calm or honest. 'I should have guessed, shouldn't I? You and the Reeve were the only fat men in the village. At least that means the Priest isn't in on this. I will be watching you,' Richard said before he turned and left.

'Well?' Sophie said as he went back out into the daylight.

'He will pay the Reeve now,' Richard tried to stifle a grin. He felt good, he felt important.

'Don't puff your chest out like a peacock,' Sophie said, 'there is more to be done. Come with me.'

Richard remounted and they rode back towards the castle. The sun was in Richard's eyes above the orchard in the distance, and he had to squint. After a while he felt the need to break the silence. 'I'm sorry for what has happened to you,' he said.

'So sorry that you plan to cross the sea and leave me here as soon as you can?'

'Did you not see Eustace Martel escape? What do you think he did to my sister?'

Sophie thought as the palfrey carried her on. 'He was beastly. What is your sisters name?'

'Adela.'

'Secure this land for Adela then, Richard. Make it a place you can bring her back to,' Sophie said.

'Thank you,' Richard said. Some birds flew overhead and landed in Richard's desolate demesne fields. 'But I had thought to reclaim my family manor of Keynes while I was in England.'

'Another manor?' Sophie looked at him, 'how are you going to manage estates on opposite sides of the sea? You can't trust even your own Reeve here.'

Richard didn't reply and pursed his lips together because she had a point. Many great lords did it, but they had a staff of lawyers and clerks. Richard had some insubordinate friends, a jealous horse, and wife carrying another man's child.

'You are young, you need to learn patience,' Sophie said, 'we are not in England either. Normandy is different.'

'I know,' Richard said flatly.

'You own this land, you even own some of the people. There might not be many slaves in England, but here most of the farmers are literally your property. They expect to be told what to do.'

They rode between the village houses and the hedge enclosed common land.

'Does the pond ever flood?' Richard asked. The pond was a good step down from the surrounding land, a greyish body of water with patches of green algae floating on the surface. A few ducks swam on the surface and in the warmth of the morning, insects flew above it.

'No, it used to be the lord's fish pond, but it had lost its fish even when I first arrived,' Sophie said.

'We should restock it,' Richard said.

'With what? We have de Cailly's wedding silver, but is the fish pond the best use for it? Be patient.'

'Well, what about the villager's houses? We could pay for them to be fixed and then they would be happy,' Richard said.

Sophie laughed. 'You have so much to learn, my boy.'

'Don't call me that.'

Sophie smiled. 'Yes, husband.'

That made Richard feel even more uncomfortable.

'If you spend your money directly on them, these animals will sense weakness,' Sophie said.

'What can I do then? As you know best, what do we fix first?'

'That,' Sophie pointed to the church as they rode around the pond. The fallen masonry of the arch still stood in a small crater of its own making in the doorway.

'We need the church on side, the church controls most of what they think. The Priest is an odious little man, but he needs to be your friend.'

'So I can't just threaten him with my sword like I did the Miller?' Richard asked.

Sophie rolled her eyes. 'You men are all the same. Use your words, Richard. Find a way for him to like you. He preaches to them every day. I have stood in that church and listened to him pronounce that women are the root of all evil. A few hours later and they were knocking down the palisade to burn me. They believe him.'

Richard left her outside, squeezed past the fallen stonework, and pushed the door open. It creaked on its rusted hinges.

'Hello?' rang out from the dark interior.

'Priest?' Richard walked in and closed the heavy door behind him. The church was a rectangular building of stone walls and a wooden roof. It was not a tall building, but it was big enough for the villagers to all stand in for services. The cool walls blocked out the sun and Richard's eyes took a second to adjust to the dimness.

'My lord,' the Priest bowed. He was standing by the altar at the end of the church, a cloth in one hand and a pewter bowl in the other.

'I didn't see you at my wedding,' Richard said.

'I'm very sorry, I had matters of faith to attend to.'

Richard remembered what Sophie had told him and sighed. 'How long have you been the priest here?'

'A few years,' the Priest put down the pewter bowl.

'Do you like Yvetot?'

'Our Lord above places us where we are most needed. There are positions in more comfort and status than here, but it is a good village.'

'Is it? Everything is falling down,' Richard said.

'Nonsense,' the Priest jumped on the spot, 'Yvetot is a fine village full of fine god-fearing folk.'

Richard suppressed a splutter. 'It is a fine village,' he tried to sound sincere.

'The souls of the villagers are safe in my hands,' the Priest said.

'Yes,' Richard's eyes lit up, 'that is your realm and you are clearly doing wonderful work there. My realm is their physical wellbeing.'

'Is it?' the Priest asked, 'you are a knight with his golden spurs, men like you only care about how much money you can squeeze out of their tenants.'

'That is not true, I wish to help them. May I offer to repair the archway that fell down yesterday?'

The Priest placed his polishing cloth onto the altar and walked towards Richard. 'That was either an act of God or an act of the Devil. Until I know which, I cannot accept your offer. If the Devil threw down the stone, then I cannot accept anything from you.'

Richard sighed to himself but kept it quiet.

'I saw you here when you rode east, and I saw the bandages on your hands as you rode by. I also heard from the priest at Castle Tancarville, he is a relative of mine. My uncle in fact.'

Richard closed his eyes. 'What was he calling me? The English Devil by any chance?'

'Yes. Well, the son of the Devil,' the Priest closed in on Richard until they were only a foot apart. The tall man looked down at Richard and Richard could smell cheese.

'Do I look like the son of the Devil?' he looked up at the Priest and into his eyes. There was no way he was backing down to a priest.

'Who am I to know that. He told me that you threw a monk from a tower.'

'God judged me innocent in the trial by fire,' Richard said.

'They call it the tale of the dancing monk, although my uncle thinks the monk was thrown from the tower instead of falling.'

'The monk danced and the monk fell,' Richard said, 'he fell down from the tower.'

'All I know is that death and destruction have followed you here. Both times you have visited our peaceful village people have died,' the Priest said.

'Peaceful? The villagers have tried to attack the castle twice in the past few weeks. I cannot be blamed for either of them.'

'I will not take your English charity. Neither it nor you are welcome in Normandy, and the broken arch will remind every farmer here of that when they walk around it to enter their church.'

'I'm just trying to help,' Richard said.

'Then you should not have come here to begin with,' the Priest spat and Richard had to wipe his face clean. He put his hand onto his sword and the holy man's eyes followed him.

'I won't draw it,' Richard released his hand, 'and I won't

threaten you with it. I have come here to tell you that I wish to work with you. How can I show you my honesty?'

The Priest watched him intently for a while. 'I believe a Devil can still be honest, honestly evil that is. There is nothing you can do. Keep that bloodthirsty Sir Thomas away from us, and the younger Tancarville too, that would be a start. Stop blood from spilling in this village. You will never live up to Sir Arthur, so stop trying.'

Richard didn't know where to begin, but he felt that the conversation had ended. He held himself for a moment face to face with the Priest, but then turned on his heels. 'Thank you for your time.'

'Mind the masonry on your way out,' the Priest said as Richard opened the church doors. He blinked in the light and scuffed his foot on the stone as he left the building.

'Well?' Sophie said.

'Less successful,' Richard said after he'd shut the door.

'He is braver than the Miller,' Sophie said, 'try again in a few days.'

'I would rather ride into a battle than do that again,' Richard moaned, 'there is nothing I can do to make him change his mind.'

'Maybe you should spend some time at Sir Arthur's grave?'

'Why?'

Sophie shook her head and her hair shook with it. 'Richard, you need to think beyond yourself. Think about what others want and need. Not everything is about you.'

Richard was waiting for her to tell him what others wanted and needed when Sir Wobble appeared from the orchards that ran up to the graveyard and church.

'There are some good apples if you find the right trees,' he said to Richard.

'Leave some for everyone else,' Richard said.

Sir Wobble swung a bag down off his back and onto the ground. He opened it up. 'See how many good ones I found.'

'You have never introduced me to this one,' Sophie said.

'You don't need to know him,' Richard replied, keenly aware that Sir Wobble was nearer Sophie's age.

'I'd like to know her,' Sir Wobble said, 'especially if I am the knight of this village.'

'I'm the knight of this village,' Richard said.

'You're the lord, I'm the knight.'

'Enough,' Sophie said. She lifted herself up then swung her leg around to dismount. She reached the ground and had to rub her inner thighs.

'The wedding night was successful, then,' Sir Wobble said.

'I haven't ridden a horse for years, that's all,' Sophie shot him a stern look.

'We need the wedding night to have been successful though, don't we?' Sir Wobble's face lost its certainty.

'Stop it,' Richard said, 'but fine, I shall introduce you. This is a friend I met at Castle Tancarville, his name is William Marshal. We call him Sir Wobble because he wobbled when he was knighted. That's about all of it.'

'That's really not all of it,' Sir Wobble frowned.

'I have heard enough bickering, I would like to get out of the sun now,' Sophie turned to Richard, 'I suggest you kneel by the grave all day and all night. Everyone will see you. The Priest might even soften a little, but everyone else will then see a link between Sir Arthur and you.'

Richard looked over at the brown earth under the hot sun.

'Sounds like a great idea,' Sir Wobble grinned, 'I will go and check the orchard on the other side of the track.'

'I think you must do it,' Sophie said as Sir Wobble left and Richard stared forlornly down at the ground.

'If you want to be a lord, you need to act like one,' she said.

'I feel like a lord who doesn't have any real choice about anything,' Richard said.

'Taking good counsel is the most important thing you can do,' Sophie said, 'tie your horse up and I will send a squire to fetch him.'

Sophie left Richard on his own to kneel on the baking earth by the wooden cross. The flowers were already heavily wilted and had started to smell. At least Richard hoped it was the flowers. He put his back to the sun and held his vigil at the cross as the sun peaked and started to fall in the sky. The Priest came out of the church, watched him for a while, then went away. Richard's neck felt like a pig roasting on a spit as the sun relentlessly shone down, but it was a pain he had to ignore. He became thirsty as the early evening arrived and the air started to cool and smell fresher.

Bowman arrived with the cooler air. 'I wasn't sure if they were joking, but here you are, kneeling in the dirt,' he said.

'Here I am, could you bring me some water?'

'No, the villagers want to see you suffer a bit, young lord. Lady Sophie was very clear about that. I've been riding around your land all day. Nothing for miles east. To the north is a small Templar manor with an impressive barn. I think they have moved their fences onto your land, by the way,' Bowman said.

'I don't really care,' Richard said.

'You should, or they'll keep moving them. They could be at the mill in a few months. But that is the most interesting thing I came across, this should be a very boring castle to run.'

'I wish it was a bit more boring.'

'It looks pretty boring to kneel down there,' Bowman laughed.

'You know what I mean.'

'I do,' Bowman said. He ran his hand through his blonde hair and studied the cross.

'I think I want to return to England as much as you do, young lord. Normandy has been the wrong type of excitement, the type of excitement that keeps nearly getting me killed.'

'If we get back the silver we hid, we can go to the holy land after England and live in peace once we return,' Richard said, his mind tempting him away from the hard work he knew was required in Yvetot.

'Whatever you wish, young lord,' Bowman said, 'but there are parts of England I wish to see again. It surprises me to say it, but there are a few of my family left and I would like to visit them.'

'We will be back as soon as we can, I'll retake Keynes and find Adela,' Richard said.

'Your new lady wife is right, Richard, you need to make this land safe first,' Bowman said.

'So everyone keeps telling me. That's what I'm doing now.'

'What about when they rebel against your new demands?' Bowman asked.

'You and I will draw our swords and they will back off.'

'You want me as an instrument of law?' Bowman laughed.

'I know it's ironic, and you won't tell me anything about yourself still,' Richard said, 'but you are bigger than all of them, and they will not want to fight you.'

Bowman chuckled and left Richard to his vigil. No one brought out food, so Richard assumed that vigil also needed to be a fast. The moon eventually rose and the air chilled and darkened. He heard his first owl hoot and made the sign of the cross. The Priest came back and watched for another while, and Richard noticed a group of villagers study him from across the fish pond until it was too dark to see over it any longer.

Once he felt alone, Richard fought hard the urge to sit down. His eyelids grew heavy and a fox skulked by and watched him for a while too.

'Even the wildlife distrusts me,' Richard mumbled as he looked into its yellowish eyes.

Richard woke up when it was still dark, but rays of yellow reached up from the woods in the east. Richard found himself lying down and quickly got back into position. There was not yet any movement in the village and he hoped his failure hadn't been spotted.

Sarjeant was the first to visit, his large frame wondered around the pond and his kind face smiled as he neared.

'You made it, my boy,' he said.

'I think so,' Richard wiped some sleep from his eyes, 'am I finished?'

'When the sun fully separates from the horizon,' he said.

'What have you been doing, everyone else has been finding things to amuse themselves with?'

'Speaking to the villagers. They are a poorly educated collection of souls, they just lack proper direction,' Sarjeant said.

'And how do I fix that?' Richard asked.

Sarjeant laughed. 'Not on your own, my boy. The Reeve is cunning and the Miller is dishonest. The Priest is, well, he's a priest, but the people are just people. If their lives were prosperous and a little more enjoyable, it would not occur to them to start storming the castle whenever they got upset.'

'You are speaking like you have an idea,' Richard said. The sun breached the treeline to the east and the sky yellowed. A blanket of mist hovered above the ground all around. Richard shivered.

'I will show you when you are finished,' Sarjeant said then yawned, 'it is quiet here, I like it.'

'You didn't like it last time when you stood watch on the wall in case the villagers came back.'

'Last time your joke provoked the Little Lord to murder their lord,' Sarjeant said, 'and I had to stay up all night on the cold stone of the battlements because of that.'

'I'm sorry,' Richard said.

'It is no matter, the real fault was not yours,' Sarjeant looked across the fish pond. 'It looks like the greedy knight is already up to scavenge for food.'

Sir Wobble made his way over to the graveyard. He had returned with an empty sack.

'More apples?' Richard asked, 'how many do you need?'

'I'm going to make cider,' Sir Wobble said.

'Cider? Do you know how to make cider?'

'No, but if peasants can do it, I can work it out,' he replied.

'If you manage, we could get a lot of cider out of that orchard,' Richard said out loud, then had an idea. 'When you're done, I'd like you to round up some villagers and set them to work clearing those ditches,' Richard pointed to the ditches that funnelled water from the pond out into the common land. They were dried up, clogged with mud, and in some places bushes had even started to grow in them.

'I'm not a foreman, I'm a knight,' Sir Wobble crossed his arms and the sack flapped through the air.

'Exactly, I need someone who the villagers won't ignore. This is quite an important task, if this one fails, I won't be able to get them to do anything else.'

Sir Wobble looked over at the ditches and back to Richard. 'Very well, I will make them clean those ditches out to their very bottom. The water will flow like never before.'

'Thank you,' Richard said.

'I think your time here has done you good,' Sarjeant said.

Sir Wobble flung his empty sack over his shoulder and strode off to the orchards once more.

'I'll ask him to organise de Cailly's squires to help repair the castle next, I'll tell him to make the most impressive palisade in Normandy.'

Sarjeant grinned. 'You are getting good at this,' he said.

'We need to repair the stables too, and build more. We can't have all these horses hobbled in the inner bailey forever. We should have fenced paddocks outside the castle too. If we buy some mares we can breed horses to ride and sell.'

'Careful, my boy, one thing at a time.'

The sun was now a ball in the sky, only its very bottom still clung on to the horizon.

'Do you think this has worked?' Richard asked.

'I do, but the test will be how clean your ditches are this evening.'

'I don't want to end up like Sir Arthur,' Richard said, 'if I fail I'll never get Keynes back.'

'You wont fail, and I think you can stand up now.' Sarjeant said.

Richard glanced at the sun, now free in the sky, and got to his feet. Everything ached and he was tired.

'You can breakfast on your apples,' Sarjeant suggested.

Richard nodded and they walked down the track and into Yvetot's orchards. His legs felt dead and his back hurt. There was still dew on the ground and on the leaves of the short and stocky apple trees.

'They will be ready for harvest soon,' Sarjeant said.

'How do you know so much about apples?'

'They make cider.'

'Of course,' Richard rummaged in the nearest tree for a red apple. Drops of dew fell onto his face, but it refreshed rather than annoyed him.

'There are still plenty here, our other young knight's foraging seems not to have dented our supply. I suppose these apples are the only thing Yvetot has as an asset.'

'Can we sell them?'

'The apples, no,' Sarjeant said, 'their cider, yes.'

'Everyone wants to make cider,' Richard took a bite of an

apple. It wasn't sweet, but it wasn't too sharp either. They walked through the trees and after a while came to the hedge that separated the orchard from the main road.

'I think my land ends here,' Richard said.

'I'm sure we can find a lawyer to tell you,' Sarjeant said, 'but back to cider.'

Richard sighed. He really wanted to go to his bedchamber now.

'We could sell it, and there would be plenty left over,' Sarjeant said.

'You mean left over for you to drink,' Richard said.

'Well, yes,' Sarjeant scratched his chin, 'but mostly to sell, of course.'

A trio of horsemen rode slowly east along the road towards them.

'I think we could sell cider to them,' Richard felt his mind working.

'We haven't made it yet,' Sarjeant watched the riders.

'Not them, all travellers,' Richard said. He looked around the orchard. 'All we need to do is clear a few trees and build an inn. We can stock the cider round the back and serve drinks to travellers.'

Sarjeant beamed. 'We are right on the main road, you could make a fortune. Think of all the stories we would hear.'

'If it went well, we could add a hall for sleeping,' Richard said.

'Normandy is famous for its cider, travellers will all expect cider,' Sarjeant said.

'We should start clearing the trees as soon as possible,' Richard felt excitement course through him, but he could hear his wife's caution too.

'What shall we call the inn?'

'I don't know, maybe the Leaping Horse or Sleeping Knight?' Richard suggested.

'Those are terrible names. They're boring and don't mean anything.'

Richard nodded to the trio of riders as they went along, and by their dress decided that two of them were monks. Sarjeant watched them too. His face burst into a wide grin.

'Richard, I know what we will call it,' he said.

'What?'

'The Flying Monk.'

'That is a cruel joke,' Richard scrunched his face up, 'we aren't calling it that.'

'The Dancing Monk then?'

'I'll choose the name, it's my inn,' Richard said.

'But can I run it?' Sarjeant's eyes pleaded.

Richard took a deep breath as the sun's rays started to warm the back of his neck, which he was sure was burnt from the previous day. Sarjeant had a lot of experience of inns and drinking establishments, but always on the wrong side of the bar.

'How can I be sure that I don't leave you in charge one day and come back to find you dead in a pool of cider?'

'I am a changed man, my boy. I want a quiet life with some good conversation and a modest amount of cider,' Sarjeant said.

'A modest amount?' Richard snorted, 'and who judges what modest is?'

'I am responsible for myself,' Sarjeant said.

'You really want to settle down here?'

'I do. I am too old for battles and marching. I can look after the Flying Monk for you.'

'I'm not calling it that. But I do need a steward. The Reeve should run the village, but I need a steward to run the castle.'

'I think Lady Sophie can run the castle,' Sarjeant said.

'I want you to run the castle, or at least look like you're running the castle, while my wife really runs everything,' Richard said in a tone of resignation.

Sarjeant grinned. 'All of the benefits but none of the work. That sounds good,' he said.

'Some of the work. Will you be my steward?'

'Of course, my boy, it would be a great honour,' Sarjeant said.

Richard nodded, someone would have to stay behind while he went to England anyway, and that clearly shouldn't be Bowman or Sir Wobble.

'Thank you, it means a lot to me.'

'We are all in this life together,' Sarjeant said, 'I will stay sober while you are in England.'

'You better, you will need to look after my wife while I am away. Find out how to re-stock the fish pond too, then you can serve fish alongside bread and cider.'

Sarjeant nodded, his smile showed half his teeth and his blue eyes gleamed.

As the sun set behind him, Richard stood over the drainage ditch with Sophie and peered down into it.

'It really is clear,' Richard said.

Sir Wobble stood beside it in his white under-tunic and wiped some sweat off his brow. 'I told you, the best ditches in Normandy,' he said.

'You are far too proud of that,' Richard said.

The ditch leading from the fish pond drained out into the common land, and for the first time in probably a decade, water flowed along it. Sir Wobble let out a deep breath and stretched out his back. 'I was just going to watch and tell them what to do, but I actually enjoyed digging,' he said.

A mound of dark and damp earth stretched along the side of the ditch, the removed earth, and it stung Richard's nostrils.

'The villagers did a good job too,' Richard said.

Sweat had matted Sir Wobble's brown hair onto his face. 'They worked harder than I thought they would,' he said.

The villagers had dispersed, although one had only made it as far as the nearest hedge and was drinking something in its shade.

'He barely dug though,' Sir Wobble looked at the him, 'I think he was drunk when we started.'

'At least they helped,' Sophie said, 'maybe we won't be lynched after all.'

'We can go to England soon,' Richard beamed.

'We spoke about that, not yet,' Sophie said.

Richard frowned. 'I have a plan, for the first time in my life I have a real plan. We'll fix the palisade and the stables. The Reeve will work for us now, he'll get the demesne land farmed. We'll be able to sell crops next year. We'll make cider, refill the fish pond and sell it all in an inn at the edge of the village on the main road.'

'One day. There is a lot to do before that is all in place,' Sophie said. She glanced at Richard from the corner of her eye and he felt her hand slide around his. He felt warmth rush to his face.

'I must confess,' Sophie said, 'I am surprised how quickly you have made a difference,'

'It has taken all of us, soon we will be safe here. Sarjeant will be my steward,' Richard said, 'and he can have everything running without me before winter, so we can cross the sea.'

'Do not go too fast, the people do not like change. They still haven't accepted me and I've been here for years. You are asking a lot more of them than even that,' she said.

'They will not argue anymore, not while men with swords are here.'

'You want to take all the men with swords away with you to England,' Sophie said, 'leaving me with no one to defend the walls if they come back with their ladders and torches.'

'I need the men to retake Keynes,' Richard said.

'You'll have me,' Sir Wobble said, 'I can take Eustace Martel. If your uncle is anything like you, I can deal with him too.'

'Is he always this confident?' Sophie asked.

'Yes,' Richard said, 'although he is getting worse.'

Sir Wobble grinned at Sophie. 'I need to go to England too, so Richard does have to come with me. It is only a matter of when.'

Richard looked over to the villager's fields. In ones and twos those who hadn't been on drainage duty made their way back towards the houses for the evening.

'It's been a long day, we should find you some food,' Richard said.

Sir Wobble picked up his tunic from the ground. 'I am really hungry, but clearing ditches might even keep me fit to fight. I think it has actually loosened my shoulder up,' he said.

Richard watched him put the tunic back on, and noticed him wince when he pulled it over his head. Despite his words it would be a little while before he was fully fit.

'We won't leave yet,' Richard said, 'and I won't take the squires.'

'Good,' Sophie said.

'I will worry about Keynes another time, this is about getting my sister back.'

'Really? Only this morning you were very set on fighting over your English land,' Sophie said.

Richard turned to his wife. 'I listened to you, you need to be safe here while I'm gone,' he said.

Sophie raised her eyebrows. 'If this is a ruse,' she started.

'It is not, you told me to heed counsel, and you know Yvetot better than I do, so I am listening to you,' Richard said.

'Lord Tancarville never listens to his wife,' Sir Wobble said.

'Are you saying I should be more like him? Richard asked.

Sir Wobble shrugged and adjusted his tunic. 'I don't really care. Are you really going to build an inn?'

'Yes we are.'

'Good for you. It's not very knightly though, is it?' Sir Wobble said airily.

'For heaven's sake,' Sophie said, 'being knightly isn't about riding around the countryside burning things. It is about managing estates and making farms productive.'

'They don't sing songs about that, though,' Sir Wobble said.

'Songs don't keep families alive,' Sophie said.

Sir Wobble shrugged. 'They keep names alive, and mine will be kept alive. If Richard spends his time building inns, his will not be.'

'Maybe I can have both,' Richard said.

Sir Wobble started walking back to the castle. 'Maybe. You should name the inn after me.'

'What would that be, the Prancing Peacock?' Richard laughed.

'Very funny, but I think the name you've already chosen is better,' Sir Wobble said.

'What name?' Richard asked.

'You know it, everyone thinks it's hilarious, and think you are very gracious for going along with it.'

'Sarjeant. He's told everyone, hasn't he? What has he told you?' Richard asked.

'The Flying Monk,' Sir Wobble replied and walked off towards the orchard.

'Why is that so funny?' Sophie asked.

'That's not a story for today,' Richard said, 'or tomorrow. Tomorrow we start on the demesne land and the palisade, so I can get to England before the seas turn for the winter.'

FAMILY FIRST

Rain clattered onto the thin strips of horn that glazed the window frames of the hall at Yvetot. Richard sat in his chair and rubbed his fingers along the stained armrest. He'd done it every night for weeks in the hope that eventually he'd wear the blood away, but it hadn't worked. The fire crackled over in the hearth and the smell of burning wood was a comforting one in Richard's nostrils.

'You see, my lord,' the Reeve said as he stood in front of Richard, 'the Miller has indeed paid me.'

'Good,' Richard looked up from the armrest. The Reeve held a handful of coins out and Richard pointed at the single table in the hall.

The Reeve set the coins down and glanced up. 'We have two more barrels of cider ready for the town, too.'

'Good,' Richard's eyes wandered back over to the burning logs in the hearth. He yawned as the horn windows rattled in the wind. Only dim light made its way through them even though it was the middle of the day.

'I told you the cider was a good idea,' Sir Wobble said as he shifted on the bench by the table. He burped.

'You ate that fast,' Richard looked at his plate.

'I was hungry,' Sir Wobble replied.

'It should be easy to keep selling the barrels in the town,' the Reeve said.

'We will just need to help the last villagers fix their roofs if this weather keeps going,' Richard said.

'How long until we can cross the sea?' Sir Wobble asked.

'When the weather settles, I will speak to my wife.'

'God's legs,' Sir Wobble said, 'there is one lord here for sure,

43

but they don't wear spurs, do they.'

'I don't need her permission, I'm just trying to get along with her,' Richard said.

Sir Wobble laughed and pushed the empty wooden plate away. 'We only have perhaps two weeks until there's no chance of good weather for sailing. We need to leave now.'

Richard sighed and took a deep breath of woodsmoke. They'd exchanged the same words each day for a week, but his friend was getting more insistent now.

The door flew open and a man in a sodden dark blue tunic rushed in. He was covered in a brown cloak and despite his hood, his dark hair was stuck to his face and dripping wet.

'Who are you?' Richard pushed himself to his feet and his hand dropped to his sword.

The man took a few breaths and shut the door behind him. 'I apologise for the intrusion, are you Richard of Yvetot?'

'I am,' he replied.

The man pushed his cloak behind him and ran his hands over his face to clear some of the water. 'I have a message from Castle Tancarville.'

Sir Wobble looked up from his place. 'Tancarville? What do they want?'

'They want nothing, they sent me with a message for William Marshal.'

'Him?' Richard said.

'Me?"

'You are William?' The messenger asked.

Sir Wobble nodded.

'I am very sorry to tell you that your father is dead.'

Richard glanced down at his friend. 'I'm sorry,' he said after a moment.

Sir Wobble blinked a few times but didn't say anything.

'Reeve, will you find my wife, please?' Richard asked.

The Reeve jumped as if hit, scuttled around the messenger, and went to the door. He drew his cloak around himself and pushed out into the rain.

'Are you well?' Richard asked.

Sir Wobble slowly turned his head to Richard and shrugged. 'I haven't seen him since I left to go to Castle Tancarville. I'm not even sure how long ago that was, maybe eight years? I am trying to remember what he looked like.'

Richard turned to the messenger. 'I can give you a space in this hall for the night if you wish to rest?'

'No, my lord, I am to ride back to Tancarville. Good day,' the messenger bowed and left.

The door closed behind him and all Richard could hear was rain on the horn slats. Sir Wobble twisted himself around and held his hands up to the fire. It reflected back in an orange glow on his face.

'Do you need to go back to your family? Do you inherit his land?' Richard asked.

'I've told you before that my older brother will get the land,' Sir Wobble said.

'I'm sorry.'

Shades of yellow danced with the orange on the man's face. 'I should visit my brothers, though. It would be seen as very bad courtesy if I ignored them.

'I don't know what to say. May the lord have mercy on his soul,' Richard said.

A gust of air blew open the oil covered cloth that served as a shutter on the back window. The cold air sent a shiver down Richard's neck and made the fire dance and roar before it settled back down.

'It gets easier,' Richard said.

'What does?'

'Losing your father.'

Sir Wobble looked up from the flames. 'He was a great man, I've told you about him,' he said.

'You have, he was the marshal to the last King Henry. He rescued Matilda during the Great War. You told me the story about King Stephen putting you in his catapult at least six times,' Richard said.

'He was a warrior, he was strong, he was cunning and he was loyal. At least I think he was, but he was hard,' Sir Wobble said, 'once he was covering Empress Matilda's retreat when King Stephen's men forced him into an abbey. They set it on fire, because even though he had only one man with him, they were afraid of him. They wouldn't go in to fight him, so they set the abbey on fire. They burnt it down around him, but even the fire couldn't kill him. I think he was too angry to die. The fire was so hot that the lead roof melted all around him. My father was burnt, his skin blistered, and the roof dripped on his eye and he lost it, but he walked out the next morning alive. I always remember that story because that is what is expected of us, Richard.'

'To never give up?' Richard asked.

'No, to scare your enemies so much that they dare not fight you when they have you cornered,' Sir Wobble said.

'That's not the lesson I took from that,' Richard said.

The door opened and out of the storm Sophie appeared under a mustard-coloured cloak. 'Did you want me?' she asked.

'William's father has died.'

'Oh, my,' she unfastened her cloak, revealing a bump under it, and hung it on a hook on the wall. It started to drop water onto the floorboards immediately. She raced over to the table and sat next to Sir Wobble. She put an arm around him and squeezed. 'How are you? Tell me.'

'I'm fine actually, the cheese goes really well with the cider,' he replied.

'I don't think it has sunk in yet,' Richard said.

'There isn't much to sink it, my father is gone. My family lands move to my brother. Although, I suppose until he has a son, I'm the heir now,' Sir Wobble said.

'That's why you want to go back,' Richard said, 'to check how likely that is.'

'Of course I should, the lands are actually worthwhile,' Sir Wobble said. 'I really am fine,' he said to Sophie.

'Are you sure?'

'Yes, really.'

Sophie leant back and looked at Richard.

'He probably is fine,' Richard said, 'but now we have to go to England quickly.'

Sophie turned and stared at her husband. 'We had an agreement. You can go to England when Yvetot is safe and ready.'

'Sir Roger said I can cross the sea when you are with child,' Richard said.

Sophie's hand went down to her stomach without thought.

'I can go now, and the village is fine. Even the Priest has stopped preaching against us in the church. You will have both Sarjeant and de Cailly's squires to man the walls if anything goes wrong.'

Sophie frowned. 'I can't stop you, just don't ride off with all of our money or the silver.'

'You can keep the coins, but I will take the silver for our passage,' Richard said.

'The silver is worth more than you'd need,' Sophie said.

'We need to lodge and feed ourselves in England,' Richard said, 'I'll try not to spend it all.'

'Can we leave in the morning?' Sir Wobble asked.

Richard knew there were boxes and boxes of silver coins buried in a crypt under a nunnery in the Eawy Forest, but getting there and back would delay them by days. That was even if they could even get it out without the builders noticing. He would get it next year. Keynes and the Holy Land could wait, too, family came first. Adela came first. 'We can leave in the morning,' he nodded.

Sophie let out an audible breath. 'I would rather you didn't do it at all, but I understand that helping your sister is the right thing to do. Please do not be away longer than you need to. I don't want to spend the winter here alone.'

'We will ride to my grandfather in London first, he might have heard from uncle Luke where she is. After we find her, then we will find Sir Wobble's brothers, that should be easy,' Richard said.

'I don't like that name,' Sophie said, 'you are both grown men, can you not call him William?'

'There are too many Williams,' Richard said.

'I really don't mind it,' Sir Wobble turned back from the fire and stretched his arms up into the air.

'Children,' Sophie said wryly.

'I would rather we didn't sail from Harfleur though, I don't want to ride past Castle Tancarville,' Richard said.

Sir Wobble shook his head. 'Me neither, with your luck the Little Lord would stumble into us in the woods and murder us,' he said.

'What other ports can we use?' Richard asked.

'There are some to the north east, but I don't know how welcome we would be. But Fecamp is only a day's ride to the north. It is mostly a fishing port, but a fisherman might be cheaper to convince to take us to England than a merchant who only has coins for eyes,' Sir Wobble said.

'Close and cheap sounds good, do you know if we need to worry about the lord?'

'I don't know who the lord is, but the castle was the palace of the dukes of Normandy until William the Bastard moved it to Caen after the Conquest. The King was there a few years ago when he was in this part of Normandy, but I haven't heard about it since,' Sir Wobble said.

'We shall sail from Fecamp then,' Richard said, 'if you can go and find Bowman, tell him to get ready for the morning.'

'You should ask me instead of commanding me, Richard,' Sir Wobble frowned, 'landed knight or not, my family is more noble than yours.'

'Enough of that,' Sophie said and walked over to Richard.

Sir Wobble unhooked his tattered knighting cloak from the wall and went to brave the rain.

'That thing won't keep him dry,' Richard said.

'That's not why he wears it,' Sophie said. She walked behind Richard and put her arms around his neck. 'I might actually miss you,' she said.

He hesitated too long in his reply and she pushed herself off him. 'I'm going to rest, the rain has tired me,' she said.

Richard let her go, his feelings on her too mixed for him to know himself. The baby needed to come out a girl. He sighed as the fire crackled and rain battered the tower around him. He had more immediate things to worry about. He needed to gather some food for the journey, check his mail shirt hadn't gone rusty, and pack his silver candlestick for the journey. That would be his emergency currency, the only cause he would willingly sell it for was for Adela.

Luckily the next day it didn't rain. Thick grey clouds rolled across the sky as the three men rode north east towards the port of Fecamp. Their progress was slower than expected because the roads in places had become muddy tracks from the previous day's downpour. Solis kept his footing and Richard was sure he was glad to be away from home, the palomino had a spring in his step. After hours and hours of travel, Richard realised he'd thought of Yvetot as home for the first time.

Ahead in the distance, a dark shape on the horizon loomed.

'We should have arrived here in daylight,' Sir Wobble grumbled from under his cloak.

'I can't help the roads, don't blame me,' Richard glanced around but it was so dark he could barely see the trees that lined the track.

'I wasn't. That should be Fecamp though, the abbey should give us somewhere to sleep,' Sir Wobble said.

They rode over the last hill and Fecamp came into view. The abbey sat at the bottom of the valley that the town nestled in, modest hills to the left and larger ones to its right. Richard could smell the saltiness of the sea ahead, but it was too dark to see it. He thought the port must be beyond the abbey, presumably with some houses down on the seafront.

'Is that the castle?' Bowman asked.

'I can't see anything except the abbey's spire,' Richard said.

'It's not a castle, it's the old palace,' Sir Wobble said.

'Same thing,' Bowman said, 'it's right next to the abbey, can't you see it?'

Richard squinted his eyes and had to ride on before he could make out the outline of a castle's battlements in the dark. The abbey was closer and he could see lights flickering in it. It was a tall building of stone, but they first came across a wall that Richard assumed marked its grounds.

'There are fires in the castle's keep, too,' Bowman said.

'It's a palace, and I don't think there should be,' Sir Wobble said, 'I think I heard it has been abandoned.'

'Trust me, I can see light,' Bowman said, 'in the castle.'

Richard could almost hear Sir Wobble's teeth grinding. 'It looks like a castle to me,' Richard said, 'even though it may once have been a palace, can we not argue about that?'

'There's a gate,' Bowman pointed ahead to a wooden gate in the abbey's wall.

They dismounted and when Richard hit the ground his

legs were stiff. They led their horses into the abbey grounds, through what he thought were paddocks, and towards the main building.

'I have a mind to go and see who is in the castle,' Bowman said, 'they probably are having more fun than the monks.'

'That is clearly a bad idea,' Richard said, 'I would like to avoid dangers and surprises while we are here.'

'That's no fun though, is it?' Bowman laughed.

'Quiet,' a monk appeared in the doorway and hissed at them.

Richard and Bowman exchanged a glance.

'There's one surprise for you already,' Bowman said.

'Please, be quiet,' the monk whispered. He was young, thin, and his eyes looked like a cornered deer's.

Richard led Solis over to him. 'What is it?'

'They could be watching, they could be near,' the monk replied.

'Who?'

'Shhhhh, put the horses in that stable,' the monk pointed to a wooden building, 'then come inside. Quickly, and quietly.'

'Very well,' Richard looked at Sir Wobble and shrugged.

The other knight shrugged back, and they set off towards the stables with their horses. There were many stalls, but no other horses in them. Richard ignored that, and brought his saddle and bridle inside the abbey with him.

'You do learn, then,' Bowman grinned.

'What?' Sir Wobble asked.

'He doesn't want his things stolen,' Bowman said as he walked towards the abbey with his own saddle in his arms.

Sir Wobble watched them go and glanced back to his stall. He sighed and stomped off to bring his horse tack and belongings along with him too.

'Quickly,' the monk leant out of the doorway and ushered them in. He shut the door behind them gently. 'I hope you weren't followed,' he said.

'Why would anyone be following us?' Richard asked.

'They're in the palace,' the monk said.

'I told you it was a palace,' Sir Wobble said.

'Fine, it's a palace,' Bowman said, 'still looked like a castle, though.'

'Follow me,' the monk said and hurried off down a stone corridor.

'I think we're about to have another surprise,' Bowman said and readjusted his grip on the wooden saddle under his arm. They followed the monk round a corner and through a doorway that opened up into what Richard assumed was a hall for visitors. A long hearth smouldered in the centre of the room and biblical tapestries hung along the walls.

'That was not the surprise I was expecting,' Bowman looked over to a set of chairs at the far end of the hall.

'What is it?' Richard put his saddle down by the wall and laid his bedding over it.

'The Queen.'

'What queen?'

'THE bloody Queen,' Bowman said.

'Have some manners,' the monk hissed, 'I will introduce you to the abbot.'

Three women and one man sat in the chairs by the hearth. The man must have been the abbot, for he was dressed in a billowing rich red tunic edged in gold. The Queen was obvious too, in her fur lined dress with a fur lined cloak hanging over her shoulders. Richard's eyes were drawn to the bulge in her dress and he guessed she was as far along as Sophie was.

The monk rushed ahead and spoke to the abbot.

Richard looked at Sir Wobble. 'How do we speak to a queen?'

'Sparsely,' he replied, 'I can do the talking.'

'Can you, now?' Bowman said, 'the peacock wishes to advertise himself.'

'Shut up,' Sir Wobble turned to Richard, 'can we not let him talk at all?'

'That's probably for the best,' Richard said as they walked to the hearth and the monk drew chairs out for them. He placed them as far away as he could from the Queen, but the abbot spoke first.

'I am Abbot Turold,' the old man said. He was clean shaven but his face was furrowed and his eyes tinged with red.

'I am William Marshal,' Sir Wobble announced.

'I see your spurs, whose knight are you?' the abbot asked.

'That's a good question,' Bowman chuckled.

Sir Wobble set his face still for a moment. 'I am riding with my friend Sir Richard of Yvetot,' he waved at Richard.

'And whose knight are you?'

'I serve Sir Roger de Cailly,' Richard said.

The Queen and abbot exchanged glances. 'A Tancarville knight,' the Queen said. The Queen was older than Richard, he guessed by ten years, but her face was smooth and her eyes bright. She had a long oval face with a long and strong nose at its centre. She wore a thin golden crown over hair wrapped in white linen.

'I do not want Tancarville knights in this abbey,' the Queen said sternly.

'Of course,' the abbot said, 'you three must leave now.'

'We serve Sir Roger,' Sir Wobble said, 'we do not serve Lord Tancarville so much.'

The Queen studied the young knight. Her eyes examined his strong and tall body, then made their way around his dark face. 'You look like someone I know. Who is your father?'

'John Marshal, Your Majesty.'

'From England?'

'Yes, Your Majesty, he was loyal to Empress Matilda and King Henry when he ascended the throne,' Sir Wobble said.

'Good, you can stay,' she turned to Richard. 'You?'

'Your Majesty,' Richard began slowly, fumbling his words, 'my father was William Keynes. He captured King Stephen at the Battle of Lincoln during The War.'

'I do not know him personally but I have heard his song,' she said, 'you may remain.'

The Queen looked at Bowman, noticed the iron spurs on his heels and looked back to the knights. 'How did you get in, were you not stopped on the road?'

'No,' Sir Wobble said, 'we just rode right up to the abbey.'

'Maybe they were drunk, it is night?' the abbot said.

'There were lights in the castle,' Bowman said.

'Palace,' Sir Wobble shot him a look.

The Queen raised her eyebrows at Bowman, who dropped his own and backed away. He took the chair furthest away from the Queen and sat down.

'The brigands are not disciplined,' she said, 'had they not

taken our horses we could escape now. Not that I fancy riding anywhere in a hurry,' she felt her belly.

'Could I politely ask what is going on here?' Sir Wobble said.

The abbot leant forwards. 'Two days ago three ships sailed into the harbour. They were pirates from Brittany. An oaf calling himself Conan of St Malo pillaged and fired the town, he even stole our horses. Our Queen was about to take a ship across the sea, and they had the audacity to take her horses as well. They baulked at capturing her, lest her husband hunt them down in person, but they have been eating and drinking in the old palace ever since. We fear they will torch the abbey when they leave, but what can we do? They have had men guarding the road until, it seems, tonight.'

Sir Wobble looked over to Richard. 'See, fear of the man saved the wife,' he said under his breath.

Richard ignored him. 'You may have our horses,' he offered.

Bowman groaned behind him.

The Queen studied Richard's face as the hearth sent columns of smoke up into the rafters. 'That is a very selfless offer. But it is dark and I am with child. My previous babies were hardy, but this one complains whenever I move too much,' she said.

'The pirates may find their bravery in the morning and come for the Queen,' the abbot said, 'I fear we have no way to save her.'

'Are there any ships in the harbour?' Richard asked.

'Plenty, but their crews are locked below decks and Bretons are guarding them. The Queen's ship itself is heavily guarded,' the abbot sighed.

'We are trapped,' the Queen said, 'my travelling companions all taken captive, my horses and baggage all gone.'

'How far is it down to the harbour?' Richard asked.

'A short walk downhill through the town,' Abbot Turold said, 'even in the dark it should be lit enough from the houses to find your way.'

'What if we can get to a ship?' Richard wondered.

'The Queen's ship is heavily guarded, the Bretons have claimed it as a great prize,' the abbot said.

'Not the Queen's ship,' Richard grinned, 'the least guarded ship able to take our three horses.'

The abbot turned to the Queen. 'Eleanor,' he said, 'I am too old for such excitement, but that is bold enough to get you safely out to sea. But the choice is of course, yours.'

She rubbed her belly and her two ladies shifted nervously on their chairs. 'I fear I have nothing to lose. Ladies, you will have to be brave for me.'

The elder nodded, although the younger remained tight lipped.

'You can ride my man's horse down to the waterside,' Richard said to the Queen.

Richard heard Bowman groan behind him again, but luckily he kept his mouth shut.

'We should go now,' the Queen said, 'we have no possessions to carry or prepare.'

'We will ready the horses,' Richard nodded to Sir Wobble who followed him out of the hall.

'We only just got here,' Bowman mumbled but he got up eventually and reluctantly went with them.

Richard rode Solis out of the abbey gate and back onto the track. Dark clouds overhead drifted by but occasionally the light from the crescent moon flooded Fecamp.

Sir Wobble rode up beside him and winked. 'This is exciting,' he said.

Behind them Queen Eleanor rode Bowman's horse as he walked by its head. Her ladies walked at the back, wrapped in cloaks and staying close together.

Richard led them around the abbey building until they came to its main entrance. Directly opposite, only a bowshot away, was the old palace. Its walls stood tall on a mound surrounded by a moat, and the shadows of fires inside the keep lit up its windows. Solis pricked his ears towards it, and Richard thought he could hear human voices and maybe even music floating out of the windows.

'I can't see any guards or lookouts,' Sir Wobble said.

'That's either stupid or lazy,' Richard said.

They slowly walked on past the palace and down the gentle slope that led to the sea. The track meandered between a number of houses and a warehouse, all gutted by fire and some still smoking. The warehouse wall had collapsed into the street, charred posts stuck out and Richard had to pick his way around them. Richard's eyes looked for movement in alleyways and in the shadows, but he saw nothing and heard only a dog barking in the distance.

'I can see masts,' Sir Wobble nodded ahead and Richard squinted to see. The moon came out for a moment and reflected on the timber and rigging before a cloud smothered it again.'

'What is the plan?' Sir Wobble asked.

'I haven't thought that far,' Richard said, 'I was hoping something would work itself out.'

'That's probably not going to happen. We need to have a look at what ships there are without being seen, and then make a real plan,' Sir Wobble said.

'That does sound like a real plan,' Richard took a left at a junction. They turned right again and a seagull squawked overhead.

'Are we going to try to fight our way onto a ship, or try bargain our way on first?' Sir Wobble asked.

'I suppose we can try to bargain first,' Richard said, 'that would be the safest way to get out to sea.'

'And what about sailing the ship, do we just hope the crew want to help?'

'I don't have a better idea than that, let us hope the abbot was right and they are at least on the ships. Or we had better find one with oars,' Richard grinned.

They rode out onto the harbourside without realising. It was long, as long as Richard could see in either direction in the dark, and various ships were moored along it. At the limit of his vision to his right, a large cog bobbed up and down gently, a red flag hung from its castled and raised rear platform. A handful of shadowy figures stood by it in a group. Closer ships had the odd guard, but a galley directly in front of them had two. The men stood either side of a plank of wood that led across from the harbourside onto the galley itself. The low keeled vessel was lower than most of the other ships. It had only a single mast and Richard thought it was too small for rough seas.

'That will have oars,' Sir Wobble nodded at it.

Unfortunately, the guards had seen them ride out of the town and turned to confront them. They shouted something that Richard didn't understand. 'We'll try that one first, then,' he said.

'Are we going to try bargaining?' Sir Wobble asked.

Richard shot him a glance as he drew his sword.

'I thought not,' his companion smiled and drew his own.

The two ladies at their rear screamed as shouts rippled down the harbour-front. Richard spurred Solis towards the plank and said a prayer that his horse wouldn't refuse to charge onto the ship.

'Come on, Soli,' he shouted and raised his sword. Hooves clattered on the uneven stony surface, and one of the guards raised a crossbow at him. Richard looked straight down it and saw the top of the bolt. He was dead, this was it. The guard squeezed the trigger and the bowstring twanged. The bolt fell harmlessly from the incorrectly loaded crossbow and Richard reached the man and cut at his head.

He hit something and Solis did indeed refuse to stand on the wooden plank. The stallion jumped over it instead, straight onto the deck of the galley. His metalled shoes clattered and he slipped as he scrambled right up to the mast before he stopped. Richard spun him round and saw Sir Wobble use his horse to push the second guard into the sea. The guard tumbled in with a yelp. The splashing seawater covered Bowman as he dragged his horse onto the galley, the Queen still on its back.

'Hold Soli for me,' Richard shouted to Sir Wobble, and jumped from his saddle. He could hear shouts on the land in what must have been Breton.

'We need to find the crew,' Richard shouted.

'Leave him loose, he won't jump into the sea,' Sir Wobble shouted and jumped off his own horse. The horse ran over to Solis while Sir Wobble ran back to the plank.

Bowman led the Queen to where the two confused horses stood now. He shouted at the terrified ladies to hold the horses for him.

Richard ran to the back of the galley to what looked like a cabin door.

Sir Wobble reached the plank as a crossbow bolt thudded into the galley by his leg. He ignored it and started to lift the plank up. It was heavy and he strained to tip it into the sea.

Richard heard it splash as he kicked at the door. On the third kick the wooden lock snapped and it flew open. It was pitch black inside.

'Hello?' he said as he stepped inside. He smelt them before he saw them. The air was thick and reeked of urine and human waste. He heard a cough as his eyes adjusted and he could make out the shapes of a dozen men sitting on the floor, all with their hands behind their backs.

'Hello?' he said again and approached them slowly.

'Now would be good, Richard,' Sir Wobble shouted from the front of the galley.

Richard pressed on. 'Are you the crew?' he asked.

A reply came but it was in a language he couldn't make any sense out of. Some of the others started talking or shouting, their desperation and fear clear even if their words were not.

'Are you going to kill me or help me?' he asked out loud before realising the pointlessness of it. If they didn't kill him, the Bretons were going to, so he reached over with his sword. The man nearest to him shrank back and started to cry.

'I'm saving you,' Richard pushed him aside to cut his hands free.

The man pulled his newly free hands out and stared at them. He shouted happily and started to untie his fellow prisoners.

'Richard, I really hope you have a crew in there,' Bowman appeared in the doorway, 'Christ burn me, it smells bad in here.'

'Help me free them,' Richard shouted.

Bowman rushed in and started to untie the single rope that bound them all. Freed captives started to rush outside.

'I hope they can sail this thing,' Bowman said as the last man was set loose. The man said something to Richard, then followed his companions out into the night.

'Me too,' Richard rushed out after him.

The Queen dismounted and led the three horses to the back of the galley with her ladies, away from the crossbow bolts that rained down on Sir Wobble. He was lying flat on the deck, the short front of the galley only just tall enough to cover him. Bolts thudded into the side of the ship and skidded off the deck and flew away into the sea.

'They could hit the Queen,' Richard said.

'Get her inside, then,' Bowman said.

'Your Majesty, please go inside the cabin,' Richard shouted.

Long wooden oars appeared out of the side of the ship from a level below and Richard breathed a sigh of relief.

The Queen stopped at the entrance to the cabin and turned around. 'The Queen of England and Duchess of Aquitaine will not be setting foot in such a foul place,' she said.

A bolt embedded itself in the opened cabin door an arm's length from her head. She looked at it but her face remained unimpressed.

'What about now?' Richard asked.

'Never,' she turned to face the Bretons and folded her arms.

A bolt hit Richard's empty saddle and Solis kicked his back legs out at the impact above his back. His hooves crashed into the side of the galley and broke some of the wood free. On the harbourside a group of Bretons carried another boarding plank over towards the galley.

'Come on, row,' Richard said to himself and went to stand in front of the Queen. Why hadn't he brought his shield, he asked himself. He felt the galley shift beneath him and had to move to steady his balance.

The Bretons raised their plank and wedged one side on dry land. The galley heaved itself into motion and the Breton's dropped their plank. All three horses jumped at the ground moving under them and Solis broke free from the lady holding him. He bucked and spun.

The new plank crashed down, but instead of landing on the galley it scraped the side and fell into the sea in a huge splash.

The galley's crew synchronised their oar strokes and the vessel started to cut through the calm waves.

Richard walked to his horse with his hand out. Solis stopped jumping around and snorted at him. 'I'm sorry, I said I would never put you on a ship again,' Richard said.

The Queen watched him and unfolded her arms. She clutched her stomach and looked down. 'I fear this baby is a coward,' she said, 'but you, young man, are not.'

Sir Wobble got to his feet and brushed himself down. He

rotated his shoulder around a few times, winced and walked over.

'Neither are you,' the Queen said to him, 'it took four Bretons to lift that boarding plank, yet you threw yours overboard with no aid.'

'None of those Bretons was William Marshal,' he grinned.

Richard looked around the deck. 'The horses are going to have to stay up here, but if there is a storm, they'll be overboard.'

'I will pray for no storm, but fear not,' the Queen said, 'these Castilians will row all night and all day for us.'

'Castilians?' Richard asked.

'They are from Iberia, I know them well. These men are good sailors and they will want to settle their debt to you for freeing them,' she said.

'Are you hurt?' Richard asked her.

'No, but I owe you, too,' she said, 'I will not forget either young William's strength, nor how you stood before me.'

Richard's cheeks burnt up and he had to look away.

'He is a small country knight,' Sir Wobble said to the Queen, 'don't mind him and his embarrassment.'

'Without him, tomorrow I would be a hostage of Conan of St Malo, left to rot in the old palace, to die of shame or hunger,' the Queen said, 'I can speak to these men and steer them for England's nearest port.'

Queen Eleanor did exactly that, and the oldest captive turned out to be their captain. He appeared the next day in his mail shirt, and in the daylight Richard noticed his dark complexion and eyes. The man clasped his hands over Richard's and spoke words to him. Richard nodded and smiled. The horses were given bread and water, and although Richard had to tie Solis to the mast, they settled down and accepted the voyage. The wind picked up in the morning as the sun rose to their east, and the crew hoisted their sail, which after making Solis jump, sped the galley up as they rowed.

The sun was only just clinging on to the sky when they saw land break up out of the watery horizon before them. It wasn't long before he could make out a settlement on the shore, and Richard was told that it was the port of Hastings. The galley furled its sails and rowed in as dusk darkened the English town. Before he knew it, the Queen of England had departed and he was back on English soil with his two companions.

'I thought it would feel different,' Sir Wobble said as he looked around the Hastings seafront.

'It just feels like another new place,' Richard said.

'I've been away for so long,' Sir Wobble said, 'I'm not sure I actually belong here.'

Richard wasn't sure if he belonged on either side of the channel, but he understood.

'Cheer up,' Bowman said, 'if it helps, I definitely belong here.'

'It doesn't help,' Richard said, 'come on, we need to find somewhere to sleep, we didn't really get much last night.'

'No, I need some decent food first, not ship food,' Sir Wobble yawned.

'Then we're going to London to find my grandfather,' Richard said.

'Then we'll find my brothers,' Sir Wobble said,

'No, then we'll find my sister. After that we will find your brothers.'

Sir Wobbled groaned. 'We'll do your family first then, Richard, don't worry about me.'

They found an inn and slept well, before starting their journey north to London at dawn the following day. While the roads were not busy, they were muddy and the horses slipped and stumbled their way towards the city. It stayed dry but the wind began to bring a chill to the air.

They reached the city walls at midday and once through, immediately felt warmer.

'I won't miss the wind,' Bowman said as he looked up at the two storey houses in the middle of London. They rode past a number of churches with bells which rang loudly as they went by. Richard could smell far more woodsmoke than when he'd visited with Bowman, the air was thick from the fires used to warm houses and smoke seeped out from every door frame and window. A few wagons bustled along the roads, but traffic was light.

'Do you know where we're going?' Sir Wobble asked.

'We came here on my way to Normandy,' Richard said, 'although it was warm then.'

'Your grandfather's hall better have a decent hearth,' Sir Wobble said.

'It has a hearth,' Richard frowned and checked the horizon for the churches he was navigating by.

'I think it was just down this road on the right,' Bowman pointed.

Richard wasn't sure, so they followed his advice and soon came to the road with the banners hanging from the buildings.

'This was it,' Richard spotted the white banner with the blue line through it. He smiled and dismounted by the front door. 'Do you want to come in this time?' he asked Bowman.

'Why not,' he swung himself down from his saddle and handed the horse to Sir Wobble.

'The Queen's favourite knight can hold the horses,' Richard said with a grin.

'She liked you more,' Sir Wobble said with a shrug.

Richard knocked on the old wooden door and after some time Sir Hugh's servant Edith opened it.

'Master Richard, I thought you would never be coming back?' she said. Her eyes scrunched up and her head tilted to one side.

'I nearly didn't,' Richard smiled and followed her into the hall.

The hall had not changed in the months since Richard's previous visit. The roof was still high and still collected the hearth's smoke. The fire crackled away in the centre of the hall, but this time Sir Hugh was sitting in a chair by his high table. The old man peered through the hearth smoke at Richard.

'Who is that?' he said in a voice that was hoarse and cracked.

Richard walked around the fire. 'It's me, grandfather,' he said.

'No. You? It can't be,' Sir Hugh recoiled in his chair.

'Who is this?' the man standing next to Sir Hugh asked. He was of middling height, with light hair and a flat nose. A second man sat at the table with a quill in his hand and parchment before him.

'You can't come back,' Sir Hugh raised his voice.

Richard's face fell. 'Grandfather, what's wrong?'

'No, no, he told me you were dead,' Sir Hugh said.

'Who did?'

'Your uncle.'

The man with the flat nose squinted at Richard. 'You must be the dead grandson.'

'Do I look dead to you?'

'Obviously not,' said the standing man, 'I am Sir Hugh's lawyer, Thomas of Chiswick.'

Richard looked at him and wasn't sure how much he needed to care about that. Then he turned to Sir Hugh. 'Well, I'm alive, why do you look like you have seen the Devil?'

'I'm so sorry, my boy,' Sir Hugh's body slumped into the chair as if he'd melted into it. The lines on his face were no deeper than before, but his grey hair could have been a shade whiter.

'If this is the grandson, do you still require my services?' the lawyer asked his employer.

Sir Hugh groaned and coughed. 'I have done a terrible thing, Richard, please forgive me.'

'What have you done?' Richard walked over to his grandfather and squatted down in front of his chair. The old man's small eyes flickered back at him.

'Your uncle left me with no choice. He said you were dead and told me to make him lord of Keynes. I was weak so I believed him. It is so hard to object when you're old and tired,' he said.

'You are still alive, you can just remove uncle Luke and replace him with me,' Richard said.

'It is too late for that, Saint Peter will cast me down into the pits of hell,' Sir Hugh wailed.

'Why are you crying, grandfather?'

'Because it is too late, I cannot reverse it.'

'Why not?'

'Because Luke swore fealty to King Henry for Keynes, in exchange for the King recognising his legitimacy,' Sir Hugh said.

'From a legal standpoint, the matter has been closed,' Thomas the Lawyer said, 'the manor of Keynes no longer belongs to Sir Hugh so he cannot assign a lord or heir. Luke of Keynes holds the manor directly from the King now. That ceremony has been done.'

'The King?' Richard stood up, 'the King owns Keynes now?'

'I'm sorry, I should have checked if you were alive,' Sir Hugh dropped his head down into his hands.

'I'm not just alive, grandfather, but a knight. Look at my heels.'

Sir Hugh and the lawyer glanced down and saw the yellow of the fire reflect off his golden spurs.

Sir Hugh's eyes lingered on them, then he burst into tears. 'Had I but known,' he sobbed.

Richard felt his heart beat faster. His palms sweated and he didn't know if he was angry or sad.

'Your uncle convinced me he was better suited to run the manor than you, the king even knighted him to raise him to the station required. I thought that even had you been alive, you were but a boy who had seen nothing of the world. There was no chance you could run Keynes at your age. Then the King raised Luke up, and Luke pulled out your father's knights spurs.'

'He has my father's spurs?' Richard tried to remember what spurs his uncle had been wearing when he had killed his mother. He couldn't.

'Yes, my boy, I have failed you.'

Richard wanted to throw something. 'Grandfather, I am a knight. I have actual land in Normandy, I am a real landed knight. I could have taken over Keynes without you giving it away from our family.'

Sir Hugh jerked his head up and Richard saw despair in his eyes. The old man sucked in one sharp breath and then another.

The lawyer crouched over him. 'Sir Hugh, are you alright. Get him some water,' he shouted.

Sir Hugh's breathing shortened and sharpened as his eyes looked into Richard's.

The clerk knocked his chair over getting up to run and find some water.

Richard felt a cold stab of energy surge through his belly and fear bubbled in his mind. He reached over to Sir Hugh's hands and picked them up. They were cold. The old man sucked in one large breath.

'Grandfather?' Richard whispered.

The air rushed out like a cold winter wind and Sir Hugh's eyes glazed over. His final breath hung in the air and mixed with the fire's smoke.

Richard stayed still.

Bowman walked slowly up and put a hand on his shoulder. 'I'm sorry, young lord.'

The clerk rushed back in through the back door carrying a jug of water. He crashed to a halt when he saw Sir Hugh and dropped the jug. It hit the ground and smashed, sending shards of pottery across the reeds that covered the floor.

Thomas the Lawyer sighed and looked at the clerk. 'Go and fetch a priest.'

The clerk gasped for air and shuffled out of the hall as quickly as he could.

Thomas sat down on the chair next to Sir Hugh. 'I'm not going to get paid now, am I?'

'That depends,' Richard broke eye contact with his dead grandfather. 'What can you do about my uncle and the manor that should be mine?'

'Seeing as it isn't your manor, not much,' Thomas the Lawyer said, 'but, it isn't his manor either. We were re-writing his will to make that official when you burst in here and killed him.'

'I didn't kill him,' Richard said.

'Aye,' Bowman said, 'let's be very careful about accusations like that, shall we?'

'The will that the clerk has nearly finished states that the manor of Keynes shall go to Luke, and Sir Hugh's own manor of Bletchley will do the same upon his death.'

'Bletchley?' Bowman asked.

'That's where he lives. Or lived,' Richard looked down at the body, 'it is no bigger than Keynes and is poor, but it was our family's original home. It would have gone to my father, and then to me,' Richard said and looked over to the lawyer. 'What about Bletchley, won't that come to me now?'

'No, this will gives it to your uncle.'

'That will isn't finished, what about the old will?' Richard asked.

Bowman laughed. 'I suppose that would count as a good surprise,' he said.

'Bletchley is not a great prize,' Thomas the Lawyer said, 'plague took half of its inhabitants last year, only a priest and four families still reside there. If you claim it, it will have to go through the courts.'

'I hate lawyers,' Bowman mumbled and went to poke the fire.

Richard thought about the will and his uncle. Luke may have bullied his grandfather into yielding, but he was going to fight. He was a knight now, he had killed, and he no longer had but a candlestick with which to fight his uncle.

'Lawyer, I would like to pay you.'

'Really?'

'Yes, but not for this new will,' Richard said.

'The will has been written. Sir Hugh even signed it, the clerk was merely adding the witness statement.'

Richard knew he was getting angry. His thoughts were rushing too quickly to violence and part of him was shouting inside his head to calm down. It was Sophie's voice.

'This is what is going to happen,' he said in a tone that made the Lawyer shrink, 'I am going to pay you in silver to write a document of whatever legal name is correct, to say that Bletchley and Keynes should come to me by law. Then you will take it to whatever court there is in London, even if it is the King's, and tell them about it. I'm going to come back, Thomas, and I'm going to pay you more silver if you have succeeded.'

Thomas the Lawyer looked over at Bowman then back to Richard. His face twitched. 'That is against the law, that is coercion,' he said.

'Call it what you want,' Richard said, 'I'm calling it justice. My uncle Luke is the criminal here, we shall make that right.'

Richard reached over to the parchment on the table. The ink was still wet on it as he picked it up. He read it. His anger pulsed stronger and he was sure the lawyer deserved to feel the edge of his sword.

Bowman watched him. 'Young lord, your plan is a good one, but it does depend on the lawyer being alive,' he said.

'It doesn't depend on him having all his fingers though, does it,' Richard said and put his right hand on his sword.

'Now, there is no need for that,' Thomas the Lawyer held up his hands as if they would stop Richard.

65

'Richard,' Bowman stepped closer, 'it is a good plan.'

Richard read the last of the will. 'Why did my grandfather want to give some money to a nunnery in Nottinghamshire?'

'I don't know,' the lawyer said.

Richard's mind raced and he felt his veins cool. 'I've never heard of it, why would grandfather care about it?'

'Nottinghamshire?' Bowman's eye twitched.

'He didn't tell me, but it isn't in the old will. That was the only thing we added,' Thomas said.

Richard looked at Bowman. 'Are you thinking what I'm thinking?'

'I don't think so, young lord.'

'Eustace locked Adela away in a nunnery. This might be my grandfather's way of providing something for her,' Richard said.

'Does it say which nunnery?' Bowman asked.

'Newstead, do you know it?'

Bowman shook his head. 'Not the nunnery, but I know where a town named that is. It is further north than I would like to go,' he said.

'Then we're going to Newstead,' Richard nodded, 'she must be there.'

'Don't get your hopes up,' Bowman said, 'even if she is there, she may not be your sister anymore.'

'I have to try, we are going north,' Richard felt better. There was a plan and he wasn't going to let Adela down again. 'Lawyer, do you accept my offer?'

'It is immoral and dangerous, of course I do not,' he replied.

'Dangerous?' Bowman said.

'The King has effectively sided with your uncle, and all the other laws of the land mean nothing against the decree of the King. He could hang me for treason,' Thomas the Lawyer cried.

'He could,' Richard said, 'maybe. But if you don't accept my offer, I'm going to cut your fingers off for certain. I swear it on the Holy Trinity.'

'You wouldn't,' the lawyer shuddered and gripped his chair.

'This young knight,' Bowman started, 'do you know what he did to a monk that he didn't like?'

'No, don't,' Richard hissed.

Thomas the Lawyer's wide eyes stuck on Richard.

Bowman grinned. 'The monk flew, lawyer, from a tower. Flew a long way, he did. Didn't bother this young knight after that.'

'Fine, fine, I'll do what you ask,' Thomas said, 'please don't hurt me.'

'Good, and I want you to include in that document that Edith is given this house now my grandfather is gone. Give it to her and not my uncle,' Richard said.

'Do you not want it?' The lawyer asked.

'No, I have no use for a house in London and it is a place of darkness,' Richard said, 'give it to the servant.'

'Really?'

'Really. She can have everything in it too. We will check for blankets and weapons, but she can have everything else. She can sell grandfather's sword too,' Richard said.

'Very well, if you insist.'

'I do,' Richard said, 'and don't forget any part of it.'

The lawyer took a few deep breaths. 'I can hardly forget,' he said.

Richard nodded and turned to the hearth. He read the will one more time and crouched down.

'That is a legal document, young man. It is a crime to destroy it,' Thomas the Lawyer said.

Richard held the parchment into the flames and drew his sword.

'No, you said you wouldn't, I need my fingers,' the lawyer's eyes welled up.

Richard dropped the parchment onto the fire and it started to catch. He held out his sword and just as the parchment started to rise in the heat, he pushed the sword gently onto it to keep it down.

'Oh thank the Lord and Mary the Virgin,' the lawyer moaned and made the sign of the cross.

'Pathetic,' Bowman said.

Richard held the sword in the fire until the flames consumed the whole document. He took it out and checked the blade which glowed red at the tip. Now he was going to do what he had promised to do all those months ago when he rode away from Keynes to save his own life. He was going to save his sister.

OUTLAW

The flames licked the underside of the deer. Its skin had darkened already and the legs that stuck out from the body had gone black at the bottom. The large fire was so hot that Richard sat far away from it despite the chill in the air. It burnt his face while his back seized up from the cold.

'I think I've been on the road too long,' Richard rubbed his hands together.

'It would have been four days instead of five had you not made us go around Keynes,' Bowman said.

'Everyone knows the Great North Road is the safest route north,' Richard said, 'and I don't want to run into my uncle until I'm ready.'

Sir Wobble's eyes didn't waver from the deer and he huddled inside his tattered green cloak to turn the spit. 'This is going to be amazing,' he said.

'It will get us the rest of the way to Newstead,' Bowman nodded.

'Thank my grandfather for the old hunting bow,' Richard's breath came out as a fine mist then disappeared into the air.

'They don't make bows like that anymore,' Bowman said.

'Who cares, it worked,' Sir Wobble grinned. His face was red from the fire's heat.

Richard cast his eyes around the forest that enveloped them. They had followed Bowman off the road at a distance while he hunted, but once he'd made the kill they'd gone most of the way back to it. The trees were dark and contorted, their dark trunks blocked his vision and Richard couldn't see far through their leafless branches.

'I know this forest,' Bowman said, 'few will travel up the

Great Road at this time of year. Certainly no merchants will be trading, nor farmers driving animals to market.'

'It isn't merchants and farmers I'm worried about,' Richard said.

'It's late enough that no one will see the smoke,' Bowman said.

'The fire is big and bright, though,' Richard said, 'and the trees have no leaves to hide that.'

'Well I'm sorry, young lord, do you want me to build a fence around us?'

'It's just that this is clearly poaching, and we aren't ready for a fight,' Richard said.

'I am,' Sir Wobble turned the deer over onto another side.

'You're not, I saw your shoulder when you heaved the plank into the sea.'

'I still did it though,' Sir Wobble said.

'I still can't believe that was Queen Eleanor,' Richard shook his head.

'It is a good thing you didn't get her killed,' Bowman said, 'the King would rip your entrails out and feed them to you.'

'Me? I saved her,' Richard said.

'I think it was me that saved all of us,' Sir Wobble yawned.

'What was that?' Bowman snapped his neck around and looked into the trees.

Sir Wobble lifted his hand from the spit.

Richard searched out into the night but his eyes saw nothing. All he could hear was the fire fiercely burning away, cracking and popping. He suddenly realised that embers had constantly been floating quite high into the sky.

Bowman looked over to where the bow was unstrung and wrapped up in a cloth. 'Someone's out there,' he said.

A branch cracked in the darkness.

'They have horses,' Bowman got up and rushed over to the bow.

Sir Wobble threw off his cloak and jumped to his feet.

'I'm blaming you for this one,' Richard stood up, 'which direction?'

'Towards the road,' Bowman said, but he never had time to get to the bow.

A set of shadows shifted and solidified in the dim light and Richard made out the silhouettes of two horses being led by two men.

'Only two,' Bowman said as the shadows coloured and morphed into men. The first man was tall, his green eyes were the first colour Richard's eyes caught in the darkness. The man pushed back his brown cloak and scratched his blonde hair as he strode up to the fire.

'Would you accept two strangers by your glorious fire on this cold night?' the man asked. His voice betrayed his age, Richard thought the newcomer couldn't be older than himself.

Sir Wobble relaxed and sat back down by the spit.

'Of course,' Richard said. The gaze of the young man was constant and unwavering, it made the hairs on Richard's neck tingle.

The green-eyed young man handed his horse to his companion and stopped at the fire.

'I am Nicholas,' he said, 'who are you?'

'Richard, and this is William and Robert.'

Bowman squatted down by the bow bag and waited, his eyes on Nicholas.

'This is my servant,' Nicholas said, 'Gerold.'

Gerold didn't tie or hobble the horses, which seemed strange to Richard, especially as he left their tack on. He slipped his right hand inside his cloak so it was on his sword but not visible.

Nicholas walked up to the fire and stopped a few paces away. He held his hands out and the fire shone shades of orange on them. 'It is a cold night, you have my thanks for allowing me to warm up,' he said.

'No need for thanks,' Richard said.

'What are you three fellows doing out on the road at this time of year?' Nicholas asked.

'Travelling to visit my sister,' Richard said. He looked over to Bowman who was dead still. Sir Wobble turned the spit, yawned and idly scratched his face.

Gerold came over and stood next to Nicholas to warm his hands too.

'Where have you journeyed from?' Nicholas asked.

'London,' Richard said.

Nicholas peered down at Sir Wobble over the fire. 'Is that your servant?'

'Yes,' Richard said.

Sir Wobble looked up and opened his mouth.

'Quite an insolent servant,' Richard said, 'he has come newly to me. Quiet, William.'

Sir Wobble furrowed his brow at Richard but closed his mouth.

'My father always says insolent servants should be beaten,' Nicholas said, 'you should not let insolence pass.'

'I'm not beating anyone in this cold,' Richard said.

'It would warm you up. You don't look like a merchant or a priest, are you noble?'

Sir Wobble snorted.

'If you don't beat him, I might,' Nicholas said.

'I'm not beating him,' Richard swallowed. He opened the cloak up round his neck to let some heat out. He ached to throw it away but held firm.

'Whose service are you in?' Nicholas asked.

Richard was tired. He'd been too cold to sleep well for the past three nights, and now this young interloper had heated him up so much he was sweating inside his clothing. He was a knight and they outnumbered the newcomers. Annoyance started to push his worry and tension aside. 'Why do you care?' he snapped.

'Now, no need for that,' Nicholas said, 'I'm just making conversation, showing you my courtesy.'

'Who are you, then?'

'No need to be rude,' Nicholas dropped his hands from the fire.

'I'm not being rude, I'm just making conversation,' Richard tried to mimic his tone.

Bowman remained still on the ground, his face set.

'I am Nicholas.'

'Who do you serve?' Richard asked.

'Would you be so kind as to share some of that deer once it is ready?' Nicholas asked.

Sir Wobble frowned. 'Maybe two of the legs,' he said.

Nicholas laughed loudly. 'That's two beatings your servant has earned himself. If the deer is no good, I will make that three and do it myself.'

Sir Wobble's eyes narrowed.

'We can give you as much as you can eat,' Richard said.

'I should think so,' Nicholas said, 'because that deer is more mine than yours.'

Gerold stepped towards Bowman and threw his cloak over his shoulder. His hand rested on his sword.

'Wait,' Nicholas said, 'everybody stay where they are.'

Richard's hand gripped his sword under the cloak. This was no time to be getting into a fight. Breath steamed out into the chilled air and the fire spat. Richard smelt the meat cooking but his mouth was dry.

'I do not wish for violence,' Nicholas said, 'just for a fair outcome.'

Richard licked his lips and waited.

Nicholas's green eyes bored into him with more confidence than he should have had for his age.

'I will take payment for the deer in addition to two legs. Then we will be on our way,' the tall young man said.

'What do you want?' Richard asked.

'All of your coin and all other valuables with you,' Nicholas's face remained firm as he spoke to Richard.

That couldn't happen. 'We don't have anything valuable,' Richard said.

'That's what everyone says,' Nicholas said, 'but it is never true. Which means you are lying to me.'

Richard stared back at him.

'You think that because there are three of you, you need not fear us,' Nicholas said.

Sir Wobble stifled a chuckle.

The tall youth raised his eyebrows. 'If he's a servant, then I'm the king of England,' he narrowed his eyes.

'But I'm not the King of England,' he continued, 'although I am the son of a man who knows him. The son of the man who owns this land you're poaching on.'

A gust of wind blew through the empty branches and blew the flames to one side for a moment.

'My father doesn't take kindly to outlaws poaching his game,' Nicholas said, 'but if you pay me, we can all be friends.'

'I'm not going to pay you,' Richard said.

Gerold drew his sword a fraction out of its scabbard and Bowman shifted his balance.

'Then you have a choice,' Nicholas said.

'What's that?'

'Pay me, die, or tell me who shot the deer so I can take him back to my father.'

Richard glanced at Bowman without realising.

'Him? He does have the look of a hunter,' Nicholas said and looked around the fire, 'I had not seen you down there.'

Bowman's lips pressed together and Richard primed himself to fling aside his cloak and draw his weapon.

'Your hair is blonde and you are a poacher. I wonder if I might know who you are. There are two outlaws in this forest you could be. Stephen of Calverton has blonde hair, but he is supposed to be a decade older than you appear to be.'

'He isn't an outlaw,' Richard said.

'I think he is. The other outlaw said to roam this area, killing good men and robbing merchants, is Robert of Shelford.'

Richard looked for Bowman's reaction as another gust of wind blew through their camp. It caused Nicholas's horse to jump and the shield hanging from its saddle rattled. The light from the fire caught it. The shield had a chequerboard pattern on it, and Richard had a fleeting thought in the night that it could have been yellow and red.

Bowman saw it too, but he did not hesitate. He pounced up at Gerold. Gerold started to draw his sword but Bowman knocked him to the ground and they disappeared in a ball of woollen cloaks.

'Gut him, Gerold,' Nicholas shouted and turned to Richard, 'let them fight.'

Richard and Sir Wobble paused.

'I am Nicholas, bastard son of Geoffrey Martel, and if you harm me you are all dead men.'

'There is a reward for that man's capture,' Nicholas shouted, 'let me have him and you can live.'

Bowman and Gerold unravelled from each other and

Bowman came up on his feet. Gerold lay on the floor and cried out loudly.

Nicholas's eyes lost their confidence and he flashed his sword free from his cloak. Bowman was already going for him, his knife tight in his hands. Nicholas stepped aside and dodged the thrust. Bowman, who was larger, turned to wrestle the Martel man, but the youth was quicker. He stuck a leg out and Bowman tripped. As he fell to the ground, Nicholas slashed out with his sword and Bowman's cloak tore. Nicholas started to run back to his horse and Richard snapped out from his inaction. 'Get him,' he cried.

Sir Wobble flew from his position and ran. Nicholas vaulted into his saddle as Richard made it past Bowman. The Martel bastard kicked his horse on as Richard tried to slash him with his sword. The blade hit the saddle and he felt the wood resist him. Nicholas shouted at his horse and it burst into a canter, branches snapped underfoot and around Nicholas's body as he flew from the camp and disappeared into the night.

Richard grabbed Gerold's horse and caught his breath. The sound of hooves quickly faded and he turned to see Sir Wobble bending down over Bowman.

Gerold called out in pain but it was faint.

Richard looped the horse's reins around a stout branch and went to where Bowman lay. The big man had rolled over onto his back and lifted up his left arm.

'I knew a Martel man was going to be the death of me,' he said.

'That's just a cut,' Sir Wobble said and pulled apart the split tunic to look at the wound.

Richard knelt down and looked too. The wound was deep and the flesh torn apart rather than neatly cut. Rich red blood oozed out onto his green tunic.

Bowman turned his neck to look. 'That's deep, the pain is going to hit me soon, give me all the cider,' he said.

Sir Wobble went to rummage through his bags.

'What do I do?' Richard asked.

'We need to burn it and pack it with moss,' Bowman said, 'damn those Martel bastards to hell.'

'Here,' Sir Wobble said and thrust a leather covered bottle

at Bowman. He took a long drink and passed back the empty container. Sir Wobble frowned.

'Richard, heat your knife up in the fire, it needs to be as hot as the fire,' Bowman said.

Richard took out his eating knife and had to use his cloak to cover his hands and face to get close enough to get it into the flames.

'It hurts,' Bowman cried out in frustration.

'We can keep the new horse for Adela,' Richard said as he felt the heat creep up the blade and into his hand.

'Is that really what you're thinking about right now?' Sir Wobble asked.

'You're thinking about how he's just drunk a whole bottle of your cider, so don't judge me,' Richard said.

A fain groan escaped from under the cloak that covered Gerold.

'We need to do something with him, too,' Sir Wobble added.

'I'll kill him before I die, don't you worry about that,' Bowman gritted his teeth together and clutched his bleeding arm. He muted a howl of agony.

'What we should be thinking about is the Martels,' Sir Wobble said, 'from what you've told me, their lands are here, and they will come looking for us tomorrow. We need to be thinking about moving. And you mentioned your sister.'

'So what?' Richard said from under his cloak.

'Nicholas Martel knows Bowman is here. If your uncle or Eustace is here with them, then they will know who you are, and Eustace knows where he put your sister,' Sir Wobble said.

An icy finger stretched around Richard's heart and gripped it tightly. 'Oh Christ, they could go to Adela tomorrow, and if we are going to the wrong place they will get there first,' he said.

'Exactly, so we need to be moving now,' Sir Wobble said.

'Only once he's ready to,' Richard said.

'It's got to be hot enough now, get it over and done with,' Bowman hissed as blood seeped between his fingers and down his arm.

'I don't know how to do it, what if I do it wrong?' Richard said.

'Hold the knife against the inside until it stops bleeding,'

Bowman said, 'it goes wrong if I don't hold still.'

'Do you want me to do it?' Sir Wobble said.

Richard pulled the knife out of the fire and went to Bowman. 'No, he's here because of me so this falls to me,' he said.

Bowman removed his bloodied hand and set himself. 'Do it.'

Richard pressed the knife into Bowman's arm. He screamed a scream that hurt Richard's ears as skin was cauterised and blackened. Steam roared out into his face and Richard recoiled at the smell, images of the village of Fallencourt burning flashed back into his mind, and he flinched the knife away.

Bowman howled and looked down. 'It's half done, boy, reheat the knife.'

Richard felt giddy but went back to crouch near the fire. He plunged his knife back into it and threw his cloak back over himself. This was bad, this was very bad.

'How does it feel?' Sir Gobble asked.

'How do you think it feels?' Bowman replied.

'I don't know, that's why I'm asking,' Sir Wobble said, 'no one did this after my wound at Castle Peacock.'

'They should have,' Bowman said and looked down at his arm, 'I'm feeling cold, you need to hurry.'

'I can't heat it up any quicker,' Richard said, but decided the knife would be hot enough anyway. He went back to Bowman and pressed the blade into the other side of the wound. All of Richard's sense repulsed and he choked on the taste that rose up into his mouth.

'I'm not going to be able to eat the deer now,' he said as he removed the knife.

'More for me then,' Sir Wobble grinned.

Bowman checked his arm and leant back to lie on the ground. 'Oh, Jesus that hurts so much,' he said.

'Is it done?' Richard asked.

'No idea, but it will go bad, I know it,' Bowman said, 'I've got a feeling, I just know it.'

'You'll be fine,' Richard said.

Bowman tried to lift his left arm up off the ground but grunted and failed. 'I can't move it, young lord, I'm done for. I'm so cold.'

'Calm down,' Sir Wobble said, 'have a rest for a while, you can have some sleep before we need to be gone.'

'Who cares, I'll be dead in a week,' Bowman said, 'my life was a waste, what have I done with it?'

'You helped me,' Richard said hopefully.

'Have I? You're about to get murdered by the people who killed me and half my family,' Bowman said.

'I will kill Eustace,' Richard looked around for a large leafed weed to wipe his knife on.

'Or I will,' Sir Wobble went back to the spit to turn the deer. It had gone completely black on the side it had been sat on, which only added to the stench of burnt flesh around the camp.

'Someone has to,' Bowman said, 'they mutilated my father and sent him to a monastery. Eustace took my sister and kept her locked away. Until he sent her to the same monastery that is, just so that her and my father could see how broken each other were.'

'That's terrible,' Richard said and his mind went back to Adela, 'what happened?'

'My father was a tenant of Geoffrey Martel,' Bowman said.

'Wait, was he a knight?' Sir Wobble asked.

Richard looked at Bowman. 'Are you the son of a knight?'

The wounded man hesitated. He exhaled deeply. The steam from his breath drifted upwards into the cold night sky and diffused away into nothing.

'I was,' Bowman sighed.

He looked up through the branches above and the dull clouds drifting along overhead.

'I think Geoffrey wanted my mother, because he told my father they were divorced and that he was to leave Martel lands. Geoffrey must have given the task of removing my father to Eustace to prove himself, because he was young at the time. Like me he was probably not even thirteen. I remember men bursting into our manor house and taking my father out. He fought them for sure, but Eustace had big men under his command and my father stood no chance. Eustace gave him a choice from his father. Leave or have his family killed. He chose to leave. Eustace ordered his men to remove one of his hands, and I saw them do it from where I was hiding.'

'Christ save us,' Richard muttered, 'I don't know if I want to hear any more.

'I do,' Sir Wobble turned his spit.

'Eustace took more than the hand in the end. He took an eye with his own knife,' Bowman said, 'then his men bundled off my mother.'

'What happened to her?' Richard asked.

'The story told is that Geoffrey Martel kept her for a while. I don't know what happened,' Bowman said, 'have we got more cider?'

'Go on, give him some,' Richard said to Sir Wobble, who trudged off to find another bottle.

'Do you know which monastery they are in?'

'No,' Bowman replied and drank from the bottle Sir Wobble came back with.

'You should have told me, it is half the same story as mine,' Richard said.

'What good would it have done?'

'I don't know,' Richard looked over into the burning fire, 'but I ran away. What did you do?'

'I was too young to do the sensible thing that you did, young lord. I found a sword and then I found Eustace Martel,' Bowman said.

'Why?' Sir Wobble asked, 'what could you have done?'

'Nothing, but I thought men should fight for what was right. And family, men should fight for family,' Bowman said.

'What happened?'

'Obviously he didn't kill me, but when I found him he had men with him,' Bowman said, 'my anger disappeared and fear replaced it. I was so young.'

'But he spared you,' Richard said.

'He did, but he gave me a choice after his man swatted my sword out of my hands. He told me that someone had to die for my insolence. Either me right there and then, or my sister. I ran. And I will go to hell for it,' Bowman said.

'I ran too, and I was years older than you,' Richard said.

Bowman shook his head. 'It doesn't matter now though, does it, I'm dead anyway.'

'We can still fix things,' Richard said.

'Only if we leave before morning,' Sir Wobble said.

'Yes, you've made that clear,' Richard said, 'what happened, did Eustace kill your sister?'

'Eustace took my sister but he didn't kill her. The story is the same as my mother, except for ending up in the monastery with my father,' Bowman said.

'No wonder you wanted to kill him,' Richard said.

'If anything, I'm surprised you showed so much restraint,' Sir Wobble said.

Richard nodded.

'I've had probably more than fifteen years to think about it,' Bowman said, 'and I had managed to avoid all Martels for that whole time. At least until this young one showed up.'

'I'm very sorry, this is all my fault,' Richard said.

'It is really,' Sir Wobble said, 'but I think that's just life.'

'Or death,' Bowman groaned.

Richard looked over at Gerold's horse. It had a shield hanging from it just as Nicholas's had, but it was plain red. 'Is Gerold not a Martel man?'

Sir Wobble looked over at the blanket over him. 'I think you meant, was.'

Richard sighed and looked back at the shield. 'Did anyone else notice Nicholas's eyes?'

'Typical Martel eyes. They had evil in them,' Bowman said.

Richard looked at Bowman. 'But did you also notice his hair?'

Bowman's eyes wrinkled, then his face drained of colour and froze.

'What?' Sir Wobble asked.

'Did you notice what colour his hair was?' Richard asked him.

'Blonde I think, I didn't really get a good look.'

'And what colour is Bowman's hair?'

'Blonde?'

'So?' Richard said, 'have you listened to his story at all?'

'I wish I had died before you said that,' Bowman groaned.

'Hold on,' Sir Wobble stood up, 'but Eustace never seemed to recognise you?'

'I told you, I was a boy, and so was he.'

Richard put his head down into his hands and let out a deep breath. 'I can't keep up with this, everything is already complicated enough.'

'I can't believe I've been killed by my own half brother,' Bowman said.

'Do you think he knows?' Sir Wobble asked.

'Who?'

'Nicholas.'

'He must do, if he knows who Bowman's mother is,' Richard said.

'Curse them all,' Bowman pushed himself up with his good arm, 'let us eat this damned deer that's cost me my life and be gone.'

'He has gotten rather dramatic all of a sudden,' Sir Wobble said to Richard.

'I'm getting bored of it, to be honest,' Richard replied.

Sir Wobble started to push out the logs burning in the fire so it would start to break up.

Bowman watched and kept looking down at his arm.

Richard swore under his breath and tried to clear his nose of the smell of burnt flesh. 'If any of us survive this, we need to do something about the Martels,' he said.

'I agree,' Sir Wobble said.

Bowman nodded. 'I'm might be dying, but my anger will keep me alive long enough to have a second go at my so-called brother,' he said.

Richard believed him.

HOLY SISTER

Richard thumped on the big wooden door and stepped back to look up at the building.

'Are you sure this is a nunnery?' Sir Wobble asked from his horse behind.

The stone block walls were put together in a way that reminded Richard of London's ancient city walls. The building was only one storey high though, and didn't seem all that wide.

'No, not really,' Richard said.

'The farmer said this area was Newstead,' Sir Wobble said, 'but this could be anything from a monastery to a royal hunting lodge.'

Richard stepped away from Solis and banged on the door again.

'We're going to have to reheat this thing now, it's stone cold,' Sir Wobble complained.

Richard turned to him and the deer carcass that was strapped to the back of his saddle.

'It did keep my back warm for a while, though,' Sir Wobble grinned, 'and tonight it will keep my belly warm from the inside.'

'How is he?' Richard gestured at Bowman on his horse. Bowman himself was slumped forwards in the saddle.

'I think he's more asleep than dead,' Sir Wobble said.

'Either way, we better be in the right place,' Richard said, 'and I could do with some sleep myself.'

'We aren't supposed to need much of that,' Sir Wobble frowned, 'you are not hardy enough.'

'What are you talking about?'

'You're a knight, you're supposed to be out hawking and

hunting with hounds, living on the land and not sleeping in a bed like a fat merchant,' Sir Wobble said.

'That's rich coming from you, you don't even like hunting,' Richard said.

'All you need to do is stop complaining about being tired and cold,' Sir Wobble stretched his upper body out and yawned.

Richard ignored him and went to knock on the door again. As he hit it, it gave way, and he nearly punched a nun in the face. The startled woman froze as his clenched fist grazed her nose.

'I'm so sorry,' Richard took a quick step backwards.

The nun swallowed and her small eyes blinked. 'Can I help you?'

'I'm sorry sister, I'm looking for my, well, my sister,' Richard said.

'Is she a nun here?'

'I don't know.'

'Is she at least a nun?'

'She wasn't,' Richard said.

The nun frowned and shook her head. She was short and on the edge of looking old. 'Why do you think she's here?' she asked.

'That is a long story,' Richard said, 'but the short version is that my grandfather told me she was.'

Sir Wobble let out a laugh mixed with a snort, and started to cough to suppress it.

The nun cast her eyes at him and frowned. 'Really. What is her name?'

'Adela.'

The nun looked at Richard. 'I know of no one of that name, but I will fetch the mother superior.'

'Thank you,' Richard said as the nun retreated back inside and shut the door behind her. He heard a bolt slide across.

'Not very welcoming,' Sir Wobble said.

'I think that was your fault,' Richard said, 'and you undermined me by laughing.'

'Undermined?' Sir Wobble lifted himself up and out of his saddle, 'you are not my lord.'

The bolt slid open with a clunk and the door swung back open.

The nun returned. 'I could find no one called Adela among the sisters,' she said.

Richard's world caved in. They were in the wrong place, which probably meant Adela's death. His eyes blurred and dizziness sent his vision spinning. He stumbled to one side, and leant on the wooden walls.

'Not very knightly,' Sir Wobble walked towards the doorway and peered at his friend.

Richard shook his head and tried to catch his breath. How could this have happened? How did he come to the wrong nunnery? He had no idea at all where Adela was.

Another nun walked out of the nunnery behind the first and looked at Richard. She was of average height, had dark hair under a linen headdress, and a straight nose. His family's straight nose. The nun had said she wasn't there, but standing before Richard, was very definitely his sister.

'Richard?' she said.

'But. How?' Richard cried and ran to her.

Adela back-pedalled but he was too fast, embraced her and pushed her back into the nunnery.

'What are you doing here?' she shoved him away.

'I've come to find you,' tears rolled down his eyes.

'I told you this was the right place,' Sir Wobble walked forwards.

'I missed you so much,' Richard stepped back, 'how are you?'

'Quite well,' Adela said.

'Really?'

'Of course, it has been a long time, brother.'

'Not that long, I've longed for this moment since we were torn apart.'

'Come, brother, we should go inside,' Adela said. She waved Richard into the nunnery and turned to the other nun. 'The man on that horse is either drunk or in need of our help, gather the sisters and see him to the infirmary.'

The nun nodded and scurried away.

Richard narrowed his eyes. 'You can order older nuns around?'

Adela smiled faintly, so faintly that Richard wasn't even sure it was a smile.

A group of nuns who had gathered to eavesdrop responded to the order and went outside to carry Bowman in.

'Stable their horses for them,' Adela said.

'Thank you,' Sir Wobble said, 'I'm William Marshal.'

'That's very nice,' Adela said, 'follow me, we have somewhere to sit down.'

Richard had long let go of Solis and a nun already stroked him on the nose while she whispered to him. Happy his horse was being well cared for, Richard went in after his sister.

Sir Wobble followed him along a cloister, one side open to a courtyard that one could ride into from the entranceway.

A nun rushed up behind them and bowed to Adela. 'The guest is wounded not drunk, they will tend to him,' she said.

'He's probably both, actually,' Sir Wobble said.

'Thank you, sister,' Adela replied, 'what happened to your friend?'

'A run in with some bad people. A bit of a family disagreement actually, it was his half-brother,' Richard said.

'I hope you haven't killed anyone?'

'I didn't, not here at least,' he dropped his eyes and wondered why he felt any guilt at all about those who he had killed. Had not all of them wanted to harm him?

Adela turned into a room. 'This is our refectory, it is where we eat,' she said.

Richard turned away for a moment to compose himself and saw his horse being led through the courtyard and into a stable block. Nuns were around all the horses and he could hear their excited voices from the cloister. Inside the refectory however, it was quiet, cool and surprisingly small. Sparsely furnished only with wooden tables and chairs, no fire lit it and shadows stretched out from the doorway. No windows let light in either, and Richard frowned at the prospect of spending time there.

'Sit,' Adela said and Richard found a chair for himself.

Sir Wobble inspected the room, shrugged and sat down. 'At least we got here first,' he said.

'First?' Adela glanced at Richard.

'Worry not,' Richard said, 'I can't believe we found you.'

'How did you find me?'

'Grandfather left a clue in his will,' Richard said.

'His will? Is he dead?' Adela asked.

'He is,' Richard sighed, 'it's just us now, everything we had is gone. They're all gone.'

'They told me mother died,' Adela's eyes dimmed, 'but I didn't know if it was true.'

'I'm so sorry, it is true. I watched uncle Luke kill her myself,' the words tumbled from Richard's mouth and he felt more tears build in his eyes. 'Who told you about it?'

'They did,' Adela nodded, her face impassive other than her eyes, 'uncle Luke was with them. She paused and stared intently at Richard. The *voices* told me that they will take him, though.'

'The voices?' Richard asked.

'Yes,' she said softly, 'but why are you here, brother?'

'We came to rescue you,' Richard said, 'I've brought a horse for you to ride away with us. So much has happened since we were last together, I own a village and castle in Normandy where you can be safe. I'm even married now.'

His sister raised her eyebrows and sighed. 'You have read too many tales of knights and princesses, brother. Not all women need saving.'

'What?'

'Not all women need saving, Richard,' Adela repeated.

'But you can't be happy here, you were imprisoned,' Richard said.

'Yes I was, but it was the start of a journey that led to my redemption.'

'But you're stuck in a nunnery,' Richard said.

Sir Wobble rocked his chair back onto two legs. 'Maybe she likes it here, Richard. There are many nuns you know, surely not all of them can hate their condition.'

'You're not being helpful,' Richard snapped.

'He is not wrong,' Adela said.

'Could we light a fire in here and reheat my deer?' Sir Wobble asked.

'I was going to gift that deer to the abbey in thanks for finding Adela alive,' Richard said.

'It's not yours to give,' Sir Wobble slammed his chair back down to floor onto four legs. One of them creaked a little too much.

'It isn't yours either, did you hunt it?' Richard asked.

Sir Wobbled scrunched up his face.

'I took the candlestick from the chapel at Keynes,' Richard said to his sister, 'I have brought it with me and I think I want you to have it. I must confess that I hit our uncle in the head with it and the blood has stained it,' Richard said.

'Why did you do that?'

'He was about to kill me, sister.'

'Seems fair to me,' Sir Wobble said.

'Can you fetch it for us, please?' Richard asked him.

His friend groaned and got up. Sir Wobble mumbled something on his way out but Richard let him be to avoid further complaints.

'You never had a friend when we were growing up, this is good for you,' Adela said.

'I don't know what you're talking about. You didn't either.'

'Don't be petty. Tell me about your village in Normandy,' Adela asked.

Richard did. He left out the part where he killed a man in an alleyway that wasn't an alleyway, and also where the monk flew from the tower. He also neglected to mention that he'd recently had very satisfying dreams where he throttled Yvetot's priest. His sister nodded along in the washed-out light.

Sir Wobble returned with the candlestick as the story landed at Hastings, and Richard skipped over his grandfather's death and the ambush by Nicholas Martel.

Sir Wobble placed the silverware onto the nearest table. It had nothing to reflect and looked duller than Richard had ever seen it before.

'Here you are, my lord and master,' Sir Wobble said and slouched back down into his chair.

'Thank you, Richard,' Adela said, 'we are very happy to receive your gift.'

Richard stared at the dull candlestick. 'Why did the nun not know your name?' he asked.

'I do not go by my old name here,' Adela said.

'Why not?'

'I was brought here very soon after I was taken, for Satan's man did not find me agreeable.'

'You mean Eustace?'

Adela's eyes lit up like a fire that Richard could only interpret as hatred.

She nodded. 'We do not speak his name. He deposited me here as a frightened child, crying and alone. The abbess took me in, for most of the sisters here share my story.'

'They can't all have been abused by Eustace, surely?' Richard asked.

'He is not a bad apple on a good tree. His whole family and their followers make up an orchard that is an affront to God,' Adela said and her eyes glazed over. 'But they do fill this nunnery, and good work is done here.'

'You can't be saying that what they've done is a good thing?'

'It is neither good nor bad, Richard, I have learnt that here. We help our community, we employ their wage-men on our fields. We sell them our produce, teach them, and improve their lives. These are all good things, and few of the sisters would be here without the satanic family's evils to bring us together,' Adela said.

'I wasn't expecting her to say that,' Sir Wobble said, 'but we still want to kill Eustace and the bastard, yes?'

'Killing is a sin,' Adela said calmly but her eyes flickered when he said Eustace.

'They must face justice,' Richard said.

'By killing them?' Sir Wobble checked.

'Blood should not be spilt in vengeance,' Adela said.

Richard looked between his friend and his sister, and couldn't find an answer that would satisfy both.

'The Lord forgives, so should we,' Adela said, 'and I can see how much you hurt, brother. You need not torture yourself for fleeing Keynes. You could not save me, and it was best that I was not saved. I forgive you.'

He had to wipe away a tear. 'I have been self-centred and childish,' Richard said, 'I have only thought about my own grief and guilt. I wanted to rescue you to make myself feel better. I can see that you are not in need of my help. They called you the mother superior, yet you have been here less than a year. I thought you had to serve for fixed terms to be able to advance?'

'You do. Normally. The Lord spoke to me as soon as I arrived here. He told me that I should use my suffering to heal others, to transfer their ailments to myself. The sister I hugged when I arrived had terrible back pain, but once I let her go she was cured of it.'

'Can you touch my shoulder?' Sir Wobble asked.

'I thought knights shouldn't complain about pain or discomfort?' Richard arched his eyebrows.

'I haven't complained about it, have I? I'm just seeing if she can help me.'

Adela got to her feet and approached Sir Wobble. He pointed to his shoulder. She put both of her hands around it and gripped.

Richard saw his eyes bulge. 'Remember, that's my sister,' he said.

Sir Wobble's face turned bright red despite the lack of light in the refectory. He strained under Adela's hands and after a while exhaled deeply. His eyes closed and his whole body relaxed.

Adela released her hands. 'It is done,' she said, 'the shoulder was holding all of your guilt over the lives you have taken.'

'I'm quite sure that he doesn't know how to feel guilt,' Richard said.

'His body does,' Adela returned to her seat.

Sir Wobble rotated his shoulder and grinned. 'That worked,' he said.

'Has the Lord said anything about our father?' Richard asked, 'or does he only speak of healing.'

'The voices say many things, but they speak to help people, they guide me to help people,' she said.

'So, nothing about our father?'

'No,' Adela said.

'Did they guide you to become the mother superior?'

Sir Wobble yawned, slouched into his chair, and closed his eyes.

'No, my miracles convinced the abbess that I should follow her when she leaves us. She thinks I'm touched by the divine.'

'If you finally fixed his shoulder, then I think you must be,' Richard said.

'The Lord has a plan for us all, Richard. Mine is to help the people in this growing town.'

'Mine is to bring justice to the Martels and uncle Luke,' Richard hardened.

Adela's eyes raged again. 'Our uncle will rot in hell, he will be torn apart by wild beasts each day for eternity, his eyes will be pecked out by crows and he'll watch wolves fight over his entrails.'

Richard blinked. 'Where is my younger sister?' he asked.

'He will die a thousand times every day, brother.'

'He should be punished in this world first,' Richard said.

'Do not put on the cloak of justice to cover a lust for vengeance,' Adela said, 'justice should be pure and clean.'

'Am I not pure and clean?'

'No, Richard, you are a warrior and a husband. You have killed, and killed more than you've told me,' Adela said, 'it should not be you that brings justice to our uncle.'

Richard frowned. 'Someone has to, and I will if I get the chance.'

Adela looked at him. 'Trust in the Lord's plan.'

A quiet snore escaped from Sir Wobble.

'You really aren't going to leave here, are you? The horse I brought for you to escape on - I suppose I will donate that to the nunnery instead,' Richard said.

'Again, that is most generous of you,' Adela said, 'although I think the sisters will find having a horse here too much of a distraction.'

'You can sell it for all I care,' Richard yawned, 'do you really like it here, isn't it boring?'

'Boredom is a luxury of the rich and the sinful. I manage the labour we hire and deal with the merchants too, I have work that keeps me busy,' she said.

'What I've learnt from trying to manage Yvetot is that those things are boring and terribly complicated,' Richard said, 'they make me bored and confused.'

Adela's eyes sharpened. 'They make me feel powerful. Have you ever felt powerful?'

Richard frowned. 'When I lower my lance,' he replied.

'My ledgers are my lance. I have power within these walls. Outside of this nunnery, and without the Lord's voices, I have nothing. Do you see?'

'I will be very sad to leave you,' Richard said.

'And I you, but we have different paths to follow.'

'Before we go, would you mind trying to heal my other friend, please?'

'Of course, I can help him now,' Adela said.

'Thank you,' Richard got up and followed his sister out of the refectory. As he walked into the cloister he glanced into the courtyard where two nuns played with Solis over his stable door. They stroked his nose and he lipped at their hands as they giggled and teased him before pulling them away. After walking back past the front door, Adela took Richard to a small dormitory where Bowman lay on one of four beds. He was awake but his half closed eyelids opened when he saw Richard.

'How are you feeling?' Richard asked.

'I thought I'd hate a nunnery, but this is more pleasant than I was expecting,' Bowman looked around at the younger of the nuns attending to him. Two inspected his cauterised wound.

'Whoever performed this had the subtly of a drunken bear,' one said.

Bowman raised his eyes up to Richard, who kept his silence.

'Can you fix it?' Bowman asked, 'it feels like a rat is gnawing around inside my arm.'

'The cut runs very deep,' a fair haired and middle-aged nun replied, 'it smells of corruption.'

'What does that mean?' Richard asked.

'It means that we will pray for your friend, and mix a remedy for him, but his fate cannot be changed by mortal means,' the nun said.

'I knew I was going to die,' Bowman groaned, 'can you bury me under a shady tree?

'Shut up,' Richard said, 'it's too early to be thinking about that.'

The nun glanced up at Richard. 'Such talk might prove prudent,' she said.

'Allow me,' Adela walked towards the wound.

The nuns peeled aside and knelt down around Bowman. They put their hands together, closed their eyes and started to pray.

'What are they doing?' Bowman asked, 'I feel like the piglet that's about to get slaughtered for a feast.'

'My sister has healing powers,' Richard said.

Bowman's eyes opened up fully. 'Does she now?'

Adela put a hand either side of the sword cut and squeezed. Bowman groaned and then cried out as her finger nails dug into his skin.

'This isn't healing me, she's going to rip my arm off,' he said.

'Quiet, let her do it,' Richard said, 'if you're so convinced you're going to die anyway, where's the harm?'

Bowman pressed his lips together as Adela kept the pressure on. The prayers of the nuns swirled around Adela in the cold dormitory, they were almost enough to warm Richard. The few candles on the stand next to Bowman flickered in the air and threw the nun's shadows up against the wall behind them. Adela held firm and it wasn't long before Bowman's face softened and he yawned.

'There,' Adela said, 'the corruption under the skin has been removed.'

'I'm so tired,' Bowman's eyes dulled.

'Sleep,' Adela gestured, turned and nodded at the nuns, 'thank you sisters, you may go.'

'Is he cured?' Richard asked.

'It is too soon to know,' Adela said, 'and not everyone deserves to be cured, the Lord sometimes chooses not to heal those I touch.'

'It did something, he's fast asleep,' Richard grinned, 'whatever happens, thank you for trying.'

'You did come back for me, even if you didn't need to,' Adela said.

Richard looked at his sister and marvelled at how much older she looked now. Her expression was now that of an adult, not a girl, and she seemed to have a weight on her shoulders.

'Can we rest here until he wants to travel again?' he asked.

'Of course,' Adela said, 'you are welcome to stay as long as you need to.'

Richard thought he heard a bang on the front door. He looked out of the dormitory and Adela frowned at him. 'What is it?' she asked.

'I thought I heard the door,' his heart sunk and remembered what had happened on the way to the nunnery.

'Should I be worried?' Adela folded her arms.

'That depends on who that is,' Richard felt a rush of fear of what he might have brought to his sister's doorstep.

'Might this have something to do with the wound on your friend?'

'It might,' Richard said, 'I'm going to wake Sir Wobble.'

'Who?'

'William, my hungry friend,' Richard said.

Adela rolled her eyes. 'I hope you are not expecting to fight inside this nunnery.'

'I don't want to, but it doesn't mean they won't come in,' he said.

Adela sighed. 'Let me see who it is before you overreact.'

'It is probably better if you don't open the door,' Richard left the dormitory and ran back to the refectory. Sir Wobble was fast asleep in his chair where Richard had left him.

'Wake up,' Richard rushed over and shook him.

'What?' Sir Wobble groaned and pushed Richard's hand away.

'There's someone at the door,' Richard said.

'So? Give them a drink and some food and send them on their way,' Sir Wobble rubbed his eyes.

'Where do you think we are?' Richard asked.

Sir Wobble yawned and looked around the refectory. 'Oh,' he said.

'Yes, oh. We need to either arm or get Bowman out of here.'

Adela appeared in the doorway and her face was white. 'I looked out of a window. There are three riders and a dozen men on foot outside,' she said.

Richard made the sign of the cross. 'If you're listening, Christ, save our souls,' he said.

Sir Wobble jumped up. 'We should have already left,' he said.

'You can't blame me for this,' Richard said, 'you're the one who was sound asleep.'

'Fine, let's kill the riders and the rest will scatter,' he replied.

'Footmen can still get in here and find Bowman, we need to get him on his horse and lead him out of here,' Richard said.

'We can't run, their riders will catch us,' Sir Wobble said.

'Hide here, I will prevent their entry,' Adela said.

Richard and Sir Wobble exchanged glances. 'I hardly think these men will respect any sanctity here,' Richard said.

Sir Wobble shook his head in agreement.

'The sisters can move your friend into one of the outbuildings and hide him,' Adela said, 'they can prepare your horses and you can ride off if I cannot stop them entering.'

'If you do that, they will probably kill you,' Richard said, 'we should just go now.'

Sir Wobble sighed and stood up.

'There will not be blood spilt on this property, it is forbidden,' Adela said.

Sir Wobble looked at her. 'I promise you there won't be,' he said and strode out of the refectory.

'Ask the nuns to tack up the horses then,' Richard said, 'but then we shall flee. Don't answer the door until we are gone.'

Another series of loud thuds came from the entrance to the nunnery.

'The door is sturdy,' Adela said, 'they cannot force their way in.'

'I hope not, Bowman can only move as fast as a one legged drunk.'

'Sisters,' Adela shouted.

'I can't leave you here, not again,' Richard grabbed her hands, 'we have the spare horse, you can come with us.'

'The Lord will protect me.'

'He won't protect you against cold steel, how do you know this is not the Lord's test for me. Whether I will fail you a second time? This might be my final chance, fail again and will I be doomed to hell?'

'You think too much about yourself,' Adela frowned.

A patter of footsteps rang out from the cloister and two nuns burst through the doorway. 'What should we do?' one asked.

'Have the sisters prepare the three horses to ride, and see if you can move the wounded man to the grain store,' Adela said.

'Yes, Mother Superior,' one said and they charged off.

'These men are not after me, brother. Only the Martel knight and my uncle know I am here.'

'What if one of them is outside? They will not let you go

unpunished for helping us,' Richard said.

'Your conscience can be clear,' Adela said, 'I neither wish to go, nor am able to.'

'If you are killed, I will have no one left,' Richard said.

'My place is here.'

Richard cried out in frustration. 'What would our mother want?'

'Our mother is not here,' Adela said, 'I will not go, I will not be harmed, and you will have to learn how to understand that. A man's job is not to control all of the women in his life.'

Richard felt angry and his nostrils flared as his breathing increased.

'Fine, if you wish to die that is your choice. I'm going to save my friend,' Richard whirled around towards the door. He ran down the cloister and past the front entrance. Muffled shouts could be heard from the other side of it and more bangs rattled it on its hinges.

Richard raced to the dormitory where Bowman was. A nun was on each side of him and they were trying to haul him to his feet.

'Let me help,' Richard said and pushed one of the nuns out of the way. He put his arm around his friend and lifted him to his feet.

'I'd like to sleep longer,' Bowman groaned.

'We need to go,' Richard said and dragged him forwards.

'Why? That bed was comfy and soft and the nuns are pleasing to my eyes,' Bowman said.

'Nicholas the Bastard is here,' Richard said.

Bowman woke up. 'Curse the Martels to hell,' he said as they squeezed him through the doorway and into the corridor.

'I couldn't agree more, but we need to get onto our horses before they know we're here,' Richard said.

'I can't ride, Richard, my head feels too light and I want to throw up.'

'I'll tie you to the saddle,' Richard said and hauled the big man out into the courtyard.

Nuns swarmed around the stables, lifting saddles onto horses and slipping bridles on over their ears.

'Someone bring me that horse out,' Richard pointed to

Bowman's horse. A nun led it over and held it while another helped Richard to put Bowman's left foot into his stirrup.

'Get ready, you'll need to do some of this yourself,' Richard said.

'Don't worry about me,' Bowman pushed his weight down into the stirrup and pushed himself up into his saddle. Except that he didn't make it. He started to swing his right leg over the horse before his strength gave out and he started to fall. Richard went to catch him, but Bowman was too big and he fell on top of Richard and they clattered onto the courtyard in a heap.

'I thought I didn't need to worry,' Richard pushed Bowman off him and rolled up on to his feet. He had to shake one of his legs back to life.

The blonde man looked up into the sky and groaned. 'Alright, I might have been wrong on that one,' he said.

A nun ran into the courtyard with one hand on her headdress. 'They are shaking the door, we must open it before they break it,' she screamed.

'Help me lift him into the saddle and we'll be out of your way,' Richard said.

Nuns converged on Bowman and five of them grabbed every part of him and lifted him back to his feet.

'Very friendly for nuns,' Bowman said with a slur. He grinned as one shifted her grip around his thigh.

'I hope that's the cider talking,' Richard said, 'everyone lift him.'

The nuns grunted and groaned and together pushed Bowman up so he could flop himself over his saddle.

'Don't let go, ladies, I was enjoying that,' he said.

'Help him sit in it properly,' Richard then looked around, 'where is Sir Wobble?'

He peered into the stable where Sir Wobble's horse was, just as the door flew open and Sir Wobble walked out. He wore his glittering mail shirt with the torn shoulder, and had his helmet laced onto his head.

'What are you doing, we're going to ride for it,' Richard said.

'Look at him,' Sir Wobble nodded to where Bowman was being spun around by two nuns who had grins on their faces.

'He can ride, and besides, there are too many to fight,' Richard said.

'Have you seen your horse? You're not ready to go,' Sir Wobble led his own horse out of its stable.

Richard looked for Solis as a nun led him out onto the courtyard's stone surface. The palomino horse's bridle was over his right eye and the saddle was so far back it was almost on his rump. Solis snorted and shook his head to try to move the bridle leather from his eyelid.

'See, those nuns are going to open that door, and then they are going to get into this courtyard. And you will still be in it,' Sir Wobble said.

'Bring him here,' Richard said to the nun holding Solis.

Sir Wobble swung himself up onto his saddle.

'We only need a moment,' Richard said as he pushed the bridle off his horse's eye and the stallion tried to rub the released eye on him.

'Get off,' Richard told him and went to fix the saddle placement.

'You know,' Sir Wobble said from atop his horse, 'I didn't really want to see my brothers anyway. They are terribly boring and I think they were going to serve me very bland food. Norman food was better. They never liked me, either, so I don't feel bad being unable to see them again.'

'Don't even think about it,' Richard moved the saddle forward and reached bellow Solis's belly to grab the girth strap.

'Everyone has taken too long, Richard, so there isn't really any choice. People will sing a song about me though, this is going to make for a good story,' Sir Wobble said, 'get Bowman out of here and take him to my uncle Patrick in London.'

'Who is your uncle Patrick?' Richard buckled the girth strap tightly.

'I'm sure you'll find him,' Sir Wobble pushed his horse into a walk out of the courtyard, 'he is the Earl of Salisbury, after all. Green and white stripes.'

'The Earl of what?' Bowman said as the nuns pushed his feet into his stirrups.

'I don't believe him,' Richard said as Sir Wobble disappeared out of view, 'I think he just wanted to make a dramatic exit.

Which is what we need to do.'

'You're going to just leave him to go and be a hero?' Bowman asked.

Richard shrugged. 'No one seems to want my help,' he said.

He heard the doors at the front of the nunnery creak and swing open. A great cry sounded out.

'We need to go,' Richard mounted his horse.

Hooves echoed on stones from outside, and Richard imagined Sir Wobble smiling as he charged.

'Idiot,' Richard said and turned Solis to point him the other way, 'do you need me to lead you?'

'I'm fine,' Bowman said and turned to follow him to the back of the nunnery.

Richard wasn't sure for how long he'd be fine. 'Follow me, our hero isn't going to buy us much time.'

They rode around the stables as the ting of steel on steel rang out in the air and mixed with screams from the nuns as they recognised their danger.

'If he kills them all he's going to be an unbearably smug little bastard, isn't he?' Bowman said.

'Yes,' Richard said, 'if.'

EMPLOYMENT

Richard rode Solis with his reins hooked onto his belt so he could blow warm air into his cupped hands. He hadn't expected to be back to London so soon, but at least that meant his memory was good enough to successfully retrace his way back to what was now Edith's house in the city.

'The banner is still there,' Bowman nodded as they turned into the street with Richard's family house.

'I expect Edith will leave it there,' Richard said, 'are you warm enough?'

'No, but we'll be inside soon,' Bowman's face was white and Richard was worried that his lips seemed to be turning blue.

'The hearth is good and warm so you can rest there while I try to find Sir Wobble's uncle Patrick. He should want to lend me men to go and find Sir Wobble.'

'He should,' Bowman said, 'but it's a shame we took all the blankets from here last time, then left them at the nunnery.'

Richard snapped his head round to look at the saddle behind him. There was nothing tied to it at all. 'My wedding silver is still bundled in the blankets, too,' he said.

'Damn those Martels,' Bowman groaned.

'We can't cross the sea without coins, we aren't going to be able to rescue another ship's crew to bargain for passage this time,' Richard said.

'I can't believe you just noticed it was missing,' Bowman said.

Richard scowled. 'I've been busy shivering while you slept under my cloak, and worrying that I got our friend killed,' he said.

'That was his choice,' Bowman said.

'Don't you feel even a little bad for him?' Richard asked.

'Should I? I don't know him, he's a strutting peacock who doesn't care about anyone but himself.'

'Then why did he ride off and get himself killed so you could live?' Richard asked.

'You heard what he said,' Bowman replied, 'he just wants his name in a song to be sung around hearths across the Christian world.'

'Maybe, but he didn't have to do it,' Richard said.

'Perhaps, but then you didn't see him die, did you?' Bowman stopped his horse by the door under the blue and white banner.

Richard sighed as he unhooked his reins, dismounted, and passed them to Bowman.

'I don't know if this place has any stables, but there must be some somewhere,' Richard said, 'wait here and I'll find out where they are.'

Bowman gathered up the reins from Richard as Solis started to lick the other horse in the face.

Richard left them and pushed the door open. The hall was dark and no warmer than outside. The air was still and the hearth was a layer of ash with a few charred pieces of old and cold wood lying on it. Smoke no longer collected in the rafters. Richard shut the door behind him and listened for noise but the house was quiet. He walked forwards towards the chairs and table and noted that someone had at least removed his grandfather's body. Richard went to walk on but his next step slipped slightly so he looked down at his foot. He had to squint in the dull light, but when he did he saw there was a dark pool of sticky liquid on the wooden floor. He squatted down and picked up a clump of straw that had made up the floor covering. Richard lifted the straw up to his eyes and caught the smell of iron. It looked like blood too, semi-congealed and sticky. He threw the straw down and slowly drew his sword. Richard held it before him and walked into the back chamber. It was just as it had been on his first visit to London, except that there was a wooden chest on the floor by the empty bed. Richard let out a long breath and sheathed his sword. He tipped open the chest's lid and the hinges squeaked to reveal an undyed linen bag. Richard went to pick it up, but it was heavy and had a texture that he recognised. It was a bag of mail.

Richard swore.

He walked out of the house and back into the daylight with the bag of mail slung over his shoulder.

Bowman, neck tilted back and snoring, was asleep in his saddle, and Solis was on the other side of the street taking chunks out of a house door frame with his teeth.

'Soli, come,' Richard said and the stallion's yellow head spun around and his ears flopped. The horse spat out some splinters and sauntered over.

Richard heaved the bag of mail up behind his saddle and tied it on to it. He knew there was no point telling his horse off.

'Bowman,' he said but the man remained asleep.

Richard mounted his horse. 'Wake up,' he shouted almost into his face.

'What is it?' Bowman groaned and massaged his neck once the life was back into his eyes, 'and you probably shouldn't shout so loudly.'

'I think my uncle has moved in here,' Richard said.

'So you're stealing his mail?'

Richard grinned. 'You're not going to tell me off for that, are you?'

'Absolutely not,' the big man grinned. He started to laugh but coughed instead.

'I think something bad has happened to Edith though,' Richard said.

'I never met her. What do we do now?' Bowman asked.

'We can't leave you here anymore,' Richard said, 'so you'll just have to come with me as I find Sir Wobble's uncle.'

'Sir Wobble isn't the nephew of an earl,' Bowman said.

'He seemed quite sure about it,' Richard looked around at the banners on the houses.

'What are you looking for?'

'He said green and white stripes, but there are none like that here,' Richard said.

'We had better find them quickly,' Bowman rubbed his hands together.

Richard nodded and they rode out to find Patrick of Salisbury. They searched until the sun had started to drop in the sky, but still the green and white banner alluded them.

'Maybe he really was just making it up,' Richard said.

'I told you, but I really hope he wasn't,' Bowman yawned.

'I think we've covered almost every street, certainly the rich ones,' Richard said, 'I think we need to try the Tower.'

'Are you sure? That's the sort of place that men like us should steer clear of,' Bowman said.

'Men like us?' Richard narrowed his eyes, 'men like you, maybe.'

'You're like me now,' Bowman said, 'at least in England.'

That made Richard think of Normandy. 'I wonder how Sophie is,' he said.

'I'm sure Sarjeant is drunk, and she is staving off the villagers with rocks again,' Bowman said.

Richard growled at him. 'You're not helping. We are going to the Tower.'

'That will not end well,' Bowman said.

'You don't have to come with me,' Richard turned his horse to the east.

'I am extremely well aware of that,' Bowman coughed again then followed him anyway.

The Tower of London sat on the north bank of the Thames and on the eastern end of the city walls. It had a large bailey surrounded by well-built wooden walls and a large ditch. Inside was the White Tower itself, a giant square building at least three storeys tall and with towers on its corners. It had large windows and its entrance was a staircase that climbed up to a door on the first floor. Richard and Bowman however, only got as far as one of the gates in the wooden wall.

'Get away,' the short and stocky guard said when Richard asked for entry.

'Is Earl Patrick of Salisbury here?' Richard asked

The guard sighed and scratched his short ginger beard. 'I don't know, but you still can't come in.'

'Why not?'

'We can't just let anyone into the castle, that's the whole point of a castle,' the guard replied.

'Just tell me if he's here, then,' Richard said.

Bowman started to look drowsy in his saddle again and Solis

spat out one last saliva-covered piece of door frame, which hit the guard on the chest.

'I could have your head for that,' the guard wiped it off.

'Just tell me if Earl Patrick is here, and whatever the answer, we'll go,' Richard said.

The guard studied Richard and Bowman. 'I don't trust you, but I'll ask the captain of the guard,' he turned and went off into the castle, leaving Richard looking up at the imposing walls. You would need a decent ladder to scale them, he thought.

Bowman snored gently in his saddle by the time the guard came back. 'No one wants to see you, and you can't come in,' he said.

'Ask Earl Patrick, please,' Richard said.

Bowman awoke with a snort and looked around. 'What's going on?' he asked.

'You're leaving,' the guard said.

'Is the Queen in?' Richard said, 'we know the Queen.'

'You know the Queen?' the guard started to laugh, 'of course you do, God's teeth, what do you take me for?'

'But we do,' Richard said, 'we helped her to cross the sea. We rescued her from Breton pirates.'

'Breton pirates,' the guard laughed so hard tears ran from his eyes, 'this is one of the better stories I've ever heard on guard duty.'

'It's true, we escaped on a Castilian galley.'

'A what? You made that up,' the guard said, 'now go away before someone important comes along and has you kicked aside for getting in their way.'

Richard sighed, this was not going to work. 'Come on, we might as well go,' he said to Bowman.

'Where to?'

'I have no idea,' Richard said and considered the church spires he could see over the rooftops of London.

'Who can we go to?' Bowman asked.

'No one I know,' Richard said, 'what about you?'

'I think I'm all out of friends,' Bowman sighed.

Richard patted Solis on his yellow neck. 'It's a hard time of year to become an outlaw,' he said.

'There isn't really a good time,' Bowman tried to flex his arm but cried out and swore.

'We need somewhere warm to stay until you're better,' Richard said, 'and I really need to go back and look for Sir Wobble. We at least owe him that.'

'Maybe. He's more likely to be rotting in a Martel castle in chains than dead, though,' Bowman said.

'I hope so,' Richard said, 'can you imagine how angry he'd be at the bad food?'

Bowman laughed but it triggered a coughing fit. Richard was worried about that, but he didn't have time to think about it. A string of riders on their ambling horses left the city and rode quickly towards the gate.

'Bowman, look,' Richard nodded at them, 'look at the banner.'

'I can't see it,' Bowman squinted and coughed again.

'Green and white stripes,' Richard said, 'we didn't find Earl Patrick, but Earl Patrick has found us.'

At the head of the column rode a tall man with long dark hair that rolled down to his shoulders. His thick black beard was heavily specked with grey, and his brown eyes picked out Richard.

'What do you want, why are you staring at me like that?' the man eased his horse gently to a stop.

'I'm sorry, are you Earl Patrick?' Richard asked. He suddenly felt self conscious, his own tunic was stained and unwashed, whereas the earl's dark red tunic with gold lined sleeves glimmered in the light. The earl's cloak was a rich blue and it's ornate cloak pin was bright gold.

'I am, who are you?'

'I am Richard of Keynes.'

'You mean Yvetot,' Bowman said.

'Yes, sorry, Richard of Yvetot.'

'You don't know where you are the lord of?' Earl Patrick frowned, 'enough, get out of our way.'

'We need to speak to you, my companion needs a healer and your nephew needs your help,' Richard said.

Solis sniffed in the direction of the Earl's tall black horse.

'My nephew? Which one?'

'Sir Wob, I mean William Marshal,' Richard said.

'You are not very convincing, if you wish to defraud me

you should have spent more time preparing yourselves,' Earl Patrick said.

'William has been taken or killed by the Martels in Nottinghamshire,' Richard said, 'we must go and rescue him.'

The earl's horse strained its neck forwards to sniff back at Solis.

'My nephew William is in Normandy, not Nottinghamshire, although I suspect they are just about the same to the likes of you,' Earl Patrick said.

Solis squealed and threw a leg out at the black horse. The horse threw one back and Earl Patrick hauled him away.

'I'm feeling quite dizzy,' Bowman said, 'can you stop them being so loud?'

'Clear the road and ensure I never set eyes on you again,' Earl Patrick said.

'We do know William,' Richard said, 'he's tall and dark and has legs that wrap around any horse.'

Earl Patrick held his horse back for a moment and studied Richard. 'That just means you have actually seen him, it doesn't mean you know him.'

'He only really cares about food. He eats everything, and when he can't eat, he sleeps. When he can't eat, and he isn't tired, he rides and fights,' Richard said.

Earl Patrick sniffed and glanced over at Bowman. 'He does look bad,' he said.

'His father has just died and William is not in the will.'

'Is that so?' Earl Patrick smiled, 'I had not heard about the will. You can come inside with us. We will put your friend in a warm room and see if he recovers. We will continue this conversation when I am by my fire.'

'Thank you,' Richard turned Solis around and grabbed Bowman's reins to lead him into the castle.

Earl Patrick's chamber was within the White Tower itself. It was larger than Richard's hall at Yvetot, and he found himself with his nose up to the wall tapestries marvelling at their detail. One hunting scene featured a palomino horse that looked just like his own, its ears back whilst trying to bite a raging boar.

Earl Patrick flung his cloak at a young man to put away and sat down by the fire that had clearly been kept burning in his absence.

'Very well, Richard of Wherever,' the earl said, 'sit down and tell me about my nephew. I haven't seen him for years.'

Richard sat on a carved wooden chair that had a sheepskin seat, and told him everything. Or rather, he told him of his adventures with Sir Wobble except for when his friend had stolen Lord Tancarville's falcon, or when he had been embarrassed for taking no spoils after the Battle of Neufchâtel.

'I did not even know he'd been knighted,' Earl Patrick nodded and gazed into the fire.

'So you see that I owe him. At least to find out what happened,' Richard said.

'I do, it is an obligation you must keep. I can spare three knights and their men to accompany you, but they must be back thirty days after Christmas as we are due to travel to France in the spring,' Earl Patrick said.

'We are looking for employment in France,' Richard said, 'and we need to get across the sea, but as I told you, I lost my silver.'

'I do not need you. I have enough men already, and we expect to fight so I do not wish to take any I do not trust,' the earl said.

'Thank you for your offer of knights, I would be honoured to accept your help,' Richard said. He hoped that, if all went well, the knights might put in a good word for him.

Earl Patrick nodded and turned to some of the knights who stood behind him. He was about to speak when a boy rushed in. 'My lord, there is something happening in the courtyard,' he said in his high voice.

The earl sighed and stood up. 'Well, we better see what it is,' he said.

Richard got up from his comfortable chair and followed him down and out of the Tower. It was dark when he stepped out onto the first-floor staircase and looked out over the bailey. Light flashed from braziers dotted around the walls, but Richard couldn't make out any of the figures in the bailey at all. He descended down the stairs behind the earl and his knights. A mounted figure stood surrounded by a huddle of men, their long shadows stretched out on the ground around them.

'What is all this?' Earl Patrick pushed his way into the crowd.

Richard craned his neck to see over the collection of nobles and soldiers, and could see that the mounted man led two riderless horses behind him. They were saddled.

'He fought twenty men on his own,' a man in a green tunic said.

Richard dared to hope. 'Sir Wobble,' he shouted.

No one heard him in the excitement, but Earl Patrick quickly forced his way to its centre.

'Ha, it is you, my lad,' the earl said.

Richard used both hands to push a mailed guard out of his path and caught up with the earl. 'Sir Wobble,' he cried.

'Richard,' the mounted rider said, 'I can't believe you made it here.'

'Me? I can't believe you're alive,' Richard said.

'Of course I am, I'm William Marshal,' he grinned.

'I was not convinced this boy's story was true,' Earl Patrick nodded to himself.

'Where is your helmet?' Richard asked.

'Somewhere in the forest near the nunnery,' his grin faded, 'it was like the last moments of Castle Peacock all over again.'

'Are you hurt this time?' Richard asked.

'Where is Castle Peacock?' Earl Patrick asked.

'A small but fine fortification in Normandy,' Richard said.

Sir Wobble laughed but then clutched his side.

'You aren't fine, are you?' Richard said.

'Enough of this,' Earl Patrick said, 'stable these horses and take this man into my chamber.'

His knights relayed the orders and some younger men took Sir Wobble's horses and helped him to dismount.

'I don't much fancy climbing those steps,' Sir Wobble said when he reached the ground.

'I thought knights didn't complain,' Richard said.

His friend shot him a look and Richard noticed how much dried blood was on his face and mail shirt. His right hand was dark red from blood, and mud was rubbed into the metal rings of his armour. Richard let him go ahead and noticed his scabbard was empty.

Earl Patrick led them back to his chamber where Sir Wobble

stood in the middle of the room and was unarmed. Two taller men lifted his mail shirt up and over his head. Sir Wobble stifled grunts of discomfort at lifting his arms up, but sighed once the armour was gone. His thick woollen tunic was removed in the same way and Richard winced at the slashes in it. The slashes matched the wounds on Sir Wobble's bare chest. Blood encrusted three cuts and one stab wound in his side. His right hand dripped blood onto the rushes on the floorboards as he was washed clean.

'I didn't stop to rest while trying to get back to London,' Sir Wobble yawned, 'I think I went west after the fight, so I rode the wrong way all night until the rising sun pointed me to the south.'

'Whose horses were those?' Earl Patrick asked.

'The Martel Bastard and his companion,' Sir Wobble grinned, 'the Bastard could fight but his companion was weak and slow.'

'Did you kill them?' Richard glanced over to Bowman but he was asleep on the floor in a corner of the room.

Sir Wobble shook his head and winced. 'The companion yes, but the Bastard I could only drag off the horse. His infantry swarmed me by then and I had to cut my way free. Spears hurt, by the way.'

'They do,' the earl said, 'they are best avoided in my experience.'

'I didn't have much choice, I only needed to remove their horsemen from the game,' Sir Wobble said.

'The game?' Earl Patrick raised his eyebrows.

'Everything is a game, uncle. This one was to allow my friends to escape. They were on horses, so the game was to stop the opposing horsemen from getting to my friends.'

Earl Patrick looked at Richard. 'He really is an odd fellow, isn't he. But it seems that you were very fortunate to have him on your side.'

'I was, and I need to thank you properly, Sir Wobble,' Richard said.

'Sir Wobble?' Earl Patrick asked.

'There were too many Williams at Castle Tancarville,' Richard said.

'Don't worry,' Sir Wobble ran his fingers over his stab wound, 'everyone saw me arrive here, my name will be all over London by the morning. They will know my name.'

'Your father was a proud man, too,' the earl said, 'and it made him enemies that he couldn't intimidate or remove with a sword. You should remember that.'

'I remembered to take some prizes from my victory this time,' Sir Wobble smiled at Richard.

'You did, you will have something to show Lord Mandeville next time you meet him,' Richard said.

'And now I can give Sir Roger his horse back. Although I rather liked it, it got me out of that alive,' Sir Wobble said.

'I asked your uncle if we could enter his employ to earn our way back over to France,' Richard said.

The earl smiled. 'Now that I can see you are truly friends, of course I will consider your request. William here will naturally serve in my personal mesnie. You can join him, but you will need to prove yourself to me first.'

'Of course, what do I need to do?' Richard asked.

A man walked out of the group of the earl's knights, he wore a monk's robes and had a face that reminded Richard of a weasel.

'Brother Geoffrey?' he said.

'I am as surprised as you are, Richard of Keynes,' the monk said.

'I thought he was Richard of Yvetot,' Earl Patrick said.

'Richard of Keynes carried a hot iron for twelve steps to demonstrate his innocence for a murder. The Lord saw fit to judge him innocent, but Richard of Keynes has been accused of other things. This boy is indeed Richard of Yvetot, a move I confess I never predicted. Sir Roger surprised me with that one, boy,' Brother Geoffrey said.

'Me too,' Richard said.

'I also did not know you had crossed to England,' the monk said.

'I had Sir Roger's permission.'

'Does Sir Roger still harbour his grudge against Lord Tancarville?'

'I know nothing about that,' Richard said.

'Ah,' Brother Geoffrey laughed, 'what a loyal tenant you are. The king will soften his view of Sir Roger, and his tenants, if he continues to distance himself from Castle Tancarville. That is good for you, if my words are too much for you to understand.'

'Geoffrey, what are you doing here?' Earl Patrick asked, 'your arrival is always trouble.'

The monk bowed to the earl. 'My Lord, you wish to test the boy. I have a royal command which may give you an opportunity to do so,' he said.

Earl Patrick sighed. 'What is it?'

'The rebellious archbishop needs cutting down to size. More specifically, you are to find one of his horses and cut its tail down to size.'

'That is outrageous,' the earl replied, 'to dock the tail of a man's horse is to humiliate him, it is a step too far. If someone did that to me, I would have no choice but to kill him.'

'I think that's the point,' Brother Geoffrey said, 'it is supposed to send a message.'

'I want no part of such a scheme, where is the honour in it?' Earl Patrick frowned at the monk.

'Remember your history, My Lord,' Brother Geoffrey said, 'the king wishes to give you a chance to confirm your loyalty to him. He remembers that a man who has switched sides once can always do so again.'

'Will you never cease to flaunt that in my face?' The earl stomped off over to the crackling hearth. Bowman still snored softly in the corner of the room.

'Send the boy, with a guide, to dock a tail. If he is not caught, then he can gain employment,' Brother Geoffrey smiled.

Richard didn't like that smile, just as he didn't like the monk.

'He will do as we ask,' the monk looked at Richard, 'for I have a golden noose around his neck.'

'What does that mean, why do you two always talk about gold?' Sir Wobble asked. He had been wrapped in bandages then clothed in a fine new tunic. He sat down gingerly on a chair.

The monk's eyes twinkled. 'The boy will dock the tail,' he said.

'Very well, monk,' Earl Patrick said, 'but I do not approve of such pettiness. It is beneath a king and it is beneath me.'

Brother Geoffrey bowed to the earl. 'Have him do it tomorrow night.'

The earl sighed and remained facing the fire. Brother Geoffrey stepped back and left the chamber.

'Can I go with him?' Sir Wobble said.

Earl Patrick turned to his nephew. 'Of course not, look at you, I would be surprised if those wounds don't corrupt and kill you,' he said.

Sir Wobble frowned. 'Wounds won't kill me,' he said.

'One day I will teach you some humility, but until then you shall stay in the Tower to recover,' Earl Patrick said.

'Which archbishop is it?' Richard asked.

'Why do you care?' the earl asked.

'Because one of them was once very kind to me, and saved our lives from thieving pilgrims,' Richard glanced over to Bowman.

'I hope for your sake it was not the Archbishop of Canterbury,' Earl Patrick said, 'for it will be to his palace outside the city where you will go tomorrow night.'

Richard's face dropped.

'I'm sorry, neither of us have a great deal of choice, it is royal command,' the earl said.

'It is dishonest,' Richard said, 'cutting the tail is the worst thing I could have to do to the archbishop short of killing him.'

'Then find the cheapest packhorse he has and cut the tail off that. I don't care what horse you do it to, even if it's a mare. Maybe that will soothe your guilt,' the earl said.

Richard looked at Sir Wobble.

'I'm not helping you get out of it,' his friend replied.

'Do this for me and you will serve in my mesnie alongside young William. After the spring campaign you will be released and can return to wherever Yvetot is.'

'It's in Normandy,' Richard said.

'I don't care,' the earl said, 'just bring me back the tail so I can give it to that wretched monk.'

'Does the monk serve the king?' Richard asked.

'Obviously,' Sir Wobble said, 'surely that is obvious?'

'I didn't ask you,' Richard said.

'Enough,' Earl Patrick said, 'get some rest and tomorrow I will send you out with a squire, Long Tom, and you will bring me back a tail.'

Long Tom put his hand on the wooden gate and gently swung it open. He was a tall, slightly built man a few years older than Richard. His face was wider at the top than the bottom and Richard thought that his mouth was too small for his head. Nevertheless, he had been pleasant enough on the ride over to the archbishop's property.

'What if there are guards?' Richard whispered in the darkness.

'Then we have to be quick on our feet,' Long Tom grinned and let Richard through the gate and into the paddock. The grassy field was huge and stretched off into the distance until it met some woodland. Off to one side Richard could see a manorial complex, and attached to it were some wooden walls enclosing what looked like a stone built stable building. They headed towards it.

Long Tom walked much quicker than Richard due to his long legs, and Richard had to almost jog to keep up. 'Slow down,' he said between breaths.

'We need to cover this ground quickly,' Long Tom replied.

'If we move too fast we might catch someone's eye,' Richard said.

'You just can't keep up,' Long Tom smiled and broke into a jog of his own.

Richard had to outright run to keep up, but he kept a hand on his knife so it didn't fall from its sheath.

They reached the stable compound and crouched down by the wall to catch their breath.

Long Tom edged around to the gateway and stuck his head around the corner. 'I can't see anyone,' he said.

'I think we should wait a moment to listen for movement,' Richard said.

Long Tom looked at Richard then back into the stable yard. He thought for a moment. 'That is actually a good idea,' he said.

They waited in the moonlit night until they were sure no one was still working in the compound. Richard looked up at the moon, which was half full but quite bright. In the distance an owl hooted and both men made the sign of the cross. They noticed each other and had to hold down laughs.

'I hate owls,' Richard said.

'Everyone hates owls,' Long Tom shivered, 'I think we are safe.'

The tall man got up to a crouch and moved to open the wooden gate into the compound. Richard followed and shut it gently behind him. The yard was a large area of beaten earth with a well, a few barns, and the stone stables. Long Tom considered each building and then crept over to the stable doorway.

Richard followed and heard a horse snort. He swallowed his distaste for their mission and went inside.

'Let's find his finest horse,' Long Tom said.

'No, I want to do it to his worst horse,' Richard said.

'Hey, no need to be rude, we're supposed to humiliate him, so let's find his finest riding horse.'

'I just can't do it, Earl Patrick said I could dock a cheap packhorse,' Richard said, 'I'm the knight here, so that's what we're doing.

Long Tom raised his hands in mock surrender. 'You pick the horse then, I'm going to look for something valuable to take back as a trophy.'

'You can't steal things,' Richard said.

'You're going to dock a horse, what is stealing against that?'

'Fine, but be quick,' Richard said.

Long Tom disappeared down the corridor of the unlit stables and Richard peered into the first stall. It looked like a decent brown riding horse so Richard moved on. He looked in on four more horses before one turned on him and tried to bite him over the stable door. It was a black mare who turned to threaten him with her hooves, and swished her tail in his face over the door.

'You deserve it at least,' he gritted his teeth and opened the door. The mare ran around the stable and faced him with bared teeth. Richard stood up straight and put his hands on his hips. The mare lunged towards him, but not at him, and Richard stood his ground. She backed off, spun around and threw her back feet at him. Richard had done this with Solis when he'd been a colt. But the colt had been much smaller.

Richard closed his eyes and felt the rush of air as the mare very nearly connected with his face. She looked round and blinked at the unmoving Richard.

'Got you,' he walked forwards. The mare turned around and went to eat from a pile of cut grass with a snort. She ignored Richard entirely as he drew his knife, held her dock, and started to saw off her tail. He felt better about doing it to a bad horse, but still sawed as quickly as he could. Richard finished the last strands of hair just as Long Tom sprinted past the open stable.

'Run,' he shouted and disappeared.

Richard swore, and tail in hand, kicked the stable door ajar and ran out after him. At the end of the corridor where Long Tom had come from, he glimpsed a light, but didn't want hang around to look at it. He scrambled out of the stables and made for the compound gate.

Long Tom reached it first, just as a man walked in front of it and blocked his way. They collided in a heap and hit the ground together.

Richard reached them as the archbishop's man got to his feet. He was large, a bear of a man, and his eyes seethed with surprise and anger.

'God's toes,' Long Tom sprung up. In his hands was a leather bridle with golden decorations riveted onto it.

Richard still had his knife in his hand and he flashed it in the big man's face to try to ward him off.

'I'll rip you both in half,' the big man said and went to grab Long Tom.

Richard slashed at the man's arm and cut a red ribbon along it. The man howled and turned to Richard.

Long Tom used the bridle as a flail and flung the leather and metal at the side of the giant's face. The metal horse bit at its end connected with his head and the big man crumpled over. Richard gave him a hard shove and ran past him. Long Tom joined him and they sprinted back across the paddock as fast as they could.

Shouts and cries rose up behind them but neither looked back as their feet pounded the short grass.

Long Tom reached the paddock gate first and clean vaulted over it.

'Hey,' Richard shouted as he slammed into the gate,

rebounded, and had to open it normally for himself.

'Hurry up,' Long Tom shouted as he ran for the horses.

Richard was out of breath as he shut the gate behind him. He ran to Solis who sniffed at the tail he held. Richard mounted as quickly as he could and Long Tom already spurred his horse on down the track that led back to London. Richard urged Solis into a canter, which turned into a gallop as Solis decided he was racing. His stallion quickly caught up with Long Tom's palfrey.

'They don't have horses, we can slow down,' Richard shouted as the cold night stung his face.

Long Tom dropped his horse back down to a walk and took a deep breath. 'That was close,' his toothy grin reflected the moonlight.

'Why did you have to take the bridle?' Richard asked.

'Why not, this is worth a half decent warhorse,' he held the bridle up proudly.

Richard took a few deep breaths and felt his body calming down. 'You're an idiot,' he started to laugh.

Long Tom laughed too and they rode back into London under the silvery moonlight.

Richard passed the black tail over to Earl Patrick in his chamber.

'I don't want it,' the earl said, 'Long Tom can find Brother Geoffrey to take it.'

Richard swung his arm over to Long Tom, who had already deposited his new bridle in a safe place before entering the chamber.

Long Tom took the tail and shrugged. 'Yes, My Lord,' he said.

'Was it a clean job? Is there anything I need to know?' Earl Patrick looked Richard in the eyes.

'No,' Long Tom said first.

'No to which question?'

Long Tom pulled a face. 'Nothing you need to worry about,' he said.

Richard glanced at him and then shook his head. 'No, nothing.'

'Good,' the earl said, 'Richard, you will join my mesnie with William, here. Get your friend back to health if you can and we shall sail in the spring.'

Long Tom left to deliver proof of the night's success.

'We can visit my brothers over Christmas,' Sir Wobble said from his chair. Three empty wooden plates were stacked up on the floor beside him.

'I thought you didn't care about seeing them?' Richard asked.

Sir Wobble shifted in his chair. 'Well, now I'm going to be sitting around here for a few months I'm already starting to get bored.'

'He can't ride yet,' Earl Patrick said, 'a spear got him in the thigh so he isn't going anywhere for a while.'

'I'll be fine,' Sir Wobble crossed his arms.

'Wait until after the celebrations are complete, there is no use rushing the healing,' Earl Patrick said.

'If we'll be here that long I really need to write to Sophie,' Richard said.

'Your wife?' the earl asked.

Richard nodded. 'Can someone give me parchment and ink, and help me send it please?' he looked over at Sir Wobble.

His friend laughed. 'I can't write, you know that, find a clerk.'

Long Tom reappeared in the chamber with empty hands.

'You were supposed to give it to Brother Geoffrey,' the earl said.

'He did,' Brother Geoffrey entered the chamber with the horse's tail in his hand, 'I happened to be on my way.'

His face was cold and he had a frown embedded over it.

'Ah, you came back, Richard. That is a shame,' Brother Geoffrey looked at Richard.

Richard held his tongue but felt worry creep into his mind.

'What do you want? We did your dishonourable deed, what more do you need?' Earl Patrick asked.

'I want nothing, but this one,' he pointed a bony finger at Richard, 'is trouble wherever he goes.'

'What do you want?' Richard said.

'Your uncle is in the Tower,' the monk said.

Richard felt a chill stab deep into his core.

'And he has laid an accusation against you,' Brother Geoffrey said, 'you were seen outside your grandfather's house on the day of his death, and again yesterday when you and your man were heard shouting in the street.'

Richard sighed and looked over at Bowman, but he was still asleep.

'Your uncle has accused you of murdering your grandfather, and coming back yesterday and killing his servant. His lawyer is drawing up documents to present to the king as apparently the lawyer and some clerk actually witnessed you killing your grandfather.'

'That's absurd,' Richard cried, 'he died of shame, his heart gave out.'

'Do you have proof?' The monk asked.

'Of course not.'

'Then you will struggle to argue your case,' Brother Geoffrey said.

'My uncle killed Edith,' Richard said, 'there is no question about it.'

'Who is Edith? Earl Patrick asked.

'The servant,' Richard said, 'when my grandfather died I gave her his house.'

'I doubt the house was yours to give,' the earl said.

'I'm the heir, my father was his eldest son, and he is dead,' Richard felt his eyes start to water. He clenched his fists.

'The royal court will make a judgement on the matter when it is ready,' Brother Geoffrey said, 'I honestly don't know what I believe.'

'I'm going to kill him,' Richard said through his teeth.

'Words like that won't help you sound innocent,' the monk turned on his feet and left the chamber.

Earl Patrick let out a breath. 'It isn't boring having you around, is it?'

'That's why I like him, uncle,' Sir Wobble said.

'But do you trust him?' Earl Patrick asked.

Sir Wobble tilted his head from side to side. 'He has never lied to me. I didn't go into his grandfather's house so didn't see what happened, but I do believe him. He is kind to horses,' he said.

'But you didn't see how the old man died?'

'No, but I think he is telling the truth,' Sir Wobble said.

'How sure are you?'

'I rode out against fifteen, or maybe it was twenty men on my own to save him,' Sir Wobble yawned, 'I wouldn't have done that for many others. Probably anyone else, actually.'

Earl Patrick turned and considered Richard. 'I think your anger is genuine and I know William never lies. I fear that the only way for you to survive the judgement is to silence the two witnesses.'

'You want me to murder two people?' Richard blinked, 'to prove that I didn't murder two others?'

'That does sound crazy,' Sir Wobble said.

'Then at least if they do hang you, you'll have done something to deserve it,' the earl grinned under his greying beard.

'The monk will know who did it if they suddenly turn up dead,' Richard said, 'and I'm not killing anyone in cold blood.'

'What about the flying monk?' Sir Wobble said.

'Shut up,' Richard snapped and the earl looked at him.

'A flying monk?'

'The monk wanted to kill me, he was sent by my uncle,' Richard said, 'and I'm not murdering anyone, I'm a knight and I need to act like one.'

'I think murdering people is acting exactly like a knight,' Long Tom added as he leant on the door frame.

'No one asked you,' Earl Patrick said, 'very well, consign yourself to the royal court. You will have to stay here until called. If you leave, someone may take that for guilt.'

Richard stood in the large banqueting hall on the middle floor of the White Tower. He was in a queue, carefully arranged by two clerks, and he was lining up to stand before the royal court. Nothing but a short space of time stood between him and the king's justice, and his palms were clammy. He had waited days for a summons to come. Days had turned into weeks and even Christmas came and went in a state of apprehension. Bowman started to recover as the weather hinted at warming up and the days started to lengthen again. Sir Wobble's thigh had mostly healed and he had ridden off to visit his brothers on his own. Richard had slept in the corner of Earl Patrick's chamber next to Bowman, wondering when the call would come, and what being hung would feel like.

Looking around the banqueting hall now though, Richard wished he could be back there again as he ran his fingers around his neck. The queue hadn't moved for some time when he saw Brother Geoffrey slink over from the stairwell.

'Ah Richard, are you looking forward to your judgement?' he asked.

'Not really,' he felt his stomach tie new knots in itself.

'Only the guilty need fear, boy,' the monk said.

'I only fear being unjustly convicted,' Richard said, 'give me a trial by ordeal and I would prove it again.'

'That will not be done here, we are in the heart of a modern government. You will have the chance to tell your story,' Brother Geoffrey said.

'It is the other side of the story I'm worried about, all they need to do is lie, and I'm finished.'

'Do you not believe in royal power?' The monk squinted at Richard.

A man exited the court chamber and into the banqueting hall. His eyes were wide but he looked relieved.

'I have no idea,' Richard said.

'It seems to have worked for that defendant,' the monk watched the relieved man as he almost ran down the stairwell.

'I will be giving evidence,' the monk turned to watch Richard's reaction.

'And whose side will you be taking?' He asked.

'I have not decided yet,' the monk tilted his head, 'I know the Lord exonerated you at Castle Tancarville, but too many accusations of murder follow you.'

Richard sighed. 'I'm going to hang.'

'Not necessarily,' Brother Geoffrey said.

'So you're siding with me?'

'No, they might just cut off your head,' Brother Geoffrey grinned and his two top teeth slid out over his bottom lip.

'Leave me alone,' Richard said.

'You may as well make your peace, boy, the lawyer has drafted good evidence.'

Richard stood behind the next man in, and as that defendant was ushered in, Richard felt the urge to be sick. He put a hand over his mouth and contained it.

'My advice,' the monk began.

'I don't want it,' Richard said.

'My advice,' brother Geoffrey continued, 'is to tell the truth.'

'That is stunning advice, I will surely now be saved,' Richard turned his back and faced the door of the court chamber.

'Very well, but if they do hang you, I shall want to have a word about some gold first.'

'I don't know anything about it,' Richard said.

'What if the knowledge could buy your freedom?'

Richard paused. 'I still don't know anything about it,' he said, fully confident in his sincerity as he knew the buried hoard wasn't gold, but silver.

'You paused for too long, boy, I know, you know,' Brother Geoffrey said, 'but do you know that the king is not at the Tower?'

'No?' Richard turned back to the monk.

'You will not face him,' the monk said as the door was thrown open by a guard. The defendant was dragged out by two guards, crying. The man thrashed his arms but a guard slapped him around the face and he went limp. They hauled the man off towards the stairs.

Richard gulped. 'Then who is judging?'

'Oh, my boy,' Brother Geoffrey said, 'someone who is far harsher than the king in matters of family law.'

A guard appeared in the doorway and pointed at Richard.

He felt faint but forced his legs to move and carry him into the court chamber. The chamber was not as large as the banqueting hall and was well lit by fires. Clerks sat by desks and groups of other men spoke to each other around the room. At the far end was a raised platform with a set of chairs on it. The most lavish was empty, but the second most decorated was not, and on it sat Queen Eleanor. Richard noticed that the bump on her stomach was gone.

The Queen lowered her eyes down at Richard and met his. She stared at him showing no emotion or reaction.

Brother Geoffrey walked in behind Richard and went to stand off to one side. Richard noticed that he went to stand next to Thomas the Lawyer. The lawyer's eyes were stuck to the floor and Richard glared at him, and his veins started to pulse at his betrayal. The Queen still studied Richard but maybe this was a good thing. Maybe he had a chance, she did owe him.

'Who is this?' She asked the white bearded man standing beside her.

'This is, Richard of Keynes it says here,' he held up some parchment to his red rimmed eyes.

'Of Keynes?' The Queen replied.

'That is what is written,' the old man replied.

'And what is he accused of?'

'There is a lawyer to read the accusation,' the old man strained his eyes in the direction of Thomas and Brother Geoffrey.

Thomas the Lawyer stepped forwards and bowed to the Queen. He kept his eyes down and lifted up some parchment. 'Richard of Keynes was seen outside and inside the house of his grandfather last year. He was seen by myself and my clerk,' Thomas pointed at the clerk who stood at the very back of the crowd trying to blend in.

'There he is. Myself and my clerk even witnessed the brutal murder of Sir Hugh, by his own grandson. This serious matter can only be punished by death. What is more, he was seen outside the very same house the day before a family servant was found dead in the house. We believe he killed the servant as well as the master.'

The Queen levelled her eyes at the lawyer. 'Other than your own words, is there anyone else who witnessed the death of Sir Hugh?'

'There was my clerk.'

'You already mentioned your clerk, is there anyone else?' she asked.

The Lawyer shook his head.

'What do you say, Richard of Keynes?' The Queen asked.

'My grandfather died of a broken heart because my uncle had forced him to disown me on the false news that I was dead,' Richard replied.

'Were these two men there at the time?'

'They were,' Richard said.

'What happened to the servant?' The Queen asked.

'I have no idea, when I went back to the house there was only a pool of blood by the hearth. Edith was gone.'

'Is Edith the servant?'

'She was, yes,' Richard said.

'My client says that an item of his was also stolen at this time,' Thomas said, 'his mail shirt.'

'I did not,' Richard replied instantly.

'Ah,' the Lawyer said, 'but you did. Clerk.'

The clerk shuffled through the crowd with a heavy linen bag in his arms.

Richard's heart sank.

'This was found in the bed of this very man,' the Lawyer said.

The clerk tipped the bag upside down and the mail shirt slipped out of it. It hit the floorboards with a clink and a rattle, but also a thud that to Richard might just as well have been an executioner's axes.

Richard sighed. He knew he shouldn't have lied but the words had just slipped out.

The Queen tapped a finger on the side of her face and shook her head. 'This is a sorry affair,' she sighed.

The clerk sank backwards into the crowd and the Queen's eyes settled on Brother Geoffrey. 'You, monk,' she said.

He stepped forwards and bowed.

'You told me that you knew this boy,' the Queen said, 'I would like you to tell me why this boy is innocent.'

'You want me to tell you why he is innocent?'

'That is what I said.'

'Not what I think of his character?' Brother Geoffrey said.

'Speak for him, I want you to advocate for him as he has no lawyer.'

Brother Geoffrey's tiny weasel eyes glanced at Richard. 'That isn't proper procedure. Are you sure, Your Majesty?'

'I meant what I said, monk,' the Queen replied.

'Very well,' he glanced back to Richard for a moment, 'I did once watch this young man undergo an ordeal by fire. He carried the bar for twelve steps, more than required by law, and afterwards his hands were not burnt. I saw this with my own eyes.'

'Curious,' the Queen said.

Richard wasn't sure exactly what was happening, but the Lawyer mopped his brow with a cloth.

'That was for a different crime,' Thomas said, 'it has nothing to do with these ones. All three crimes he is guilty of.'

'I confess I took the mail shirt,' Richard said, 'but my uncle took my manor and killed my mother. He was the cause of all of it.'

'You didn't tell me anything about that,' the Queen said quietly to Brother Geoffrey.

'I didn't know about that,' he replied, 'I would need to investigate.'

The Queen sat back into her high chair and adjusted the crown on her forehead. 'I find that this is a regular family dispute, mixed up with a common robbery in which Sir Hugh was unfortunately killed. This boy is not guilty of his murder, and I don't care about a servant.'

'I must protest,' Thomas the Lawyer said, 'I saw him kill his grandfather.'

'And I saw him put his body in front of mine to shield me from crossbow bolts,' the Queen roared. The whole chamber fell silent.

Brother Geoffrey very slowly turned his head to Richard.

Richard shrugged and despite his best efforts a grin seeped out.

'Crossbow? What?' The Lawyer looked around the crowd for support.

'He is innocent of murder, although evidently he stole some mail. The mail is here on the floor so it can be returned. I see no need for the matter to be discussed any further. All of you, leave now, there are many cases left to judge,' the Queen said.

Richard needed no encouragement and headed for the door. He walked through it quickly and chuckled to himself. He felt lighter.

'That could have gone worse for you, boy,' Brother Geoffrey said, 'what was that about the crossbows?'

'Nothing much,' Richard walked towards the stairwell.

'I think differently, but I am curious as to your intentions towards the lawyer and the clerk.'

'I want to jam my fingers into the Lawyer's eyes for sure,'

Richard said, 'but the clerk is not his own man, I care not for him.'

'I urge you to forget about the Lawyer, his corpse may be one too many for you to dodge justice for,' Brother Geoffrey said.

'What happens between me and the Lawyer is none of your business,' Richard said.

The monk stopped and watched him him go, Richard could feel the little eyes burn into his back as he descended the spiral staircase.

Richard rushed back to Earl Patrick's chamber and found the first bottle of wine he laid eyes on.

'What happened?' Sir Wobble said from his chair.

Richard held a finger up to him as he downed the bottle. He finished it and took a huge breath. 'She let me go,' he said.

'Who?'

'The Queen.'

'You are touched by something divine,' Sir Wobble laughed, 'had it been the king you wouldn't be here drinking my uncle's finest wine.'

Bowman was awake and sat on a chair of his own. His blonde hair had been brushed for the first time in months. 'You are running out of lives, young lord,' he said.

'I think I'm done risking however many lives I have left,' Richard said.

Bowman looked at Sir Wobble. 'He doesn't know.'

'Of course he doesn't know, he's been soiling himself at the court all day,' Sir Wobble said.

'I wasn't soiling myself. What don't I know?' Richard asked.

'Earl Patrick has a man in Poitou,' Bowman said.

'Where's Poitou?' Richard asked.

'If you travel south from Normandy, you go through Maine, then you go through Anjou. Poitou is what you go through next,' Sir Wobble said.

'That sounds very far away,' Richard said.

'It is,' Bowman said, 'it's further south than I've ever been.'

'The point is,' Sir Wobble interrupted, 'that a powerful family there has rebelled and is torching the king's lands. My uncle's man from the region came and told us about it today, so we are going to muster to go and put down the rebellion.'

'What family is it?' Richard asked.
'The Lusignans,' Bowman grimaced.

AN EASY JOB

The twin towers that guarded either side of the entrance to the port of La Rochelle sharpened into view up ahead. The crisp morning air lingered even though the sky above was clear and the sun bright. A haze of mist hung over the water that the cog sailed through, and Richard could taste its freshness.

'I'll be glad to be back on land,' Richard said to Sir Wobble who leant on the side of the cog next to him.

'Me too, the ship is terribly boring,' Sir Wobble said.

'Especially for this long, I thought the voyage to Castle Tancarville last year was long enough.'

'Twice as long, twice as boring,' Sir Wobble said, 'but at least you're out of the hold now, and not huddling in a dark corner with Long Tom.'

'He's still down there,' Richard shook his head.

'He's weak, even weaker than you,' Sir Wobble grinned.

'It's not just the sea, his eyes seemed black,' Richard said, 'he seems broken down there.'

'Is that why they call him Long Tom?'

'Why?' Richard asked.

'Because when he's sad he's got a long face,' Sir Wobble suggested.

Richard almost laughed but felt bad for the young man. They'd both suffered from seasickness, but Long Tom had not been above deck for the entire journey down to the west coast of France.

'I don't care, I just want to get back on my horse and find some rebels to fight.'

'I want this to be an easy job,' Richard said, 'we need to get back to Yvetot. I promised Sophie we'd be back before the

126

winter, and now it's the next spring already.'

'She's going to hang your balls from the banner pole,' Sir Wobble laughed.

Richard ignored him and focused his eyes on the stone towers and the seagulls that whirled high above it. The cog sailed slowly because the day was calm. La Rochelle's port was fortified, and a high wooden wall went round from the towers to the stone wall that ringed the main body of the town.

'This voyage should be the hardest part of our task,' Earl Patrick walked up and slapped Sir Wobble on the back.

The sweet smell of the mist started to be replaced with the rich smell of smoke from the town.

'Will we fight, uncle?' Sir Wobble asked.

'Not even the Lusignans will cross me, and we have the Queen with us,' the earl said.

'I wouldn't mind a decent skirmish,' Sir Wobble said, 'the king would notice me if I captured a Lusignan.'

'They wouldn't dare face us, their rebellion will fade into nothing when the Queen is installed as the governor. We only need to get her to Poitiers and order will be restored.'

'How sure are we of that?' Richard asked.

Earl Patrick raised his eyebrows at Richard. 'You are one of my councillors now, are you?'

'No, I just want to know if I need to be careful here or not,' Richard said.

'My man from Poitou, Simon the Quiet, is well informed in local matters. The Lusignans still fear King Henry's wrath. If the royal army marches into Poitou, they will wreak havoc on the Lusignans, and they are clever enough to know that.'

Richard hoped so, he was a long way from home and in a land he didn't know.

'Simon,' Earl Patrick called, and a man in his thirties approached and nodded.

'My Lord,' he said.

'This is Simon the Quiet. Simon, this young knight of mine is questioning your judgement.'

'Is he?' Simon focused on Richard. Simon the Quiet was an unremarkable looking man, he had a paunch and his hairline was fading, but otherwise he had no features Richard could put his finger on.

'I mean no offence,' Richard said, 'I just don't know what lies ahead.'

'What lies ahead is La Rochelle, there you can see its shipyard,' Simon pointed to a dock within the port. 'The ship they are building is for the Templars, their fleet is based here. All the money they make is shipped out of this port and sent to the Holy Land.'

'Damned Templars,' Richard mumbled under his breath.

'The Templars here are quite reasonable,' Simon said, 'the Templars in Poitiers are another matter.'

'He doesn't care about the Templars,' Sir Wobble said, 'and I care about what sort of men the Lusignans are if we are to fight them.'

'We're not going to fight them,' Earl Patrick said.

'Poitou is widely held to be ungovernable,' Simon said, 'and that is largely because families like the Lusignans see no king as their natural overlords. So they think they should rule themselves. Guy of Lusignan is young, probably your age, but he is ambitious and independent. His father is currently lost in the Holy Land, some say captured by the infidels.'

Richard swallowed. What if his father had fought side by side with that Lusignan? What if they were imprisoned together? He didn't want to have anything in common with a potential enemy, so he pushed that fleeting thought aside.

Simon pointed beyond the town. 'We will ride east for a few days to reach Poitiers, half way is the town of Niort. The country is green and the valley-sides are full of vineyards. Later in the year they turn a reddish black with their grapes. The rivers are many and well flowing, the people are rich and independent and our settlements are fine. It is not like England where everyone lives on top of each other.'

'I would enjoy having lands here,' Earl Patrick said, 'it would cut my wine bill down.'

'Maybe you will receive some as a reward for this service,' Simon said.

'This service will be too small to warrant that. The rebellion is merely a cry for help that will cease when we show that it has been noticed,' the earl said.

'Exactly,' Simon the Quiet nodded, 'barely worth any thought at all. The Lusignans fear the king.'

'See, my boy, I told you,' Earl Patrick beamed, 'an easy job.'

They sailed into La Rochelle's port and the crew began to prepare to dock. Bowman appeared out on deck and stretched his arms and back out. The Queen also appeared, followed by four ladies and two little hairy dogs that yapped at any man that came too close.

One of Earl Patrick's squires brought up his banner and unfurled it at the front of the vessel. The blue and white horizontal lines caught the breeze only for a moment before it sank down and crumpled.

'Patrick,' the Queen said.

The earl left Richard and bowed to the Queen.

'Your colours are the same as the Lusignans. That will be very confusing,' she said.

The Earl looked at his banner. 'Yes, I hadn't thought of that. We will tie a colour onto each of our arms so we know. I saw some red linen in the hold, I shall purchase that and we will have red armbands.'

'Very good,' one of her little dogs ran up to the earl and started to bark at him. He tried to shoo it away but every time he did the little dog kept running back to bark.

'May I leave? I do not wish to have to kick your dog,' he said.

'You may, but your kindness to dogs does not seem to have stretched to the archbishop's horses.'

'What? Oh, that,' Earl Patrick sighed.

'I did hear about it, Patrick. Come, you noisy dog, stop it,' the Queen said.

'That was distasteful,' the earl said, 'speak to your husband about it, the scheme was not mine.'

'I did. He was very pleased when the monk showed him the tail. He was even more pleased when the archbishop sent a man to complain that his very best bridle had been stolen,' she said.

'A bridle? I know nothing of that,' the earl half turned to look at Richard but checked himself.

'Then I suppose you will also know nothing about the blinded stable-hand who was assaulted by your men?'

'I certainly do not,' Earl Patrick said, 'but I will be finding out.'

'Do not concern yourself, Henry threw silver coins at the messenger for making him laugh so much. Heaven knows why, but he found it delightfully amusing.'

Earl Patrick backed away from the small dog, which retreated back to the Queen with its tail wagging and head held high. The earl bowed, stood next to Richard and placed his heavy hand on his shoulder. 'Do you remember what you answered when I asked if anything had happened?'

'Yes,' Richard said.

'Would you give a different answer now?'

Richard hesitated. Long Tom had probably been the cause of the blinding, and certainly had stolen the bridle, but at the same time, he was only a squire.

'It may not have gone entirely to plan,' Richard said.

The earl groaned. 'You blinded someone, Richard.'

'That was not intended, and the man gave us no choice.'

'You know what they say,' Sir Wobble began.

Earl Patrick cut him off. 'If you say an eye for an eye, I'll poke your eye out before you finish speaking,' he said.

'No,' Sir Wobble grinned, 'I was going to remind you what they say about ships that have docked.'

'And what is that?' the earl asked.

'That you should get off them.'

'I don't know how I'm related to you,' Earl Patrick shook his head and then went to order everyone to disembark.

Solis walked gingerly onto dry land, tested it with his hoof, and sniffed the air.

'It's warmer here,' Bowman said as a porter brushed past him carrying a sack of something. Others moved back and forth between warehouses and ships and the wall of noise from them was a contrast to the quiet calm of the ship.

'I thought it was bad when we got to Normandy the first time,' Richard said, 'but I have no idea what anyone here is saying.'

'It is a different language,' the Queen walked towards a horse that was being held ready for her, 'my language.'

Bowman raised his eyes to Richard. 'That's us told, then.'

'Keep your eyes away from her,' Richard said as Bowman's

eye's followed her walking away.

'Don't you lecture me about eyes,' Bowman said, 'did you really blind that stable hand?'

'No, that was Long Tom.'

'Why didn't you say so?'

'I was the knight, it was my responsibility. I have to shield those who I am responsible for,' Richard said.

'This is you trying to do what your sister told you about being selfish, isn't it?'

'No,' Richard looked away, 'why do you care?'

'I don't, but we'll have to wait a while before the Queen's baggage will be unloaded, so I was hoping to go and find some local wine.'

Earl Patrick stood on the dockside ordering men this way and that. 'Richard, William, help unload the ship, stop standing around,' he said.

'No wine, then,' Richard said to Bowman and they went to help. Horses were unloaded and then the supplies, a pile of spears and shields, and finally the Queen's baggage. Carts were hired from the town and over the morning they were loaded with everything.

'There is a shield and lance for every man,' the earl said.

A while later Richard had removed his tunic, and sat in a linen under-shirt on a wall to wipe his face.

Bowman took a long drink from a cup of water. 'That was too much like labouring for me,' he said.

'I don't mind,' Richard said, 'it was good to move around after being on the ship. Even Long Tom's out and about now.'

Long Tom threw a sheet of canvas onto a cart and sighed. His oddly shaped face did indeed look long, and his eyes had a sunken look to them.

'I don't think he's well,' Richard said.

'Looks like he's spent a week on a ship,' Bowman said.

'We all hate ships,' Richard smiled.

The Queen's baggage train assembled into a convoy and looked ready to leave the town. One last cart trundled from within La Rochelle, and it was pulled by a shaggy little mare.

'That's Three Legs,' Richard said.

'Who?'

'You don't remember Nicola and her mare Three Legs?'

'Oh, the merchant who was looking after the silver,' Bowman got to his feet.

'Exactly,' Richard got up too and went to meet Nicola.

The cart stopped at the head of the Queen's convoy, and Nicola looked over at the two men who approached her.

'What are you doing here?' she asked. Her mousy coloured hair had increased in greyness since their last meeting, but her face was no more worn and her eyes still as full of life.

'We are in the service of Earl Patrick,' Richard said.

'I can see that by the pile of shields,' Nicola said, 'I thought the two of you would be off wasting silver and getting murdered by now.'

'What silver?' Bowman grinned.

'Quite,' Nicola replied.

'But what are you doing here?' Richard asked.

'I wish to travel inland, but will not do so without an escort.'

'I thought you traded between London, Normandy and Flanders?' Richard asked.

Nicola regarded him closely. 'You think too much for your own good. Keep that mind of yours on your own affairs,' she said.

'Is the Queen your mistress?'

'I have no mistress nor master,' Nicola said sharply, 'where is your other friend, the older one?'

'He is my steward,' Richard replied.

'Ah, Yvetot, I heard about that,' she nodded.

'I suppose your cart is full of wool and your destination happens to be Poitiers?' Richard asked.

Nicola tutted him. 'Never make assumptions, young man, but I will be going to Poitiers with the Queen.'

'So you do serve the Queen?'

'Enough, you have worn my patience out,' Nicola said, 'and the Queen will return to us now that we are ready.'

'We should mount up,' Bowman said.

Richard nodded. It sounded like they had a long way to go and had already spent too much of the day unloading and loading equipment.

Sir Wobble had three shields when they got back, and held

two of them out. Richard took one of the kite shaped shields painted with horizontal blue and white lines.

'I think they make a nice change from the red,' Bowman said.

'I did like the Tancarville red,' Sir Wobble said, 'these seem too friendly to me.'

'It's what we've got,' Richard noticed the earl busied himself selecting horses from a string of them and giving them out to his men.

'Richard,' Earl Patrick shouted, 'I've bought these palfreys and you cannot continue riding around on your warhorse. You are supposed to be a landed knight.'

Richard looked over the new horses. They had been purchased with saddles and bridles, but they did all look quite young.

'I've never bought a horse, how do I pick one?' He asked.

'You haven't bought these either, I'm letting you borrow one,' the earl said, 'just get on one, ride it to the start of the convoy and back here again, and if you haven't fallen off it when you return, it'll do.'

Richard picked the first horse that bothered to turn its head to him. It was brown with fine hair and smaller than Solis. Solis was tied to a tie-ring embedded in the dock wall, and his yellow head followed Richard and he waved a hoof in the air at him.

'Deal with it,' Richard shouted to him.

The palomino pawed on the cobbles, his metal shoes threw sparks over to the horses tied beside him and they flinched away. Richard mounted the palfrey and walked it along the convoy. As he rode away from Solis, the horse started to shout at him.

'If that was my horse,' Richard heard Earl Patrick start, but he was too far away to hear him finish. When he turned back, he could see his yellow coated horse trying to pull himself free from his tie point. Richard groaned to himself. He simply wasn't going to be able to sit on another horse if Solis could see it. He trotted the palfrey back as quickly as he could and jumped off it. Solis immediately stopped his commotion and stood still as Richard gave the reins back to the earl.

'I'm sorry, I think I need to ride him,' Richard shrugged.

'You should never let a horse get that attached,' the earl said, 'but it's your problem, not mine.'

Richard prepared Solis to ride and mounted up with Bowman and Sir Gobble.

'We'll stop at a good manor somewhere, or maybe a town, and they'll have wine,' Bowman said.

Richard sniffed the air. 'This is much more interesting than the sea,' he said.

'I can still only smell salt and fish,' Sir Wobble said, 'I can't wait to see the countryside.'

'You just want to eat everything that comes from it,' Richard laughed.

'Nothing wrong with that,' Sir Wobble replied.

Sir Wobble had donned his mail shirt and mail leggings, and slipped his helmet onto his head.

'We are in friendly territory,' Richard said, 'from what Earl Patrick and Simon the Quiet said, we don't need to arm for a couple of days.'

'Do you really trust someone called Simon the Quiet?' Sir Wobble asked as he tied the helmet's lace up beneath his chin.

'I don't know, but your uncle seems to,' Richard said.

'Doesn't mean I should,' Sir Wobble adjusted the strapping on his shield so it sat just below his eyes, 'there, all ready,' he said.

'Why do I feel nervous?' Richard asked more to himself than anyone else.

'You have responsibility now, the villagers at Yvetot might not admit it, but they have a need of you,' Bowman said.

'So?'

'I think you don't want to let them down,' Bowman said, 'so try not to get yourself killed.'

Earl Patrick rode over. 'Do you really let your squires talk to you like that?' he asked Richard.

Bowman tilted his head slightly and waited for Richard's response.

'He isn't really my squire,' Richard said.

'Why does he serve you then?'

'He doesn't really serve me either,' Richard said.

'No,' Sir Wobble interrupted, 'the only useful thing he's ever done was hunt that deer I never got to finish.'

'So,' Earl Patrick chuckled, 'he follows you around, but serves you badly.'

'Life around Richard has never been dull,' Bowman said, 'maybe I just like to keep myself entertained.'

'Nonsense, why are you with him? What is in it for you?' the earl scratched his beard.

'No idea, My Lord,' Bowman grinned.

The road east was just as Simon the Quiet had described it. The convoy snaked east along decent roads and was blessed by calm weather.

'How is your palfrey?' Richard asked Bowman.

'Comfortable,' he replied, 'how's yours?'

'Very funny,' Richard said from aboard Solis, who was a hand taller than all of the riding horses everyone else rode. Bowman's warhorse walked in a convoy of horses amongst the Queen's baggage train.

'I can't believe we have all these carts for a few knights and a few dozen squires,' Richard said.

'It's mostly the Queen's belongings that fill the carts, young lord,' Bowman replied, 'I'm sure she is slowing us all down.'

'I'm glad we've been placed at the back to guard her though, if there's trouble it will happen at the front where Sir Wobble is,' Richard said.

The convoy rumbled on over a stone road which only had the occasional hole in it. They rode directly behind one cart, and ahead of another, as trees lined the way and birds sang in far off undergrowth. The road wound down into a valley, but when the ground opened up, Richard could see a settlement ahead. Ringed by a long wooden wall, the small town nestled itself on the southern side of a river bend. Tall hills blocked the view in every direction, and in the centre of the town was a large stone fortification.

'That's a donjon,' Bowman said.

'It's a castle.'

'Well, yes, but it is just a giant keep with no walls of its own, I've heard about them,' Bowman said.

The column reached the town as darkness began to fall, but Richard could barely see the ground by the time the baggage had all been stowed and quarters found for everyone. Richard and Bowman found Sir Wobble at the foot of the donjon, looking up at its immense stone foundations.

'It's bigger than the White Tower,' he said.

'No one is knocking those walls down,' Bowman said.

'I'm glad we're staying inside it,' Richard said, 'I think I'll be able to sleep easy tonight.'

The donjon constituted of two large towers joined by a keep. Round turrets seemed to grow out of the masonry all around it, and Richard felt a tinge of intimidation just from standing beneath it.

Richard followed the earl inside and made his bed where he was told. The halls and stairwells confused him to the point where he wasn't sure how to get out of the donjon from the dormitory where the earl's men were billeted.

'I'll be glad for a fire tonight,' Bowman looked around the hall where squires and knights laid out their bed.

'I should like to be fed some decent food,' Sir Wobble said.

'Go and look for some, then,' Richard wished they'd been in a hall with a window, it was dark and there was a hint of dampness in the air. He licked his lips and was sure he could taste mould. 'I wouldn't mind finding somewhere nicer to sit down for a while,' he said.

'Let's go, then,' Sir Wobble started to walk off out of the hall.

'I'm staying here,' Bowman stretched himself out on his bed and folded his arms behind his head.

'Suit yourself,' Richard followed Sir Wobble out.

'Do you remember which way we came in?' Sir Wobble said once they reached the staircase.

'Not really, but I'd like to see the view from the battlements,' Richard said.

Sir Wobble nodded and climbed up the spiral staircase. It wasn't lit but Richard's feet knew where to go and soon they made it to the floor above. Sir Wobble stopped at the top, turned back slowly, and shushed Richard.

'What?' Richard whispered.

'The Queen is over there,' he replied.

'Why are we whispering?'

'They're arguing,' he nodded towards the back of the hall where a long table ended where the Queen sat.

'The Templars are reliable and have no interest in domestic matters. Why would he lie?' she said.

'The Templars are wasps buzzing around the good people of Poitou,' Simon the Quiet shouted. Richard was surprised he was willing to raise his voice in the presence of royalty.

'Simon has served me for years,' Earl Patrick said from the chair to the Queen's right, 'and his father before him. His family have been loyal to me without fault. Why would he lie?'

'One of them is lying,' the Queen roared.

Richard and Sir Wobble exchanged a glance. The hall was silent for a moment.

'Maybe one of them is just wrong,' the earl said.

'That is not acceptable,' the Queen said, 'this concerns the security of the realm. This is not a merchant party haphazardly going from place to place with no care in the world. It concerns the safety of your queen. Is the way ahead safe or not?'

'It is,' Simon the Quiet said.

'It is not,' a man in a Templar surcoat banged his fist down on the table. He was finely built and had a scar running across his cheek that Richard was sure could only have come from a blade.

'I care not who rules Poitou, I care not if the Lusignans capture the Queen or are themselves taken,' the Templar said, 'I wish for peace between Christians. I will however, not speak untruths. The Lusignans are between this town and Poitiers. Your party is well armed, but it is small. The Lusignans are well armed but well numbered, and they know the land. It is unsafe for you to progress.'

The Queen pursed her lips. 'The Templars are always honest, but I do not know you as a man, Master Levesque,' she said.

'He is a dishonest Templar,' Simon the Quiet said from the opposite side of the table, 'he became the Master of Poitiers through bribery.'

'That is an outrageous accusation,' Master Levesque kept his voice steady.

'I have no reason to doubt this man,' Earl Patrick said, 'but I have every reason to believe Simon. We should continue ahead tomorrow.'

'I fled Poitiers because of the Lusignans,' Master Levesque

137

said, 'they swarm around the countryside like locusts burning everything. Poitiers has no knights to defend it and the townspeople are not a reliable guard. Guy has threatened Templars in Poitou before so I came here. We can hold this donjon for a year simply by bolting the front gate.'

'That is nothing but a story woven to keep the Queen away from the seat of government,' Simon said.

'He really is angry,' Richard whispered, 'and not that quiet.'

Simon pushed his chair back and it screeched across the wooden floor. 'The Templars wish to turn Poitou into their own demesne land. Everyone knows they are greedy for wealth and power,' he shouted.

'Enough,' the Queen slammed down a wooden plate onto the table. It split in two and one half spun through the air and missed Master Levesque's face by a whisker. He blinked but didn't flinch.

'That was close,' Sir Wobble whispered.

'I am quite sure that the Lusignans wish to prevent my reaching Poitiers. Until I am installed there, there will be nothing to bridle their aggression. We must progress tomorrow. If the earl and his man say the way is safe, then we must attempt it. God will clear our path if our cause is righteous.'

'If you decide on this course,' the Templar said, 'I will follow you and defend you with my life, but I must warn you against it. I will travel next to your person and prove my loyalty and honesty with my body.'

'He wants to steal your crossbow bolt blocking story,' Sir Wobble whispered to Richard.

'He can have it,' Richard replied.

The earl stood up and held a red armband over to the Templar. 'That was well spoken. I have no ill will towards you. We are wearing red armbands in the journey and you are welcome to wear this with us.'

'I thank you for your courtesy,' Master Levesque reached to take the red linen.

Simon snorted and started to walk towards the stairwell where Richard still hid in the shadows.

'Go, go,' Sir Wobble pushed Richard up the stairs.

Richard rushed up and around the dark spiral until it emerged suddenly into moonlight on the roof of the donjon.

'He didn't go down, he's coming up this way,' Sir Wobble hissed.

'There's someone up here already,' Richard said quietly and pointed over to the far corner of the roofed area, where a human shaped shadow was visible above the battlements. Richard grabbed Sir Wobble's tunic and dragged him over to a wooden shed in the middle of the roof. They slammed down up against the wooden panels and caught their breath. Richard heard Simon's footsteps come up the stairwell and walk over towards the shadow. Stars twinkled in the sky above and a few wisps of clouds drifted slowly across the half-moon. The breeze chilled the sweat on Richard's neck as he stuck his head around the shed to look at Simon.

'Ah, Simon,' the shadow said and floated towards him. It turned into a man wearing a dark coloured tunic but Richard couldn't make out any of his features.

'Did it work?' The shadow asked. His voice was deep and deliberately quiet.

'I think so. The Templar is being troublesome but the Queen's pride will win out,' Simon the Quiet said.

The shadow nodded. 'Good, but if they change their minds be sure to send word,' he said.

'Of course, I have no wish to displease him,' Simon said.

'They are arrogant and their empire is monstrous. We must cut its head off to free Poitou from tyranny.'

'Amen,' Simon said, 'we have suffered under them for too long, this is our moment.'

'Our path is dangerous, tread carefully, Simon,' the shadow said.

'They suspect nothing,' he replied, 'we will decapitate the serpent coiled around all Aquitaine,' Simon said.

'Enough of this talk here,' the shadow said, 'go back and act as if you are bored and relaxed.'

'Very well,' Simon the Quiet bowed and made his way back down the staircase. Richard watched the shadow follow him. For a brief moment he saw the man, he wore a surcoat over his tunic with blue and white horizontal stripes.

'One of my uncle's men?' Sir Wobble said as he disappeared, 'but that makes no sense.'

'No,' Richard said, 'he wore no red armband.'

'You're right, but that can only mean his lord is a Lusignan.'

'We must warn your uncle.'

'Of course, but we need to be careful. My uncle likes Simon and will need to be persuaded gently.'

'We only have until tomorrow morning,' Richard said, 'it sounded to me like we will be riding into an ambush.'

'That would give me a chance to show my uncle my prowess,' Sir Wobble said.

'If you live through it,' Richard said, 'stop being selfish. You heard them, they are planning to take the Queen herself.'

'I suppose that would look bad on me,' Sir Wobble frowned, 'we will try to warn my uncle. I shall do it though, he trusts me more than you.'

Richard went to argue but closed his mouth because he knew it was the truth. He wanted to look out over the battlements and pretend everything was fine, but instead he followed his friend back to the blackness of the stairwell. They crept down slowly and stopped at the hall again. The Queen drank wine and the earl spoke to the Templar. Simon had gone to sit on his own and there was no hint of the other man who had been on the roof.

'Do we just go in?' Richard whispered.

'No, we can't say anything while my uncle is with Simon.'

'We can't sit here on the cold stone all night, either,' Richard said.

'Fine, once Simon leaves, I'll go in,' Sir Wobble said.

'That could be all night.'

'True,' Sir Wobble considered his options, 'you wait here for a while and I shall get some sleep. Wake me if he leaves. I'll be back after a while and we can swap.'

'That's fine if you remember to come and relieve me,' Richard said, 'I know what you're like.'

'I promise I'll come back soon. My uncle likes a drink so it could be some time.'

'Swear it,' Richard said, 'these stones will be cold if I sleep on them all night.'

'Don't worry, trust me,' Sir Wobble walked down the staircase and left Richard alone to spy on the chamber. He moved up a few steps so he was totally in the black and sat down on the stones. Arguments continued in the chamber.

'I'm told the Templars want to tax the whole of Poitou for their own gain,' Earl Patrick said.

'And who told you that, Simon the Quiet?' Master Levesque asked.

Richard was too far away to catch the reply and he soon stopped trying to listen. He wished he had his cloak as the cold started to seep into his feet and every part of him that touched the cold hard stones. It wasn't long before he had to fight to keep his eyelids open, and Richard cursed Sir Wobble for taking his time. Richard's stomach rumbled and he yawned.

Before he knew it, Richard heard footsteps enter the chamber.

'Hurry up, it's the Queen, we can't be late for her breakfast,' a voice said.

'Who cares,' another replied.

Richard rubbed his neck which was unbearably sore, and one of his legs was full of pins and needles. He hopped down the steps on his other leg and peered into the chamber. The Queen walked out of a door at the far end of the space, wearing a different dress to the day before. As he saw Earl Patrick walk over to the table and yawn, a sinking feeling hit him. He was going to kill Sir Wobble.

'Did you sleep well, Your Majesty?' The earl asked.

'No, the bed was so hard it might as well have been made of stone,' the Queen sat down heavily at the table.

'Mine was,' Richard mumbled to himself.

Simon the Quiet lay on a bed roll up against a wall, and the Templar Master already sat at the table. Richard went down the stairs before the servants came back out of the chamber. He made his way back to the hall where his unused bed lay and saw Sir Wobble under two large blankets. One of them was his.

'Where have you been?' Bowman sat up his bed.

'Waiting for this lazy oaf,' Richard walked up and kicked Sir Wobble where he thought his ribs were.

Sir Wobble cried out and his eyes shot up to Richard. 'What

are you doing that for?'

'Remember last night?'

'No? Oh.'

'You promised, you said to trust you,' Richard wanted to kick him again.

'I'm really sorry,' Sir Wobble said, 'I must have been more tired than I thought.'

'What about me? I'm now tired and sore and cold. Not to mention hungry,' Richard said.

'What is going on?' Bowman asked.

'This idiot left me to sleep on the stone floor all night,' Richard decided to kick Sir Wobble again anyway.

'Ouch, stop it,' Sir Wobble wriggled out of bed and stood up.

'I really want to keep kicking you,' Richard said.

'Was Simon still in the chamber when you left?'

'Yes,' Richard said.

'Damn it,' Sir Wobble's cheek turned a shade of pink despite his darker complexion.

'What are you going to do about it?' Richard asked.

'About what?' Bowman said, 'you never tell me anything anymore.'

'I'll tell you later,' Richard said then turned to Sir Wobble, 'you created this mess, you clean it up.'

'Why should I?'

'You left me to sleep on the stones, William, you go and tell your uncle,' Richard said.

'You left me to fight the Martel Bastard by myself,' Sir Wobble crossed his arms.

'Me? I didn't want you to, you rode off all on your own,' Richard started to roll up his bedding. He swiped his stolen blanket off Sir Wobble's bed with a flourish and packed his things.

'Do I need to worry about anything?' Bowman got to his feet.

'Yes,' Richard and Sir Wobble said at the same time.

Richard knew he was too angry to be of any help to anyone. 'I need to go outside,' he said to Bowman, 'but Sir Wobble needs to stop us riding into an ambush.'

'Ambush?' Bowman said.

Richard nodded and trudged out of the hall. He wasn't sure

how to get out of the donjon so he just headed down any staircase he saw. By the time he'd found the gate and walked out into the morning air, Richard's temper had cooled. He went to find the paddocks where the horses had been left, and dropped his bedding bundle there. The grass was still dewy from the night but the sun reflected and sparkled in the droplets across the paddock. He looked up at the grassy hills that surrounded Niort and marvelled at how different the landscape was to Keynes. Or for that matter to Normandy. He wondered how Sophie fared, and hoped that Sarjeant had kept his promise of sobriety. He wondered if the Miller was paying the Reeve, and if the Reeve had paid Sophie. That thought made him half remember a dream from the previous night where he had again poked the Priest's eyes out. Richard thought about laying his cloak out to have some real sleep when men started to file out of the donjon. The earl was amongst them and they headed over to the paddock.

Bowman appeared and slung his bedding down beside Richard's. 'Saddle up,' he said.

'Which way are we riding?' Richard asked.

'How should I know,' Bowman searched around the paddock for his horse. Squires and servants went in to fetch horses, and down in the town Richard heard the baggage carts trundle about.

'I'm arming up,' Richard said, 'if we ride east you should wear your mail.'

'Is that where your ambush is, young lord?'

'It's not my ambush,' Richard found the bag that held his mail shirt.

'Fine,' Bowman did the same and both men shook their armour on over their heads and belted their swords over the top of it.

By the time Richard had mounted Solis, slung his blue and white shield over this back and took up his spear, he still didn't know which way they were headed.

'The baggage train is still down in the town,' Bowman nodded.

'We're going to be waiting a while, aren't we?' Richard sighed.

Bowman nodded. 'Where is Sir Wobble, or have you two

really fallen out?'

'Don't ask me,' Richard said, 'it's up to him. It's also up to him to stop this ambush.'

'If you're that worried, maybe you should do something about it yourself instead of sulking,' Bowman shifted his spear so it rested on his foot and his shoulder.

'I'm tired of fixing things,' Richard glanced up at the towering masonry of the donjon.

They waited for a long time before the carts wound their way up to the donjon and the column could form up and start moving out. Earl Patrick rode at its head in his finest gold trimmed tunic, the armoured Sir Wobble at his side. At some point over the winter, he'd found someone to fix the hole in the mail's shoulder. The young man didn't turn his head to Richard as he rode by, and Richard made no effort to speak to him either.

They waited until most of the baggage had rolled by and the Queen appeared on a fine white horse. The Templar Master Levesque rode alongside her in his mail shirt, with two Templar sarjeants behind him.

'Why are you armed?' the Queen asked as Richard and Bowman fell in behind her.

'For the same reason the Templar is,' Richard said.

Master Levesque turned around. 'You do not speak to the Queen in such a manner, have some respect,' he said.

Richard considered the white and black surcoat over his mail. 'If it is any consolation,' Richard said, 'I believe you.'

The Queen slowed her horse so it fell alongside Solis, who threw his teeth at it as a warning. 'And what is it that you believe?' she asked.

'That we are riding into an ambush,' Richard said.

'And how would you know about that?'

'I saw Simon the Quiet talking to a man last night who said they wanted to attack you, Your Majesty.'

Bowman gave Richard a quizzical look.

'That man is a rat,' the Templar said.

'Regardless,' the Queen looked Richard in the eyes, 'we are now set in motion so will not deviate. Patrick is not a man to be easily swayed. If we ride into an ambush, then so be it.'

Richard frowned. That seemed like a terrible idea, but at least he'd been able to say something.

'If we are attacked and it goes badly, we will ride back to Niort,' the Queen said.

'Of course,' Master Levesque said.

'Will someone tell me what is going on?' Bowman asked.

'Keep your man quiet,' the Queen said to Richard.

Richard shot Bowman a look to do just that and the group settled into silence.

They had waited half the morning for the baggage train to form, and rode without rest well into the afternoon. As the countryside grew more remote and the river to their right wider, Richard started to relax. It felt good to be out in the country, but the increasing steepness of the hill on their left eventually started to make him feel hemmed in.

'We can't go anywhere but forwards or backwards,' Richard said.

'Stop worrying about it, young lord,' Bowman said, 'there's nothing you can do about it.'

'That doesn't help me,' Richard craned his head up to see the earl and Sir Wobble at the head of the column. He could pick them out in the distance but when they went round a corner they were hidden by roadside bushes. Between them were the warhorses, and behind Richard the baggage train had started to lag behind. Nicola's cart, pulled by her shaggy mare, was the only one that had kept up with the riders.

'The hill becomes a cliff from here,' Richard looked up at the sheer face of earth that rose up on the left of the road. Vegetation grew out from it and it rose to three times their height.

'It's going to be soon,' Master Levesque said from next to the Queen. He moved his horse to ride on her left and shifted his shield around so it was ready for action.

'He is taking it as seriously as you are,' Bowman rearranged his shield so it was ready too.

'I don't think there's much doubt,' Richard said, 'as soon as the earl calls a retreat we need to turn around and lead the baggage away.'

'The Queen is your concern,' the Templar said, 'the baggage

has no value.'

'It is easy for a Templar to say that,' the Queen sniffed, 'but we wait for the earl's signal.'

The road straightened out and sloped downwards until it was at river level. Richard could again see the earl's banner flutter at the head of their party, and Sir Wobble in his armour behind it.

Richard saw the stone fly from the cliff half way down the column before he heard it overshoot the column and splash into the river. For a moment all he could hear was the gentle flow of the river and the clomping of horse's hooves, but then the clifftop erupted with noise. Shouts rang down along with more stones. Some stones hit shields and others hit horses who reared up and span around. Arrows flew down at speed but most hit the ground. Knights looked up to face the missiles but it was obvious to everyone that the clifftop was unassailable.

'Forwards or back?' Richard shouted.

The Templar stood perfectly still and looked up. 'Patience, the earl has not yet commanded,' he said.

'Look, riders,' Richard pointed far ahead down the road to a group of horsemen cantering towards them. Their banner was white and blue.

'Lusignans,' the Queen frowned.

Earl Patrick called back for the warhorses to be mounted and servants and squires rushed back to the middle of the column to distribute them.

'No one else is armed,' Richard said as he watched the fully armoured Lusignans approach in a flurry of horses and flowing surcoats.

'I think we can safely assume we should retreat,' the Queen said calmly.

'The earl has given no order, Your Majesty,' Master Levesque said.

'And yet I am the Queen, so you will obey me.'

Sir Wobble alone was armed and ready at the head of the column, and he stood by himself in the middle of the road as the knights and squires scrambled back to arm or mount warhorses.

'They don't have time,' Bowman said.

'We can help them,' Richard started to move Solis forwards.

'Stand your ground,' the Queen said, 'you are here to guard me.'

Richard halted and looked at Bowman.

'We were told to guard her,' he shrugged back as an arrow hit his shield. Bowman looked down at it and pulled it out.

A stone hit a squire in the head and he dropped to the floor. Earl Patrick's warhorse was trotted to him by a young man. Richard counted a dozen armed Lusignans canter down the path as Sir Wobble spurred his way towards them.

'He is a fool,' Richard said.

'He is brave, though,' the Queen said. An arrow whistled by her ear and stuck in the ground behind her.

'Close on the Queen,' the Templar shouted. Richard and Bowman rode to her left side and shielded her from the clifftop as best they could.

Sir Wobble lowered his lance and the leading two Lusignans lowered theirs in response. They came together at full speed but both Lusignans missed Sir Wobble. His lance hit one of them on the top of his helmet and it flew off his head. The attackers rode by Sir Wobble and seemed to ignore him.

Earl Patrick put a foot in his stirrup just as his servant was hit in the chest by a stone. The projectile hurled him backwards and he dragged the horse's reins down with him. The animal reared up and the earl was thrown back onto the ground. He jumped up and grabbed his warhorse just as Guy of Lusignan, the only one with a white and blue surcoat, ran him through with his lance. Earl Patrick was knocked down and the lance snapped as Guy rode past.

'Patrick,' the Queen cried.

'The earl won't be giving any commands now,' Master Levesque said, 'Your Majesty, it is time to leave.'

A stone bounced of Solis's rear and he kicked out at it.

'I'll kill them for that,' Richard mumbled to himself.

'Stay your temper,' the Queen said, 'but the Master is correct. The Lusignans have made their mistake so now we may go.'

'Did you want to be ambushed?' Richard asked.

The Queen said something in reply, but Richard's eyes were drawn to Sir Wobble. He had turned back to chase Guy and must have seen his uncle as he fell to the ground. Richard heard his cry of anguish echo down the road and over the noise of missiles and screaming horses.

'He's going to try to kill them all,' Bowman said.

Sir Wobble spurred his horse and drove his lance into the back of one squire. The lance pierced mail and the man lurched forwards before he fell out of his saddle. The other knights and squires noticed him and all turned to face him. Sir Wobble swept his lance sideways into one's face and bloodied his nose. Guy rode over to where Earl Patrick lay and looked down at him.

Sir Wobble's lance snapped in two and he used the remaining half to club another knight off his horse.

'He rides like a demon,' the Templar said as Sir Wobble spun his horse around to evade a strike. He kicked on to get out of the press just before he would have been trapped, and broke free of the melee as Lusignans tried to swarm him.

'He can't kill them all,' the Queen said.

'He thinks he can,' Richard said, 'and we can still help him.'

'You will do no such thing,' Master Levesque said.

Sir Wobble turned his horse and sprung back at the pursuing men-at-arms. The dozen riders could only ride three abreast down the road, and presented Sir Wobble a dense enough target that he could reach them even with his shortened broken lance.

'We need to help him,' Richard said.

'We can't, he is giving us time to escape. Again,' Bowman said.

'Order the train to move, get the carts turned around,' the Queen shouted. The servants and squires with the warhorses had started to retreat of their own accord, and they streamed back past the Queen. Nicola unhitched her cart to turn it as the road was so narrow.

'Protect the Queen,' the Templar shouted, but no one answered his call.

Sir Wobble embedded his lance in a squire's face and the weapon wrenched free from his hands.

'Let me go forwards,' Richard cried, heat in his veins and water in his eyes, 'I can't leave him to die.'

'You will not, or I will have your head removed,' the Queen

said.

Sir Wobble took a sword blow on his repaired shoulder but blocked another with his shield.

'I don't care, if I save him you can have my head,' Richard spurred Solis away from the group.

Sir Wobble's sword danced in the air and one knight lost some fingers along with his sword, while another wheeled away with blood on his face.

'I will burn your land and kill everyone on it,' the Queen roared.

Richard slammed Solis to a stop and breathed heavily. He felt his eyes pulse but the threat cut his heart in two.

Sir Wobble wheeled around, somehow got behind a squire and lashed out with his sword. The squire almost fell off his horse, and it started to bolt down the road with him hanging out of the saddle. Guy took a lance from one of his men and lined up a charge.

'William,' Richard shouted but he was too far away, and horses and men still ran noisily back past him. An arrow hit one man in the leg and he tripped and smashed his face on the road.

Guy cantered at the unsuspecting Sir Wobble and lowered his lance. He lowered it below the man and buried it into the horse de Cailly had leant him. Sir Wobble was thrown to one side but didn't fall from the saddle as his horse staggered over and crumpled to the ground. Guy rode on and his men-at-arms circled.

'It is too late now, he was brave but he will be taken,' the Templar said.

The last of the warhorses were led behind, along with the last of the earl's fighting men.

'Fat lot of good they were,' Bowman said as they abandoned their lord and Queen.

The Queen nodded. 'Good, we can retreat with honour now, at the rear of our men,' she said.

Richard felt a tear roll down his face as Sir Gobble pulled his leg out from under his horse and struggled to his feet.

'Yield,' Guy shouted to him and drew his sword.

'You killed my uncle, stabbed him in the back,' Sir Wobble

149

cried, 'like a base coward. I'll kill you all.'

'Richard,' the Queen shouted and he heard their horses start to walk away.

The arrows and stones had ceased, and now only Sir Wobble was left to fight. He backed himself towards the river where a hedge separated it from the road, and placed his back to the thorns. His chest heaved and he raised his shield and sword.

'Anyone who fancies testing his strength, step forwards,' he shouted and spat blood out onto the road.

'Fine, whoever wants the glory of defeating this youth may indulge him,' Guy said. The three men-at-arms Sir Wobble had unhorsed approached him on foot.

'Do you have no honour,' Sir Wobble said, 'you are so cowardly that you fight me all at once?'

They ran at him all at once. Sir Wobble lunged at the squire on his left and rammed his shield up into his nose. He sprung off him and batted a sword away on his way to headbutt a knight. The knight reeled backwards as Sir Wobble danced aside to face the third man. He backed away and looked over at his companions who both clutched their faces.

'Come on and fight me,' Sir Wobble screamed.

'Richard,' Bowman shouted, 'you can do nothing for him.'

'This can't happen again,' Richard whispered to himself and he choked back tears.

The Lusignans all dismounted and four of them stood together to advance on Sir Wobble. He backed himself up against the hedge again and swore at them.

They stepped forwards gingerly, swords held ready above shields.

Sir Wobble howled a war cry that Richard was sure was his own name, and coiled to charge. A spear thrust out from the hedge behind him and burst out through the front of his thigh. Sir Wobble screamed as the spear was pulled to one side and dragged him off his feet. His sword flew from his hand as he hit the ground. The four dismounted men-at-arms took their chance and rushed him. One jumped on his bleeding leg while the others jumped on his arms and head.

It was then that Guy turned to look at Richard and he snapped out of his malaise.

'Richard,' Bowman shouted, 'you can't save him, but you can still save your Queen.'

He turned Solis around and realised he was getting left behind. He cantered back the way they'd come, up the slope and around the last bend. He was greeted by the view of the baggage train at a standstill and a scene of utter panic. Earl Patrick's knights and squires who had evaded the missiles had mounted, but rode around the stationary baggage carts shouting to each other. Master Levesque rode amongst them and ordered them to form up, but no one paid him any regard.

'Richard,' Bowman shouted, 'they are stuck.'

Richard caught up with Bowman and the Queen and looked down the line of carts. Down the road, beyond the carts and panicked riders, a tree lay across their route to safety.

'That is not an accident,' Richard said.

'Obviously,' Bowman said.

'We need to get through it, the Lusignans will be on us at any moment.'

'The Templar is trying to organise them,' Bowman said.

'He's not having much luck though, is he?' Richard said.

The Queen glanced over her shoulder back to the corner that Guy was going to appear around. He had never seen her nervous before, not even on the galley at Fecamp. Richard looked at the fallen tree. It didn't have a thick trunk but it was enough to block the carts and deter riders, because behind the tree enemy footmen had taken up defensive positions.

'We need to break through the barricade,' Richard said and pushed Solis on towards the carts.

'Do not leave your Queen,' she shouted at him.

'I'm not,' he shouted back and reached the carts. Master Levesque implored at the men-at-arms to form up to attack the tree, but they still only argued amongst themselves.

'We can charge the tree,' Richard said to him.

'I cannot take Christian blood, nor bare arms in a fight between Christians,' he replied.

Richard glanced up to the clifftop and could see men rush along it behind the undergrowth. A stone flew down and crashed into Master Levesque's shield.

He looked down at the stone as it fell to the road. 'The Devil take them, I suppose they struck me first, so God be damned I'll fight them,' he looked at Richard and grinned.

'To hell with all of them,' Richard shouted. He spotted Long Tom on top of a horse and in a mail shirt. 'Tom, protect the Queen, get some of these idiots with you,' he shouted.

'Richard, what is happening?' He said, his eyes moved from the cliff to the Queen to Richard and back again.

'We are doing our duty and saving our Queen,' he said.

'But they're all around us, we're going to die,' Long Tom said.

'Of course we are,' Richard felt his blood rising, 'that's our lot, grip that bloody lance and take one of the cursed Lusignans to hell with you.'

Long Tom looked back at his with wide eyes. 'You're mad.'

'And you're already dead,' Richard said, 'go and stand by the Queen. If the Lusignans appear, charge them.'

Long Tom stared back at him, but then moved his horse over and obeyed.

Richard clenched his own lance tightly and carried on back down the rows of carts. He thought the Templar was probably behind him, but if not they were out of time, so he pressed his spurs against Solis and locked his eyes onto the tree up ahead.

'For William Marshal,' he shouted at the top of his lungs and lowered his lance. The squires he flew by stopped to watch him. His stallion's hooves dug into the road and stones flew up from his feet. Richard didn't notice the earl's men-at-arms stare at him, open mouthed, or that some slowly turned to follow him. He shouted Sir Wobble's name again as Solis's ears flicked towards the tree.

'Just like the galley,' Richard shouted and clamped his legs onto the horse. Solis put his head down as arrows started to fly from behind the tree. Solis leapt. The yellow horse cleared the trunk and his front feet tucked up but still clipped some leaves. Richard's lance hit a spearmen in the mouth and the speed of the horse dragged the head away from his body. Solis slammed into the ground behind the tree and Richard started to turn him. He whirled around as the Lusignan infantry looked back behind them at the lone horsemen in their midst. Richard charged towards the tree, speared an archer in the stomach, pulled the lance out and ripped a spearman's jaw off. One recovered himself enough to bring his spear around to point at Richard, but he batted it aside with his lance and cantered parallel with the tree. Solis knocked a man to the ground and then his horse smashed another's kneecap with a hoof. Richard brought his lance down into an archer's thigh, it went straight through and the point dug into the tree trunk lying across the road. The lance snapped with a popping sound and it fell from Richard's grasp. An arrow skidded off the rim of his shield and flew up somewhere into the air. Richard rode sideways over a wide-eyed archer who was floored painfully, then drew his sword just in time to block a thrusting spear. He pushed Solis into that man too, who back-pedalled before tripping on a rock and crashing onto the road. A spear point appeared in Richard's eyeline and suddenly his right eye went black and pain shot across his face. He cried out and flailed his sword in the hope of knocking the spear aside. He pushed Solis on to get out of trouble as something hit his mailed leg. His right eye stayed black but he wheeled around anyway and attacked the remaining dozen men holding the tree. Richard hit a spearmen in the helmet as something bounced off his shield and he felt part of it rip away.

The infantry screamed at him but Richard didn't know their words. Solis grabbed a spearman, his teeth clenched on his spear and Solis yanked it away from the man's fingers. The shaft smacked an archer in the head and he staggered away. Solis dropped the spear as Richard's sword was blocked by a shield and snapped in two. Richard looked down at the split and useless blade with his one open eye. He sighed. He'd given it his best, he could be sure of that.

A horse flew over the tree in front of him. The rider had a black and white surcoat and rode in silence. Master Levesque speared an infantryman and wheeled his foaming horse over towards Richard. He speared the man who was about to thrust at Richard's face, and some of Earl Patrick's men started to jump the barricade and join the fight. Spearmen had converged on Richard and the Templar charged to scatter them. Richard threw his broken sword at a man, who stepped out of its way, and rode Solis towards another to run him down. A spearman stabbed up at Master Levesque's belly as he killed an archer, and the Templar slumped in the saddle. Richard felt a wave of anger and kicked Solis on right over the spearman. The man disappeared under metalled hooves and suddenly the fight was over. The earl's men-at-arms killed the last of the infantry and Richard turned to see Bowman on the ground and starting to lift the tree trunk up.

'For God's sake help me,' he shouted.

Richard reached up to his eye but only felt warm stickiness. An arrow whistled over from the clifftop and stuck in the ground nearby.

'Help him move the tree,' Richard shouted and two squires dismounted and rushed to aid Bowman.

Richard inspected his right hand and realised that he couldn't make a fist. The whole hand was bloody and pain started to seep from it. He had no idea when he'd been hit there.

A volley of stones erupted from the clifftop and one of the squires screamed. Richard turned to watch Bowman and his assistants pick up the tree and start to drag it off the road. Arrows started to fall around them. One got caught in Bowman's leg mail, the metal rings saved him from a wound. The next caught him on the hip as he was bent over and he dropped the tree.

A cart rolled around the tree, its driver whipping the horse hard as he bellowed at it. Its wheels bounced on the uneven round surface and over the body of a fallen spearmen, but it got through and began its race back to Niort.

Bowman jogged over to Richard. 'We need to get away from this cliff,' he shouted.

Richard looked over the tree to where the baggage train creaked into action like an awakening wooden snake. 'We need to shield the Queen from pursuers,' he said.

'With what? We've a handful of men and you look blinded,' Bowman pulled the arrow out of his hip.

The Queen cantered around the tree. 'Form a rearguard,' she said to Richard before she disappeared back towards Niort.

'We might as well,' Richard said to Bowman, 'our horses have been walking all day and theirs will be fresh.'

Bowman swore. 'We'll take some of them with us,' he said through gritted teeth.

A cart aimed poorly and it smashed straight into the fallen tree. The horse pulling it bolted down the road and tore itself free. The cart lost a wheel, tipped onto its side and blocked the road again.

'Move that cart,' Richard said as he saw a white and blue banner appear around the corner beyond the tree. Guy rode beside it and his men had remounted.

'There's more of them than us,' Bowman said.

'But we've got the tree, don't move the cart,' he shouted.

Two squires had their hands on it and looked up at Richard.

'Dismount and man the barricade,' he shouted, 'spear their horses if they jump it.'

One of the squires removed his hands and started to run away down the road.

'Stop or I'll run you down,' Richard cried.

The squire ground to a halt, looked up at Richard and ran back to the tree without making eye contact.

'You have either scared the hell out of them or shamed them to hell,' Bowman said.

Richard glanced over at the Templar but he was still on the ground.

'That's a shame,' Bowman said, 'I think they've killed the only good Templar.'

On another day Richard would have laughed, but instead he'd spotted Long Tom gallop his horse towards the tree in front of the Lusignans. The drivers of the carts stuck in front of the barricade abandoned their vehicles and ran for it. Moments later they all clambered over the tree and ran away down the road as fast as they could. The road was left littered by carts and the bodies of dead and wounded men.

Guy of Lusignan cantered over them.

'Man the barricade,' Richard shouted again and most of the earl's men dismounted and prepared to stand firm. A few turned their horses and rode away.

'Cowards,' Bowman said.

'We don't need them,' Richard tried to clench his hand again but it ignored him, 'all men to the tree, let your horses go.'

'What?' Bowman said.

Richard swung off Solis, winced on his way down, and left

155

the reins go. 'Let your horses go,' he shouted, 'we need everyone fighting.'

There were only two of the earl's knights left and they dismounted and repeated the order. The squires who were left obliged, and a number of horses bolted back along the road. Solis stood still and looked at Richard after he'd hung the reins back over his yellow neck.

'Hardly fair to order everyone else to do it when you've got him,' Bowman said.

Richard shrugged and went to the tree. 'Spear the horses when they jump,' he said.

Guy rode up almost to the tree and studied it. He turned back to his men. 'Dismount, we'll take it on foot,' he commanded.

'Oh,' Richard said.

'There are twice as many of them than us, young lord, and now our horses are gone,' Bowman said.

'Sorry about that,' Richard grimaced.

'If we get out of this, remind me to never let you command anything,' Bowman clutched his shoulder.

'For Earl Patrick,' Richard said more in hope than expectation, and he got little in the way of response. The Lusignans formed up into a tight line and locked their shields together. Guy stood behind them and Richard thought he had a good strong face. His men stepped forwards and held their spears over their shields.

'At least they've run out of arrows,' Bowman grinned.

'Good, I don't want to get killed by an arrow,' Richard said.

The attackers closed in step by step and the defenders started to fence against them with their spears. Spear points jostled for advantage and shafts were batted aside. The attackers closed in but their weapons were hampered by the branches sticking out of the tree. Bowman found a spear on the floor and climbed up onto the overturned cart. The Lusignans had ignored it and from his new vantage point Bowman was able to stab down and catch an unaware opponent in the neck. His victim reeled away and fell to his knees.

'Get round their flank,' Richard shouted and pointed to where Bowman was. One of the earl's knights who had put his mail on jumped over the tree to the cart, and together he and Bowman attacked the flank of the Lusignans.

'Give it up, lads,' Guy shouted at his men. Another one fell to Bowman and they broke apart and retreated. Bowman and the knight jumped back over behind the cart and the two sides separated.

Richard went to Bowman. 'I think they know the Queen has gone, and we are not worth the cost.'

'I think you're right, but they're going to help themselves to the carts anyway,' Bowman said.

'That's not our problem,' Richard said.

'You are all going to die,' Guy shouted from behind an abandoned cart. The horse still attached to it snorted and stamped its feet.

'If you killed William,' Richard shouted back, 'I will hunt you down.'

'That knight is alive, but he will cost to return him to you,' Guy replied, 'for he cost me much.'

'You will have a reckoning,' Richard said.

'Leave it, Richard, Sir Wobble is alive so we can come back for him,' Bowman said.

'Your earl is dead, you have no master. Leave the tree and we will spare you,' Guy said.

'We're not going anywhere,' Richard shouted.

'And who are you, one eyed-devil?'

'Richard of Yvetot. Remember it.'

'I will,' Guy shouted and gestured at his man to fall back. Some of them remounted and others went to jump on the carts that were furthest away to drive them away. Richard watched them back off and steal carts, while Bowman found some fabric to tie around Richard's head to cover his eye.

'Was it such a good idea to tell him your name?' Bowman asked.

'I don't know. I still can't see,' Richard said.

'The eye is still there,' Bowman said, 'give it time and your sight may return.'

'I'll get on Solis and round up the other horses,' Richard said.

'A few have stayed, but you better bring some back or we will all die on this road.'

'I'm not Sir Wobble,' Richard said, 'I'll come back.'

Richard did come back, he used Solis to herd a dozen horses up who had stopped to graze alongside the road. The knights and squires remounted, and nervously glanced back to the bend where the Lusignans disappeared with as many carts as they could drive away.

'Let's go,' Richard said once everyone alive was back on a horse. They made their way back along the road as fast as they could and soon caught up the drivers and cartsmen who had fled on foot.

Richard had no time for them and kept going until he caught up with Nicola, who pushed her mare on as hard as she could.

'The Lusignans will be busy hauling away the other carts,' Richard told her, 'you can relax.'

'I will relax when I think I should relax,' Nicola said and looked over her shoulder. She cracked her whip so Richard decided to leave her to it and get back to the Queen.

The donjon was a welcome sight, although it was so dark when Richard led his ragtag force back, that he almost wasn't sure they were in the right place. They deposited their horses in the paddocks and dragged their weary bodies back up to the hall where everyone other than Richard had slept the previous night. When Richard got there he noticed that the hall was only half as full as it had been.

'Is the Queen here?' Richard asked a knight.

'Upstairs,' he replied.

Richard's legs were almost asleep by the time he reached the Queen's chamber. She stood looking out of a window to the east, alone.

'Your Majesty,' Richard cleared his throat.

She turned and her eyes lit up. 'My dear Richard,' she said.

He let out a heavy breath. 'I am glad you made it back,' he said. Richard looked around and realised Bowman hadn't bothered following him.

'I honestly believed we would be able to fight through,' she said.

Richard said nothing. His anger started to be replaced by guilt over his failure to alert the earl of the trap.

'What happened to your eye?'

'I don't know,' Richard said, 'but it doesn't work now.'

'I will remember this,' the Queen said softly, 'and I will remember William. I have never seen two men fight like that.'

'He lives, Guy of Lusignan said so,' Richard said.

'Good. His poor uncle.'

Richard shrugged. 'What do we do now?'

'I have already sent messengers out to my husband. He will crush these rebels like vermin. They made a terrible mistake in attacking us, let alone killing Patrick. I really liked him,' she said.

Richard nodded.

'You are obviously free from his service now. You should return home to recover, for you are in no fit state to serve me further,' she looked down at his hand, which dripped blood onto the wooden floor.

'I'm sorry,' Richard picked the arm up with his left hand and tried to fold it up within his tunic.

'I will give Patrick's men a choice in the morning. They can stay and serve me, or they can leave and make their own way,' the Queen said.

'What about William?'

'What about him?' the Queen asked.

'Guy said he was alive and it would cost to buy his freedom,' Richard said.

'Of course,' she replied, 'I will arrange a ransom if needed, seeing as Patrick cannot.'

'Thank you,' Richard bowed.

'You have made a name for yourself, Richard of Yvetot,' the Queen said, 'the talk in the hall below is of your leap over the tree. They are calling you the Yellow Centaur.'

'That's just silly,' Richard said.

'So, they are wrong in saying your horse wielded a spear and struck down a man?' she smiled.

'He did, actually,' Richard grinned, 'he just didn't know he was doing it.'

'Good. I shall hope to find you in my service again, Richard of Yvetot, the Yellow Centaur. Now go and heal, after that you can bring William back.'

HAMMER OF JUSTICE

The guard in his stained padded jacket passed the parchment back to Richard.

'This looks real,' he said, or at least that's what Richard thought he heard, such was the thickness of his accent.

Richard retrieved the parchment and hid it in the pouch that hung inside his tunic.

'I must confess, I'm surprised that actually worked,' Bowman said.

'The Queen did actually write it,' Richard said, 'there shouldn't be anything to worry about.'

They rode back into the noise and swirl of smells that was La Rochelle. They went alone except for Long Tom, who had thrown in his lot with them when he'd heard Richard had not given him up to Earl Patrick for the bridle blinding incident.

'What is your plan?' He asked.

'I'd only thought about getting through that gate,' Richard rubbed his own blind eye.

'I suppose you did get an eye for an eye in the end,' Bowman started to laugh.

'Shut up,' Richard said.

'That is quite funny,' Long Tom joined the laughter.

'It isn't,' Richard wondered if that was the first time Long Tom had laughed since that night at the archbishop's stables.

'Two to one says you're wrong, young lord,' Bowman grinned, 'I say we find somewhere clean to spend the night, then look for someone to look after that eye properly.'

'Good idea,' Richard said.

'Stop rubbing it,' Bowman said as they rode into the town. Even through one eye, La Rochelle felt brighter than any of the Norman towns Richard had visited, and there were so many people. It was like London, but brighter and with more seagulls.

'The Queen's letter should get us onto a ship, but which destination do we choose?' Bowman asked.

'What's the quickest way back to Yvetot?'

'Harfleur, then ride past Tancarville and Lillebonne,' Bowman answered, 'on the assumption we don't want to go near Fecamp again.'

'We don't,' Richard stared back at a child who looked up into his bandaged eye from the side of the street.

'Then Harfleur it is, we'll just have to avoid the castle.'

'I'm sure we can go around it,' Richard said.

'Probably,' Bowman nodded.

'I don't care about avoiding it so much now, I just need to get home,' Richard said.

'Your home.'

'What does that mean? It's your home too.'

'Is it?' Bowman watched a mother drag two children into a house.

Richard sighed. 'Where do we stay here?'

'How should I know?'

'Can't we look for a guest house?' Long Tom said from behind them.

'Obviously,' Bowman said.

'Those houses look fancy,' Long Tom pointed down a wider street with two storey houses set back from it.

'No harm in trying,' Richard turned Solis down it.

'Can you do the asking?' Richard said to Bowman as they pulled up by one house.

'Why me?'

Richard pointed up to his bandaged eye.

Bowman groaned, looped his reins over a wooden fence post and stomped off towards the front door. Richard dismounted and patted Solis on the neck. The stallion bent his head around to nag for food and Richard's good eye looked over to the other side of the street. A man walked along the street and into it. The man looked very familiar but there wasn't anything particularly remarkable about his appearance.

161

'Tom, was that Simon?'

'Who?'

'Simon the Quiet?' Richard said.

'Surely not, he wouldn't be stupid enough to come here,' Long Tom said.

'I'm sure that was him. Maybe he thinks we're all dead or taken,' Richard said.

'I'll kill him for what he did,' Long Tom drew his knife.

'Put that back,' Richard hissed, 'before anyone sees it.'

'Why, I need to gut him,' Long Tom scowled.

'Then you'll hang, and they might hang me while they're at it. I promise you, we'll settle up with him before we leave La Rochelle.'

Long Tom paused and looked over towards the house. He slid the knife slowly back into its sheath. 'Before we leave?'

'I swear it,' Richard said.

Bowman shouted over from the house. 'There are stables attached, they say we can stay here,' he said.

'What happened to your eye?' The owner of the house asked. He was a stout and generously bellied man with a ring of curly grey hair around his head. He squinted his eyes at Richard.

'Don't be rude, Pierre,' his wife said from the far corner of the chamber.

'The boy is missing an eye,' Pierre said, 'and blood is pouring from the dressing.'

'It's not pouring, it is seeping, and how do you know the eye is missing, foolish man, you can't even see it,' his wife said.

'The eye is still there,' Bowman said, 'but this is Pierre and Garsende, the owners of this property.'

'Thank you for letting us stay,' Richard said.

'Your man promised a lot of coin,' Pierre rubbed his hands together.

'Did he?' Richard looked at Bowman.

'He did,' Garsende said. Pierre's wife was thinner than he was, and a good deal younger. Her long dark hair was tucked into the back of the belt she wore around a dark blue dress.

'That coin is not yours to be free with,' Richard said.

'It isn't yours either, it's from the Queen,' Bowman said.

'The Queen?' Garsende asked enthusiastically.

'Which Queen?' Pierre narrowed his eyes.

'Which Queen? You idiot,' Garsende said, 'there is only one Queen here, the young man means the Duchess of Aquitaine.'

'Eleanor,' Pierre nodded quickly.

'Of course, who else could he be talking about?'

'Are you important? Why did Eleanor give you coins?' Pierre asked with wide eyes.

'Now, don't overbear yourself on these poor men,' Garsende said.

'It's fine,' Richard said, 'we did her a service, so she has given us passage home and money to help us get there.'

'What service did you do?'

'Pierre, be quiet.'

'We were attacked on the road,' Long Tom said, 'someone tried to kill the Queen.'

'Maybe they just wanted to capture her,' Bowman said.

'Simon said they wanted to cut the head off the serpent,' Richard said, 'so I'm pretty sure they wanted to kill her.'

'Simon,' Long Tom said, 'we just saw him go into the house over the road.'

'What?' Bowman said.

'I think so, anyway,' Richard said, 'but he is just over there.'

'Over the road? That's Raymond the Vintner's house. He is a terrible fellow,' Pierre shook his head.

'Shush, husband.'

'Do you know Simon the Quiet?' Richard asked.

'That depends on who you are,' Garsende said.

'The duchess gave them money, dear, we can trust them.'

'You are so simple,' Garsende turned and went back to the hearth where another woman stirred a cooking pot.

Pierre walked to Richard and looked up at him. 'There are many in Raymond's household, it may be that he has a Simon. However, they steal our wine and illegally undercut our prices,' he said.

'If you say so,' Richard said.

'Raymond is from Poitou, they are all outsiders. They don't belong in La Rochelle,' Pierre said.

'We aren't from La Rochelle either,' Long Tom said.

'The duchess favours you, so you are one of us,' Pierre said, 'La Rochelle is ruled by its people, we are free from royal taxes and mint our own coins. We have the duchess and her family to thank for that, you see.'

'We don't much like her husband, though,' Garsende said from the hearth.

'No, he's from the north, and northerners are uncivilized,' Pierre puffed out his already ample chest.

Richard exchanged a look with Bowman. 'Can you help us with Simon?' He asked.

'What can we do?' Pierre asked.

'He planned the ambush,' Richard said.

'Kill him,' Pierre jumped on the spot, 'we can go there and hang him now.'

Long Tom started to draw his knife, 'good, let's do it,' he said.

'Everyone stop,' Richard said loudly.

Pierre paused and Long Tom raised his eyes to the ceiling and backed down.

'He needs to be punished, but we all need to sail away from this town alive,' Richard said.

'That eye also needs some attention before you men get carried away,' Garsende said.

'I think she's right, it doesn't look good to me,' Long Tom said.

'Can we have something to eat and rest for a while,' Richard ordered more than asked.

'There will be food soon,' Garsende said, 'rest with us.'

Richard collapsed down into the tall armchair Pierre pushed over to him. It was painted blue and as comfortable as a knight's chair. Which he supposed was probably why he'd been given it. The chamber was well lit by a number of windows covered with slats of horn, and even had a few tapestries on the wall.

'They live better than you do,' Bowman looked around at the walls.

'I didn't realise that being a merchant could be so...'

'Profitable?' Bowman said.

'Apparently,' Richard could smell the sea coming from the cooking pot and wondered what it held. While it cooked, the other woman removed Richard's dressing and mixed up a paste of something to put over his eye. Whatever it was it stung but Richard didn't let it show. Finally, with his head wrapped up in a new bandage, the meal was served. Bowman poked it suspiciously with a spoon and pulled a face when we ate the slippery seafood. Long Tom ate everything except the seafood, but Richard thought the whole dish tasted quite good.

Bowman drank the soup straight from the bowl. 'I can taste the wine in this,' he said.

'It's one of ours,' Pierre told him.

'Is everyone on this street a vintner?' Richard asked.

'Of course, it is Wine Street.'

'Do you all fight each other over wine?'

'Naturally, don't you knights fight each other over power?' Garsende said.

Richard gazed at her tanned face. He decided that she was probably the brains behind whatever operation was run out of this house.

'We have an idea,' Pierre said.

'About what?'

'Simon the Traitor.'

'Oh, what is it?' Richard said.

'The wine purity laws in La Rochelle are strict, if an accusation is made the magistrate will order a seizure of tainted goods. The magistrate of our quarter is the head of a vintner family too, and he dislikes Raymond as much as we do.'

'Does Raymond have illegal wine?' Richard asked.

'Not yet,' Pierre smiled so much his eyes nearly disappeared.

Richard sat by a window facing the street and peered out through the yellowy horned slats. On the main table a large pouch sat with its drawstring tightly shut.

'We are in the wrong profession,' Bowman sat with his eyes on the pouch.

'Why?' Long Tom asked as he paced up and down the chamber.

'These merchants do not ever have to risk life and limb, and yet they can afford to use this much cinnamon just to spite a rival,' Bowman said.

'I've never even seen cinnamon before,' Richard said.

'A whole pouch,' Bowman raised his voice, 'and I get shot in the hip for nothing more than a bowl of soup with strange slippery sea creatures in it.'

'How is the hip?' Richard asked.

'That's the first time you've asked,' Bowman sank into his chair and folded his arms, 'but it's fine, actually.'

'I'm sorry, I've been a bit busy wondering if I'm going to have one eye for the rest of my life. Would Sophie even want to look at me?'

'Oh, who cares,' Bowman reached over and grabbed a pewter cup, 'you barely even know her.'

'Are you drunk?' Richard asked.

'Of course I am, I've been drinking this all night,' Bowman took another mouthful of wine.

'Tom, it will have to be you who does it,' Richard said, 'he's too drunk, and I'm too recognisable with this bandage.'

Long Tom got to the end of the hall and turned. 'If I meet him in there, you know what I'll do.'

'That's why I'm watching for him to leave,' Richard said.

'How do we know no one will see me?' Long Tom asked.

'We don't, but once you're back here, you can stay hidden until we catch a ship,' Richard said.

'Then we recover at your manor, and then go and get William back from the Lusignans?'

'Yes,' Richard said, 'then we go and get William back.'

'He's going to be furious with you,' Bowman picked up the pouch of cinnamon, 'you left him again.'

'He left me on the stone stairs,' Richard replied.

'Not quite the same thing, is it?' Bowman opened the pouch and sniffed it. His head recoiled. 'God's nose that's sharp.'

'You're not supposed to breath it in,' Richard said.

'This is worth more than your horse,' Bowman closed the drawstring.

'I know, the world has gone mad,' Richard said, 'look, the door is opening.'

Long Tom ran over and looked out of the window next to Richard. Two men walked out of Raymond the Vintner's house. One was Simon the Quiet.

'That's him, that's his fat belly,' Long Tom said.

'Right, here we go, get ready, Tom.'

Long Tom grabbed the pouch from Bowman, who watched it go and sighed.

'Go now,' Richard said, 'they've gone.'

Long Tom opened the door.

'And Tom.'

'Yes?'

'Try not to blind anyone,' Richard said.

Long Tom grinned and shut the door behind him.

Richard peered out through the slats for what felt like an age before Long Tom reappeared from the vintner's house. He slammed the door behind him and sprinted down the street.

'That isn't good,' Richard said.

'What?' Bowman said from the table.

'He's running away.'

A man left the house behind him and ran after Long Tom.

'At least he didn't run straight here,' Richard said.

Pierre entered the chamber. 'I have tipped the magistrate off, he was enraged,' he smiled.

'Good, let us just pray that Long Tom is a faster runner than whoever is chasing him,' Richard said.

'It is no matter,' Pierre said, 'if the wine is bad, the wine is bad.'

All three waited for Long Tom to return, but in the end it was the magistrate and his militia that arrived first.

'They're here,' Richard called Bowman over to watch.

A dozen men armed with cudgels were led by a tall man dressed in a bright green tunic. A red cloak flowed behind him as he strode up to Raymond's door and banged a fist on it.

It opened and the magistrate and his militia flooded in. A while later they dragged out two barrels of wine, and some of the men ran off back the way they'd come.

'They will need a cart to move those,' Pierre nodded.

'That means it worked, doesn't it?' Richard asked.

'It does.'

A while later a cart arrived and the barrels were taken away. The militia waited around until Simon and his companion returned. There was an argument between his companion and the magistrate, but eventually the militia marched Simon off with them and left the street empty once again.

When they'd gone, Long Tom walked causally back down along it and into their house.

'What happened?' Richard asked him once he was inside.

'I poured it in the three barrels like I was told to,' Long Tom said.

'What happened to the man who chased you down the street, did he get a look at your face?'

'Yes, very close, actually.'

'God's legs, we're done for,' Bowman groaned.

'You were supposed to do it quietly,' Richard said.

'It's not my fault, he came in just as I finished, I didn't know he was there.'

'You're not very subtle, are you?'

'It worked though, didn't it?' Long Tom said.

Bowman nodded.

'Not if they come for you next and hang you,' Richard said, 'you shouldn't have let him see your face.'

'I don't think he's going to be telling anyone about my face,' Long Tom walked over to the table and searched for his wine cup amongst the empties on the table.

'What did you do?' Richard sighed, 'if you blinded him you'll need to have taken both of his eyes.'

'I can promise I didn't blind him,' Long Tom drank some wine.

Richard rolled his eyes. 'Did anyone see you kill him, and what did you do with the body?'

'It is all taken care of, Sir Richard, don't you worry about the details,' Long Tom said.

'He never worries about the details,' Bowman burped.

'I think you've had enough,' Richard said.

'You can never have enough of our wine,' Pierre said.

'Stop telling me what to do,' Bowman sat deeply into his chair and yawned.

Richard decided that ignoring him was the best option, and decided that the same probably applied to Long Tom.

They waited for a week in the merchant's house to see what would happen with Simon the Quiet. Richard's eye had paste rubbed into it again and by the end of that time the bandage was taken off permanently.

'That is going to be a nasty scar,' Bowman said, 'it goes right over the eye.'

'I think it makes him look dangerous,' Long Tom said, 'which is useful.'

'It's ruined my face, hasn't it?'

'Completely,' Bowman said.

'I can see through it though,' Richard said, 'everything is blurry but I'm not blind.'

'That is wonderful news,' Pierre said, 'and I have some more for you. There will be a judgement of Simon the Traitor tomorrow. We can go and see what the magistrate does with him.'

The cobbled town square was lined with colourful and bright buildings, and Richard saw masts above the houses down a road to the south-west that led to the port. The cathedral towered above the buildings to the west, but the crowd in the square was focused on the raised platform next to the town hall. The magistrate sat on it in all his finery, a long golden chain hung around his neck and his cloak was lined in fine furs.

Simon the Quiet looked less fine. He was flanked by militia before the magistrate, and looked tired.

Richard edged his way through the crowd with Bowman and Long Tom behind him. Seagulls screeched overhead and the bells at the top of the cathedral started to chime loudly.

The magistrate had to pause his speech until the bells ceased. 'You have heard the accusation. Bring forth the barrels,' he said.

Two barrels were rolled over onto the platform. A guard knocked the top off one and stood back. The magistrate went to stand over the exposed wine. 'All have seen the barrel opened. Three members of the vintners guild will taste the wine, and if the spice is found, Simon the Quiet will be judged to be guilty.'

'It's not even my wine,' Simon said.

'Your cousin has given me his word that if cinnamon is found in the wine, then it was your doing and not his,' the magistrate said.

'Raymond is his cousin?' Long Tom said.

'Seems so,' Richard said, 'and it seems Raymond has thrown him under the cart to protect himself.'

'Good,' Long Tom craned his neck to get a better look.

Three men lined up and scooped out wine from the open barrel. They each tipped the drink into their mouths and swirled it around.

'This wine has truly been spiked,' the first said.

'I agree,' the second nodded.

The third said something Richard didn't understand while he gestured violently at Simon.

'The guild has found cinnamon in the wine. Simon is guilty of breaching the wine purity laws,' the magistrate said to the crowd.

They cheered and booed back.

'Simon the Quiet is sentenced to have two fingers on his left hand removed.'

'Two fingers?' Long Tom cried, 'is that all?'

'We never did ask what the punishment was,' Richard said.

Bowman groaned. 'That was pointless then, wasn't it.'

'I'm not sure what we can do about it,' Richard said.

Long Tom swore and pushed Richard out of his way. He surged through the throng of townspeople until he was at the front of the press.

'He's a traitor,' Long Tom shouted.

The crowed still jeered and a wooden block was carried up onto the platform. Simon the Quiet remained still and quiet.

'Simon is a traitor,' Long Tom shouted again.

The man next to him stopped booing. 'What did you say?'

'He tried to kill the duchess,' Long Tom said, 'he's a traitor.'

'Traitor,' the man shouted.

'We should probably leave,' Bowman tugged on Richard's sleeve.

'He tried to kill the duchess,' Long Tom shouted and more of the crowd took notice.

'We should, but I want to watch,' Richard said.

The magistrate turned to the crowd and listened to them as they took up Long Tom's accusation. 'Silence,' he shouted after a while.

The mob hushed. 'Simon lured the duchess and the Earl of

Salisbury into an ambush, where he was killed,' Long Tom said.

'We heard about that,' cried an on-looker.

'It was him,' another pointed at Simon and they all erupted into jeers and taunts.

'Enough,' the magistrate shouted and stamped his foot on the platform.

'He is working with the Lusignans,' Long Tom said, 'they plotted against us. And they killed the Templar Master of Poitiers.'

The magistrate walked to the back of his platform and spoke to the dignitaries assembled there.

'That's a Templar, isn't it?' Richard looked at the dignitary he spoke to the longest.

'It is, they won't like this,' Bowman said.

The magistrate returned to the edge of the platform. 'People of La Rochelle. A letter had been sent from the Templar Master of Poitiers a fortnight ago warning of treachery. This man's accusation confirms it. We judge that Simon the Quiet plotted to kill our duchess.'

The crowd shouted and called and swore.

'What's happening? Surely it should take longer to decide his guilt than that?' Richard asked.

'I think our Tom is not settling for two fingers,' Bowman said, 'and I think they are looking for someone to blame.'

'Bring forth the wheel,' the magistrate shouted above the clamour, which only served to make the mob even louder.

'The wheel?'

'I've never seen it, young lord, but I think they are going to break him on the wheel,' Bowman said.

Long Tom pushed his way back from the front of the crowd.

'Can you let me know if you're going to do something like that again,' Richard told him.

'It worked though, didn't it?' Long Tom grinned.

Richard wondered if it was such a good idea for Long Tom to go with them back to Yvetot, but there wasn't a lot he could do about it now. He resigned himself to Tom's company.

'This is for Sir Wobble,' Richard mumbled to himself.

'For Earl Patrick,' Long Tom nodded.

Richard nodded back.

A large cart wheel was hauled up onto the platform and laid down. Ropes were used to secure it to the platform and Richard saw Simon drop to his knees. Over the sound of the mob he couldn't hear him, but he liked to think Simon was pleading pathetically for his life.

Simon the Quiet was dragged up onto the wheel and pushed over onto it. Guards tied his hands and feet to the rims so that his limbs crossed the heavy wooden spokes.

A man with a hammer came forwards. It was long handled and its head had as much iron as a tree-felling axe. Richard was as familiar with blood and death as any other man would be, but the sight of the axe grated him.

'This is fair, isn't it?' Richard said to Bowman.

'Sir Wobble is probably still in agonising pain from that spear thrust through his thigh,' he replied.

Richard pursed his lips. 'Traitors should be punished,' he said, but mostly to convince himself.

'Remember what you did to a monk who hadn't even hurt you,' Bowman said.

'Yet, he hadn't hurt me, yet,' Richard said.

The hammer raised up into the air and the crowd fell silent.

'No, please, God save me, I didn't do anything,' Simon wailed.

'The hammer of justice falls on all traitors,' Long Tom said.

The hammer indeed fell. Its iron block arched down between two of the spokes and straight onto Simon's lower leg.

Richard winced as the bone snapped.

The crowd cheered.

Simon screamed the loudest scream Richard had ever heard, and a flock of seagulls perched on the roof of the town hall flew up into the air screeching.

The executioner held the hammer aloft to the crowd who cheered back at him.

'This shouldn't be fun,' Richard said.

'He deserved it,' Bowman said, 'simple as that.'

The next hammer blow fell onto Simon's arm and it snapped just the same as his leg had.

'I don't need to see any more,' Richard turned to leave.

Bowman grabbed his shoulder and the big man held him still. 'This was you, Richard. You did this. You have to see it through. You are a landed knight and one day may have to order an execution. You need to be able to stand and at least watch it,' he said.

Richard turned back as the hammer cracked Simon's other leg but didn't break it.

'He's getting tired,' Long Tom said, 'and it's only been three blows.'

The executioner finished the job on the leg to the joy of the crowd.

'They really do like the Queen, don't they,' Richard said.

'It is the same everywhere,' Bowman said, 'this place is no more entertained by a killing than London or Nottingham.'

The hammer landed on a hand and mushed it into a pulp of bone and skin. Simon howled so much Richard wondered how he was even managing to breathe.

The next few blows destroyed the last of his limbs, and because he was a traitor to their precious duchess, the magistrate didn't allow the executioner to finish with a blow to the head or lungs. Instead, Simon the Quiet died a long and agonising death, during which he was not very quiet at all.

THE RED BABY

The white crenelated tower of Castle Tancarville loomed up over the trees and hedges that lined the sunken lane.

'I preferred the south, it was warmer there,' Bowman said.

'You didn't prefer the food,' Richard said.

'The company wasn't great either,' Bowman looked at the tower, 'but then it was not particularly welcoming here, either.'

'We'll just ride by, we don't need to go inside or let anyone know we're here,' Richard said.

'I've heard about this place,' Long Tom said, 'they say Lord Tancarville murdered another noble a few years ago.'

'We heard that one,' Bowman said, 'it's probably true.'

They rode around the last hedge and the front gate of the castle came into view.

'You have got to be joking,' Bowman said.

The two guards by the gate recognised Bowman at the same time. 'He's back,' Jean the crossbowman pointed.

'I bet he hasn't brought any wine with him,' the other crossbowman said.

'Don't tell them we've just been to Aquitaine,' Bowman whispered to Richard, 'they'll be beyond jealous.'

'No wine, I'm afraid,' Bowman shouted back and rode over.

'We were talking about you the other day, weren't we, Jean?' The bearded crossbowman said.

'We were,' Jean said, 'we wondered what happened to you.'

'Nothing much,' Bowman said.

'Something's happened to his eye though, look, Rob,' Jean nodded at Richard.

'That looks nasty, Jean, I wonder if he slipped when eating his soup,' Rob laughed.

'Are you two ever sober?' Richard asked.

The two crossbowmen looked at each other and burst into laughter.

'What's been happening here, then?' Bowman asked.

'Same as usual,' Rob said, 'the lord is terrifying and his son is a brat.'

'Although,' Jean said, 'they've just ridden out with all their retinue. Even took the young aspirants.'

'Where to? Have they gone to war?' Richard asked. His mind went straight to Yvetot and he prayed that Tancarville hadn't gone there.

'I don't know, no one told us,' Jean said.

'Maybe it was a tournament,' Rob said, 'I'm sure someone said it was a tournament.'

'You mean Lord Tancarville and the Little Lord aren't here?' Bowman asked.

'No, there's barely anyone here at all,' Jean said, 'you may as well go in for something to eat. Maybe you would bring us something on your way out?'

'You don't want cider or wine, by any chance?' Bowman asked.

Richard walked his horse on towards the castle. He felt a certain urge of nostalgia pull him inside, and the guards stepped out of his way.

'Golden spurs?' Jean said as Richard went by.

'He's gone up in the world, then,' Rob said.

'Tell me about it, Bowman replied as he and Long Tom followed.

Castle Tancarville was much the same as it had been the previous year. The grass in its triangular courtyard was still marked and flattened by hoof prints, and the keep and Tancarville's chambers to their right still stood proudly on their raised mound.

'It's quiet,' Bowman said.

'I don't like it,' Richard said, 'it makes it even more threatening here.' He noticed that there were now a few paddocks down at the far corner of the yard, with horses that he thought looked Italian grazing in them. They rode past the chapel, which made Richard shudder.

175

The door opened and the priest looked up at Richard. 'You? What are you doing here?' He asked.

'I'll go and find food,' Bowman said.

'I'll go with you,' Long Tom said quickly.

'Don't steal anything,' Richard said, 'or hurt anyone. Only do what Bowman tells you.'

Richard didn't miss Long Tom roll his eyes, or that the priest waited for an answer.

'We're just passing through,' Richard said, 'we mean no trouble.'

'No trouble?' the priest said, 'last time you were here you caused me nothing but trouble. Everyone still thinks you are either a devil or an angel, and I am fed up of hearing about it.'

'I'm sick of it too,' Richard said.

'I have heard what you've been doing, I hear all in Normandy,' the priest said.

Richard laughed. 'You are all seeing now, are you?'

'The Lord speaks to his chosen people.'

'Don't lie to me. You are not chosen by anyone, your nephew just happens to be the priest in my village,' Richard said.

The priest stood still and went red.

'You aren't as clever as you think you are,' Richard said, 'you're just a horrible little man.'

'You cannot speak to me like that,' the priest's eyes flared, 'and I know of events at your dung heap of a village that you do not, so do not mock me.'

'What happened?' Richard asked, 'is that where Lord Tancarville has gone?'

'Oh look, you aren't so sure of yourself now, are you?' The priest straightened himself up.

'Just tell me whatever story you have, and then I can be rid of you,' Richard said.

'If you insist on disrespecting me, boy, I will not reveal anything.'

Richard sighed. He really wanted to push the priest back into the chapel and slam the door in his face, but Yvetot was more important. 'Fine, what is it?'

'That's better,' the priest said, 'your so-called wife has given birth.'

'Did she survive?'

'Surprisingly, considering what flew out of her womb, she did,' the priest replied.

Richard felt a weight fall from him. His grandmother had died giving birth to uncle Luke, and he knew that at Keynes, women were buried a lot younger than men tended to be.

'What do you mean, flew out of her?' He asked.

'A wild storm raged across Normandy, even here the thatch half blew off the stables. Some of the horses went mad with terror from the winds and driving rain. At Yvetot the tracks turned to rivers and the sky turned dark red. Blood red.'

'Did it,' Richard said flatly.

'My nephew never lies.'

'I think he does,' Richard said, 'but continue.'

The priest raised his eyebrows but threw his arms up into the air. 'Lightning burst forth from the red sky and thunder split the heavens in two. The lightning, clearly the Lord's wrath, struck the village down. It crumbled under flame and now stands only as piles of sinful ash.'

Richard blinked and tried to decide how much to believe.

'A dragon with blue wings and a yellow head circled the moon, and cried down to the village,' the priest said.

Richard sighed and decided he didn't need to believe very much of the tale. 'Does the baby live?' He asked.

The priest nodded. 'The last I heard it did.'

'What did it look like, what colour hair did it have?'

'How should I know?' The priest asked.

'I thought you knew everything that happened in Normandy?' Richard put his right hand on his hip.

'Do not scorn me, boy,' the priest said, 'the Red Baby lives but your village does not.'

'The Red Baby? Did it have red hair?' Richard asked.

'I told you, I don't know. Why would it have red hair?' The priest narrowed his eyes at Richard.

'Why are you calling it the Red Baby, then?'

'Because of the sky, you foolish boy,' the priest said.

Richard let out a breath. Maybe the baby wouldn't obviously be the Little Lord's, and the whole issue would blow over.

'As soon as I told Lord Tancarville, he flew into a rage,' the priest continued, 'he left this very morning to find the king or the archbishop at Rouen. He shouted that he would have Sir Roger evicted from all land and cast him out of his service.'

'What did Sir Roger do?' Richard asked.

'Ask Lord Tancarville,' the priest said, 'I assume he rightly blames Sir Roger for installing you at Yvetot. Lord Tancarville was also very angry at his son, but not as angry as he was at you.'

'Me?' Richard's optimism faded away.

'He wants to burn you as a heretic who has brought the Devil himself to his lands.'

'Yvetot isn't his lands,' Richard said.

'It is, through Sir Roger it goes back to Lord Tancarville,' the priest said, 'and he wants to see you burn.'

'Maybe the fire won't touch me,' Richard suppressed an urge to ride his horse over the priest.

'Perhaps,' the priest's eyes moved to Richard's now healed hands, 'but how sure are you of that?'

Richard wasn't too sure of that, but didn't feel the need to answer the priest. His eye was still blurry and his stomach now rumbled.

Bowman and Long Tom led their horses over from the kitchen building.

'No meat was on, can you imagine that?' Bowman said.

'I think we need to go,' Richard told him.

'Obviously,' Bowman slung a small cloth bag over to Long Tom, 'we did at least get a little bread.'

'Good,' Richard said, 'we need to get home as quickly as we can.'

'We can't make it tonight,' Bowman said.

'Then we'll ride through the night.'

'Through the night?' The priest said, 'yes, ride through the night like a servant of darkness.'

'What is wrong with him?' Long Tom asked as he remounted his horse.

'Quite a lot,' Richard said, 'but Sophie has given birth so we must hurry.'

'Oh, has she?' Bowman asked.

'Yes, and this priest has a wild story about Yvetot burning

down, so we need to go and find out how much of it was real,' Richard said.

'I am a man of God,' the priest said, 'I only speak the truth.'

Bowman laughed.

Richard turned Solis around and started to walk back out of the castle.

'You'll burn,' the priest said after him, 'you'll never be back here again.'

'You should pray for that,' Richard shouted back, 'for if I do, you might just fly from a tower.'

Bowman trotted up to Richard. 'Was that a sensible thing to say?' He asked.

'Probably not,' Richard muttered, 'but I really don't like him.'

The guards protested that Bowman hadn't brought them any food, but Richard ignored them. They pressed on east towards Lillebonne and Yvetot, Richard's mind running through possibilities of how ruined his village might be. They rode through the lanes of Normandy, retracing their steps from a year earlier when they'd gone to war. At Lillebonne, Richard rode by the gap in houses where the disfigured war veterans had been, but there was nothing there but beaten earth. It was dark as they crossed the river at Lillebonne, and it grew cold as they pressed on towards Yvetot in the dead of night.

The sun crested the horizon and a yawning Richard squinted to look for the entrance to Yvetot.

'Do you have a good fire for me to sleep by?' Long Tom asked.

'As long as the priest was full of lies,' Richard replied.

'Then yes,' Bowman yawned, 'I just want to be out of the saddle.'

'We're here now,' Richard had spotted the left turn ahead that led to his village. The sky rippled reds and yellows as scattered small clouds drifted above him. The hues gave a certain glow to the dawn.

'I smell ash,' Bowman said.

Richard swallowed hard and looked up for the moon but couldn't see it, or any dragons. He made the sign of the cross as they reached the turning.

'Look,' Bowman pointed to the side of the road where burnt

179

logs and piles of ash still smoked.

'Sarjeant managed to get the Flying Monk built, then,' Richard said to himself. He'd doubted the project would get off the ground, although it seemed that it was back on it now. Tendrils of smoke drifted skywards.

'The whole village can't be gone,' Richard said in hope.

'We better find out,' Bowman turned his horse towards Yvetot.

'What was that?' Long Tom looked down at the smouldering wreckage.

'That was my inn,' Richard said, 'but if the village survives, we'll rebuild it.'

Solis sniffed the air and snorted at the smoke, but Richard pushed him past it and on through the orchards where green leaves had started to grow.

The village emerged from through the trees and then the church.

'They aren't burnt down,' Richard said.

'Being burnt down might improve it,' Bowman grinned.

'That's not funny,' Richard said.

'It isn't very big,' Long Tom looked around, 'and the church doorway has fallen down.'

'Only part of it. The Priest refuses to move the stone,' Richard said.

The Priest himself emerged from the half-blocked doorway and peered out at the new arrivals.

His eyes widened as he recognised his lord. 'You should go,' the Priest shouted over to them.

'Go? This is my village,' Richard shouted back.

The Priest scuttled over. 'The villagers are very good people, you must understand, and their intentions are always honest,' he said.

Richard looked down at the tall, thin man. 'What have you done this time?'

'Nothing at all,' the Priest said, 'all you need to do is come back later. Or even better, go back to England.'

'You are mad,' Richard said, 'I've just been to see your uncle, too. You're both quite mad.'

'Of course, just please leave,' the Priest put his hands together in prayer and held them up to Richard.

'What is wrong with him?' Long Tom asked.

'I don't really know,' Richard said, 'but where are the villagers? They should be in the fields at this time of year.'

'I told you, they are honest folk,' the Priest's eyes darted from Richard and back towards the castle.

'If they are trying to push the palisade down again,' Richard said.

'Please don't go,' the Priest dropped to his knees.

Richard frowned. 'I will deal with you later,' he said and pushed Solis straight into a canter. The tired horse flew down the track and clumps of mud flew up from his hooves. Richard arrived at the castle and was greeted by the sight of the villagers fanning the flames of two fires burning at the foot of the wooden palisade.

'God help me, not again,' Richard slammed Solis to a halt.

'That's what happens when you're nice to them,' Bowman said as he caught up.

'I wasn't even that nice,' Richard said.

Over the wooden palisade Sarjeant's head appeared, followed by a wooden bucket. His blue eyes flashed anger as he tipped the bucket down onto one of the fires. It half worked.

'Lady Sophie is up there,' Bowman pointed up to the tower where Richard could see his wife shout down to de Cailly's squires who were arrayed along the inner stone wall.

'At least we aren't too late,' Long Tom took in the scene, 'but is this normal around here?'

'No,' Richard said.

'Yes,' Bowman shrugged.

'I'm going to kill them,' Richard said as Sarjeant emptied another bucket onto the fire.

'Maybe don't quite kill all of them,' Bowman said.

'Where's the Reeve? I'll start with the damned Reeve,' Richard searched the villagers crowded around the walls for his plumb body.

Richard drew the new sword the Queen had given him and spurred Solis on. 'Reeve,' he shouted.

The Reeve stood literally fanning the flames of the other fire with the bottom of his tunic. The villagers around him heard

Solis approach in a thunder of hooves, and scattered.

The Reeve spun around and looked up at his lord with disbelieving eyes. 'You're dead,' he yelled.

'Do I look dead?' Richard swung his sword above the Reeve as Solis cantered past.

The Reeve fell to the floor and stayed there with his hands over his eyes.

Richard wheeled around and came to a stop just before his horse trampled the Reeve into a pulp. 'I saw what you were doing, tell me why I shouldn't cut your lying head off?'

The Reeve turned his eyeballs just enough to look up at Richard. 'Please don't kill me, we thought you were dead,' he cried.

'Why should my death mean you burn my castle down?' Richard asked.

The Reeve started to cry. 'The storm, my lord, the storm.'

'Get up,' Richard said and turned to the other villagers, 'and put that fire out.'

As they ran to obey, Sarjeant pushed the main gate open and sallied out with a group of the squires.

'I do not wish violence on others often, my boy,' Sarjeant said to Richard when he reached him, 'but this one and the Priest should have their noses cut off.'

Sarjeant's wrinkles were much deeper than when Richard had left him. 'What in God's name has happened here?' Richard asked.

'There was a storm,' Sarjeant said.

'See, I told you there was a storm,' the Reeve said from the ground.

'Shut up,' Richard said, 'I wasn't asking you.'

'Your wife gave birth and the sky turned red,' Sarjeant said.

'Did any dragons circle the moon?' Richard asked dryly.

'Dragons? That's absurd,' Sarjeant said.

'I'd heard about the storm,' Richard said, 'but why were they trying to attack the castle? Again.'

'They already think you come from Hell, and the red sky and storm made them take action. That and the Priest telling them to,' Sarjeant said.

'I'll kill him,' Richard said.

'You can't really kill a priest,' Sarjeant said, 'for then they will have a real reason to hate you.'

The squires rounded up the villagers who were pushed towards Richard with bowed heads.

'See, they're sorry,' the Reeve looked up and Richard felt him look at the scar across his eye.

'You see that?' Richard pointed his sword blade at the scar.

The Reeve nodded frantically.

'That was from a sword, and do you know what happened to the man who wielded it?'

The Reeve shook his head.

'I killed him,' Richard turned to the villagers, 'and I will have blood for this. You should be in the fields, go back to work.'

As they shuffled off, the Reeve got up to his knees. 'Please spare me,' he said.

'I think I'll take your nose,' Richard said.

'No, please no,' the Reeve clasped his hands together, 'I'll do anything, please spare my nose.'

'Or maybe some fingers,' Richard said.

'I think his head,' Sarjeant growled and the Reeve jumped up and backed away from him.

'Perhaps,' Richard said, 'but I need to see my wife. Begone, but I will take something from you for this.'

The Reeve ran back to the village as quickly as he could.

'He can't be trusted,' Sarjeant said.

'I know,' Richard said, 'and I'm sorry for what happened here.'

'They burnt the Flying Monk, Richard,' Sarjeant said, 'it wasn't the lightning. They set it alight to ward evil spirits from turning off the main road and into Yvetot.'

'That is as stupid as it is blasphemous,' Richard said.

'They also want to kill the child before it draws the evil spirits into their homes,' Sarjeant said, 'the Priest has been speaking to them.'

Richard turned to one of the squires. 'I need you to ride to Sir Roger and tell him he needs to come here. Tell him Lord Tancarville thinks Yvetot is his and has marched to Rouen to claim it,' he said.

'Of course, I'll leave at once,' the squire nodded and headed off to the paddocks outside the castle.

'Now I need to see Lady Sophie,' Richard said.

Sarjeant looked at him. 'She has not taken the birth well, and this attack has left her wild. She is like a crazed mother boar, but she has also refused to see the baby since it was born.'

'Thanks for the warning,' Richard swung himself out of his saddle. He patted Solis on the nose and handed him to a squire. Richard walked into the lower bailey and saw Sophie standing in the open gateway of the stone wall. She wore a faded blue dress and had her hands on her hips.

'Where have you been?' She shouted as he neared.

'Did you get my letter?' He asked.

'Yes, but you promised you would be back before Christmas, and Christmas is now a distant memory,' she said.

'I couldn't help it,' Richard said, 'and Sir Wobble has been taken prisoner.'

'What?' Sophie blinked at him, 'William?'

'Yes, William. In fact, if he hadn't been captured, we'd probably still be in Aquitaine.'

'Aquitaine? I thought you were going to Northern France?' Sophie said.

'It changed,' Richard said, 'can we go inside? Everyone can hear us.'

Sophie turned to go, and her dress whirled around with her as she went up into the keep. Richard ignored the squire by the gate who pretended not to have heard anything, and followed his wife inside.

'How was the birth?' Richard asked.

'How do you think?' Sophie replied, 'a baby came out of me. It was hideous. And it is his. His.'

'I had hoped the red name was because of the red sky,' Richard said.

'It isn't, it has red hair,' she collapsed into her chair and put her head into her hands, 'and it is a boy.'

'But are you well?' Richard knelt down before her.

She looked up into his eyes and Richard thought she looked lost. 'No, I am not well. My body feels as if it has been wrenched in two, and then the villagers do the only thing they are good at, and come here again with flaming torches.'

'At least I came back in time,' Richard said.

'Do not look for a compliment or for thanks,' Sophie said, 'had you stayed at home as you should have done, they wouldn't have done anything to begin with. The inn would still be standing.'

'I am sorry for what happened,' Richard said.

'Did you at least save your sister?' Sophie asked, 'was all of this worth it?'

Richard swallowed. 'She did not need rescuing,' he said.

'So you could have stayed here.'

'I didn't know,' Richard stood up, 'this is not all my fault.'

'Then whose is it? I am going to blame someone for this,' Sophie said, 'and at the moment it is all on you.'

'What do you want me to do about it?' Richard threw his hands up.

'Go upstairs and kill the baby. Burn it in the fire,' she said.

'You can't kill your own child,' Richard said.

'That's why you need to do it, you're not its father so it is fine,' Sophie said.

'That doesn't make it fine,' Richard said, 'I will not kill an innocent baby.'

'Either you are to blame for everything, or it is,' Sophie said, 'so you can either kill it or you can leave.'

'You can't evict me, I'm the lord here,' Richard said.

'I can make you want to leave,' Sophie dug her finger nails into the armrests of the chair.

Richard didn't doubt that for a moment. 'I will go and bring you some cider, but I will see the baby for myself first. What are you calling it?'

'It has no name,' Sophie said, 'and I will never give it one.'

Richard sighed and went upstairs into their chamber. He pushed the door open to find the servant with a mole on his face holding a small baby in his arms. The servant held a piece of bread to the baby who ignored it.

'Have you ever tended to a baby?' Richard asked.

'No, my lord,' the servant said.

'He can only have milk for a while, although I'm not sure how long,' Richard said.

'Oh, I didn't know,' the servant ate the bread himself.

'How is the baby?' Richard asked.

'Why are you asking me? I'm apparently trying to feed it food it can't have,' the servant said.

'I think we need to find it a nursemaid,' Richard said.

'Our lady can't go near it, I fear what she will do to it if he leaves my sight,' the servant said.

'She just asked me to kill him.'

The servant pulled the tightly wrapped baby back.

'I'm not going to,' Richard said, 'what do you think I am?'

'With that scar across your face and all the stories,' the servant said, 'I think you are a dangerous man to be around. The baby has harmed no one and deserves his chance at life.'

'We can agree on that,' Richard said, 'if he reaches his fourth summer we can worry about him then, God will likely take him from us before then anyway.'

'It is our Christian duty to look after him,' the servant said.

'I'm trying to agree with you,' Richard said.

'I will find a woman in the village to be his nurse,' the servant said, 'and he can sleep in the basement so our lady can have this chamber back.'

'Very well, look after him, and if he survives we can name him.'

The servant nodded and looked down at the sleeping baby. 'I'm surprised he's lived this long,' he said.

'I'm sure his life will be difficult and bloody,' Richard said, 'so we will call him the Red Baby until he reaches a safer age.'

'You may be right,' the servant said, 'I will remove him from here and maybe that will be enough for Lady Sophie to recover herself.'

'Thank you,' Richard said as the servant took his ward out of the chamber. Richard sat down on the bed and let himself fall backwards onto its straw filled mattress. He tried to relax his body and felt tension in his back and neck. He looked up at the wooden beams on the ceiling and tried to breathe deeply. A wave of drowsiness fell over him and he thought it would be nice just to sleep for a while.

The chamber door flew open just as he drifted away.

Sophie strode in. 'Why is my servant carrying the baby, alive, down into the cellar?'

'I'm not murdering a baby,' Richard kept his eyes on the

ceiling.

'Why not? How many men have you killed?'

'I don't know,' Richard said, 'not that many.'

'What about women and children?'

Richard sat up. 'None, never, who do you think I am?'

'I don't know,' Sophie shouted so hard that the horn slats on the windows rattled.

'We will find a solution, maybe the Little Lord and his father can be convinced to leave us alone. What is Yvetot worth to them anyway?'

'You are no better than them, you men who love fighting more than life. All any of you can do is kill and destroy, what is the point of you?'

'We can protect too, and that is what I am doing,' Richard said.

'How? How are you protecting me by disappearing over the sea for the whole winter? I managed perfectly well without you, and if it wasn't for that thing that came out of me, I would be managing still.'

'It is done now,' Richard said, 'we can move on from this. I have sent word to Sir Roger that Lord Tancarville is coming here, and he will protect us.'

'Tancarville is coming here?' Sophie stilled.

Richard sighed. His instinct was to lie to calm her down, but he thought she probably deserved the truth instead. 'Yes, and his son. They have heard about the Red Baby.'

'No, you can't name it,' Sophie said, 'if you name it, we can't kill it.'

'I have named it, so can we stop talking about murdering babies now?'

Sophie collapsed onto the bed and Richard caught her in his arms. She started to cry so he held her. Richard said nothing as the tears flowed and flowed. She wrapped her arms around him and gripped so tightly he couldn't fully breathe, but he decided he'd wait it out.

When she finally looked up, her face had puffed up and her eyes were red. 'Why did you leave me, Richard? You promised, you promised to stay.'

'I'm sorry, I thought it was safe to go, but maybe I was too

187

hasty,' he said.

'I understand why you had to leave, but you could have gone in the spring,' Sophie said.

'I was impatient,' Richard said, 'I would do it differently now. But you survived the baby, and now we can work for our own future.'

'With the Tancarvilles marching towards us we have no future,' she said.

'I don't fear them,' Richard said, 'God is on our side, and so is Sir Roger.'

'You cannot be sure Sir Roger can, or will, help us,' Sophie said, 'not now that thing came out with red hair.'

'He is a man of honour.'

'Honour is no good when he has only a few knights,' Sophie said, 'this castle can barely keep out its own peasants.'

'I'm back now, we will gather supplies in the cellar and hold the stone walls with the squires. We just need to stand firm for a few weeks and Lord Tancarville will get bored. He is only doing this because of his son, I think it's expected of him. He doesn't care about Yvetot at all.'

'Don't promise what you can't deliver,' Sophie said, 'and do not lie to me.'

'I'm not lying to you. Lord Tancarville might find the king at Rouen and he might be told to leave us alone. Let us hope for that,' Richard said.

'I'm not hoping for that,' Sophie said, 'kill the baby and we remove his reason.'

'I've made it very clear that I'm not killing him.'

'It's not a him,' Sophie said.

'You don't have to like him, or even see him for a year for all I care,' Richard said, 'just don't murder him.'

'You should hate it, its birth will be the death of you.'

'There is a queue of things waiting to be the death of me,' Richard sighed, 'I'm not going to worry about a Red Baby.'

'You should.'

'I need to worry about Yvetot first.'

'Did Sarjeant tell you about what he's been doing?'

'No,' Richard replied.

'He's spent the last few months arguing with Templars

188

about boundaries. He beat one of them around the head with a shepherd's crook last month. They came here for compensation and I had to give them a barrel of cider to make them go away,' she said.

'I'll speak to him about it,' Richard said.

Sophie let go of Richard, spread out across the bed and closed her eyes.

'Have you ever had cinnamon before?' Richard asked.

Sophie looked up at him. 'No.'

Richard pulled an underarm pouch out and dropped it onto her stomach. 'This is from a merchant in La Rochelle.'

She sat up and pulled the pouch open. 'Is this really?'

'It is, and it's yours,' Richard said.

'I'm not saying thank you,' Sophie said.

'You don't have to.'

THE RED BANNER

The next morning Richard went to see the Priest. He'd waited until the morning in order to cool off, but as he approached the church he felt his heart thump in his chest. The Priest had nearly cost him everything, and he couldn't be allowed to continue. Richard stepped around the fallen masonry and banged on the church door.

There was no answer. 'If you don't open the door, I'll set a fire alight under it and burn my way in. Which I think is only fair considering what your parishioners tried to do yesterday.'

'There is no need for that,' he heard from behind the door.

A bolt clunked and the door opened. 'Come in, my lord,' the Priest said.

Richard entered and his eyes adjusted to the darkness. 'Why did you try to turn me around when I arrived yesterday?' He asked.

'I did no such thing,' the Priest said.

'No such thing?' Richard folded his arms, 'you ran outside and told me to go away.'

'I would never do that,' the Priest turned away and walked over to his altar.

'You want to pretend nothing happened?' Richard said, 'well I can't. Some lords would have your head for that disrespect.'

'My lord, you are young and I didn't want you to see anything offensive.'

'I'm not a child, Priest, this is my village. I'm a knight with golden spurs and I have seen men die. You do not need to shield me from the world.'

'Very well, I apologise for my considerations,' the Priest

bowed to Richard.

'Do you? You're just trying to slope your shoulders and have my accusation roll off them,' Richard said.

'I am an honest man,' the Priest tilted his head up.

'You're not honest, the Reeve told me that you incited the villagers to burn the inn and storm my castle. Is he lying?'

The Priest frowned. 'The Reeve is a good honest man, he would never lie. He cannot have said such a thing.'

'He did, so I'm cutting his fingers off. Or maybe yours. One of you is responsible for the scorch marks on my palisade, so one of you will pay the price for them. Is that not fair?'

The Priest stroked his chin. 'Of course that is fair, but perhaps no one man is responsible for what happened.'

'Then I'll take fingers from both of you,' Richard put his hand on his sword.

The Priest gulped. 'If you insist on placing blame, which is very unchristian, then of course the Reeve is the head of the village and your representative here. His loyalty should be directly to you, so his involvement would, strictly speaking, place the blame on his head.'

Richard shook his head. 'You have the backbone of a blade of grass. Christ was willing to die on a cross for you, and you're not willing to lose a finger for the treason you clearly committed.'

'There has never been any treason in my village,' the Priest said.

'You mean my village.'

'Of course, your village.'

Richard's grip on his sword constricted. 'And why did you feel the need to send word of the Red Baby straight to your uncle at Castle Tancarville?'

'I would never collude in idle gossip,' the Priest straightened his back up.

'We rode here from the castle,' Richard said, 'I spoke to your uncle.'

The Priest's face dropped.

'Just another lie, then,' Richard sighed.

'It was just sharing news with him, perfectly harmless.'

'You just said you told him nothing,' Richard said.

'No idle gossip was shared, just common news,' the Priest said.

'I should cut your tongue out,' Richard twisted his hand on his sword hilt and almost drew it, 'to finally end the lies that gush forth from your mouth.'

'There is no need for that, there are no lies in Yvetot.'

Richard shut his eyes and exhaled. 'I think I know why Sir Arthur stopped bothering to come into the village,' he said.

'Sir Arthur was a great man.'

'Stop it,' Richard said, 'just stop talking. I'm going to decide who to cut some fingers from, or maybe an ear, and then I'll be back.'

'Please, not my ears,' the Priest said, 'I need them to hear God's words.'

'I have had enough of you. Lawful punishments will be applied, and if there is one more rebellion, even if you have nothing to do with it, it will be the end of you.'

'You do not have the right to try a member of the clergy, let alone kill one,' the Priest said.

'I won't have to kill you,' Richard grinned, 'I'll just bury you alive in the graveyard and let the earth do the killing. I'll break no rules.'

'That is barbarous,' the Priest cried.

'Then think very carefully about it,' Richard said.

'When you were last here you wished to be a kind ruler, what happened to you?' The Priest asked.

'You did,' Richard walked up to the Priest and poked him in the chest, 'you made the villagers rebel again, you filled their heads with poison. You burnt my inn, and you have taught me that I can't rule these people as a good Christian.'

The Priest shrank backwards until his back was against the cold wall of the church.

'Remember the teachings of Christ,' he said, 'forgiveness is the path to righteousness.'

'Fear not, I will forgive you, even as I swing an axe down on your fingers,' Richard raised his voice and it echoed around the walls.

The Priest winced.

'I'm going to have to be like every other knight now, and that is on you. You ruined it, and this is your last chance to stay here. That is me displaying Christian values. One more false move and you're gone, clergy or not.'

The Priest sank down the wall and put his head in his hands.

Richard looked down at the piteous figure. 'For the next mass, I'm going to be standing at the back of this church, and I'll be listening as you tell the villagers how wrong you have been. And you better make it convincing.'

'Of course,' the Priest started to sob.

'Why did you make them burn the Flying Monk?' Richard asked.

The Priest sniffed. 'I didn't.'

'Don't lie, I'm very fed up of it,' Richard said.

'I was scared,' the Priest burst into a flood of tears.

Richard sighed. 'Scared of what?'

'The sky, it was red and the thunder was loud. It crashed over us and we thought the end times had finally come. The inn was a place of sin.'

'So you tried to redeem the village at the time of the rapture?'

'Yes,' the Priest wailed.

Richard turned away and looked up at the wooden beams under the roof. 'I don't know if I'm more disgusted with you, or embarrassed for you,' he said.

The Priest hid himself under his hands.

The church door creaked open and Sarjeant stuck his head around the door. 'Lady Sophie said I'd find you here,' he said.

'I think I'm done, anyway,' Richard said and left the Priest alone in his corner.

It was brighter outside but the wind had started to pick up.

'You need to get a new priest,' Sarjeant said, 'this one will be the death of you.'

'Everyone will be the death of me,' Richard mumbled.

'I thought we could go for a walk,' Sarjeant made his way towards the orchard.

Richard followed. 'I heard you have had some run-ins with our Templar neighbours,' he said.

Sarjeant kicked at a tall weed. 'They are overbearing and jealous. They moved their fences closer to the mill again,' he said.

'And what did you do about it?'

'I knocked them out,' Sarjeant said.

'I hope you mean the posts and not the Templars,' Richard laughed.

Sarjeant kept walking ahead of Richard.

'Did you move the posts back?'

'I did. I put them back to where they should be,' he replied.

Richard pushed aside some branches and they made their way onto the village road.

'What happened then?' Richard asked.

'They moved the posts back.'

'And what did you do then?'

'I caught them doing it that time,' Sarjeant said, 'so I convinced them to stop.'

Richard groaned. 'Just tell me if I need to worry about them.'

'That depends if they move their fence again.'

'I'll have to go and speak to them,' Richard said, 'I hope you didn't hurt any of them too badly.'

'Nothing they won't recover from. Or didn't deserve.'

'We don't need to be fighting with the Templars, we've got enough problems already,' Richard said.

'The inn was doing well before the storm,' Sarjeant said.

'I think you're trying to change the subject.'

'The inn is a better subject, or at least it was until those fools torched it.'

'How much of the cider have you been drinking?' Richard asked.

Sarjeant stopped and turned to Richard. 'The right amount, I have not slipped,' he said.

Richard nodded. 'Good, thank you.'

'The inn was a success,' Sarjeant said, 'travellers frequented it, and all said it was in the perfect place. If we rebuild it, they shall return. A year of profits and we will be able to afford to restock your fish-pond. We need to get a falcon or some hunting dogs, too.'

'Coins don't fall out of my ears,' Richard laughed.

'More is the pity,' Sarjeant continued to walk towards the charred remains of the inn. When he got there, he shook his head at the heap of blackened wood and grey ash.

'We will rebuild it,' Richard nodded, 'and maybe change its name for better luck.'

'Luck was not the cause of this,' Sarjeant said, 'it was the Priest.'

'I know,' Richard said.

'You should petition the Archbishop of Rouen to replace him.'

'I think Lord Tancarville is going to get there first, that's where he's taken his army,' Richard said.

Sarjeant walked over to the main road. 'That is not good news,' he said.

'No, but I sent word to Sir Roger, so hopefully his arrival will be enough to defuse things,' Richard said.

Sarjeant stamped a slow burning ember out with the heel of his leather shoe.

'How has Lady Sophie been?' Richard asked.

Sarjeant looked up. 'Each day you were away she grew angrier. Since Christmas I have tried to avoid her where I can. They say a pregnant woman can be taken with madness, so I hoped her normal self might return after the baby came.'

'I don't think that's happened yet,' Richard said.

'Not yet,' Sarjeant said, 'but time heals all things.'

'Not everything,' Richard scratched his scar. It itched constantly, but the blurred shapes he saw through the eye had hardened slightly over the past few days.

'Does she hate me?' He asked.

Sarjeant laughed. 'Don't ask me, I'm a drunk who was kicked out of the Templars. What do I know of women?'

Richard smiled. 'About as much as me, I think.'

'Lady Sophie doesn't hate you, she is just scared of being left alone,' Sarjeant said.

'Yes, she's made that fairly clear,' Richard said, 'I know I need to be here long enough that the village doesn't erupt when I leave again.'

'If you have any choice when that is,' Sarjeant added.

Richard frowned. 'There is that,' he said.

'I think you won't be leaving anytime soon, though,' Sarjeant looked down the road to the east.

'Why is that?' Richard followed his gaze.

'Because there is a red banner marching along the road,'

Sarjeant said.

Richard's guts turned to ice. 'Already?'

'Look,' Sarjeant pointed.

Richard did, and saw a body of riders coming towards them from the east. At their head he could see the red banner.

'I can't make out their faces,' Richard said.

'I don't know who else's red banner it will be,' Sarjeant said.

'We need to get everyone inside the palisade,' Richard said, 'now.'

Sarjeant turned away from the road but Richard was already running back along the track into Yvetot.

'You tell the Priest,' Richard shouted as the church came back into view, 'I'll muster the squires.'

Sarjeant ran to the church and Richard kept going back to the castle. When he reached the open gate he had to stop. He lent on the gate for a moment as two of the squires took water to some horses.

'Lord Tancarville is here, get everyone and the horses into the palisade,' he said.

The squires rushed off and shouts rang out from around the castle. Richard saw the first of the villagers running over from their houses.

Sophie's head appeared from their chamber window. 'What is it?' she asked.

'Tancarville,' Richard said.

Richard once again stood on the stone walls of the castle as an attacker arrayed itself beyond them. In the distance palls of smoke rose up from the village, and Richard wondered if the church had been torched along with everything else. Frankly though, he thought that the destruction of their homes was God's judgement on his villagers disloyalty.

Bowman sighed beside him. He wore his mail shirt and his helm sat on the stone wall.

'I suppose the good thing is that even if the villagers hadn't burnt down the Flying Monk, Lord Tancarville would have just done it anyway,' he said.

'That doesn't make me feel much better,' Richard said, 'and I'm a bit more worried about us in this castle than the inn right now.'

'He looks smug,' Bowman turned his eyes towards the Little Lord. The younger Tancarville sat atop his horse in his armour and looked back up at them. His red hair could be seen under his helmet.

'I really, really, do not like him,' Richard said.

'No one likes him,' Bowman said.

The Little Lord's red Tancarville shield hung on his left side, but to his right stood his father. Lord Tancarville was distinguishable from his son by his barrel-like chest and the sword he waved around in the air. His men moved to where he pointed, some started to inspect the wooden palisade.

'They'll breach it before the end of the day,' Richard said.

'We've got these stone walls,' Bowman said, 'and they don't deserve saving.'

Richard looked at the villagers cowering in the lower bailey. 'I can't let them in here, there isn't room,' he said.

'Kick them out of the gate, that's my advice,' Bowman said.

'I will leave their fate to God's will,' Richard said, 'he can judge them for me.'

Bowman shrugged. 'I've no love for them,' he said.

'I'm going to go and talk to Lord Tancarville,' Richard turned and stomped down the stairs and into the lower bailey. He walked to the front gate where two nervous looking squires were stationed. One held a loaded crossbow.

'Put that down,' Richard said, 'the last thing we need is for someone to shoot Lord Tancarville by accident.'

The squire leant the weapon against the palisade.

'Open the gate,' Richard said.

'Are you sure?' One asked.

'Just open it,' Richard tapped his foot on the ground.

They unbarred the gate and swung it open. Richard stepped out of the safety of the castle.

Tancarville looked at him and raised his eyebrows. 'You have become brave since we last met,' he said.

'I think I'm just fed up, actually,' Richard said.

'You are still insolent then,' Tancarville laughed.

The Little Lord pushed his horse forwards. 'Get out of my castle,' he said.

Richard folded his arms. 'You've already burnt my village so this place is now worthless, why don't you just leave?'

'I've got a mind to storm the castle just for that,' Tancarville said, 'I am your lord and you need reminding of it.'

'I'm not leaving,' Richard said.

'We have ridden directly from Rouen,' Tancarville said, 'and the ecclesiastical authorities there have declared your marriage void.'

'How can they do that?' Richard asked.

'You are from England and your wife is from England, so it was not easy for them to decide that you are too closely related,' Tancarville said.

'Not all English people are related,' Richard said.

'All good Normans know they are,' the Little Lord said.

'I'm a Norman, I'm just born in England,' Richard replied.

Both Tancarvilles laughed.

'You can leave now with all your people,' Tancarville said, 'I will grant you safe passage back to England. I'll even pay for a ship.'

The Little Lord coughed. 'Pay for a ship? For him?'

'Quiet, boy,' Tancarville said, 'this is politics, something you don't understand.'

'We aren't leaving, I was given Yvetot and I intend to keep it,' Richard said.

'Lady Sophie will stay,' Tancarville said.

'You want to give her to him?' Richard looked at the sneering Little Lord.

'We heard about the baby, and it's obviously mine,' the Little Lord said.

'You can't prove it,' Richard said.

The Little Lord pointed to his hair.

'This is all your fault,' Richard said, 'you got drunk and slipped on some pottage.'

'Don't you dare mention pottage,' the Little Lord said.

Richard thought about it and decided he didn't have much to lose. 'You are welcome to come in and have pottage with me,' he said, 'and I will even let you eat it out of a bowl.'

The Little Lord kicked his horse forwards and drew his sword.

Richard stood his ground as the horse cantered towards him. The Little Lord screamed and raised his sword arm.

As he neared, Richard gritted his teeth. The Little Lord swung his sword down at Richard's head, who ducked away from the blow and latched on to the young Tancarville's arm. Richard pulled the arm down and the Little Lord was tugged from his saddle and fell from his horse.

Richard yanked the sword from his grasp and threw it over onto the grass.

The Little Lord rolled over and jumped back to his feet. 'I'll stab your eyes out,' he yelled.

'A better man than you already tried,' Richard turned and walked back into the castle, leaving the seething young Tancarville behind him.

'You can shut it now,' he said to one of the squires as he walked past.

They bolted the gate and Richard went back to the inner wall. All of the squires cheered him. They shouted his name and he felt the hairs on the back of his neck stand up.

Bowman watched him return. 'He'll be the death of you,' he told Richard.

'Which one?'

'The younger one,' Bowman said, 'he hated you already, even before you pulled that stunt.'

'It was his fault,' Richard said, 'I went to talk, it was clearly out of order for him to draw his sword.'

'It was, but he will want your head now,' Bowman said.

'He can try to take it,' Richard looked back over the palisade to where some Tancarville men had gone to chop down some trees in the far wood.

'You are very brave while you're behind your walls,' Bowman said.

'I just want to sit by the fire for one night and not have to worry about someone coming to kill me. Or burn my village down.'

'They did just burn your village down, so that's one less thing to worry about,' Bowman said.

Sophie walked up the stone steps to the ramparts. Her face was set and white. 'Is he here?'

Richard nodded.

'Didn't you see?' Bowman asked.

'See what?'

'Your husband just unhorsed the Little Lord,' Bowman said.

'Oh, that's what the cheers were for,' Sophie frowned, 'so now they have another reason to force their way in.'

'He chose to attack me,' Richard said.

'You chose to unhorse him,' Sophie said, 'that doesn't sound like it happened by accident.'

'They want to break into the castle anyway,' Richard said.

'I think it won't take them too long,' Bowman said, 'they'll have a ram and some ladders made before the end of the day.'

Sophie stared out into the distance where the sound of axes biting into trees echoed out from the woods. Tancarville's men had fanned out and some were erecting a couple of large tents on the flat ground in front of the castle. Their horses had been put into Richard's paddocks, which made him frown. He'd have to check their droppings for worms himself.

'They are planning to be here a while,' Bowman said.

'So am I,' Richard said.

'Did they say anything about me?' Sophie asked.

'They did, and I think you know what it was,' Richard replied.

Sophie took a deep breath, shot Richard a disdainful look, and walked briskly back down the steps.

'What are you going to do when they breach that wall?' Bowman asked.

'What can we do other than man this one. We can defend against ladders, we have more than enough squires to hold on,' Richard said. He looked down into the inner bailey. He couldn't see the Miller, and hadn't seen him since his return, but the Priest wasn't there either.

'Can you see the Reeve?' Richard wondered out loud.

'No,' Bowman replied, 'he'll have made a run for it though, like a rat.'

'Get your fellows back behind the stone wall, then shut the gate,' Richard said loudly to the squires manning it.

'You're sure you want to leave the peasants out there? I'm not asking for my sake, but for all your future guilt I'll have to deal with,' Bowman said.

Richard didn't reply but instead looked out as the squires left the bailey.

Bowman shrugged. 'Very well. I didn't think you had it in you, I really didn't,' he said.

'They have betrayed me,' Richard said, 'and I think they only understand force. If they want to see what another lord will do with them and their village, let them see it now.'

As the gate in the stone wall slammed shut, the more astute villagers realised their predicament. They ran up to the walls beneath Richard.

'Let us in.'

'You can't leave us out here.'

Richard stepped back from the battlements. 'We need to come up with a plan,' he said to Bowman, 'let's go inside, we can do no more here.'

Long Tom already sat in the hall by the fire. 'What exactly is going on?' He asked as Richard entered.

'Lord Tancarville thinks his son has a claim to Yvetot.'

'From what you told me, Lord Tancarville does hold Yvetot from the king, so he is your lord,' Long Tom said.

'I'm in arms against him now, so it hardly matters. If I go out there again and beg forgiveness, the Little Lord will kill me anyway,' Richard replied.

'Don't you worry, Long Tom,' Bowman said, 'our young lord is blessed. He always finds a way out of all the corners he's been backed into.'

'This is quite a corner,' Long Tom said.

'We can hold it,' Richard said, 'we have good walls and Sir Roger's squires. They have no wish to let Lord Tancarville in. They know he won't go easy on them. I don't think he'll spare them.'

'There was no time to gather provisions,' Bowman said, 'we can't sit here for more than a few days.'

'Nor can they,' Richard said, 'they just burnt the village, and most of our food along with it. There isn't much left for them to steal to sustain themselves.'

'It's Lord Tancarville, the Chamberlain of Normandy,' Long Tom said, 'even Earl Patrick found him worrying. Everyone knows he's violent and disloyal. If you force him to storm the walls, you know the laws of war. We're all dead, not just you.'

Richard sat down and let his eyes fall to the fire. 'You want me to walk out?'

'I didn't say that,' Long Tom said.

'It's what you meant though,' Bowman said, 'but luckily it isn't your choice.'

'We'll man the stone walls and wait for Sir Roger,' Richard said, 'if he arrives, then Lord Tancarville might at least be willing to compromise.'

'We don't know if Sir Roger will come,' Long Tom's face reflected the shadows from the fire, and Richard thought he was starting to look more like he'd done on their first sea voyage.

'He is my lord. He will come,' Richard nodded.

'Well,' Bowman took a deep breath, 'truth be told, your self importance has been annoying me lately, but I will stand by you, young lord.'

Richard looked over. 'Thank you,' he said.

Bowman grinned. 'After this, you'll owe me.'

'I'm sure you won't let me forget it,' Richard said.

'No chance, and while I'm at it I'll remind you about the alleyway in Hampstead,' Bowman said.

'That wasn't an alleyway,' Richard said.

Bowman chuckled and went over to the window, 'They're already ramming the palisade with a tree trunk.'

There was a shriek from the doorway. Richard turned just in time to see the blue of Sophie's dress disappear upstairs.

'I better go,' Richard said.

'Don't forget to come and get slaughtered with us, young lord,' Bowman said behind him.

Richard heard Long Tom snort at that, but he pushed on into the chamber upstairs as fast as he could.

'Are you alright?' He asked his wife when he reached it.

Sophie breathed heavily. 'They're coming, you can't stop them,' she said.

'Only into the lower bailey, they won't get any further,' Richard said.

'They could, they will, it's only a matter of time,' Sophie looked to the window and back to Richard.

'I will defend you.'

Sophie's gaze went to the door before she walked closer to Richard. 'What if you can't?' She screamed into his face.

Richard recoiled. 'I will fight until my last breath,' he said.

'What good is that to me?' She said, 'you can die heroically and have a song sung about you, but how does that help me when the Little Lord drags me into bed every night? I want to take your courtesy and prowess and ram it down your throat.'

Richard held his hands up. 'Sophie, calm down.'

'I can't calm down, I gave birth to one monster, and now two more are going to knock our door down.'

'We shall deal with the monsters one at a time.'

'You could have dealt with the first one already, Richard. Kill the baby now and throw it outside, then the monsters out there have no claim over me,' Sophie cried.

'I'm not killing the baby.'

'Then you're killing me,' Sophie shouted and pushed past him. She ran up the spiral staircase towards the roof. Richard stood for a moment before he realised what she might have meant, then bolted up after her. He ran up onto the roof and saw the dark smoke rise from his devastated village. In front of the smoke Sophie started to clamber up onto the battlements.

'This isn't a romance story,' Richard shouted as he ran to her, 'you can't just throw yourself off the roof.'

'Why not,' Sophie spun round, 'you threw a monk off.'

'Who told you that? And it was nothing to do with this. Come here,' he said.

'The Devil take you and all your kind,' Sophie said and turned back to the wall.

Richard ran over to her as she climbed up onto the stonework and readied herself to push off.

He grabbed her body. 'Stop it, this is foolish. Suicides can't get into heaven,' he said.

'Hell waits for me already for the monster I spawned,' she shouted and tried to wrench herself from his grip.

'The Lord forgives,' Richard said, 'all sins can be atoned for.'

'Look,' Sophie said, 'more banners are coming. You'll be overrun before nightfall.'

Richard looked out towards the village and his wife was

right, more banners approached.

'The thought of the young Tancarville makes me sick, Richard. Let me go and let me have some peace.'

'Sophie, no,' Richard tried to haul her back but her fingers clung onto the corners of the stone.

'Let me go.'

'Sophie, those are not Tancarville banners,' Richard shouted into her ear, 'the new red banner isn't his.'

Sophie softened for a moment and Richard took the opportunity to pull her from the wall. They fell back and landed in a heap on the wooden floorboards.

'That isn't Sir Roger's banner,' Sophie said, 'so what good is it.'

'Didn't you see,' Richard said, 'that is the royal banner. The actual King is here.'

'The King?' Sophie sat up.

'Yes, so now Lord Tancarville either submits to his judgement, or will have to face the King. The King has brought an army, Sophie, wait and see what happens before you do something final.'

Her face stayed white but she nodded and got to her feet.

Richard did the same. 'Go into the hall and we'll see what Lord Tancarville does,' he said.

She left, still shaking, and Richard walked over to the battlements overlooking the lower bailey. The royal army filed out of the track and onto the open area in front of the castle. Horsemen lined up opposite Tancarville's, who formed up on their lord. Richard squinted to try to make out the King, but he was too far away. He could see red banners though, and the multicoloured de Cailly banner seemed to be next to it. The only thing Richard could be sure of, was that King Henry had far more fighting men with him than Tancarville did. A few riders rode out from the royal line, and Richard thought it was the two Tancarville's who rode out from theirs to meet them.

He ran all the way down and out of the tower, only stopping once he was on top of his stone wall.

'I told you he was lucky,' Bowman said to Long Tom.

Sarjeant stood on the wall too. 'Nothing good ever happens when great men meet angrily,' he said, 'this may not be our salvation.'

'Have you met the King before?' Long Tom asked Richard.

'No,' he replied.

'I have been at his court,' Long Tom said, 'and he can go from angry to happy and back again in a moment. Don't upset him.'

'You could just as well be talking about Lord Tancarville,' Richard said, 'I think he even liked me for a while.'

'The mix of the two of them worries me,' Sarjeant said.

'Everything worries you,' Bowman said.

They had all donned their mail shirts and a pile of spears leant against the inside of the stone wall.

'How long are they going to be?' Richard asked.

'That depends on how angry the King is,' Sarjeant said.

'Lord Tancarville is moving,' Bowman said.

Tancarville and his son rode back to their assembled horsemen. Richard heard a shouted order, and the horsemen rode over towards his demesne land and halted. That cleared the way for the king, who rode towards the castle with his bannerman and two others.

'That's Sir Roger and his banner too,' Bowman nodded.

'We might be able to survive this after all,' Richard smiled.

'Don't count your blessing yet,' Sarjeant said, 'but I suggest you open the gate before you make the King knock.'

'Good idea,' Richard looked at the nearest of the squires, 'come with me and unbar all the gates.'

He rushed down into the lower bailey and caught his breath as the squires opened up the palisade's gate. As it swung open, he saw de Cailly standing next to Henry, the King of England and Duke of Normandy.

He bowed. 'Your majesty.'

King Henry wore a shimmering blue tunic under a silken red cloak. The golden crown on his reddish hair gleamed even in the shadow of the smoke that floated up from the burning village. Richard's eyes were drawn to his fine sword belt, studded with golden fittings.

'What, have you never seen a king before?' the King laughed to himself.

'No,' Richard looked up, 'nor such a beautiful belt.'

The King laughed louder. 'You dive straight in with flattery. I do not think you are as foolish as the Chamberlain says.'

'Richard,' de Cailly said, 'is it true about the baby?'

'Yes,' he replied firmly. De Cailly's face looked worn and under his eyes were dark patches.

'Are you going to invite me in?' The King asked, 'or are you going to leave me standing outside like some sort of farm hand?'

Richard stepped aside and bowed again. 'Of course, the castle is yours.'

'I know that, it is all mine,' the King waved around himself and strode through the gate.

De Cailly raised his eyebrows to Richard as he followed the monarch in.

'Is that all of them?' The King looked at the villagers who stood near the stone gate, still being kept out of it by squires armed with spears.

'Yes,' Richard struggled to keep up with the King's pace, 'it isn't a large village, and thanks to Lord Tancarville, it isn't really even a village anymore.'

The King ground to a halt and spun round to Richard. 'Do not speak to me of the Chamberlain, I know perfectly well what he has done,' he roared.

Richard backed away and swallowed down an urge to be sick.

The King wheeled around again and the villagers and squires all scattered as he stormed through the gate in the stone wall.

De Cailly greeted his squires, but Richard tried to keep up with Henry as he flew up the stairs and into the castle's hall.

'I'm sorry for the state and size of it,' Richard said when he caught up.

'Why, did you build it?' The King asked.

'No, no I didn't,' Richard's eyes dropped to the floorboards for a moment but he hauled them back up.

The King laughed. 'I have ridden along that road a dozen times, but I never even knew there was a village here,' he said.

'That's why we built an inn by the entrance,' Richard said.

'That's what the ruin was,' the King nodded to himself, 'what did you call it, because if you named it after me and allowed it to be fired, I will not be pleased.'

'We called it the Flying Monk,' Richard said.

The King turned and studied Richard. 'That is a most curious name. Why?'

Richard ran through his options as the king's dark eyes bored a hole into him. 'A monk flew from a tower,' he said.

'Did he throw himself, or did you throw him?' The King asked.

Richard's eyes flickered for a moment before he could control them, and the King bellowed with laughter so much he had to clutch his belly.

'You did,' he staggered to Richard's chair and threw himself into it, 'I did not expect that.'

Richard steered his eyes to the fire which was only really alive on one last log.

'What did the monk do to you?' The King asked.

'He was going to deliver me to my treacherous uncle who wants to kill me,' Richard answered.

'That sounds perfectly fair, then,' the King said, 'I have my own problems with troublesome churchmen. Maybe I should throw them off towers.'

Two of the King's knights entered the chamber with hands on their swords, but they were waved away. 'I need no babysitting, this one couldn't kill me even if he wanted to.'

The knights bowed and withdrew out of the hall.

'Your hall is small, but it is still a hall,' the King chuckled, 'ha, I made a rhyme.'

Richard didn't know what to say so smiled.

'So, who are you, then, boy?' The King asked, 'thrower of monks?'

Richard told him. Except for the murders, thefts of the King's silver, and the poaching of deer in England.

'William Keynes was a good man, I was sorry to hear of his death,' the King said, 'his loyalty is not forgotten. Fortunately, it seems that his loyalty passed down to you. I must thank you for rescuing my Queen at Fecamp, for although she had told me about it, I had not realised it was you. I will also be paying Conan of St Malo a visit in Brittany shortly, so that we can ensure he does not inflict piracy on my property again.'

Richard nodded away, a feeling of uneasy hope growing steadily inside him.

'If Conan had harmed my Queen or her unborn child I would

have had to kill him. Although I might do that anyway,' the King said, 'that child I think will be my favourite if he lives. I am calling him John.'

'That's very good,' Richard said.

'But the news of the Niort ambush is new to me,' his face blackened and somehow reddened at the same time.

'I'm sorry about Earl Patrick,' Richard said.

'I regret his death, but his loyalty was only ever conditional,' Henry said, 'but the Lusignans must be punished for their impudence. No one can attack a royal personage and live.'

Richard nodded because he didn't dare say anything. He had left out his tree jumping exploits too, but realised he hadn't mentioned Sir Wobble's heroics or captivity either.

'His father was also a loyal man,' the King said once Richard had informed him, 'I will think on him, but we shall resolve matters here first.'

Lord Tancarville and the Little Lord walked into the hall. Both had angry red faces and the Chamberlain's fists were clenched. Richard saw both defiance and uncertainty all at once.

'Ah, Chamberlain,' the King pointed at one of the logs by the table, 'sit down.'

'That is not a chair,' Tancarville said.

'And I was not asking,' the King said.

Tancarville paused to glare at Richard then sat down on the low log. He had to look up to meet the King's eyes.

'Chamberlain. Tell me why you have fired one of my villages.'

'It is my village,' Tancarville said.

'It is mine first,' the King thumped his fit onto the armrest.

'The lady of Yvetot has given birth to my son's bastard child,' Tancarville said, 'so I am replacing this boy with my son as its lord.'

'Is this true?' The King looked at Richard.

Richard shrugged. 'I am no wise man or lawyer, I can't say for sure who anyone's father is,' he said.

'Anyone's?' The King widened his eyes.

'Except for you, of course,' Richard said quickly.

The King smiled. 'The young are so much more fun that the old. What's the point being King if you cannot make a few men cower?'

Richard decided that was probably meant as a joke so did his best to look amused.

'Why do you think the baby is yours?' The King asked the Little Lord.

The young man looked over to Richard. 'When I was last here I lay with her, and they say the baby has red hair,' he pointed to his uncovered head of bright red hair.

King Henry chuckled. 'I think it is time I saw this baby. Who can bring me the baby?'

'I will,' Richard said and gladly left the chamber. He walked down into the darkness of the cellar and took a moment to breath in the cool air. He had the King of England upstairs in his hall. Butterflies played around in his stomach and he felt sick again.

When he found the servant he told him to carry the baby up with him, and when they entered the hall, Sophie stood before the King.

'Young man,' the King said, 'your wife's beauty is unmatched, at least in England.'

Sophie grimaced and took a step backwards.

The King watched. 'I know, I know, you do not want me leering over you. My Queen has spoken to me about that before,' he waved her away.

'Is that it?' Henry noticed the servant with a mole on his face.

'Yes,' Richard said as the servant came forwards.

He held the baby out and it opened its eyes at the King. The King studied it and held a finger out for the baby to hold on to. 'What are you calling it?' he asked.

'The Red Baby,' Richard said.

The King turned his head to look at him, then laughed. 'The Red Baby? That is the funniest thing I've heard all year.'

Richard didn't think it was that funny, but kept his opinion to himself.

The Red Baby gripped the King's finger tightly.

'He likes me,' the King grinned.

Richard noticed Sophie had turned her back and looked out of a window.

The Red Baby gurgled and the King tickled him under the

chin. He looked up. 'This baby is strong and full of vigour. Do you know why that is?'

Richard shook his head and Tancarville frowned.

'It is because,' the King's eyes twinkled, 'he is clearly one of mine.'

Tancarville's mouth dropped open and the Little Lord blinked.

'I too visited Yvetot last year,' Henry looked over to Sophie who had turned around with a questioning face, 'and left her with no choice. I am the King after all.'

'That is preposterous,' Tancarville stood up, 'sheer fantasy.'

'And yet it is my word against your son's,' the King said.

'Father,' the Little Lord said, 'that can't be true.'

'Silence,' the King's spit flew towards the younger Tancarville.

Richard looked at Sophie, whose eyes met his. He knew she was as surprised as everyone else, and he also knew the King had only just told him he didn't know Yvetot even existed.

'I recognise this child as my bastard. The Red Baby. I love that,' the King said, 'I will have my boring lawyers draw up whatever it is they need to in order to make it official.'

'The church will not stand for it,' Tancarville said, 'it is clearly a fabrication.'

'It is mine,' the Little Lord pointed repeatedly to his own red hair.

The King laughed and pointed up to his own head. 'If hair colour is your only argument then I can meet you on that.'

The Little Lord sank within himself.

'The Red Baby is mine. I even like saying it,' the King grinned, 'but I will call him Henry, just in case anyone forgets who his father is.'

Tancarville stamped his foot on the floorboards and they shook.

'Richard is to be the child's guardian. He is to raise him, and when Richard is gone I will decide who will run Yvetot.'

'You'll be dead by then,' Tancarville said.

'Is that a threat?' The King pulled his finger away from the baby.

The Red Baby reached for the withdrawn finger and started

to cry.

'Look what you've done,' the King shouted, 'you meddling, disloyal Tancarvilles should be lucky that I'm on my way to flatten the rebels in Brittany. Now I'm going to take Yvetot away from you entirely.'

'What?' Richard asked without realising.

'Yvetot is mine,' Tancarville shouted back.

'We've already had this argument, and I won it,' Henry roared.

The baby cried louder and Sophie put her hands over her ears and walked straight out of the hall.

The King watched her go. 'That one has spirit,' he said to Richard.

'You can't take Yvetot away, it has been with my family for generations,' Tancarville said.

'I am the King, and Richard will pay homage directly to me for this little place. You will be compensated for your meagre loss, Chamberlain. We are riding to Brittany to put down a revolt there. We will grant you some lands from the rebels that are far larger than Yvetot.'

Tancarville sighed. 'Very well,' he said.

'You can go now,' the King said, 'but seeing as your warriors are arrayed here and stand ready for war, you will accompany me on my campaign.'

'To Brittany?' Tancarville asked.

'Yes, you are my vassal so for once you can act like it,' Henry said, 'sleep outside with your men, and march with us in the morning.'

Tancarville shot Richard a look before he stormed out of the hall. His son followed and slammed the door behind him.

'An odious little couple,' the King said to Richard.

Richard shrugged. 'Thank you,' he said.

'For what?' The King winked at him.

'For removing Lord Tancarville from Yvetot,' he said.

'That was certainly my pleasure. It is your reward for saving my Queen and baby John, a reward for loyalty. You will perform the homage in the morning before we march, in full view of everyone,' the King said.

'It would be my honour,' Richard said, although his voice

shook from the idea of standing in front of so many men.

'Now to the matter of William Marshal,' the King waved the Red Baby away, 'he is captured, you say?'

'Guy of Lusignan took him. He's badly wounded,' Richard said.

'He sounds like a fine warrior. Maybe he could teach my eldest son a thing or two about war,' the King snorted.

'I cannot afford the ransom, and I think his brothers have little care for him,' Richard said.

'The ransom I will account for. On two conditions. Firstly, that you do not tell anyone I am paying it, else they will double the amount.'

'Of course,' Richard said.

'Secondly, you must earn it.'

'I will,' Richard said. He at least owed Sir Wobble that much.

The King smiled. 'Good. You shall accompany me into Brittany along with the Chamberlain's forces.'

Richard's face dropped. 'I promised my wife I wouldn't leave her alone again. I've only been back here for one night,' he said.

Henry burst into laughter. 'My boy, is she such a foolish woman that she thinks a knight can stay at home like a farmer?'

'She is scared,' Richard replied.

'Of what, the Chamberlain and his flopping son?'

Richard nodded.

'Well, they shall be with me, won't they?' The King said, 'so she will be perfectly safe here. We will employ some builders to rebuild your little inn, some of the village and maybe even strengthen those flimsy wooden walls. I cannot have my royal land looking like some rustic backwater.'

'Thank you,' Richard said.

'We will leave a garrison too, so your pretty wife does not get too upset with you. Now you should go to her and make her happy.'

'I will,' Richard said.

'You do understand what I mean?'

'I think so.'

'You need to have a son that is yours, boy, then we can deal with the Red Baby,' the King said with a knowing grin.

REEMPLOYMENT

The heat from the flames warmed Richard's face and he could smell the burning bodies. He pulled his cloak up over his head.

'You can't hide from it, young lord,' Bowman said.

Richard thought he could try. The village had been a large one, not far from the north coast of France but now it was gone.

'Do you know what it's called?' Richard asked.

'No idea, they should really put signs up,' Bowman said.

Solis snorted at the flames that raged through the windows of a two-storey building to their left.

'It's alright, Solie,' Richard wanted to pat him on his neck but the lance he held prevented him. The previous villages along their route from Rouen and Caen had all greeted the royal army as friends, and the towns had provided lodgings and good food.

'I suppose this means we're in Brittany now,' Richard said.

'I suppose it does,' Bowman replied, 'the meaning of a warm welcome has changed.'

Richard frowned and saw the first of the bodies that his nose had already sensed. Villagers had been cut down along the street, and as he rode by side-streets, he caught glimpses of lumpy piles of tunics on the floor that were probably people.

'I can smell pork,' Richard said just before he saw some slaughtered pigs. The fires burnt high and dark pillars of smoke twisted up into the cloudy sky. Richard tried to spit the taste of ash out of his mouth.

'You have to just accept it,' Bowman said, 'we'll be through here before you know it.'

Richard was trying not to be effected, then he saw a pile of bodies by the side of the road, their bent and lifeless forms thrown up against the wall of a house. On the top of the pile was a young woman, her face forever stuck in an expression of horror.

Richard's mind flew back to the equally charred ruins of Fallencourt, and the young woman who'd been cruelly killed there because he'd tried to save her. His stomach churned and he dropped his cloak to put his hand over his mouth.

'Hold on a little while longer,' Bowman said from alongside him.

Richard's eyes only saw the young woman from Fallencourt, but on her face was now the pained last look of the girl from the new village. He shook his head to free himself from the vision, but it was movement out of the corner of his eye that did the trick.

'What are they doing?' Richard asked.

Bowman looked out through a gap in the houses and into the fields beyond. A line of horsemen cantered through the crops.

'They're ruining the fields without the effort of having to fire them,' Bowman answered.

'I trained Solie in ploughed fields,' Richard said, 'it made him pick his feet up when he was young.'

'It's harder when the fields are full of crops,' Bowman said, 'I'd wager a few will end up on their backs before they're done with the field.'

'Have you done it before?' Richard asked.

'Only once,' Bowman said, 'someone once told me that the easiest way to defeat an enemy is through famine.'

A squire riding ahead of Richard threw up from horseback and it splashed down onto the street. Solis stepped around the result and snorted again. The street had taken a thousand hooves that day already, and the horses had to raise their feet to avoid tripping in the deepening mud.

Some of the ill squire's companions laughed and mocked him. Richard caught a glimpse of his pale face and felt slightly better about his own feelings.

'I wish we'd got here in time to kill some of them,' one of the other squires shouted.

Bowman shook his head. 'This is their first war,' he said.

'I hope it's my last,' Richard fixed his eyes ahead and tried to imagine the smell of Keynes in the spring.

Bowman wrinkled his nose. 'You never really get used to the smell, though,' he said.

The stench grew stronger as a church came up ahead. Richard saw the door was open but grey smoke plumed out of it. It was as if the church was angry. The smell of burning flesh took a hold in the back of Richard's throat and he pulled his horse down an alleyway. He rode a few steps and was sick. It didn't clear his nostrils and only served to unsettle his stomach further. Richard turned his stallion back to the street and trotted past the column of horsemen to catch up with Bowman.

Bowman ignored him and Richard was thankful of it. The church was to his left, so he turned his head to the right until it was behind them. The village square lay beyond the church, a partially stoned area surrounded by the best houses in the village.

'What's that?' Richard nodded towards the centre of the square.

'Turn your eyes the other way, young lord,' Bowman suggested.

Richard couldn't, and realised that the man-high lump in the middle of the open space was a stack of bodies. Their tunics ranged from blues to yellows, but all were covered in red streaks. Out of the centre of the mass, sprouting like a flower, was a banner pole with a flag hanging from it. The wind flicked the flag up and Richard saw the red and yellow chequerboard pattern on it.

He swallowed down what tried to come out.

'Bowman,' he said faintly.

'I saw it,' his friend looked straight ahead.

'They're here,' Richard said.

'I know, I saw it.'

'Eustace could be here too, his ransom could have been paid,' Richard turned his eyes away from the square.

'Aye, he didn't come to Yvetot with Lord Tancarville,' Bowman said.

Long Tom rode behind them and Richard had forgotten he

existed. 'Is that the Eustace you told me about?' He asked.

'It is,' Bowman said without turning to face him.

Richard had told him about Eustace and the Martels. Except for Bowman's half-brother, because Bowman had shot him an angry look when he'd tried.

'Earl Patrick never liked the Martels,' Long Tom said, 'he told us you couldn't trust them to do anything other than look out for themselves.'

'Sounds about right,' Bowman said.

The column snaked along the road and Richard's nose was glad that the smells of the countryside started to take over again. Fields opened up before them and a seemingly endless flatland stretched out into the distance.

Richard thought of the white shield he wore with its blue horizontal stripe. He could see Bowman's beside him, and Long Tom had one, too.

'Eustace will notice these shields eventually,' Richard said.

'And your saddle, young lord,' Bowman reminded him that the back of his saddle was also white and blue, although these days the white was scuffed and chipped.

'And your horse is not exactly a common colour,' Long Tom added.

'I can't do anything about the horse,' Richard said, 'but maybe we can do something about the shields. We can do without the Martels knowing we are in the army.'

'You want to paint our shields?' Bowman asked.

'No,' Richard said, 'I've got another idea. Wait here.'

He pushed Solis to the side of the column and trotted him up it. He rushed past riders with banners and shields of all colours, but not the red and yellow chequerboard. He knew the King would be in the middle of the convoy, and searched ahead for his red banner. Richard dropped Solis back down into a walk when he saw a banner that he recognised. It had a blue bottom, green top and a yellow line through the middle.

Richard reached it. 'Sir Roger,' he said loudly.

A dozen knights and squires turned to him, all with the same colours on their shields. De Cailly did too, Richard recognised him from his slight hunchback and dark face.

'Richard,' de Cailly greeted him.

'I'm sorry we haven't spoken since we left Yvetot,' Richard said.

'No need to apologise, the army is large and you are in a different division. What are you doing here?'

'I'm riding to speak to the King,' Richard said.

'Ah, your new lord,' de Cailly kept his face unreadable.

'I didn't plan for that,' Richard said.

'I am not offended that the King took Yvetot from me,' de Cailly said, 'I never had a penny from it, nor a single crossbowman.'

'If it's caused any offence, I want you to know it was entirely the King's idea,' Richard said.

'I still have these to remember you by,' de Cailly's eyes twinkled as he looked down at his iron spurs.

'How are they holding up?' Richard asked, 'the leather was starting to go on the right strap when I gave them to you.'

'I've had that replaced,' de Cailly smiled, 'to tell the truth, I was proud to see you put your hands inside the King's at Yvetot. And you speak today with more confidence than you did before. You are safer as the King's tenant than you were as mine.'

Richard felt better. 'I will not forget what you did for me,' he said.

'You almost look like your father now,' de Cailly said.

Richard felt his cheeks redden. 'Thank you, may the Lord preserve you in this campaign,' he said.

De Cailly nodded and Richard sped Solis up again.

The road cut arrow-straight through the open countryside and Richard passed a dozen more banners before he saw a red and yellow one. He squinted his eyes and sighed when he realised the two colours were quartered not chequered. He'd seen that banner before, but it wasn't until he reached it that he remembered whose it was.

Sir William Mandeville rode beside his red and yellow banner, his curly brown hair spilt out from underneath his helmet. The next banner along was the royal banner.

'You can't go further,' one of Mandeville's men said to Richard as he slowed down to their pace.

'I need to speak to the King,' Richard said.

The man laughed and Mandeville turned to see what the commotion was about.

'I remember you,' he said, 'from Neufchâtel.'

'That's right,' Richard said.

'I can't remember anything else about you, who are you?' Mandeville asked.

'Richard of Yvetot.'

'Ah, the friend of the peacock knight who took no prizes from the battle.'

Richard nodded.

'How is your imprudent friend?' Mandeville asked with a grin.

'Imprisoned in Poitou,' Richard replied.

Mandeville laughed. 'So he isn't the greatest knight that ever lived, then. What are you doing here, you should be organising his ransom.'

'I'm here to earn it,' Richard replied.

Mandeville nodded. 'Now I remember who you are, I watched your ceremony in your little village. I was most amused that you angered Lord Tancarville so greatly, too. He deserved to be brought down to earth so publicly.'

Richard wasn't sure it was going to end so well for him.

'From your look,' Mandeville said, 'I see that you're worried he will blame you for the whole episode.'

Richard nodded.

'You should be worried,' Mandeville said, 'from what I heard it is entirely your doing, and I doubt the Chamberlain will forgive you.'

'Can I see the King?' Richard asked. He noticed that Mandeville's company was large, and although men with his personal colours rode around him, behind them over a hundred men rode with red shields.

'Why do they all have red shields?' Richard asked.

'As the Constable of Normandy, I command the King's mesnie,' Mandeville said.

'I see,' Richard replied. He was looking at the King's household troops for the campaign.

'I think I would like to join them,' Richard added.

Mandeville laughed. 'Would you, now? Bored of straggling in

the rearguard, are you?'

'Something like that,' Richard replied.

'If you insist on it, I won't block it,' Mandeville said.

'Thank you,' Richard said.

'I'll go with you and tell him,' Mandeville rode out of the column and next to Richard.

They rode as a pair up the line.

'What was that village called?' Richard asked.

Mandeville shrugged. 'Who cares, it's gone now,' he said.

'Who owned it?'

'Seeing as we torched it, I presume Viscount Odo, as he is the rebel Henry wishes to suppress.'

'Who is Viscount Odo?'

'A major landowner in Brittany, his stronghold is Josselin Castle. Which is all I know of him, other than he has risen in revolt,' Mandeville said.

Richard heard King Henry's laugh before he saw him. The King wore a bright red cloak that spread all the way down his horse's tail, and would have reflected the sun, had there been any.

'Stay here,' Mandeville left Richard and rode up to the King.

Soon he rode back. 'You're in,' Mandeville said.

Richard breathed more easily. 'Thank you,' he said.

'Don't thank me, thank Henry. You will need to swap that shield out for a red one,' Mandeville said.

'I will,' Richard said.

'I must confess,' Mandeville said, 'he agreed more readily that I expected. Normally Henry is suspicious of anyone who wants to be near him or join his service.'

'Maybe he likes me?'

Mandeville chuckled. 'Perhaps, but I don't care enough to find out. Go back to the carts and swap shields, then return to me,' he said.

Richard saw the smoke from the second village rise from a treeline long before he smelt it. Bowman and Long Tom rode with him at the back of the King's mesnie, red shields on their shoulders. Behind them, nearly thirty greyhounds and other hunting dogs walked, and occasionally Richard heard the cry of a bird of prey from the rest of the King's hunting staff. Their presence was the closest thing to luxury in the army, for the baggage train was solely for provisions and weaponry.

Richard reached the treeline under the smoke and entered the village.

There was no bravado or illness from the household knights, they rode through in silence. Their heads turned from side to side, their eyes checked streets and doorways.

The smell of burning hair hit Richard and he retched. He felt a wave of panic build inside him and his breathing became shallow and rapid.

'Look ahead, young lord,' Bowman said, 'think of home and try to breath normally.'

Richard tried. He locked his eyes onto the small metal rings on the back of the man directly in front of him and thought about his orchard.

'Maybe you should have gone into the church,' Bowman said.

'Maybe you should have,' Richard replied.

'Perhaps,' Bowman said, 'but luckily my father had other ideas.'

'I don't know what mine was thinking,' Richard said, 'leaving his family to go to the Holy Land.'

'You can hardly complain, are you at home now?'

Richard frowned and realised they were nearly out of the village already. It was smaller than the last one, but the fire was just as hot and smokey.

'Did you see the banner in the village?' Bowman asked.

Richard shook his head, for he had seen nothing of the village.

'The pile of corpses wasn't as large,' Bowman said, 'but the Martel flag was planted in them just the same. I wonder how many of their banners they are carrying with them?'

'I don't care, so long as they don't see me,' Richard said.

A horse in front slipped on the churned up road and fell over onto its side. Its rider tumbled from the saddle and his lance flew from his hand and clattered off a building. He got up and no one paid him much attention after that.

'It gets easier, as I've told you before,' Bowman said.

Richard took the deepest breath he could to clear the village from his airways. 'I can handle the fighting, I just hate this,' he said.

'We can't do anything about it,' Bowman said, 'say your prayers, and you'll soon harden to it.'

'How many campaigns have you been on?' Richard asked as the column entered a wood and the village faded behind them.

'Not many, young lord. I made some coin in the service of others, including this King, and the war there was the same as here.'

'Riding and burning, that's all this is,' Richard said.

'Aye, but it works. There'll be no crossbowmen or knights raised from these villages to fight the King in the future,' Bowman said.

'Who did you fight?'

'Rebels, the Welsh,' Bowman said, 'until the money ran out, then we all went home.'

'That's not very honourable,' Richard said.

'Mercenaries have a bad reputation for a reason,' Bowman grinned under his iron helmet.

The third village soon loomed on the horizon, and Richard found himself gazing at the rising smoke stacks with a surprising indifference. They made their way through the muddy streets and through the destruction of this village as they had the previous two. Even Solis didn't bother to snort at the corpses or the flames any longer, and Richard didn't feel his stomach rebel on him. If anything, as he rode between burning buildings, Richard felt like he was seeing the world through someone else's eyes. Dead animals by the side of the road were just dead animals, and even the human victims failed to stir up the sickness he'd felt before.

Bowman looked at him as they rode past a raging barn full of straw. 'I thought it would take a few days of this, young lord, but you've already got the stare,' he said.

'The stare?'

'Watch how the royal household knights are,' Bowman said, 'the way they look. That's you now, you aren't a child anymore.'

'I don't feel like one,' Richard said, 'I'm old enough to know hell awaits me for my part in this.

'Don't be so dramatic,' Bowman said.

'We are going to hell though, aren't we.'

'I'm no churchman, don't ask me. But remember that cross on your tunic?'

Richard had forgotten about that. The cross, made out of his old bandage, still clung onto his tunic under his mail armour. 'No, I haven't thought about that for a while,' he said.

'You took the cross. If you fulfil that vow, they say all sins are cleaned,' Bowman said.

'When this is done, then,' Richard said.

Bowman laughed. 'Already forgotten your complaint about your father?'

Richard frowned. He would go on crusade, but it would have to be at the right time. His immediate worry however, was the first target of the King's campaign, because up ahead was a nest of pirates, Saint-Malo itself.

A mist hung over the sea as the sun crept up onto the horizon behind Richard. The air was chilled and still, noise only from seagulls and their horse's hooves. Richard rode with Mandeville and five other knights towards the fortress of Saint-Malo, along the northern Breton coast. A causeway led towards the stone fortification in the distance, and Richard started to hear the faint sounds of waves break on the sandy beach to his right. The castle sat on the seashore, a bastion of stone amongst the sea and sand. A long finger of grey rocks stretched out to sea away from it, culminating in an outcrop upon which a three story wooden watchtower had been built. To the left of the causeway was the port from which Conan of Saint-Malo had launched his raid on Fecamp.

'Easy, now,' Mandeville said, a red cloak around himself, 'we're not trying to be noticed.'

Richard wasn't sure why he'd been asked to join the party sent to scout out the castle that morning, but he hadn't minded.

'If anyone has better eyes than me and sees movement, tell me,' Mandeville said.

Richard wished Bowman had been there, his eyes seemed to have been taken from a hawk. What he could see himself, was that Saint-Malo's castle had long walls of stone with a number of robust looking towers along it. A tall keep stood proudly in the centre of it all.

There was a small town to the south, but the pirates were clearly going to be in the castle.

Richard pushed Solis on as Mandeville rode his horse forwards. They'd left their shields behind to look a little more innocent, but if the pirates had crossbows, Richard knew they'd regret it if they strayed too close.

'Look for weak points,' Mandeville said, 'or guards. Hopefully they are both lax and lazy.'

'The wall isn't level all the way along the top,' Richard said.

'Isn't it?' Mandeville squinted.

'No, it's lower in three places.'

'You have good eyes,' Mandeville said, 'mind you, you are the youngest here so you should.'

Mandeville rode closer to see for himself.

A few minutes later Richard could make out a figure on top of one of the towers, but he was sure the man was looking in a different direction.

'I can only see one lookout,' Richard said.

'Pathetic,' Mandeville said, 'and I see the walls. They either aren't finished, or are in bad repair. Henry will be most pleased to hear this.'

Richard glanced over into the port. Some medium sized fishing vessels looked ready to sail, but the lack of wind seemed to have prevented their crews from launching. A few ships had oars, but they looked very empty. Richard squinted at those ships, there were some galleys just like the one he'd liberated from the pirates at Fecamp.

'I know those ships,' he said.

'Really?' Mandeville asked, 'are you a naval expert now?'

'No, those galleys were taken at Fecamp,' Richard said.

'Were they now,' Mandeville looked over towards them and narrowed his eyes.

'You should recognise that one,' Richard pointed towards the larger English ship that was unmistakably too well built to be sitting in a pirate's port.

'That's Eleanor's ship, the one she said was taken,' Mandeville said.

'Exactly, which means Conan is here, with all of his men,' Richard said.

'If you're right, there will be enough men inside to hold even a run-down castle,' Mandeville said.

Richard nodded, those walls looked thick, even if in some places the wall was half the height it should have been.

'I have an idea. We will wipe out this nest of pirates,' Mandeville said, 'but we need to ride back to Henry and tell him what we've seen.'

Once he'd returned to the army's camp, Richard waited around for half the day before a squire appeared with a message.

'You and your men are required by the Earl of Essex,' he said.

'Who is that?' Richard asked.

'The Constable of Normandy,' the messenger said.

'He means Lord Mandeville,' Bowman said from the pile of blankets he lay on with closed eyes.

'Oh, I didn't know he was an earl,' Richard said.

'His father died last year,' the messenger said, 'but hurry up.'

'We better go,' Long Tom said, 'we don't want to keep an earl waiting.'

Their fire was only three away from where Mandeville had set up, and they found him quickly.

'Richard, are those your men?' Mandeville asked him from behind a table. A number of men stood around it, all dressed far better than he was.

Richard glanced at Bowman and decided to ignore him. 'They are,' he said.

'I'm not, not really,' Long Tom said.

'Then what are you doing here?' Mandeville asked.

'He is, ignore him,' Richard said.

'If he isn't sure if he's even your man, he's not coming on the mission.'

'What mission?' Bowman asked.

'Get rid of him,' Mandeville said.

'Just go,' Richard said to Long Tom.

The young man sighed. 'Fine, it's probably safer here, anyway,' he said and trudged off.

'What about this one?' Mandeville looked at Bowman.

Richard waited for him to reply.

Bowman coughed. 'I sleep in his hall, so I suppose you could say I'm his man,' he said.

Mandeville grunted an acknowledgment.

The man next to him tutted. 'This is a bad idea, this man is always trouble,' he said.

'Brother Geoffrey?' Richard asked out loud, 'what are you doing here?'

'See, impudence,' Brother Geoffrey's little eyes searched him. The monk walked around the table and prodded Richard in the chest. 'Watch him carefully, but I want it noted that I object.'

'Fine, it's noted,' Mandeville said, 'but he's coming. We need a young man to look like an apprentice. We also need a man who is good with horses to drive the mule.'

Richard's eyes lit up. 'A mule?'

'Stubborn creatures,' Brother Geoffrey said, 'so I suspect it and you shall get along well.'

'Henry wants us to try to get into the castle and open the gate,' Mandeville said, 'because we don't have time to sit here for weeks laying siege to it.'

'So, he called for me,' the monk said.

'Have some humility,' Mandeville looked down at the shorter man.

'Someone fetch the cart and mule,' Brother Geoffrey said and a young clerk left the table. He returned with a young looking mule hitched up to a four wheeled cart.

'What's in it?' Richard asked.

'Stone mason's tools,' Mandeville smiled, 'you spotted the weakness, so you are entitled to help us exploit it. Unless you'd rather not?'

'Of course I will,' Richard said.

Bowman groaned.

Mandeville looked at him, then back to Richard. 'I'm told you're good with horses, and I heard about the little incident with the tree at the Queen's ambush, so you are our driver. The rest of us will take normal clothes and walk alongside. We'll offer our services to repair the walls, but once we're in we'll open the gate. The army will pour in and put down this nest of vipers for good.'

Richard didn't need to crack the whip to make the mule move. Instead, he'd asked it to move, and when it did, he gave it a pod of sweet beans to eat. Shortly after, the mule walked on happily enough with its load.

'Not bad, boy,' Mandeville said. He was dressed in a white linen tunic and a beige hood. Richard was too, and felt very out of place.

'There's scaffolding around the walls already,' Richard pointed as the cart rumbled up to the castle.

'So there is, maybe they won't have room for us,' Brother Geoffrey frowned from next to Richard. He'd refused to walk, and had mounted the cart as soon as it had left the encampment.

They approached the main gate, which was open, but a solid portcullis of latticed wood blocked their path.

'Is anyone there?' Mandeville shouted into the castle.

'Try to sound less noble,' the monk hissed at him.

Mandeville turned around with a grin on his face. 'That is almost a compliment,' he said.

'It isn't,' Brother Geoffrey said, 'you're supposed to be a tradesman.'

A guard appeared on the other side of the portcullis. 'Who are you?' He asked.

'Stone masons,' Mandeville said.

'You're late,' the man said in a deep voice. His accent was strong and Richard had to strain his ears to catch the words.

The guard walked out of view and the portcullis lifted to the sound of clunking wood and chains.

'In you go,' the monk whispered in Richard's ear.

Richard shivered, but asked the mule to enter the castle. The animal flicked his ears as he obeyed, and his hooves echoed on the stone under the gatehouse.

The guard who called them in went and stood by a huge windlass. It had a chain that went up the wall and into the gatehouse above the portcullis. Three other guards stood by the windlass. 'Come on, I'll show you to the wall,' the first guard said.

Brother Geoffrey, who looked very different in a plain linen tunic, nodded. 'Thank you, please show us the way,' he said.

The guard, who wore a moderately padded woollen gambeson as armour, walked along the base of the wall to Richard's right. To his left, Richard heard the sound of horses and saw a wooden stable block built up against the inside of the stone wall.

'You need to work fast, our lord is paying extra to the workmen who finish their section before the Angevin King gets here.'

'How long do we have, do you think?' The monk asked him as Richard moved the cart along the wall behind them.

'We think ten to fifteen days,' the guard said.

'I am quite sure we can make good work in that time,' Brother Geoffrey said.

'Good, if the walls are ready, no Angevin is ever getting in,' the guard said.

They walked past the first tower, after which the wall looked like it had suffered a landslide. Stones poured down from a breach that ended half way up the intended height of the wall. The stones were large, but it looked like you could climb up them and reach the hole in the fortification easily enough.

'There you are,' the guard said, 'the stone is already here, so get on with it.'

Brother Geoffrey bowed to him and turned to the cart. 'Unload the tools and put the mule away,' he said.

The four of them unloaded the cart of its selection of chisels and hammers.

'This isn't a full set of tools,' Bowman dropped two heavy iron chisels onto the floor.

'No,' Mandeville smiled, 'and we aren't proper stone masons.'

'Quiet,' the monk said, 'we will act like we are for now.'

Richard turned the cart around and drove the mule back towards the stables by the gatehouse. As he went, Richard thought that the keep in the centre of the bailey looked sturdy, its entrance was up some wooden stairs onto the first floor, and its walls looked very thick. He could smell baking bread from it and his stomach rumbled.

Richard left the cart beside the stables and found an empty stall inside for the mule. It had a full water bucket, so he shut the mule in it. As he exited the stables, a cart laden with cut grass caused the portcullis to be raised again, and Richard assumed some of it would be thrown into his mule's stable.

Back at the wall, Richard found Bowman on the top of the breach rolling down loose stones from the solid part of the wall.

Mandeville and Brother Geoffrey watched from the bottom.

'Aren't you going to help him?' Richard asked.

'I'm an earl.'

'I'm a monk.'

Richard sighed. 'Fine,' he mumbled and clambered up the light coloured stone blocks. They were dusty and his footing wasn't secure. Richard reached the top and looked out over the causeway and the port. 'It's not a bad view,' he said.

'No. I'd rather be tucked up in here than outside trying to storm my way in,' Bowman said.

'Can you see our army?' Richard asked.

'There are two men on foot in the far distance,' Bowman said, 'but I think I can only see them because I know they are out there.'

'So we're to work on the wall until dark, then open the gate?' Richard said.

'That's their plan,' Bowman replied. He rolled a large stone down the pile. It cracked in two half way down and hit the bottom close to Brother Geoffrey's foot.

'Mind yourself, don't ruin the stones,' the monk shouted up.

'Why should I care?' Bowman said quietly enough that only Richard could hear.

Richard picked up a stone, felt his back brace and heaved it down the slope. 'Sir Wobble would like this, hurling stones is one of his favourite pastimes,' he said.

'Aye, and he can have it,' Bowman clapped his hands to clean from as much dust as he could.

'I hope he's alright,' Richard said.

'I'm sure he is,' Bowman sighed, 'he would survive the second coming. It is us that I'm worried about.'

Richard thought about his friend. 'I suppose we're doing all we can by earning his ransom here,' he said.

'I'm doing all the earning at the moment,' Bowman said, 'and

I don't even like him.'

'You don't like anyone,' Richard smiled.

'I bet I won't like him, either,' Bowman nodded down to a group of men who left the keep and walked towards them.

'Four guards,' Richard said, 'do you think the other man is Conan.'

'For sure, he looks like a pirate king to me.'

Conan of Saint-Malo strode purposefully across the beaten earth of the bailey. His mustard coloured tunic was shorter than Richard was used to seeing, but his fur lined cloak was unmistakably rich. A sword belt was complimented by two others with daggers.

'Maybe he thinks he's from Iberia,' Richard said.

'Why? Maybe he's just a posturing peacock,' Bowman snorted, 'he'd get on well with Sir Wobble.'

'When will you be able to complete this section?' Conan asked Mandeville. The pirate king's voice was higher pitched than Richard expected, and his face was smooth and clean shaven.

'I'm not altogether sure, as of yet,' Mandeville said.

'A stone mason should know just by looking at this pile of rubble,' Conan said.

'Well,' Mandeville replied, 'some of these stones have been broken, so until we sort them we won't know how long the repairs will take.'

'Give me a time.'

'I don't know it,' Mandeville stood tall and faced the pirate king.

Bowman stepped closer to Richard. 'The monk is right, the earl is too posh,' he said.

'You don't know it?' Conan shouted, 'what am I paying you for?'

'Nothing yet,' Mandeville said, 'maybe we should discuss terms.'

Conan's hand slipped down to one of his daggers.

'He's going to give us away,' Richard whispered.

'Do you know who I am?' Conan stepped forwards.

'Back away,' Bowman said to himself.

Mandeville didn't back away, instead he puffed his chest out and looked the pirate king straight in his eyes.

'Hit me,' Richard said.

'I have no idea who you are,' Mandeville said to the pirate king.

'What?' Bowman said.

'Just hit me,' Richard said.

Bowman grinned and punched Richard on the side of his face.

Richard recoiled and threw a punch into Bowman's ribs.

'What are you doing?' Brother Geoffrey shouted up onto the wall.

Bowman pushed Richard gently down the slope, and he staged a theatrical fall down the rubble. Richard hit the bottom covered in dust and with a few cuts, but he jumped up as Bowman ran down the stones after him.

'Cease,' Conan shouted.

Bowman swung at Richard and caught his shoulder.

Richard spun around and raised his arms to retaliate.

'Seize the big one,' Conan shouted and his four guards charged over.

Bowman grinned and caught the first one on his nose. The man fell away with his hands clasping it. His companions mobbed Bowman, and after a struggle succeeded in restraining him. Blood poured from his nose as Conan walked up to him. 'Throw him out of my castle,' he said.

The guards dragged Bowman towards the gate, their captive fighting with them all the way.

Conan spat onto the ground and walked off the other way along the wall.

Richard wiped some dust from his face.

'That was actually very clever,' the monk said.

'Why?' Mandeville asked, 'I had that perfectly under control.'

'You were moments from giving us all away,' Brother Geoffrey said.

The earl sighed.

'He's coming back,' Richard nodded to where Conan had turned around.

The pirate walked back. 'We had not finished our conversation,' he pointed at Mandeville.

Brother Geoffrey rushed up to block his path and held his hands up to Conan. 'Please, my lord, he meant no offence.'

Conan pushed Geoffrey away so hard that he fell over in a heap. The pirate strode towards Mandeville and drew one of his daggers.

Mandeville stepped back and raised his hands. 'There is no need for violence, I can give you a date,' he said.

Conan walked past Richard with the tip of his blade pointing at the earl.

Mandeville back-pedalled.

Richard picked up a shovel from their pile of tools. He ran at Conan and swung the shovel at the back of his head. The shovel connected with a clang and the pirate dropped onto the ground. The dagger spilled from his grip and Mandeville picked it up.

'Don't kill him,' Brother Geoffrey said from the ground where he'd managed to sit up.

'He was going to kill me, why shouldn't I?' Mandeville asked.

'Because the King will want to deal with him personally. We should hide him in the cart and smuggle him out of here,' the monk said.

'Henry will kill everyone in this place, they are all pirates,' the earl said, 'I can cut the head off the viper now and be done with it.'

'Either way,' Richard said, 'we need the gate open. I can go and open it.'

'Go on then boy, and don't mess it up,' the monk said, 'I'll try and signal the army.'

Richard turned and walked as calmly as he could back towards the stables, while Brother Geoffrey made his way up the slope and onto the wall.

When Richard got back to the gatehouse and stables, his heart dropped. The four guards who had ejected Bowman were all hauling on the wooden pegs on the windlass to lower the portcullis back down. The latticed wooden gate landed on the ground with a thud, and the four guards all let go of the windlass. Richard realised that it took all four of them to raise it, which meant he wasn't going to manage it by himself.

He walked over to the stable and watched as the four

guards walked back to where they'd come from. Where Conan currently lay unconscious on the ground.

Richard swore, and ran over to the windlass in the hope that he was strong enough to turn it. He gripped a wooden peg with both hands and pushed as hard as he could.

It didn't budge. He tried to pull it, but that did nothing either.

He gave up on the windlass and ran into the stables. He found the box where their mule was and ran inside. The mule put his ears back when he entered.

'Don't even try it,' Richard shouted and the mule gave up its idea and went back to eating. Richard slipped its bridle on and led it outside. He went to find the harness for it and put that on the mule, then led it over to the windlass. He backed the mule up to it.

'Stand still,' Richard told it, 'or we'll cook you.'

The mule shook its head and its ears flopped from side to side, but stayed where it was.

Richard tied the ends of the harness around one of the windlass pegs and went back to the mule.

'Walk on,' he said.

The mule took a step, which took up the slack, paused for a moment, then pushed on through the pressure from the windlass. Which turned. Richard breathed a sigh of relief and kept the mule turning the windlass until the portcullis was open enough for a horseman to ride under it.

'Stay,' he ordered and ran in the direction the guards had gone.

Richard arrived back at their place of work to find Mandeville perched upon a large stone up on the rubble heap. He swung a long handled hammer around in large circles to keep the guards at bay. They drew swords and one tried to get close, but the hammer sent him jumping backwards.

'Fetch some spears, we can't reach him,' one guard said.

One did as he asked and ran off towards the keep.

Richard could see Geoffrey on the top of the wall waving his arms out towards the causeway.

Whatever happened, he thought, was going to happen fast.

Mandeville stepped down onto a lower stone and swung his hammer.

The closest guard had to duck it.

The pile of tools lay on the other side of the guards, so unable to reach them, Richard ran at the middle guard.

Mandeville saw him approach and attacked the same man. The guard stepped back out of the way of the iron hammer, but it meant Richard was free to take him down. Richard grabbed the guard, stuck his leg out behind him and tried to smash his head down onto the ground. The guard's face, wide-eyed, flashed past Richard's and hit the ground with a crack. His skull smashed open and Richard sprung up as the first guard ran at him with his sword.

Richard picked the dead guard's sword up just in time to parry the first attack, but it knocked him down onto the ground. Richard braced as the guard went to strike him again, but the iron hammer connected with the side of his head and tore his jaw half away from his head. Richard sprung up and drove his sword at the guard's neck. The blade slid in and ended his brief misery.

'Behind you,' Mandeville shouted.

Richard turned as the third guard thrust his sword at him. Richard knocked it aside, but it caught his tunic and ripped it. He went to counter with the hilt of his sword but mistimed it. The guard swung back at him, and Richard stepped sideways to evade him. Richard heard Mandeville jump from the stones and land back on the bailey floor.

The guard attacked Richard who parried it, but his sword was knocked from his hand. Richard swore at Sir Wobble, who had never actually followed through on the promise to teach him how to use swords properly.

The guard grinned but Richard wasn't done. He leapt at the Breton before he could attack. Richard didn't knock him off his feet though, instead he bounced off the gambeson of the bigger man, who laughed.

The laugh stopped mid breath as Mandeville swung the hammer into his back and the air was pushed out of his lungs.

The guard tried to scream, but looked around in disbelief as he couldn't take in air. Richard looked into the guard's eyes as the hammer's second blow caved his skull in.

The man dropped to the ground, but Richard could still see

his eyes looking back at him.

'Snap out of it,' the earl shouted.

Richard blinked and saw movement in the corner of his eye.

Conan struggled to his feet and jogged off towards the keep.

'Chase him,' Mandeville shouted.

Richard put his hands on his knees and tried to catch his breath. 'In a minute,' he said.

'They're coming,' Brother Geoffrey shouted from the wall.

'You could have helped,' the earl said to him.

'I'm a monk.'

'You have mentioned that,' Mandeville said and lowered his blood-soaked hammer.

A horn blew from somewhere in the keep. A long note droned through the air, followed by another.

'That can't be good,' Richard said.

'Back onto the wall,' Mandeville said, 'we'll make our stand there. Did you open the gate?'

'I did,' Richard said, 'if I trained the mule well, it'll still be up.'

Mandeville frowned. 'That had better be a joke.'

'I'll tell you later,' Richard said as men started to run out of the keep.

'Get up on the wall,' the earl started to clamber up himself.

Richard climbed up the dusty blocks with his reclaimed sword until he reached Brother Geoffrey.

'They've got bows,' the monk said.

'Then you'll have a fine chance to suffer for your God,' the earl snapped. He grasped the hammer with two hands and faced the oncoming pirates.

The horn sounded again and kept going. Richard counted at least thirty pirates swarm in the bailey below, and those with bows drew arrows and pointed them up towards him.

An arrow sailed up and clattered off the wall not far from Mandeville.

The earl sniffed. 'You'll have to do better than that,' he shouted.

A flurry of arrows loosed, and one sank into the shaft of his hammer. Another skidded off the stone by Richard's foot and grazed his shin. The rest sailed over the wall.

Mandeville laughed and held the hammer above him. 'Come

and fight me like men, not pirates,' he yelled.

Horses burst into the bailey from the direction of the gatehouse. A rider near their front held a red banner, and Richard felt himself relax.

'I suppose the mule did his job,' the monk said from behind Mandeville.

'Unlike some,' the earl replied.

The pirates below faced the incoming cavalry and made to form a line. Some arrows flew flat and straight at the horsemen, but the flood of attackers surged irresistibly as they poured into the castle.

Mandeville threw his hammer to the ground. 'I might add a hammer to my banner,' he said.

Richard shrugged. 'I might add a mule to mine,' he said.

The earl burst into laughter. 'I like you. Your arrogant friend from last year I did not, but you, you I like.'

The King's knights lowered their lances, and a moment later they had trampled and skewered the pirates. They carried on and killed the archers who tried to flee.

'I told you,' Mandeville said, 'he's going to kill everyone.'

The more reticent pirates had already started running back to their keep, and arrows started to fly out from the arrow slits.

Some knights continued their charge around the castle, while others dismounted and rushed up the wooden staircase.

'They haven't even set the stairs alight,' the earl shook his head, 'but that's pirates for you.'

Brother Geoffrey sat down on a large stone and folded his arms.

'Ah, Henry is here,' the earl looked down towards the gatehouse where a body of knights with red shields had entered.

The King wore his armour but no helmet, instead his golden crown sat atop his red hair. He rode over towards the rubble and dead guards by the wall.

King Henry looked down at the bodies. 'William,' he shouted up, 'I see you have been enjoying yourself.'

'I thought I would try a new weapon,' Mandeville looked at his iron hammer and grinned, 'it seems to be effective.'

'Between that and the mule,' the King said, 'we are going to have ourselves a fine story to tell.'

'The mule?' Mandeville looked at Richard.

'There is a mule tied to the portcullis windlass,' Henry laughed, 'it is a matter of luck that they are so stubborn, else it may have wondered off and closed the castle to us. That mule is the only reason you three are alive.'

'I take it back,' the earl looked at Richard with a grin, 'you are an idiot.'

Richard laughed. 'You wanted a man who was good with horses,' he said.

'And we got one,' the King said, 'and soon we shall have a pirate king.'

King Henry turned his horse and rode towards the keep. He stayed just outside of arrow range and watched as his knights entered. It wasn't long before arrows ceased flying from the first and second floors.

'Should we do anything?' Richard asked.

Mandeville sat down on a stone. 'No, we have done our bit. We can watch now,' he said.

Richard rubbed his grazed shin, but he knew he'd got off lightly. Bowman had hurt him more than the guards.

It was only a short time later that pirates started to be led out from the keep. Some were bleeding and one cradled a hand that lacked all of its fingers. They were pushed down onto their knees in front of the King. The last man out was Conan, walking on his own in front of two knights. He stood before Henry and the knights pushed him down onto the ground.

'What did you think would happen?' The King shouted at Conan.

The pirate king knelt motionless.

'What did you think would happen when you raided my town?'

Conan looked up at the king but said nothing.

'If you don't speak, I'll just have your tongue cut out,' Henry raged.

'Fecamp is deserted, there was no royal garrison,' Conan said.

'No,' the King said. He shook his head then roared, 'but there was my bloody Queen.'

Conan looked down at the ground.

'And you tried to kill her.'

'We did not,' the pirate looked up, 'we didn't know she was there. We left her alone in the abbey when we found out.'

'Your men shot crossbows at her,' the King said, 'at the Queen. Did you not think there would be consequences?'

'We didn't know it was her.'

'Absurd,' Henry cast his eyes over the dozen or so surviving pirates.

'Is that all?' Henry asked the knights standing behind Conan.

'All the ones who could walk,' one replied.

'Hang them from the towers,' he cried, 'all who come here will see what happens when you raid my property.'

Knights ordered squires to take the prisoners. Some scurried off to find rope, others herded their captives together and walked them towards the walls.

'If you cannot stomach watching this, boy,' Brother Geoffrey said, 'no one will think less of you if you leave.'

Richard glanced at the monk. 'My stomach is strong enough, monk. I will see plenty of this in hell, so I may as well acclimatise now,' he said.

Brother Geoffrey narrowed his eyes at Richard. 'One day, you will burn,' he said.

'I'm sure of it.'

Mandeville laughed. 'Leave him alone, Geoffrey, he's more of a man than you are.'

The monk pursed his lips. 'I am a man of God.'

'No, you're not,' the earl said, 'so shut up and watch our King's justice at work.'

The squires had worked quickly and hung nooses around the necks of their victims.

They dragged the pirates into the tower nearest Richard, and one by one, threw them off the battlements. The ropes jerked them to a stop as they fell, and their bodies twitched and swung back and forth, bumping into each other before they became eternally still. Richard heard some cry out before they were pushed, but it was over quickly.

'All your pirates are gone,' the King looked down at Conan, 'so there is just one viper left to deal with.'

'Your empire is unholy,' the pirate king said, 'it will not last. It is against God and the people.'

'Stop talking, I'm bored of it now,' Henry said.

'Your cruelty and arrogance will be the end of you,' Conan said.

'A bit like you then,' the King laughed.

'You can hang me from the walls, but more will take my place.'

'I'm not going to hang you, that would be too easy,' the King turned his horse away and rode back to the wall.

'William, would you mind bringing down that hammer?' He shouted up.

Mandeville picked his bloodied hammer back up and gingerly picked his way down the rubble.

Richard watched as the King dismounted and took the hammer from Mandeville. He ordered four squires to hold Conan down. The pirate protested and tried to push them away, but they overpowered him and pinned him to the ground.

The King spun the hammer through the air and nodded to Mandeville. 'This will do.'

Conan stared up at the King, his eyes hard.

'This is for attacking my port,' Henry shouted and raised the hammer. He bent his back and brought it down onto Conan's thigh.

The sound made Brother Geoffrey wince.

'What's the matter, have you never seen a hammer beat someone into a pulp before?' Richard asked him.

Conan howled and the King prepared another strike. 'This one is for attacking my Queen,' he brought the iron hammer down onto Conan's hand.

Brother Geoffrey retched over the wall.

'If you have to leave, no one will think less of you,' Richard said to him.

King Henry pulled the hammer back up. 'The last one is for my baby. This one is for John.' The hammer fell right between Conan's legs with a squelch.

Richard had to wince at that, but the monk beside him leant over the wall and coughed.

The pirate king screamed, he screamed loudly, and Richard

wondered if he had time to regret his choices.

King Henry dropped the hammer. 'Prepare the keep, I'm sleeping here tonight. In the morning we'll tear it down. Every last brick,' he said.

Richard felt a momentary urge to push the monk off the wall while he had the chance.

Brother Geoffrey turned round, his face pale, and caught Richard's eye. He shuffled quickly away from the edge of the wall.

The King's knights hauled the suffering and broken pirate king up to the tower, and dangled him from it alongside his comrades. Conan of Saint-Malo suffered greatly for crossing the King of England.

THE BLACK TOWER

The Black Tower stood atop a small mound, a mound that was littered with bodies and two overturned carts. A basket of apples had rolled off the cart and spilled its contents across the grass. Solis pulled the reins from Richard's hands and started to crunch his way through them.

'We keep arriving when everything is over,' Richard said.

'It's not over yet,' Bowman looked up at the stone tower. It was square and four storeys high, the stone around it's exterior a dark black. A wooden palisade ran around the outside of it to protect a few wooden buildings. Men-at-arms ran into the bottom of the tower while others held their horses outside.

'They've got the shields,' Richard looked at their red and yellow chequerboard patterns.

'Exactly, look at the top of the tower,' Bowman said.

Long Tom rode up beside them. 'That man is a beast,' he looked up.

Eustace Martel picked up a Breton with both hands and held him over the battlements. The man squirmed and screamed, but it didn't stop the Martel man from hurling him from the tower like a throwing stone.

The Breton screamed for a second before he hit the ground with a slopping noise.

'Ouch,' Long Tom said, 'I'd hate to die like that.'

'I'd like to move on,' Richard looked away.

'We can't until the earl says so,' Bowman said.

'I know,' Richard replied, aware that he was in a column and couldn't leave it unless ordered to. He glanced down at his red shield and hoped it would be enough to evade Eustace's attention.

King Henry sat on his horse next to Mandeville and surveyed the scene. He pointed at the tower, said something, and Mandeville nodded. The earl turned away and rode down the column behind Richard.

'They'll be garrisoning it,' Bowman said.

'Why? It's tiny,' Richard wondered.

'It's a supply base, so when we leave Brittany, we can come back this way and know we have some food waiting,' Bowman said.

Long Tom coughed. 'It feels very far from home, here,' he said.

Richard thought his face had been darkening every day. 'I'm sure we'll be home soon,' he said.

'We're half way through this at best,' Bowman said, 'the rumour is that Viscount Odo will hole himself up either at Josselin or Becherel, and Josselin is on the west coast.'

'Hopefully he is at Becherel, then,' Long Tom looked at the ground.

Solis ate the last apple within reach and popped his head back up. White foam fell from his mouth and he coughed out a piece of unchewed apple.

'Idiot,' Richard said to him.

Mandeville rode back up and past them, and shouted to the royal mesnie. 'Move on, we ride to Becherel.'

'I told you,' Bowman said.

Richard sighed. 'I just hope it will be a quick siege.'

Richard's first thought on viewing Becherel Castle, was that it was not going to be a quick siege.

'It's almost as big as Castle Tancarville,' he said as they halted on the plain that surrounded it. A village around its base was already consumed by flames, but the walls were tall and stone, and it was situated on a modest hill. The castle walls were a square with solid towers at the corners, and a towered gatehouse faced Richard.

'We aren't going to batter that down any time soon,' Bowman said.

Richard could see carts being unloaded ahead along the

plain.

'The vanguard are already making a camp,' Long Tom said.

'That's where the Martels are,' Richard said, 'so at least we know where not to go.'

Mandeville rode to the royal household troops. 'We camp here,' he shouted, 'opposite the gatehouse.'

The earl pointed out the sites for the royal tent, the hunting hounds and birds of prey. Then he told the knights where to sleep, and finally rode up and pointed to Richard. 'You are wherever you can find space,' Mandeville said, 'but before you get too comfortable, we will raid the area for supplies before they get wind that we are here and hide everything.'

Richard nodded.

'Do we have to?' Long Tom said quietly behind him.

Bowman turned to him. 'If you want to eat while we're stuck in front of this place, then yes,' he said.

Mandeville selected a dozen other knights and ordered some now empty carts to follow them. They turned east and rode away from the growing camp and along a new road. Trees flanked them tightly and soon all Richard could hear was hooves and snorting horses.

'It's not a warm summer,' Bowman flung his cloak around his body.

Richard looked up at the white clouds that floated above the trees.

'It's like the summer just didn't want to go outside. I mean, what's the point?' Long Tom said.

'We need to find that man a good drink,' Bowman laughed.

Richard wasn't sure that drink would help Long Tom very much, but his attention was grabbed by the mill-house that appeared through the trees. At the head of the raiding party, Mandeville cantered his horse on and some of his knights dismounted to enter the two-storey building. A wheel turned slowly on the other side of it and Richard could hear gently rushing water.

'We should head into the village,' Bowman looked further down the leafy road.

'We should wait for the earl,' Richard said.

'We should go back,' Long Tom halted his horse.

Richard backed Solis up and grabbed Long Tom's reins by the horse's head and dragged him off towards the village.

'Stop that,' Long Tom said as his horse went along next to Solis, 'give those reins back.'

Richard laughed. 'Cheer up, maybe some pear liqueur is what you need. Bowman says they love it around here.'

Mandeville watched them ride by and ordered the rest of his knights to raid the village. Horsemen flew into the small farming settlement, which was nearly empty of people.

'They're in the fields,' Bowman said, 'it'll only be the very old and young we find here.'

Richard pulled up in the middle of the village and let go of Long Tom's reins.

The young man's eyes were wild. 'Who do you think you are?' he cried.

'Relax,' Richard said, 'go find something you like. Apparently that's what we're here for.'

Bowman looked around at the small dwellings. 'There'll be pigs inside, and I'm getting hungry.'

'I just can't do it,' Richard said, 'I just see Yvetot burning.'

'Do you think you're better than us?' Bowman looked him in the eyes behind his iron nasal-helm.

Richard successfully fought an urge to look down, and held his friend's bright gaze. 'Of course not, and I'll eat whatever we steal, but I can't help thinking there is a better way to campaign.'

'When you think of it,' Bowman jumped off his horse, 'be sure to let the King know. In the meantime, hold my horse so I can find something for you to eat for the next few days.'

Richard frowned but took the reins that were offered to him. He watched as knights with red shields rode up and down the village and their empty carts parked up in the centre of it.

Mandeville rode into the village. 'Once we've taken everything, torch it,' he shouted.

'You can't just burn it,' Richard said.

'I'm sorry, what was that?' the earl turned his horse to face Richard.

'They're just farmers,' Richard replied, 'they might not even know who Viscount Odo is.'

'Never question my orders,' Mandeville said.

An old woman ran out of a house and tried to make it into the trees on the other side of the village. A knight chased her on his horse and spilt her brains onto the mud.

'Where is the honour in that?' Richard asked.

Mandeville rode closer. 'Where is the honour in a failed campaign due to starvation?'

'Take their food,' Richard said, 'just not their homes.'

'If we take their homes, the rebel lord will not be able to use their taxes to raise warriors, nor their labour to farm his own lands,' Mandeville said.

'Brittany is supposed to owe allegiance to our King,' Richard said, 'so these people are ours, at least once their rulers have been replaced.'

Mandeville looked down at the old woman, her blood seeped down and pooled in some hoof prints. He sniffed. 'A knight must look after himself first,' he said.

Richard frowned. Bowman emerged from a house dragging a pig by its collar, but stopped when he saw how red Mandeville's face was.

'You were happy to spill blood at Saint-Malo,' the earl said, 'so I will refrain from accusing you of cowardice.'

Long Tom, who had gone back to the edge of the village, cantered his horse into the centre. 'Someone's coming,' he said.

'Who?' The earl asked him.

'I don't know,' Long Tom said, 'their banner was red.'

'The King?' Richard asked.

'I doubt it very much,' Mandeville said, 'just a red banner?'

'No,' Long Tom gulped down some air, 'it had white or silver bits around it.'

'White or silver bits?' The earl laughed, 'you would be no good as a herald.'

Richard looked at Bowman, who let go of his pig and ran over to reclaim his horse. The pig squealed and ran back into the safety of its owner's house.

'Lord Tancarville,' Richard said.

'Him,' the earl spat onto the ground.

Bowman remounted just in time to see the Little Lord enter the village at the head of twice as many horseman as

Mandeville had brought.

'This village is ours,' Mandeville said to him, 'you can have the next one.'

The Little Lord brought his horse to a sudden halt with his reins and Richard winced. The young Tancarville considered the village. 'This one looks good to me, I think we'll have this one. You can move on to the next one,' he said.

Mandeville's face already pulsed red, but Richard could have sworn it found a new, darker shade.

'We forage for the King's table,' the earl shouted, 'you will obey me and leave.'

The Little Lord looked over to the knight next to him, who Richard recognised to be Sir John.

'Sir John hates the English,' Richard told the earl.

Mandeville scowled. 'They all hate us.'

The Little Lord rode forwards. 'You don't seem to have many men,' he said.

'Do not threaten me,' Mandeville said, 'to disobey me is to disobey the King.'

The Little Lord's hand went to his sword.

'Draw that, and you have committed treason,' the earl shouted.

Richard backed Solis up in the hope of not being noticed.

'You?' The young Tancarville noticed his movement, 'you can't have my village.'

'It isn't your village,' Richard said.

'I'm not talking about this one,' the Little Lord chuckled, 'I'm talking about my village in Normandy. I will have it.'

Richard pressed his lips together, nothing he could say would defuse the situation.

'Get out,' Mandeville shouted. His knights started to muster behind him, but Richard could see that the Little Lord was right, they were half the number of the Tancarvilles.

Sir John pointed at Mandeville. 'Our lord should be the Constable, he at least is from Normandy,' he said.

Richard was struck by how Sir John and Mandeville shared identical curly blonde hair, although that was where the similarities stopped.

Mandeville held himself much higher in the saddle. 'Sir John, this is not the correct time nor place to debate the King's allocation of titles.'

The Little Lord drew his sword.

'At least you didn't kill someone this time,' Richard said.

Bowman laughed, then clapped his hand over his mouth.

Mandeville's eyes flicked between them with raised eyebrows.

The Little Lord raised the sword. 'I'm going to take Yvetot back, Devil's Centaur, but first I'm going to take this village from you.'

In one moment the two sides went from a stand-off to a full charge with raised swords. Richard drew his just in time to dance Solis away from the Little Lord who howled at him as he missed.

Mandeville raged, and his pommel caught Sir John on the shield and sent him reeling back in his saddle. Richard parried a swipe aimed at his head by a knight, and jumped his horse out of the way of the rest of the attackers. Tancarville knights and squires clashed with the red shielded royal household, and a full battle erupted in the unnamed village.

Some of the Little Lord's men took over the carts and continued the process of loading them with looted goods. Richard thought about attacking them, when he saw the Little Lord turn his horse and ride at him.

'Leave me alone,' Richard turned Solis to face him and they cantered at each other. The Little Lord aimed a cut at Richard's face as they passed and Richard pushed it aside. Both knights turned their horses and charged again.

'Leave me alone,' Richard repeated. His adversary repeated his attack, and Richard knocked it aside again.

'You can't kill me, and I won't kill you,' Richard shouted.

He saw Bowman cut a man's sword-hand down to the bone.

'You have ruined my life,' the Little Lord shouted back at him.

Richard laughed. 'You are possessed, just forget me and you will be fine,' he said.

The Little Lord spurred his horse again. He repeated his attack for a third time, but this time Richard tried to counterattack at the same time as parry. Except it didn't work, Richard collided with the Little Lord and their legs tangled up.

Their mail armour caught together and both horses stopped. The young Tancarville's eyes burned as he raised his sword to strike. This time Richard lowered his head and used the top of his conical iron helmet to headbutt his opponent. He rammed it into the Little Lord's face and the young man cried out and almost flew out of the other side of his saddle. Richard's sword fell out of his hand, so he used both hands to push the Little Lord clean from his horse. The youth hit the ground head first and Richard regained his balance.

'See, just leave me alone,' he said, as a hand appeared on his shield. Another joined it and suddenly Richard was dragged from Solis. He smacked into the mud and banged his head on his shield. He looked up to see Bowman ride by and arc his sword at one of his attackers. It knocked him over and Richard could get up to his knees. He looked around for a sword, but the second attacker grinned at him and thrust for his face. Richard pulled his shield up and knocked the sword away.

'He's mine,' the Little Lord shouted from a few paces away. His helmet was off his red head, and blood poured from his nose and mouth. 'And I'm going to kill him.'

Both of his attackers stepped aside and went to fight other battles, leaving Richard alone.

'At least give me a sword for a fair fight,' Richard said.

The Little Lord raised his shield up to his eyes and walked forwards. 'You'll die quicker this way,' he said, 'you should be thankful.'

'You've gone mad,' Richard stepped backwards. His eyes scanned the road for a weapon, but nothing was nearby. Horses cantered back and forth all around, and he had no idea what was going on.

The Little Lord ran at him. Richard couldn't back-pedal quick enough, so had to stand his ground. He used his shield to block the incoming sword, but the Little Lord used his own shield to punch Richard in the face. It grazed his chin and Richard spun around to get away from him.

'You can't beat me without a horse,' the young Tancarville smiled a red smile.

Richard knew he was probably right. 'Solie,' he shouted.

The Little Lord looked at him. 'What's that?'

'My horse, you idiot,' Richard grinned.

Solis cantered straight past the Little Lord, brushed his shield on the way and put him off balance. Richard guided his horse to his left and threw his foot into the stirrup in one movement.

'Go,' he shouted and grabbed the yellow mane with his left hand. Solis pushed with his back legs and sprang away from the Little Lord. Richard catapulted himself up, but landed on the back of the saddle rather than in it. He cried out in pain before slotting himself into the correct place. He wheeled the horse around and halted.

'What, what?' The Little Lord steadied himself.

Richard grinned. 'It's your choice. I can run you down, or you can ride away from the village,' he said.

The Little Lord looked at the stallion. Solis pawed the ground and steam escaped from his nostrils.

'I can't hold him back for long, give the order,' Richard said.

The Little Lord took a step back.

Solis leapt a stride towards him and Richard made a show of stopping him. Yellow hooves drummed the ground and his neck arched, veins bulging.

The young Tancarville backed off some more. He backed straight into Mandeville's horse.

'I think you better go,' the earl said.

The Little Lord turned and looked straight up into the eyes of Mandeville's white horse. He jumped away and ran back towards the carts. 'Someone get me a horse,' he shouted.

Richard rode up to Mandeville and the two sides started to separate.

Bowman trotted to Richard, breathing heavily. 'I don't know why you even bother to carry a sword,' he grinned.

'I have never seen a man with golden spurs wield one so badly,' the earl said.

Richard ignored them because the Little Lord had found a new horse. The Young Tancarville ordered a retreat, and a few moments later the village was cleared of his men.

'That traitorous little rat,' Mandeville wiped some blood from his sword onto his tunic.

A wounded Tancarville squire picked himself up from the mud and tried to move an injured shoulder.

'Someone help him,' the earl shouted, 'but I will crush that little red headed worm with my hammer.'

'You kept the hammer?' Richard asked.

Mandeville nodded. 'It is good for putting down criminals.'

Richard felt his face, his nose stung to the touch.

'I can see why they keep calling you a centaur,' the earl said, 'most of us can vault onto our horses, but I've never seen anyone call it over first. During a battle.'

Richard patted Solis on the neck, who tried to bite the face of the earl's horse.

'We'll finish taking supplies, then go back and tell the King what he did,' Mandeville said.

Richard nodded.

'And we won't burn the village.'

Richard watched the catapult's arm being tied down before the engineer placed a rock in the bucket at the end of it.

Bowman stood beside him with his hands on his hips. 'I heard that Lord Mandeville found the elder Tancarville before he found the king.'

'I don't care as long as they all stay away from me,' Richard said.

Long Tom stood on the other side of Richard. 'They argued.'

'Of course they argued,' Richard said, 'all they do is argue.'

'The cooks told me that they've been ordered not to serve the Tancarvilles,' Bowman said.

The engineers cleared the area around the catapult and one pulled a rope that released the bucket. The arm snapped upwards and cracked into the beam that stopped it vertically. The stone flew from the bucket and towards Becherel's gatehouse.

It thudded into a burnt-out village building and sent charred wooden beams spiralling through the air.

'Range looks a bit short,' Long Tom said.

'It's their first shot,' Richard said.

'Shame they fired the village,' Bowman said, 'otherwise we could have got right up to the walls behind cover.'

The village still smoked, even though it had been days since their arrival. King Henry had ordered ladders to be made, and piles of them lay about the camp ready to be used.

The engineers cranked the catapult arm back down and loaded another stone. A second catapult loosed its projectile, which spun through the air and hit a gatehouse tower near the ground.

'I can't see that it did anything,' Long Tom said.

'I think it knocked a stone or two from the wall,' Bowman said.

'We're going to be here for months, aren't we,' Richard groaned.

The engineer closest to them suddenly ran away from the catapult and squatted down behind a low bush.

'That's a bad sign,' Bowman said.

Richard didn't need to be told what that was. 'Maybe it's just something he ate,' he said.

Bowman frowned as the rest of the engineers launched another stone towards the castle. It hit the road in front of the castle gate and smashed into it. The huge wooden door rattled in the distance and dust floated into the air around it.

'Didn't even move,' Long Tom said.

'Someone cheer him up,' Bowman folded his arms.

'Why?' Long Tom said, 'Our lords will fall out amongst themselves, as they always do, and we'll all go home empty-handed.'

'As long as we get that ransom,' Richard said.

'If the King's mood is bad, good luck with that,' Long Tom said.

'Right, that's enough of that talk,' Bowman said, 'I need to go and do something less depressing than standing here listening to this one spout his black nonsense.'

'What are you going to do?' Richard asked.

Bowman grinned. 'Follow me,' he said.

Richard followed his tall friend back into their part of the camp, near the royal banner. Fires crackled away everywhere with men sat around them. Bowman found his way to the largest crowd of men, who erupted in a cheer.

'Oh, no,' Richard said, 'this is a bad idea.'

'Worse than listening to Black Tom's doom mongering?' Bowman asked.

'Fair enough,' Richard replied. The knights, mostly out of their mail shirts, sat on logs around a space next to their fire. On the open ground in the middle of them, a knight threw three dice.

'What are they playing?' Richard asked.

The dice landed and the knight who rolled them dropped his head into his hands. Half of the crowd cheered.

'Raffle,' Bowman said, 'you need all three dice to land the same number, otherwise the highest pair wins. You roll until you get a pair.'

Richard frowned.

Long Tom craned his neck to get a better look at the dice. 'Seems like a quick way to lose coin,' he said.

'With that attitude, it is,' Bowman said. He elbowed his way to the front of the group.

'I don't feel great,' Long Tom said.

'I'm surprised you bothered to come with us,' Richard said.

'There's nothing else to do,' he replied, 'and it's my stomach.'

'Stay away from me, then,' Richard said.

Bowman was pushed back by a knight. 'You know the law, only knights can place dice,' he said.

'Come on,' Bowman said, 'who cares, I'm just another man who has time to kill.'

'Let him play,' a knight with a grey beard said, 'it hardly matters what his spurs are made out of.'

The first knight relented and sat back down on his log. He had long brown hair and a face with a chin that jutted out. 'Sit,' he told Bowman.

Bowman rubbed his hands together and sat on a log.

'We're wagering food,' the old knight said, 'seeing as the supplies are about to run out. What have you got?'

'One bottle of that pear liqueur they like around here,' Bowman said.

'Where is it? We need to see it,' the well-chinned knight asked.

'Calm down, Lambert,' the old knight said.

Bowman produced the bottle and placed it on the floor.

'That's not food,' Lambert said.

'And I'm not a knight,' Bowman said.

All the knights burst into laughter and the elder knight slapped him on the back. 'It will do,' he said.

Lambert put a loaf of bread down.

'Mine's got to be worth two loaves,' Bowman said.

'I can gut you for speaking to me like that,' Lambert hissed.

'Enough,' the old knight said, 'we're here to pass the time, not kill each other. Just put another loaf down.'

Lambert put another dark coloured loaf next to the first and scooped up the three dice.

Richard felt a breeze on his neck and looked up. The clouds were dark and moved in a different direction than they'd been going all day.

'I think I can smell rain,' he said.

'I don't feel well,' Long Tom said.

'Go and lie down, then,' Richard said.

Lambert shook the dice in his hand and the knights cheered. He threw them onto the ground. 'Two threes,' he said.

'Not bad,' Bowman reached for the dice, 'for a knight.'

Lambert scowled but sat back.

Bowman rattled the dice in his hands.

Richard looked at the bread and knew he was hungry. Food had been rationed down over the past day, and his stomach rumbled and complained at being empty. Or at least he thought that was why it bubbled.

Bowman threw the dice. 'Three ones,' he jumped to his feet and waved his arms in the air.

'Threes beat ones,' Lambert said.

'You only rolled two of them,' Bowman said.

The knight growled. 'I'm not giving my bread to a squire.'

'I'm ready to wager for more, if you've got any,' Bowman faced him.

The knight stood up and showed himself to be the equal of Bowman in height.

'That's enough,' Richard said.

Bowman ignored him.

Lambert looked Richard up and down. 'What happened to your eye? Cut yourself looking after some sheep?' He said.

'Don't you talk to him like that,' Bowman said.

'Or what?'

'Enough,' the grey-bearded knight got to his feet, 'if you cannot play nicely, then you cannot play. Take that bread and go away.'

Bowman picked up the bread and handed the loaves to Richard.

'Now go,' the old knight said.

'I will wager again, I need more bread for tomorrow,' Bowman said.

'Wager more than liqueur if you want to stay,' Lambert said.

Bowman thought for a moment.

'Let's go,' Richard said.

'No,' Bowman turned to Lambert, 'I'll wager my mail shirt for three loaves of bread.'

Some of the knights gasped.

'Bowman, don't do that,' Richard said.

'You'd wager mail worth a thousand loaves for just three?' Lambert asked.

'Armour is of little use to me if I die of starvation in a week,' Bowman said.

'You can't do that,' Richard said, 'we'll find more food somewhere else.'

Drops of rain started to fall onto the group. Some knights reached for cloaks to hide under.

'Look,' Richard said, 'God is giving us rain to tell you to leave.'

Bowman looked up and rain hit him in the face.

Lambert sat down and reached for his own woollen cloak.

Long Tom ran off towards a hedgerow and disappeared behind it, but not because of the rain.

Richard grabbed Bowman's arm and tugged. 'We're leaving, you can't lose that mail shirt. They'll kick you out of the royal mesnie without armour.'

Bowman grumbled. 'We need to eat.'

'They say Viscount Odo's son is on the way to lift the siege, if he arrives before starvation, then you'll need the shirt,' Richard said.

Bowman softened, shook Richard's hand off and walked away from the gamblers.

'We've got some bread, though,' Bowman said.

'We do,' Richard said, 'and you know what, you're right, I'm not bored now.'

They went back to their fire, threw some logs on it, and hung their cloaks over a frame made out of their lances. Under their shelter, Richard watched the flames of the fire fight the rain that started to come down harder. Bowman opened his pear liqueur and started to drink it. He held it out to Richard.

'No thanks,' Richard said.

Bowman shrugged. 'Suit yourself, but this would warm you up,' he said.

Richard shook his head and waited for the rain to stop. Which it didn't, and soon the grass around them ran with water and the fire spluttered and waned.

'Where's Tom?' Richard asked after a while.

Bowman's eyes were only half open, and his bottle was half empty. 'How should I know?'

'It's been too long,' Richard said.

Bowman burped and took another drink. 'He's depressing anyway, we're better off without him,' he said.

Richard rubbed his hands together. 'I might go and check on him,' he said as a gust of wind blew rain into their shelter.

Bowman coughed.

'We need to get him under some cover if it keeps raining,' Richard said, 'I'm going to look for him.'

Bowman drank some more and didn't look up, let alone get up.

'Fine, I'll go on my own,' Richard got to his feet. The rain hit him in the face when he straightened up, and he looked around as sheets of water drove across the camp. Fires were dying and men had hunkered down under cloaks, canvas, trees or even carts.

Richard walked back towards the hedge where he'd last seen Long Tom, his feet sank into the mud and cold already clasped his toes.

The knights around the gambling fire had dispersed, although Richard could make out Lambert under some blankets. The hedge dripped with water, but there was no Long Tom behind it.

Richard searched around and tried to work out where Long Tom might have wanted to go. He could see back along the camp with the castle in the distance, trees far to the east, and the camp of the rearguard to the north. There were more trees in their encampment, and they had also most of the carts. Long Tom would look for shelter, Richard thought. He pulled his hands up inside his sleeves and trudged towards the rearguard.

The rain pelted him in the back, and he could see the hobbled horses had all stopped grazing and turned their backs to the rain. A thousand horses, he thought, and there was no more grass to feed them.

He left the camp of the main division of the army, and started to walk across the open space between it and the rearguard. A rider rode past him and water splashed up onto Richard's legs. He swore at the horseman and carried on.

When Richard was close enough to see the faces of the sentries around the camp, he stopped. Where his camp had been motionless and quiet, part of the rearguard's encampment was full of slow but steady movement. Maybe they were going on a raid? Maybe they were going home. Richard squinted through the rain and thought he could see the Tancarville banner moving above some tents. The white tent canvas folded in on itself and folded down out of sight. That was clear enough, Richard though. Tancarville must have been fed up with the King and decided to leave. Water dropped from Richard's nose and he sneezed.

He shook his head and droplets flew from it. He sighed. A gust of wind almost lifted him off his feet, and when he recovered Richard noticed that men walked towards the sheltering horses. Tancarville was surely leaving, Richard thought, the King should know about this. He bunched his fists and said a prayer for Long Tom, then spun around to go back. His face was immediately hit by driving rain and it brought him to a halt. When Richard opened his eyes, he saw a figure walking towards him.

The man stopped and rain stung Richard's face. A shiver went down his spine and chilled his bones, because he knew the figure. It was uncle Luke.

Even in the rain Richard recognised the sinewy figure of his uncle. Luke stopped in a puddle, his feet sunk and disappeared under water, but his eyes fell on Richard.

Richard heard the rain spatter into the puddles all around him and could taste the cold in the air.

'Do you know how much trouble you have caused me?' Luke shouted above the clamour of the weather.

'You?' Richard shouted back, 'you have caused me to lose everything. How dare you speak of your trouble.'

His uncle looked him in the eyes. 'You've grown, boy,' he said.

'I saw what you did to my mother,' Richard said.

Luke stayed silent. A sheet of rain cut between them so heavily that for a moment it hid him.

'She did that to herself,' his uncle said.

'No,' Richard said, 'she invited you into our home and you murdered her. You were going to kill me, too. Don't bother lying about it.'

'It cost me a fortune in legal fees after you killed my father,' Luke said.

'I didn't kill him, he died of a broken heart,' Richard said, 'and you broke that heart.'

'You stole my mail too, you're still a dishonest child.'

Richard wiped some rain off his face. 'I took the mail, it's true, but you took my manor and my family. Did you take my father too?'

Uncle Luke sank slightly deeper into his puddle and whatever spurs he wore were submerged. The rain beat down around them and Richard struggled to breathe, so strong was the wind.

'Did you?' He asked again.

Luke's right hand moved inside his cloak.

'That won't work,' Richard said, 'did you know I'm a knight?'

'I do,' Luke replied, 'we were all in your little village when you knelt before the King. We found out who you were. I must confess, your rise in station surprised me. Your insolence in going after your sister, too, that will not be unpunished. Once I am finished here, I will see to her.'

'If you go near her, I'll kill you,' Richard said.

'You will already be dead,' Luke said, 'I can't let you live any longer. No one will look twice at a body on the ground after this storm.'

'You should repent,' Richard said, 'the Lord forgives. Join a monastery and pray your way out of hell.'

His uncle laughed and dragged his feet from the puddle. 'Hell? I think we're already there.'

Richard moved his hand onto his sword hilt. The leather grip was wet, but that wouldn't matter. 'You can't bully me anymore, uncle. You should fear me.'

'I've heard the stories they tell,' Luke said, 'they are just rumours and gossip.'

'As you lie broken on the ground, at the moment of your death, I will show you the scars on my hands, and you will look up at the scar on my face,' Richard said, 'and you will know fear.'

Luke stepped forward, mud stuck all around his leather shoes.

Rain blew into Richard's eyes and he had to shut them. He wiped them clear and saw two things when they reopened. One was a figure in the rain behind his uncle. The second was his uncle's fist.

Richard awoke and looked up at a clear blue sky. Birds sang. The air was fresh and his back was cold. So were his legs. And his hands. He was lying on the ground and everything was freezing cold.

'How's the head?' Mandeville asked. The earl's large frame appeared above him and blocked half of the sky. Which made Richard even colder.

Richard's hand ran up to his head and felt his face. 'My nose hurts,' he said.

Mandeville chuckled. 'He punched you right in it. I don't know what you did to deserve that, but deserve it I'm sure you did.'

'What happened?' Richard recognised their shelter, and Bowman, who was fast asleep where he'd left him.

'I was going to have another word with Lord Tancarville about his son, but we came across your duel first. The other man ran off,' the earl said.

Richard pushed himself up and his head spun.

'Take your time,' Mandeville said, 'you'll come good.'

'My body feels cold, but my head is roasting,' Richard said, 'and everything aches.'

The earl frowned. 'It's spreading around the camp. This wet weather will now also bring both biting insects and more disease,' he said.

The fire had gone out and had been replaced by half burnt wood and wet ash. Richard noticed Long Tom lying on his other side.

'I know there is no love lost between yourself and the Tancarvilles,' the earl said, 'so you'll be pleased to know that they all left during the night. In that rain, imagine that.'

'I was on my way to tell you about that,' Richard rubbed his forehead.

Mandeville nodded. 'They were, however, half of our rearguard,' he said.

Richard swallowed, which stung a bit. 'Will we break the siege now?'

'That is up to Henry,' Mandeville looked around the camp, 'but I can't see how we can stay camped here now.'

Richard kicked Bowman's leg. The tall man groaned and rolled over away from him.

'See to your men, light a fire and dry your clothes,' the earl walked away from their shelter.

Richard turned to Long Tom and kicked him as well.

He opened his eyes. 'What do you want?'

'How are you?'

'Like you care,' Long Tom closed his eyes and pulled his cloak up over his head.

'Where did you go last night?' Richard asked.

'I found a cart to lie under,' Long Tom replied, 'but I'm passing blood, so won't be a burden to you for much longer.'

Richard swore. 'Pray for good health,' he said.

'That doesn't work,' Bowman sat up and rubbed his eyes.

'What doesn't?'

'Praying,' Bowman said, 'I've done it after every heavy night and not once has praying removed my hangover.'

'Did you drink the whole bottle?' Richard asked.

Bowman picked something up, and suddenly an empty bottle flew at Richard's head. He half batted it out of the way. 'That's not funny, I'm dizzy,' he said.

'So am I, so leave me alone for the rest of the day,' Bowman lay back down and turned around.

Richard sighed, was this what having children was going to be like? He thought about the fire and wondered if there would actually be any dry wood to start one with.

He looked up when he heard a commotion at the edge of the camp. Richard pushed aside his now heavy and damp wool cloak and stood up. The world spun for a moment and he had to shield his eyes from the low sun that crept above the woods in the east. Out towards that way Richard saw men scurry around the camp. Shouts floated over the crisp air and some horsemen tore through the diminished fires and huddles of soggy men.

'Bowman,' Richard shouted.

'I'm trying to sleep,' he replied.

'Get up, something is happening,' Richard said, 'something is wrong.'

Bowman threw his blanket aside and looked up. He listened. 'We need to arm,' he said.

Richard kicked Long Tom. 'If you can get up, you need to do so now.'

Long Tom groaned and sat up. His eyes were bleary and he had dark circles around them.

Richard jumped back to the end of the shelter and looked for the linen bag that held his mail. Bowman did the same and they retrieved their armour.

'It's soaking wet,' Richard held up his shirt.

A white-faced rider cantered by and his horse threw up clumps of mud onto them. 'Guy is here, Odo's son is here,' he cried and went on his way.

'No time for the legs,' Bowman said and slid the mail shirt on over his head.

Richard put his on and belted his sword over the top of it.

'Hurry up,' he said to Long Tom, who had only just managed to get to his feet.

A horn blew from somewhere in the camp.

'What does that mean?' Richard asked.

'That we need to get onto horses really very quickly,' Bowman slung his shield over his back.

Richard picked up his red shield, which had dark mud

smeared across most of it.

Long Tom pitched over and threw up outside of the shelter.

'Bowman, fetch our horses and I'll help him,' Richard said.

Bowman swore and ran off as shouts rang out ever louder all over the camp.

Richard held the mail up over Long Tom's head and lowered it down over him. By the time Richard handed him his shield, Bowman appeared leading their horses. Solis was so covered in mud he looked brown. They threw their saddles on as other horses were dragged into the camp.

'What do we do?' Richard asked as he buckled Solis's girth strap tight.

'Get on and look for the earl,' Bowman said, 'although no one can fight in this mud.'

The whole camp was brown, feet and hooves sucked into the mud and each step was effort. Richard mounted and Bowman threw his helmet up to him. 'You'll want that,' he said.

'Are you glad you've got your mail shirt, now?' Richard grinned.

'Shut up,' Bowman helped Long Tom to struggle up onto his horse before mounting himself.

Richard looked to the east but couldn't see enemy troops. Everywhere within the camp men ran or mounted their horses.

'Muster to our banner, then,' Bowman turned his horse towards the royal banner at the centre of their division's camp.

Richard followed and Solis lifted his feet high to step through the mud. He could see the breath from himself and his horse cut through the air as he watched the royal mesnie gathering around Mandeville and his white horse. Although, like Solis, he was mostly brown now.

'A Breton army approaches,' Mandeville said when they reached him, 'remember that we are the King's bodyguards and his reserve. We hold here until needed.'

Richard and Bowman formed up with the rest of the red shields into two long lines facing the woods to the east. A plain of grass lay between the camp and those woods, where a flock of birds flew up from with a great cacophony of squawking.

'That's them, then,' Bowman said.

Richard gripped the lance he'd picked up from a cart. His

fingers were cold and his mouth was dry.

A band of loosely spaced horsemen appeared from the woods from under the startled birds. They rode half way along the plain and stopped. Richard could see the vanguard of his army move forwards on his right, and the rearguard did the same far to his left. In the centre, King Henry's infantry formed a wall of spears and marched out to the edge of the camp.

'Look, a banner,' Bowman pointed towards their left, opposite the rearguard where more Bretons emerged under a white banner with something black on it.

'They aren't riding like we do,' Richard said, 'they're in open order.'

'No, they fight differently,' Bowman coughed.

The Breton cavalry rode with space between them, and they rode quickly. Clumps of grass spun up into the air from their hooves, and they rode up to the rearguard and started to pelt them with javelins. Their riders held spare missiles in their rein hands, and soon English and Norman men and horses started to go down. The Bretons also rode towards Richard and did the same to the infantry of the main division. Crossbowmen returned fire and some Breton skirmishers fell from their horses.

'The vanguard is charging,' Bowman pointed to their right.

'Can you see the Martel banner?'

'No,' Bowman replied as the host of a thousand knights and squires kicked into canter as one, and rode out across the plain. Richard thought it was a glorious sight. Shining metal and charging horses, they looked like he had imagined the charges of Arthur did. The Bretons turned and rode away from them back towards the woods, but they were not fleeing.

'Now come back,' Richard said.

'They're won't,' Bowman replied as the whole of the mounted vanguard seemed to be swallowed up by the trees. At the other end of their line, Richard heard Mandeville swear.

A line of Breton knights filtered through the woods opposite the rearguard and started to canter towards them.

'Proper knights,' Richard said.

The Breton skirmishers got out of their way, and the knights in the rearguard counter-charged. The two lines of mailed horsemen clashed in an almighty crunch.

'That's the loudest thing I've ever heard,' Richard said.

Wood snapped, men cried and horses screamed as the two sides hit each other and fought it out. Richard sniffed the air, grimaced, and looked at Long Tom.

'I had to go,' he replied.

Richard needed to go too, and felt that soon he wasn't going to have any choice about it.

'Do it quietly,' Bowman said, 'the horses are brown already.'

Richard looked at his grinning friend and felt feint.

'Breton infantry are coming at us,' Bowman nodded ahead.

The Breton skirmishers who had used up their javelins on the infantry in the centre wheeled towards the rearguard.

'They're going to flank it,' Richard said, 'we should go and help them.'

'Not without an order,' Bowman said.

The white and black banner seemed to be pushing through the rearguard. Richard wondered if the Bretons were winning.

'Curse the Chamberlain and his treachery,' Mandeville shouted.

'I'm glad we aren't in the rearguard anymore,' Bowman said as they started to be pushed back.

Richard looked at Long Tom, whose eyelids looked to be drooping. 'We can't fight like this,' the young man said.

Bowman laughed. 'This is what war is, young lord, it's sweat, bodily fluids and icy fear. There is no glory here.'

'Or over there,' Richard nodded to the rearguard, whose knights turned and fled back behind the meagre infantry formation that stood waiting to fight.

'The King's here,' Long Tom whispered.

Richard turned around, and sure enough, the long red cloak and golden crown could be seen next to Mandeville.

Around the King there stood a dozen armed horseman that didn't look like they were Norman or English.

'They don't even have saddles,' Richard said.

'Irish,' Bowman said, 'they think armour is for cowards, but if they get close, they as good as anyone else.'

The Irish rode small horses and wore no mail, instead they only had leather breastplates and carried small round shields.

'Is their leader a woman?' Long Tom asked.

Bowman chuckled. 'Who knows, not even the Welsh women fight, but Ireland is even further away.'

Mandeville and the King engaged in a loud conversation with much arm pointing. The Irish cavalry cantered off in the direction of the vanguard, their small horses moving quite quickly enough.

'Here we go,' Bowman said, 'this is it.'

Mandeville spurred his horse in front of the waiting household knights. 'We need to recover the left flank before the Bretons turn on us,' he shouted.

A messenger left the King and tore through the thick mud to the main body of King Henry's main division. The knights, squires and infantry of it started to march forwards and out onto the plain. Richard saw de Cailly's banner at their fore, and said a prayer to keep him safe. He suddenly wished he'd been able to carve a charm into some horsebread for Solis.

'One charge from us and they could break,' Mandeville shouted.

Richard felt the hairs on his neck stand up and looked over his shoulder.

'Jesus, help us,' he muttered as the castle gates opened and horsemen started to leave it.

'One charge had better do it, or they'll finish us off,' Bowman said.

'Are you ready, Tom?' Richard asked.

'At least it stopped raining,' Long Tom held his head up to the sky, 'I didn't want to die in the rain.'

A horn blew and Mandeville shouted. Their line moved forwards but was instantly broken up by the campfires and empty field shelters.

Richard asked Solis to canter, and it felt like they had to jump each step to get through the mud. Cold lumps of it stuck on his face and horses cleared their throats almost in disgust.

'Get into line,' Mandeville ordered from out in front.

'Easy for him to say,' Bowman jumped his horse over a dead fire.

Richard rode around a fire and smacked sideways into another knight. The knight's shield tangled with his spear and

Richard nearly dropped it. Before he knew it, they were clear of the camp and out on the plain.

'Reform,' someone shouted and the knights tried to reform their line as they cantered over the muddy grass and towards the beleaguered rearguard.

Richard held Solis back as he was almost out in front, and other knights and Bowman caught up and eased back into the line. Shields banged on wooden saddles and knees. Richard licked his lips and focused on the Breton skirmishers who had ridden into the flank of the rearguard. They were going to catch them unawares.

Solis bounded over the last stretch of sodden ground quickly and Richard didn't have time to think about it. He lowered his lance along with everyone else and gripped with his thighs and legs as tightly as he could. He stuck his legs out forwards and braced into his saddle.

War-cries rang in his ears but Richard didn't shout. The royal mesnie cantered into the Breton skirmishers with so much force that they pushed them down and went over them. Solis jumped a black Breton horse which disappeared behind and under them as it was knocked over. Richard's lance sunk into something and broke as they rushed into the Breton ranks. The household's charge slowed and Richard swung his broken lance at a Breton who didn't have a helmet. He slumped in the saddle from the blow.

Red shielded knights surged on his right and pushed into the enemy. Richard tried to go with them. His shield pressed into a Breton with dark black hair, and Richard swung down over the top of it to smash down on his head. Richard beat down with the half-lance at any Breton he could reach as the mesnie surged forwards. Maybe the charge would work.

Shouts and cries rose up behind him. Richard held Solis back and a Norman knight overtook him. He looked round and saw almost no one was in their rear ranks. He was the rear rank.

Except for the King and Mandeville, that is, who rode out of the press and towards him. Richard glanced to the centre to look for de Cailly's banner. It flew high above a great mass of warriors, but Richard had no idea how he fared.

The King pointed back towards the castle, and Richard

followed his arm. The Bretons still sallied towards them from the castle. Not more than a hundred mounted men, but nothing stood between them and King Henry. Or Richard.

'To the King,' Mandeville shouted.

Richard rode over and a few knights with red shields peeled off from the combat.

Bowman appeared, sword in hand and helmet gone from his head.

Lambert the knight rode out too, and regarded Bowman. 'You do fight,' he nodded.

'We need to ride away, Henry,' Mandeville said, 'we can't lose you to their charge.'

'I'm not running from some Breton Viscount,' the King shouted.

'Then you'll be captured by one,' the earl replied.

King Henry howled and his face shone almost an orange colour. He slashed at the air with his sword.

'The skirmishers are coming back,' Bowman pointed to the distant woods.

More household knights withdrew from the melee and rallied into a line between the King and the sallying horsemen.

'Very well,' Mandeville said, 'we can match Viscount Odo if God is on our side.'

'Charge them,' the King waved his sword towards the Bretons coming from the castle.

'Here we go again,' Bowman said.

'Where's Long Tom?'

'No idea,' Bowman replied.

'They've got lances,' Richard said as the Bretons started to pick their way through the empty Norman and English camp.

'We've still got swords,' Bowman said.

Richard frowned.

'Maybe get yourself behind me,' Bowman said, 'and try not to drop it this time.'

Richard reversed his horse.

'Take them now,' Mandeville said, 'just as they hit the open ground.'

The mesnie, or at least the ones who had heard Mandeville's recall, broke straight into their charge. The Bretons picked their way through the last of the abandoned campfires.

Their shields were black and white, and Solis's hooves dug into the ground as he accelerated with a grunt.

Bowman and the other knights charged ahead of Richard. Most ducked behind their shields to avoid the Breton lances, but others like Bowman chose to swat them aside with their swords. The Bretons passed through the household and Richard swung his sword at one. It ran down the Breton squire's lance and dug into his thumb. The squire dropped the lance, and probably his thumb, but it wrenched Richard's sword from his hand.

Richard spun Solis around to chase the Bretons who he presumed were heading for the royal banner and the King.

'To the King,' Lambert shouted as his already turned horse tore past Richard. Richard pressed his legs onto his horse and the stallion lurched forwards after the enemy of his own accord.

A Breton's horse stumbled and got stuck in a patch of wet mud. Richard closed on him from behind and snatched the lance from him as he cantered by. He swung the lance into place under his armpit and lowered it as Solis caught up with the Bretons.

Richard aimed the lance at a knight's back and Solis kept his pace to push it into the man stride by stride. The knight twisted around in the saddle but the point had got in too far. Richard pressed his bodyweight into the lance for good effect, then pulled it back as fast as he could. The knight convulsed in a spasm and Richard pointed Solis at the royal banner. The opposing black and white banner headed the same way, and Richard wondered if he would know Viscount Odo if he came across him.

The Breton's hit the King, Mandeville and the banner bearer, just as Richard caught them. His lance went through the back of a knight's head just as he lowered his lance at the King. Richard wasn't sure what happened next. The melee was a swirl of red, black and white, and frothing horses. He knew he snapped his lance twice, and knew he took blows on his shield and that his right arm hurt.

Suddenly the Bretons were gone and Richard sat on his horse

next to King Henry and Mandeville. The bannerman rested the banner on the mud and examined his bloodied left arm.

'I told you, William,' the King grinned, 'this one is loyal. Takes after his father.'

Mandeville nodded to Richard. 'Well done, but this isn't over yet,' he said.

'The rearguard is gone,' the King said, 'they'll come for me now.'

'We need to leave the field,' Mandeville said.

The King spun his horse around on the spot and let out a cry of frustration. 'The centre will hold if we lead these Bretons away from it,' he shouted.

'Thank you,' Mandeville said and shouted to the few household knights standing around the King, 'follow me.'

Richard glanced down at the bodies in the mud, many of which still moved.

'Come on, young lord,' Bowman said, 'at least we're getting off this giant pool of mud.'

The King followed Mandeville, and Richard followed him. They cantered across the open plain, hooves sunk into mud as the sounds of battle faded behind them. Richard could still see the main battle in the centre of the fields, but behind them a group of Breton horsemen were chasing them.

Richard let Solis move and the horse settled into a rhythm behind the King's fine dark grey horse. He started to feel weak and light-headed, so tried to focus on gripping onto his horse. The party raced into the woods and Richard's eyes fought to adjust to the sudden darkness. Wet branches whipped his face and left cold water on his cheeks as they flew between trees and over bushes.

'Are they still behind us?' The King shouted.

Richard snapped his head around for a split moment. 'Yes,' he shouted back. He thought he'd seen Bowman behind him, but hadn't seen Long Tom since the first charge. Solis cantered on and on, and Richard could smell his sweat. The horse's heat warmed the inside of his legs. They jumped into a fenced paddock and sent a herd of grazing horses flying around it in panic.

Mandeville pulled his horse up and turned it around. Richard caught up with him and the King and they formed a line. Bowman joined them with Lambert and three other knights.

'Is this all that's left?' Henry asked.

No one answered because they all struggled to regain their breath.

'If more than five of them come through the trees, we turn and go again,' Mandeville said.

Ten Bretons rode through the trees.

'God's legs, William,' the King said, 'but I am done running. Attack, kill them all.'

The King spurred his horse and rode alone towards the enemy.

'Well, go on then,' the earl shouted and went after him.

Solis followed without being asked. A skirmisher threw a javelin into the body of the knight in front of him, but it meant Richard could stab him in the throat with his broken lance. Another skirmisher launched his missile at Richard, but it only buried itself in the wooden front of his saddle. Richard threw his shortened lance at a Breton and pulled the javelin out of the saddle before it fell out. The King rode alongside him and chopped an enemy's hand whilst shouting at him. The King's red cloak billowed behind him as he moved at speed. Another Breton lowered a lance at him.

Richard cantered to the King's aide and threw his javelin. It flew through the air, missed the Breton, skidded off his lance and into the man's mailed shoulder. The Breton jerked his lance and it skimmed the King's arm instead of his chest, even as the King's sword detached the man's jaw.

Richard stopped Solis because there were no Bretons left to fight.

Bowman gave up chasing the last enemy who galloped away across the paddock and jumped the fence to fade away back into the forest.

'We won't have long before he finds some friends,' Mandeville shouted. Blood seeped from a cut above his eye.

The King turned to Richard. 'One day, I will take you on a hunt with me,' he said.

'Come on, we need to get away from the skirmishers before we find out who won,' Mandeville said.

Richard noticed the wounded Norman knight on the floor, the javelin still through his chest. He moaned and tried to sit up. 'We can't leave him,' Richard said.

'He has served his king well,' the King said, 'we go.'

Richard tore his eyes from the wounded man and followed Mandeville as he took the lead out of the paddock and along a road that headed north. They rode on it where it fell into a valley, the sides of which grew steeper and steeper as they went. They dropped down to a walk as the sun hovered at its high point.

Bowman yawned.

'How's the hangover?' Richard asked.

'Nothing like a battle to clear the mind,' Bowman grinned, 'do you still need to relieve yourself?'

'I did that,' Richard said, 'but my guts still feel like frozen water.'

'Well, just live long enough to die from something else, that's all you have to do.'

'Helpful,' Richard sighed.

The valley curled through the hills, and the small party followed it until the sun started to set.

'I'm cold to my bones,' the King said, 'I think we can light a fire.'

Mandeville nodded and they stopped in the woods for the night. Richard stripped to his underclothes once they'd lit a series of small fires, and everyone tried to dry their sodden garments out. Steam seeped from the fabric, but without bedding it was nevertheless a cold night. Richard struggled to sleep from the pain in his belly, and the hoots from the owls he could hear in the trees. He made the sign of the cross every time he heard one.

When the light of the sun faintly lit the sky above, they remounted. Solis ignored Richard when he caught him, which he knew meant the horse was grumpy.

Bowman mounted without a word, and no one else was in the mood to speak either. They rode out of the trees and back onto the road which lay covered in a thick mist. The road became nothing more than a worn earth track, and cut a path up the hillside and out of the valley. Richard shivered, not a quick shiver, but one that kept going as the rising sun shone onto the other side of the valley.

'I can't wait until we get up into the light,' he said to Bowman.

'Won't be long,' his friend coughed twice.

Richard looked over to the sun-lit side of the valley and found himself envious of the trees there. He couldn't feel his toes. The mist that clouded the valley floor reflected the sunlight too, but when he looked up, Richard could see what looked like mist coming up from beyond the sun-drenched valley side.

'There shouldn't be mist that high,' Richard said.

Bowman looked at it. 'You're right.'

'When I used to ride Solis hard in the winter, he would steam,' Richard said, 'if the Bretons have been riding all night looking for us, their horses would be running hot. They'd be steaming.'

Mandeville stopped his horse and looked where Richard looked. 'By the feet of the Trinity, Henry, I think the boy is right.'

'We better get over the ridge before they do the same, then,' the King kicked his horse on and it cantered up the track. Richard didn't think it was a very quick canter.

They crested the hill and dropped down into the next valley before they found out what generated the steam.

'If we head north we'll reach the Black Tower,' Mandeville said, 'I think we'll reach it before midday.'

'See,' Bowman said, 'I told you the tower was a good idea.'

'I can't wait to sit by a fire,' Richard said, 'although I don't think I want to eat anything for a while.'

Richard slumped down onto the wooden floor near the fire in the Black Tower. The chamber was small and square, but it was quiet and warmth crept across the floorboards from the crackling hearth. Richard smelt the burning ash and almost smiled. He took his tunic off and threw it onto another chair.

'I was about to sit on that,' Bowman said.

Richard let out a rasping cough.

'Fine, you warm yourself up,' Bowman found another chair.

While the King and Mandeville were in the hall on the floor below, Richard and Bowman had been sent up to the top chamber with Lambert.

Richard lay on his damp cloak and rolled onto his back. It was warmer than being outside, and the pressure within his head seemed to be squeezing his eyes.

Bowman let out a loud sigh. 'Make the most of it, young lord,' he said, 'if it turns out that we lost the battle, we'll be riding away from here before dawn.'

'I don't care about the battle,' Richard's head thumped.

'Just give us one good night's sleep, Lord,' Bowman put his hands together.

Richard opened his eyes. 'Are you praying?'

'I don't know why,' Bowman said.

'We'll need more than prayers,' Lambert crouched down by the hearth and held his hands up to it.

'I wish we still had that bread,' Bowman replied.

Lambert looked over at Bowman, rubbed his hands together, then returned his gaze to the fire.

Richard closed his eyes again and tried to relax his body. His stomach refused to unlock itself so he tried deep breathing.

Footsteps pattered down the stone staircase that was part of the chamber. A man in a padded jacket and leather cap flew down the steps. 'Bretons are here,' he shouted and pointed, 'use those crossbows.'

Richard kept his eyes closed. It wasn't real. Maybe it was a joke.

Bowman let out a long sigh that tailed off, then stood up. 'Come on, I told you it wouldn't work.'

'What wouldn't work?'

'Praying,' Bowman walked over to the other side of the chamber where two crossbows lay on a wooden table.

Richard wanted to be angry but he didn't feel like he had the strength for it.

'Get up, young lord,' Bowman's shadow cast itself over Richard's closed eyes.

'I don't want to,' Richard said, 'I've had enough fighting, I've had enough of being terrified. I haven't kept any food down since before yesterday, or drunk anything today, and I still can't feel my toes. My stomach wants to escape out of my rear, and I'm worried it's passing blood but I'm too scared to check. I just want to go home and sit in the orchard as the sun goes down.'

Bowman nudged him with a foot. 'We all want that, Richard, that's why we fight.'

The man from the tower ran back up the stairs with a crossbow and bunch of bolts in his hands.

'I know it's hard,' Bowman said, 'but this is what being a knight is really about. This is why all the rich folk go on week-long hunting trips and sleep on the ground. War is hard, war is pain, war is fear and hunger gnawing at your belly. But it is the world that was made for us, so get your lazy lump of a body up and grow up.'

Richard blinked. 'Grow up?'

'I said you were a man before, am I wrong?'

Lambert laughed from the table with the crossbows. He took one and went up to the top of the tower.

Richard felt almost warm for the first time in two days, but the fire within him hadn't come from the smouldering logs in the hearth. He clenched his fists and pushed himself up, although his head spun for a moment.

'Get up, boy,' Bowman kicked him again.

Richard wanted to cry. He wanted to curl up in a ball and let someone else deal with whatever was outside. He'd had enough.

Bowman kicked him again, harder.

'Ouch,' Richard lurched to his feet, staggered a step, and pushed his chest into Bowman's. Or tried to, as the other man was taller.

'Don't ever kick me again,' Richard said.

Bowman smiled. 'There we are, young lord, you're back with us,' he said, 'now pick up that crossbow and shoot some Bretons.'

Richard growled and stomped over to the table. He picked up the wooden crossbow, drew back the string and slid a bolt into place. He strode past Bowman and peered out of an arrow slit. There was nothing there but open and empty scrubland.

'Wrong window,' Bowman stifled a laugh and pointed to the other side of the chamber.

Richard felt rage pulse through his veins and stormed over to the correct arrow slit. Outside it he could see horsemen beyond the small wooden palisade that housed their horses. The Breton horsemen wheeled around here and there as if they hadn't formed a plan yet. A bolt whistled down from the tower and narrowly missed a horse.

Richard lowered the crossbow and closed his left eye. He aimed at a rider who stood looking up at the tower. His target had a moustache under a brass or golden helmet.

'I think that's Viscount Odo,' he squeezed the trigger. The bolt flew from the crossbow with a clunk, and Richard saw it spiral down and thud into the ground a horse's length from his target. Odo didn't look down.

Bowman appeared next to Richard and handed him another bolt. Richard reloaded and tried again. The bolt embedded itself on the inside of the palisade. Richard swore.

'How about you find a spear and go and man the wall,' Bowman held his hands out for the crossbow. Richard thrust the weapon over, but stayed to watch Bowman take his first shot. The blonde man aimed for only a moment, then squeezed the trigger lever. The bolt sprang forth, arced down and hit Viscount Odo's horse straight between its eyes. The animal dropped and rolled over onto Odo's leg. The horse was dead and lay still on top of the Viscount's leg, and therefore the man was trapped.

Richard sighed. 'Good shot, I suppose,' he said.

Bowman reloaded. 'I imagine the earl will be sallying out to kill Odo while he's trapped,' he said, 'you go help him, and I'll thin out their numbers a little.'

Richard swallowed and went as fast as he could down the storeys and out into the small bailey.

Mandeville was already mounted, and some lightly armoured guards started to open the gate. 'Come on Richard, with me,' the earl shouted.

Richard remembered seeing some carts laden with supplies when he'd entered the Black Tower earlier, and ran over to them. There was no sword, but he took one of the spears and ran out towards the gate as Mandeville and King Henry charged out of it. Richard felt dizzy, so paused for a moment and leant on his spear. He heard a crossbow bolt whizz down from the tower, thought of Bowman watching him, and started to jog out through the palisade.

There were quite a lot of Bretons, and only a handful of the garrison to support Mandeville and the King. Richard felt the onset of the familiar terror of battle, but Bowman's words still rang in his ears and the resulting anger pushed the terror aside. How dare these Bretons continue to keep him awake, he thought. A crossbow bolt slammed into a Breton's chest and he half fell off his horse as it lunged away for the sudden movement of its rider.

Mandeville and King Henry charged the enemy knights trying to drag the horse from their Viscount. The men who had dismounted ducked out of the way and scattered. Their empty horses ran off in all directions, some bumped into Breton knights, and others fled away across the scrubland.

Richard ran towards the Viscount as some of the garrison fenced with the Breton horsemen that milled around.

Richard thrust his spear at a dismounted knight who went back for his lord, and caught him under the armpit. The air escaped his lungs in a rush and he fell. The spear held in both hands, Richard blocked a sword cut from above and pushed another Breton to the ground. A third caught his left arm above the elbow and Richard jumped away in pain. The Bretons cavalry started to group up, and looked to be contemplating a charge. Richard could tell that they outnumbered the English and Normans.

A Breton clutched his stomach as a bolt buried itself in him up to its fletchings. Bolts stuck out of the ground all around, and Richard could see cuts on the lower legs of some of the horses where they had run into the grounded bolts and snapped them.

The charge wasn't Richard's biggest concern though, it was that Viscount Odo was dragged away by his knights, and it didn't look like anyone would be able to capture him.

He ran to join the garrison's infantry who formed a line while Mandeville and the King cantered about chasing various Breton squires.

'While the gentry have their fun, I think we're about finished,' one of the garrison said.

'Looks like it,' another said.

'The garrisons always get it,' the first said.

'Let's just walk backwards until we're back inside,' Richard said.

The first man looked around. 'That's not a bad idea, that is. Maybe we don't die. Not yet, anyway.'

A horn sounded from the trees to Richard's right. The Bretons exchanged hurried words. The horn sounded again and Richard swore he could feel the ground rumble.

The first garrison-man looked down. 'It's shaking,' he said, 'run for your lives.'

The men from the garrison broke and sprinted back in through the palisade's gate, leaving Richard alone.

Richard sighed. He didn't think he could run, he thought he'd just pass out, so he turned back to the Bretons.

Another crossbow bolt felled one of them and some looked up nervously at the tower.

The King and the earl wheeled round, shouted and charged at the assembled Bretons.

'This is madness,' Richard said to himself, standing all on his own by the Viscount's dead horse.

Norman horsemen burst from the tree line. Their horse's heads were down and they were lathered in sweat. More and more poured onto the scrubland.

'They're saving their King,' Richard said quietly.

The Breton's horses wobbled around, they sensed the Norman's approach. Some reared and spun away.

Richard put the butt of his spear on the grass and shouted. 'They're saving their bloody King.' He started to laugh.

The first banner he saw was de Cailly's, and the knights swept over the scrubland like the water falling from a waterfall. The Bretons saw the danger and ran. They peeled off and rode away, and some of the knights chased them. De Cailly and his banner-bearer came to a halt by the King, who had stopped to catch his breath. Richard couldn't hear them, but all three men looked back over at Richard for a moment. King Henry laughed, a laugh that echoed off the wooden walls of the Black Tower. Richard leant on his spear and flexed his left arm, which was sore. He didn't mind though, because now, surely, he was going to be allowed to go to sleep.

CHOICES

In the end, Richard had got two nights of sleep by the reassuring fire in the Black Tower. He'd been able to eat a little too, and although he found walking up and down the tower hard, he felt he was over the worst of whatever had afflicted him since Becherel.

'Long Tom is still bad,' Richard said to Bowman as some time later as they stood in another camp in front of another castle.

Bowman glanced at Long Tom, who lay under blankets by their fire.

'He's shivering,' Richard said.

'I know,' Bowman looked up at the sun which was strong enough to make the day pleasantly warm, 'it's not a good sign.'

Richard exhaled and turned his gaze to the new castle. Castle Josselin sat on top of a long rock formation that ran alongside a river to its south. The walls matched the edge of the rocks and it seemed to have grown out of the natural feature rather than have been made by men. The Angevin camp lay to the north, so when the sun reached its peak, Richard had to squint to look up at the castle towers to his south.

'We aren't going to be digging under that,' Bowman said, 'which leaves through or over.'

'I feel better that this time we're fortifying our camp before building siege engines,' Richard said.

Bowman laughed. 'Our King might be prickly, but he does learn from his mistakes,' he said.

A knight rode by on a horse with visible ribs. The knight coughed as he went.

Richard shook his head. 'I don't like sieges.'

Bowman laughed even harder, then he too coughed. 'Sieges are what a knight spends most of his time doing on campaign. That, or riding around the country burning things.'

'I don't like that bit, either,' Richard replied.

Bowman looked down at the ground, which had at least mostly dried out since the storm.

'I feel like we're not doing anything here,' Richard said, 'nothing useful, anyway.'

'It's a sort of freedom, that's how I see it. No pressure to do anything,' Bowman reached down into a tattered wicker basket by their fire and found a leather container. He lifted it to his lips and took a drink.

'Which gives you an excuse to do that all day,' Richard smiled.

Bowman nodded.

Richard's eyes ran along the collection of pottery containers that were ranged around Bowman's bedding. 'I half think you're actually enjoying being here,' he said.

'I can but try,' Bowman grinned, 'otherwise what is the point of it all?'

Long Tom groaned.

'Maybe you're right,' Richard said, 'but I still have things to worry about. The Little Lord is going to Yvetot, and uncle Luke said he's going to kill Adela. I should be anywhere but here.'

'Relax,' Bowman sat down on the short grass, 'your uncle may have not survived the battle, and the Little Lord is more bark than bite.'

Richard felt his teeth grind. 'If the Little Lord had been in the rearguard at Becherel, I'd feel a lot better now,' he said.

'You can't leave, so forget about it,' Bowman drank some more.

'Sir Wobble better be grateful,' Richard held his hand out.

Bowman passed him the leather container. 'I doubt it,' he said.

Richard's stomach rumbled.

'About time,' Bowman said, 'see, all you needed was a little drink.'

'Good for him,' Long Tom mumbled from under his blankets.

'Do you want something to drink?' Richard asked him.

'What's the point,' Long Tim replied.

Richard gave up and watched the perimeter of the camp as ditches were dug and stakes driven into the ground behind them. Towards the castle, wooden screens were built and placed in position for crossbowmen to use as cover. Some already plied their trade there, sending bolts up onto the walls whenever they saw movement.

Richard hadn't seen many men on those walls so far since their arrival, and he hoped it meant the castle was undermanned. He would find out soon however, because King Henry it seemed, was in as much of a rush to leave Brittany as Richard was.

The ladder still had bark on it. It scratched Richard's hands as he waited with a dozen other men behind the wooden screens. The long ladder was one of six, and all of them waited for the command to attack.

'We didn't have to be here,' Bowman said from the other side of the ladder, 'if you had kept your big mouth shut, we could be standing by the King, protecting him with our big red shields.'

'I need to get home,' Richard said.

'Volunteering to go up the ladder first isn't how you do that,' Bowman said, 'it's how you get killed. The first man onto a wall is granted fine rewards for a reason.'

'I don't have a choice, this has to work. It could be the difference between saving Sophie and losing Sophie.'

Long Tom coughed behind Richard.

'And he shouldn't be out of his bed,' Bowman said, 'what use is a sick husk of a man in a fight?'

'I didn't make him,' Richard said.

'No, but you made the King let you do this, he didn't want you here either.'

'He understands. We both want this castle to fall,' Richard said, 'besides, it's why he gave me an extra mail shirt to wear.'

'A load of extra weight for no reason, if you ask me.'

'I wasn't asking you,' Richard said, 'I'm glad for two layers of armour. Besides, if it helps us take this castle, then it's worth it.'

'The castle will fall all right, but by sitting outside it for a few weeks. They'll lose their nerve,' Bowman said.

'I didn't make you come, either,' Richard said.

Bowman sighed. 'Aye, and I'm questioning myself,' he shot Richard a sideways glance.

Hundreds of crossbowmen lined up all along the outside castle, and their bolts flew up into the battlements. Some hit the wall and snapped, bounced back, or skidded over the top. The defenders kept their heads down, and that was the point.

De Cailly stood behind the ladders with his bannerman beside him. He was too far away to see Richard, but Richard heard him give the order to commence the attack. He unslung his shield from his back and pushed it around to the front of his body. Everyone else holding the ladder did the same.

'Let's go,' Richard said and they all started to walk. They reached the screens as crossbowmen reloaded and shot their weapons. Then they started to run. Richard's legs covered the grass, but he felt the extra weight of his double layers mail. A bolt wobbled through the air towards Richard from a tower. It thwacked into his shield and the point splintered the wood on the inside. Another bolt flew deep into the earth in front of him, and he had to hop over it.

'Nearly there,' Bowman cried, 'keep your shields up.'

Richard didn't have time to do that, because they reached the bottom of the rocks, and he needed to plant the ladder in the ground and hold it firm while others lifted it. That took both hands, and the ladder started to rise with urgency as others helped him. A stone fell from the battlements and landed next to Richard's foot. Another hit one of their companions in the shoulder, and he fell to the ground with a scream.

'Quickly,' Richard shouted as a bolt fired from a tower along the wall rebounded off the wall itself and clattered into the side of his helmet. The bolt deflected away safely, but the ladder was finally vertical.

'Push it onto the wall,' Bowman looked up and tracked its progress. It rested on the stone far above them.

Richard let go of the ladder and put his hand on the new sword the King had gifted him. 'I really hope this was a good idea.'

'It's not, let me go first,' Bowman said.

Richard frowned. 'Sophie, Yvetot, and Sir Wobble are all my problem, so I'm going first,' he said.

Long Tom pushed Richard backwards. 'And you need to be alive to fix it all. Rescue William and kill Guy of Lusignan for me,' he stepped to the ladder and started to climb it.

'Tom, no,' Richard rushed behind him and started to clamber up the rungs.

'Too late,' Long Tom climbed much slower than Richard could, but he was above him and ascending. Richard realised that they were committed. Bowman climbed behind him.

'You're an idiot,' Richard shouted up.

'We're all idiots, idiots dying for another man's cause,' Long Tom said, 'I'm dead in a few days anyway.'

Richard felt a hint of panic well up within him. On the ladder they were nothing but targets. A stone dropped down from the walls and only narrowly missed him. He wanted to look down but was too busy keeping his footing on the rungs, which bowed under his weight.

A bolt hit someone below him because he heard a scream. The ladder started to bow along its whole length, and Richard thought he heard it crack.

He whispered a silent prayer for the ladder to hold as Long Tom neared the top. A defender threw a rock at him, it bounced off Long Tom's shield and put him off balance so he nearly fell from the ladder. Richard caught his flailing leg and put it back on the bottom rung. The leg was damp and Richard could smell a foul odour.

Long Tom gasped, clung onto the ladder, then drew his sword.

'Watch out,' Richard saw the defender come back to the wall with a spear.

The man, wearing a padded jacket, thrust the spear down and Long Tom just about pushed it away. He climbed another step so his head was level with the battlement. The spear thrust down at him and it caught him somewhere in his core. Long Tom cried out, dropped his sword and held on to the spear. The defender tried to wrench it free while Richard tried to climb up the ladder, but his friend blocked him.

The Breton pushed down with the spear with a loud grunt, and dislodged Long Tom from the ladder. He tipped backwards and Richard flung a hand up to catch him. Long Tom fell too fast and Richard missed him, but his hand did land on the spear. Long Tom dropped to the ground and was gone.

Richard gripped the spear tightly and tugged. The Breton had leant too far over the wall and overbalanced. Richard pulled the spear again and the defender fell head first towards him. Richard tilted his iron helmet forwards to take the impact and tensed his body. The Breton crunched into the helmet and slid off Richard. He screamed out and tried to grab Richard or Bowman as he followed Long Tom down to the earth. Once he was gone, Richard looked up and climbed the final few rungs of the ladder.

Spear in hand, he scrambled up onto the wall and jumped onto the parapet walkway. A crossbowman three paces away turned his weapon at Richard and shot it. The bolt hit Richard square in the chest, halted his walk, and he heard the metal tip ping through at least one layer of mail. Pain exploded across his chest. He gasped a breath and lunged with the spear in two hands. The blade caught the crossbowman in the stomach and Richard drove the spear in and pushed the man over. The Breton hit the stone walkway flat on his back with a jolt. Richard withdrew the spear and stabbed it down again into his throat.

Richard jumped backwards because a Breton ran at him with an axe. The axe aimed at his head and he brought the spear up horizontally to block it. He pushed his spear to the side and threw the axe out of the way, then poked the Breton in the face with the blunt end of the spear. The man recoiled with a yelp and Richard heard Bowman shout behind him.

Richard slashed the spear point back at the axeman, whose head suddenly jerked as a bolt from outside the castle went through one ear and out the other.

'Dammed crossbows, a coward's weapon,' Bowman said as he caught up with Richard. Richard looked down and saw a bolt had slashed open Bowman's trouser leg.

'Are you alright?' Richard asked

'No,' Bowman shouted, 'I'm on a castle wall and everyone wants to shoot me.'

'Long Tom's dead,' Richard said.

'I know. Now get a move on, we need to get off this wall,'

Bowman pushed Richard along the walkway which wasn't wide enough for him to overtake. Several bodies blocked the way still further.

Richard saw the tower and started to run towards it. Each breath felt like his chest would split apart and he had to slow himself. A ladder landed on the wall next to him as he ran past it. A Breton appeared in the doorway into the tower and his brown eyes locked with Richard's. The Breton stepped back and the door slammed. Richard clattered into it and tried to batter it down with the bottom of his spear.

'It's no use, he's bolted it,' Bowman said.

Richard turned around and looked at the tower at the other end of the parapet.

'We need to get there,' he shouted.

'Why is no one else from our ladder up?' Bowman shouted as Richard brushed him aside and started to run for the open tower. A crossbow bolt hit the wall in front of him and he jumped the fragments as they tumbled down by his feet.

The Breton crossbowman lying on the wall with blood pouring from this throat tried to catch Richard's leg as he ran. Richard tumbled, dropped his spear, and fell awkwardly onto his shield.

'Keep going,' Bowman shouted and finished the Breton off as Richard scrambled back to his feet.

He glanced down the wall where they'd come up, and saw the ladder on the ground outside, snapped in two. Bodies lay around it but he didn't have time to pick out Long Tom's.

'Don't count your blessing yet,' Bowman said, 'if that door closes we're just as dead.'

Richard put every bit of energy he had into running. His lungs stung and his feet pounded the stone. The doorway came up fast, and it was still open.

A Breton appeared in it.

'Not again,' Richard shouted.

The man spat and stepped back to close the door.

'Not yet,' Richard cried and thrust his arm into the gap as the wooden door closed. The door slammed shut right onto Richard's outstretched limb. The wood crunched into his forearm and a pain seared up it.

Tears burst from his eyes and he cried his loudest cry.

Bowman crashed into the door, punched it open, and released Richard's arm. Bowman bundled into the tower and Richard heard the Breton inside die.

Men from the second ladder got onto the parapet and rushed towards the open tower. Richard stepped out of their way and looked down at his arm. The mail showed no damage, but he could feel his skin and muscles were indented in the shape of the door. Knights and squires ran into the tower and Richard started to feel light headed.

Bowman emerged from the tower, a splash of blood across his mail shirt, and held Richard's arm. 'Move your fingers.'

Richard made a fist and released it with a gasp.

'Good,' Bowman said, 'but it's that cursed bolt I'm worried about.'

Richard looked down and examined the white fletchings on the bolt that hung loosely out of his mail shirt.

'I need to sit down,' Richard slid down the wall.

'You'll feel cold soon, but that will pass,' Bowman said.

Richard hoped he was right, because the cold hit him like the waves of rain had hit him just before his uncle had knocked him out. Ice tore through his veins and stabbed his guts. He felt panic resurfacing. Even breathing softly hurt.

Bowman crouched down over him. 'Even if you die, Sir Wobble will be jealous of this one,' he said.

'Sir Wobble can rot,' Richard wheezed.

'Oh,' Bowman said, 'you're missing a finger too. That axe I expect.'

Richard's eyes crept down to his right hand, where he was indeed missing his little finger. The blood made him feel sick, and the last thing he remembered thinking was how ridiculous that was.

Richard woke up in a proper bed, in a chamber with tapestries on the wall and a fireplace rather than a hearth.

His first breath hurt, but the second hurt a little less. He lifted his right arm, which was beyond sore, and his right hand was bandaged around where his little finger had been.

'We shouldn't have done it,' Bowman sat on the bed next to

him, his back up against the wooden headboard.

'How long have you been there?' Richard asked.

'Me? As long as you've been lying here. This bed is the softest thing I've ever sat on,' Bowman said.

'Where are we?'

'Castle Josselin, in the Viscount's own chamber,' Bowman said, 'the King said as you took the castle, you could sleep in the viscount's own bed until you're able to walk.'

'We took the castle?'

'Of course. The Bretons apparently thought the castle could not be taken,' Bowman yawned, 'but they're all dead now, so what did they know.'

'Long Tom,' Richard said softly.

'He fell,' Bowman said, 'but that is why you got onto the wall.'

'He took the castle, not me,' Richard felt water in his eyes, 'and he died because of me.'

'That he did. I wouldn't take it too badly though, young lord, he only had a few days left at best. Your impatience gave him the chance for a glorious and quick death.'

'I thought you said there was no glory in war,' Richard said.

Bowman didn't reply and heaved himself off the bed. He walked over to a shelf on the wall arrayed with cups and pottery. He poured himself a drink and remained facing away from Richard.

Richard tried a deep breath but the pain stopped him half way. He thought he was going to cry, just as the door to the chamber flew open.

'The hero,' de Cailly entered with a smile. He stopped smiling when he saw Richard's expression. 'They said you were wounded, but not how badly.'

'My chest,' Richard rasped and swallowed his tears, 'the bolt ripped through both mail shirts, but barely managed to pierce my skin by a finger's width.'

De Cailly stood by the bed, his eyes wrinkled with concern. 'I'm told someone reliable treated you, but you should thank God for your second mail shirt,' he said.

Richard nodded. 'I thank the King. I'd like to keep the second shirt, do you think he'll want it back?'

De Cailly laughed. 'He'll have forgotten he gave it to you by now.'

'Both of our sets of leg mail are still somewhere outside Becherel, so I think it's only fair,' Richard said.

De Cailly shrugged.

'I think it broke a rib,' Richard felt his chest around the wound.

'Those heal,' de Cailly said, 'although they do hurt. I broke one once after a hunting accident. I fell from my horse when a boar went for it. Landed right on my chest and I felt the rib go. It was Lord Tancarville that wounded the boar and enraged it.'

Richard nodded as de Cailly rubbed his rib that seemed to remember having been broken.

'When I asked the King what your reward would be for taking the castle, he gave me a very surprising answer,' de Cailly said.

'Is he giving me the ransom?'

'He is, even though young Sir Wobble can hardly be of any account to him,' de Cailly looked at Bowman, 'and I can't believe the two of you are still together, I always thought you argued far too much.'

Bowman looked inside a second pottery jug.

'I owe Sir Wobble,' Richard said, 'we can at least ransom him now.'

'You aren't going anywhere. That rib needs to heal before you go riding across the country.'

'The Little Lord told me he was going to take Yvetot,' Richard said.

'I see,' de Cailly's face dropped, 'a traitorous brood. I can ask the King for a few of his men to take back with me to Normandy. I can go straight to Yvetot, to stop him if I can.'

'You would do that? Even though Yvetot isn't yours anymore?'

'I'd march to the Holy Land if it meant I could slap the Little Lord across the face again,' the older knight smiled.

'Thank you,' Richard felt tears on their way again.

'King Henry will remember your name,' de Cailly said, 'you have left quite a mark on him. He says you've saved his life, as well as his Queen's. When Sir Wobble finds out about all of that, he's going to be extremely jealous.'

'He helped to save the Queen,' Richard said.

'Did he? The stories are all about you, you and your horse that swings spears at your enemies and jumps trees. I confess, I don't know what to believe,' de Cailly chuckled.

'Not much,' Bowman slammed down his cup.

'Either way,' de Cailly said, 'the King will have documents drawn up to extract the ransom from his account with the Templars at La Rochelle. Then you can go and rescue Sir Wobble.'

'Bloody Templars,' Bowman grumbled.

'The bad news,' de Cailly said, 'is that the wretched monk Brother Geoffrey has been given responsibility for the ransom, so he'll be going with you.'

LEFT OR RIGHT?

Richard broke off a piece of horsebread and held it out to Solis. The horse sniffed it but turned his head away.

'Don't be like that,' Richard held up the bread higher, 'I know I promised I wouldn't put you in a ship again after we landed in Normandy the first time.'

Solis snorted.

'Fine,' Richard said, 'I know I have broken that promise three times before today, but please eat before we set sail.'

In his sling, the palomino stallion threw a leg out backwards and his iron shoe struck the side of the ship with a bang.

'Have it your way,' Richard dropped the bread in the food trough that he shared with his neighbour. The neighbouring horse was smaller and rounder than Solis, and had a much thicker chestnut coat. The chestnut horse went to investigate what Richard had dropped. Solis pinned his ears back and lashed his teeth out at the horse, who recoiled in surprise.

'Your horse is rude, does he get that from you?' A voice asked from behind Richard.

He turned to see a woman with a round face, brown eyes and long brown hair.

'Do I know you?' Richard looked hard at her. He was sure he'd seen her face somewhere before.

'I think not,' she said.

'Your accent,' Richard replied, 'it isn't Norman or French. It sounds closer to Breton, but there's something different about it.'

She looked at Richard.

'I know,' his eyes lit up, 'you're one of the Irish riders we saw

287

at the Battle of Becherel.'

'Here we have a learned man, do we?' She smiled with her eyes.

'I can read,' Richard lifted his chin, 'and write a bit, too.'

'Oh, well, somebody had better make you an archbishop before all of your talents go to waste,' she said.

'I don't have time for this,' Richard walked past her and towards the deck, 'and my horse isn't rude, he's just upset with me.'

The woman watched him go.

Richard walked onto the deck of the cog and went over to the railing Bowman leant on.

'Did it work?' Bowman asked.

'He wouldn't eat it,' Richard said.

'He nearly tore a chunk from my horse, too,' the woman said. Richard sighed.

Bowman turned to look at the newcomer. 'Young lord, won't you introduce me to your new friend?'

'She is not my friend,' Richard kept his eyes on the Breton port that started to drift very slowly away as their ship's sail began to fill properly.

'Your friend with the rude horse and a yearning for an archbishopric is a lord?' The woman asked.

'I have no idea what you're talking about,' Bowman said.

Even though he wasn't looking, Richard knew exactly the look that was on Bowman's face.

'He was just boasting to me how he can write a bit,' the woman said.

'He does like to boast, but he's a knight, they do like to do that,' Bowman said.

'You're not a knight, then?' The woman asked.

'My spurs are iron and rust,' Bowman grinned.

'Shame,' the woman looked Bowman up and down, 'you at least managed to amuse me for a moment.'

'Wait, you want a knight?' Bowman asked.

'No, I do not. Something higher,' she said.

'Who are you?' Bowman asked.

'I am Eva of Leinster.'

Bowman narrowed his eyes. 'From Leinster, or of Leinster?'

He asked.

Eva smiled and Richard turned around just to see Bowman's face.

'Why are you talking to us?' Richard asked.

'Because you had golden spurs and a well bred horse. Unfortunately, you and your horse are both intolerable.'

'You're looking for a husband?' Bowman's eyes lit up.

'Not quite, but close enough,' Eva said, 'I don't suppose either of you would fancy a very lucrative contract to fight in Ireland?'

Richard looked at Bowman, who opened his mouth.

'We do not,' Richard snapped.

'Why not?' Bowman asked, 'Ireland is very, well, very green I've heard.'

'Like you, I don't know anything about Ireland,' Richard said, 'except that it is north from here, and we are going south, because that is where Sir Wobble is.'

'Wobble? A curious name. Your Norman names sound like bad jokes to me,' Eva said.

'I find it curious that a woman from Ireland is sailing on a ship bound for La Rochelle trying to hire mercenaries,' Bowman said.

'No stone to be left unturned,' Eva said, 'that's what they say, isn't it?'

'Did the whole stone of England refuse you, then?' Richard folded his arms.

'See, you're rude. To cut a very long tale down to the length you'd understand,' Eva said, 'my father is the King of Leinster. Except he's been forced out and your King Henry said we can hire English or Normans to help us, if we can find anyone who will.'

Richard laughed and didn't bother trying to contain it. 'Bowman, you've got no chance at all. She's a bloody princess.'

Bowman frowned. 'Don't mind him,' he said, 'he is prone to rudeness and selfishness.'

'This isn't an Arthurian romance,' Richard said, 'she isn't just roaming Christendom looking for a worthy husband.'

'Well,' Eva said, 'I am supposed to be finding a husband, but one who will give my father an army.'

This time Bowman laughed. 'See, young lord, sometimes you

are wrong as well as rude.'

'Truth be told, I'm hoping for a husband who owns land in a place where it isn't always raining,' she said.

'That's why you're sailing south,' Richard nodded.

'My forlorn quest continues,' Eva walked over to the railing and watched the port get smaller. Seabirds wheeled overhead and the cog started to sway with the waves.

'I'm tired,' Richard said, 'I can hardly breathe and my arm doesn't work.'

'What happened to your finger?' Eva asked.

'His horse ate it,' Bowman laughed too much.

Richard walked away from the railing and went to find somewhere comfortable to spend the voyage, because if the weather turned and the waves grew, his broken rib was going to be unbearable.

To Richard's great relief, the weather held, and Richard managed to avoid both Bowman and Eva until La Rochelle was sighted. When he went back on deck he saw Brother Geoffrey for the first time, which made Richard wonder if the monk had hid below deck for the whole voyage too.

Richard was able to successfully feed his horse once they were both on the dry land of La Rochelle's dock. Eva led her chestnut horse from the cog, and Solis watched them walk by with his ears back.

'Neither of you like her, it seems,' Bowman grinned.

'It's not that,' Richard fed Solis another chunk of horsebread, 'it's that she clearly doesn't like me.'

'I did think she had good sense,' Bowman stretched his legs and looked down the street that led to the town square.

Richard followed his gaze. 'I'll actually miss Long Tom when we stand in the square again.'

Bowman didn't reply, so Richard led Solis away from the port. Their instructions from the King had involved seeking the Queen out, who had remained in the safety of La Rochelle. Apparently she was living in the mayor's house which was on the main square, so that was their destination.

It turned out the mayor was also the magistrate who had sentenced Simon the Quiet to death. His two-storey house was a hall that fronted onto the cobbled square, with wings that ran back from the hall to create a U shaped complex. They lodged their horses in the stables that made up one wing. The long-haired chestnut horse was already there, and Richard decided to let Bowman put his horse between it and Solis.

The mayor's hall had more windows than any other hall Richard had ever been in. Warm light spilled in and warmed the floorboards under his feet. A fireplace was being built into one of the walls, but for now a hearth crackled away in the middle of the room, filling it with a sweet-smelling smoke. Red and blue painted patterns adorned exposed beams, and clearly new tapestries, not as yet bleached by the sun, hung on the walls.

'That's the magistrate,' Bowman elbowed Richard once they'd entered. The magistrate/mayor wore his gold chain around his neck, and despite the heat, his fur-lined cloak. Beads of sweat ringed his face. In his chair however, was Queen Eleanor, and she spoke to a man dressed just as Pierre the vintner had been. Her two little hairy dogs played with each other at top speed around the hall, ignored by everyone.

The Queen's eyes briefly landed on Richard before they went back to her audience. She waved the man away and called over. 'You, was it Ralf or Richard?'

Bowman snorted a laugh.

Richard stepped forwards and confirmed his name as he bowed. As he bowed, he clutched his chest and a cry of pain slipped from his lips. One of the little dogs tore over to Richard and started barking at him. The other dog who had been chasing it tried to corner sharply and fell over.

The Queen frowned. 'I sent you home to recover, yet you appear before me in pain. And if I'm not mistaken, short of a finger,' she said.

'The King granted us the ransom for William, if I served him in Brittany,' Richard glanced warily down at the small but needle-like teeth of the dog that barked at him.

'I see,' she replied, 'I see he just had to squeeze something more out of you.'

Richard rubbed the skin above his broken rib, and made a mental note that he needed to avoid developing that as a habit.

He made an effort to go down onto one knee and hold a hand out for the yapping dog. It sniffed his hand, looked up at him, and rolled over onto its belly. Richard gave it a quick fuss.

The Queen smiled. 'I trust the revolt in Brittany has been suppressed if you are here?'

'It has,' Richard heaved himself to his feet with a flinch.

'Good, and is my husband riding south to help me?'

Richard squirmed. 'I wouldn't know.'

'I see,' the Queen sighed, 'very well. We will ransom William back and then I will see about hobbling the Lusignans, and restoring order to Poitou.'

Richard nodded.

The Queen pointed to one of the men who stood along one side of the hall. 'You, go and tell Nicola of Aachen the time has come,' she said.

The man scurried off.

'Nicola?' Richard said.

'The Lusignans have granted her safe passage to arrange the handover of the ransom and return of your friend. Now you are here and the King has approved it, she can begin that task.'

'Thank you,' Richard said.

'You look like you need the waiting time to rest,' the Queen said, 'but I have a proposition for you.'

Richard raised his eyebrows. He'd had quite enough of royal propositions.

'Even a Queen needs to surround herself with strong men, as well as the less glamorous pious churchmen and wily clerks. I am inviting you to join my household. If you so wish it.'

Richard stammered and mumbled.

'Well?' She asked.

'That is a prestigious offer, the offer of a lifetime, and I am truly honoured by it,' he replied.

'But?'

'I have land to attend to, and my absence harms it and my family,' Richard said, 'at another time I would gladly accept, but I must see to my duties at home first.'

The Queen considered Richard. 'I believe you are sincere. No matter, I extend the offer to William, provided that he survives his captivity well enough to serve me,' she said.

'Thank you,' Richard started to bow.

'You are excused bowing,' she said, 'and you are welcome to stay here until you are ready to deliver the ransom. Staying somewhere civilized will do your wounds good.'

'You are very generous,' Richard stepped back.

'So, he can be polite when he wants to,' Eva said from the side of the room. She stood with her arms folded and tapped her foot. 'Why can he skip the queue for your audience?'

The assorted onlookers, knights and dignitaries all glared at the foreign newcomer.

'Should I know you?' The Queen asked slowly.

'You should, but you don't,' Eva replied, 'I am Eva MacMurrough and I am here to ask the knights of this land to come and fight for my father in Ireland. The King of England has allowed it.'

'I know of you,' the Queen cracked a smile, 'and while I will not permit any knights in my modest household to join your venture, I shall not stop you asking others.'

'That is so very kind of you,' Eva said flatly, in such a way that Richard wasn't sure if she meant it or not.

'The rumours that have reached my court from Ireland are usually of little interest to me,' the Queen continued, 'except for the tale of a girl who rides astride like a man, wears mail, and hangs a shield around her neck. A singer from Ireland recited a poem about her, and how she challenged her future husband to a duel. He sung that she did so in order to kill him so she could avoid marrying him. The song ended in his long and painful death.'

'It wasn't a duel,' Eva said, 'and he died quickly.'

Gasps filled the hall and Richard nudged Bowman. 'You still interested?' He whispered.

Bowman only grunted in reply.

'I for one have no ill will towards a woman who can stand up for herself,' the Queen said, 'the world is changing. There is an abbey in the Alsace where a woman has just started to write a manuscript. Can you imagine that? And if the need arises I shall lead an army to restore order in Poitou myself.'

'Will you send out word of my offer across Aquitaine?' Eva stepped forward out of the crowd.

The Queen thought for a moment. 'No, I need my knights here.'

'I'll just go ask the King of France, then,' Eva said, 'he'll be east of here, am I right?'

All whispered conversations in the hall stopped.

'She's the rude one,' Richard whispered to Bowman.

The Queen pressed her lips together. 'Do not push me, but if you wish to ask that poor excuse for a man for help, then do not travel east alone. Go with Richard, or was it Robert?'

'Richard.'

Eva sank. 'Him? Is there no one else going east? In the whole of this place?'

'No, the last person to ride east was me, and I very nearly didn't come back. If it wasn't for Richard there, I wouldn't have,' the Queen said.

Eva's eyes peered at Richard. 'You don't say?'

'He will depart in a few days, two weeks at most. You are also welcome to stay here until you leave.'

'Stay here with him, but he is so very rude,' Eva said, 'all I've found is rude men. In the Breton port the men were all rude or violent. They roved around stealing and throwing their size around, like red and yellow devils in plain sight. Those monsters were the only ones willing to take up my father's offer.'

'Make a complaint to one of my clerks and be gone,' the Queen pointed over to one of the writing desks in the hall.

'Red and yellow?' Richard asked.

Eva tilted her head. 'Why, yes, red and yellow devils.'

'Red and yellow chequerboard colours?'

Eva nodded.

'Did they accept your offer? Are they on their way to Ireland' Richard asked.

'I turned them down once their ill manners became clear,' Eva said, 'they are not going to Ireland. They said they were coming here, actually.'

'Here?' Richard's stomach twisted up.

The Irish princess nodded. 'Come to terrorize the poor people here, I imagine,' she said.

'No,' Richard said, 'I think they're here to terrorize me.'

'Rude, and also over dramatic,' Eva said.

'Enough,' the Queen said over her, 'I don't have time for whatever this is, both of you leave the hall and let me get back to my duties.'

Bowman turned and tugged Richard's sleeve to drag him out of the hall.

'That arm hurts,' Richard took his leave by himself, 'let's go find somewhere to rest away from that Irish woman.'

'Of course,' Bowman said, 'you should definitely keep far, far, away from her.'

Richard successfully managed to spend the following days away from Eva because he barely left the guest chambers at all. He tried not to move much, because that seemed sensible to allow his rib to heal, but it still hurt on the day he went into the stable to see Solis, and saw a familiar shaggy mare in the stall opposite.

'We'll be going away today, then, Solie,' Richard stroked his horse's nose. On his way back to their chamber he met Bowman.

'She's back,' Bowman said.

'I know, I'm going to pack,' Richard replied.

Bowman carried his bags of mail and tied them onto the back of Solis's saddle for him. 'I know you're hurting, but I'm getting bored of being your servant,' Bowman told him.

Richard managed to put his horse's bridle on himself. 'See, I'm getting better, and I'll wear at least one of those mail shirts tomorrow,' he said.

'Whatever you say, young lord,' Bowman replied and got his own horse ready.

Eventually Nicola returned for her little horse, hitched it to her cart, and drove off to pick up the ransom from the Templars. She returned soon after with chests stacked up in her cart, Brother Geoffrey by her side, and a handful of the Queen's squires on horses.

'Don't we get more guards than that?' Richard asked once he'd mounted Solis and they'd ridden into the town square.

'Sometimes it's better not to draw too much attention,' Nicola said from her seat behind her mare.

295

'Good luck with that,' Richard watched Eva enter the square behind them. In her wake were a dozen Irish men on horseback, riding their small horses without saddles.

'Do we call them knights or squires?' Richard asked.

'Just men,' Bowman said, 'I don't know if the Irish even have knights.'

Nicola frowned. 'I had heard about her, but I was hoping she'd be less visible.'

Eva rode up to the cart. 'Are we going, then?'

'I had been waiting for you,' Nicola cracked the reins and Three Legs started to pull the cart.

'That's an awfully heavy cart for one horse,' Eva said.

'She'll manage,' Nicola replied, 'no one thinks she can haul a heavy load, so hopefully no one will bother to look at it. At least until they see you.'

Richard asked Solis to walk and they rode out of the square and out of La Rochelle. As he rode through the town gate, Richard sniffed the air and looked up.

'Is that Simon the Quiet?' He asked.

'Aye,' Bowman said, 'certainly smells like him.'

Simon's body hung in a cage from the gatehouse, and had been decomposing for several weeks.

Eva looked up but rode on impassively.

'She might be as tough as she says she is,' Bowman said.

'She has stolen your eyes,' Richard said, 'and women don't fight.'

'They do, you know,' Eva shouted from behind the cart.

'They eavesdrop too,' Richard shouted back.

Eva cantered her horse up to Richard and Bowman. It clattered on the hard road that led out into the fields around the town.

'Even your women fight,' she said, 'do you not know of Isabel of Conches, who rode in full battle dress to war a generation ago? She was a Norman like you.'

'I'm not Norman,' Richard said, 'the Normans in Normandy made that very clear.'

'You look like a Norman, smell like a Norman, and speak like a Norman,' she replied.

'Smell?' Richard turned to look at her, 'can you stop bothering me, I'm not interested.'

'Suit yourself,' Eva dropped back to ride with her compatriots.

'Speak for yourself,' Bowman said quietly to Richard, who rolled his eyes back in return.

The following day Richard struggled into his mail shirt, but not without discomfort.

'You've only done that to prove me wrong,' Bowman said as they rode out of some woods and through a village whose houses terraced up a steep hillside. The village tanner's building was on the road and Richard covered his mouth as the sharp smell of urine crashed into his senses.

'The other road was easier last time we rode east,' Bowman glanced up at the sleepy village.

'Hopefully this one is quieter,' Richard replied, 'I didn't like the donjon at Niort either, I'm glad Nicola is leading us around it.'

'That was your own fault. In fact, that whole episode was your fault,' Bowman replied.

'That's why we're here. Although I'm blaming Sir Wobble at least as much,' Richard tried to rotate his right arm around within his mail but it seemed heavier than before.

The next village also hugged a hillside, its fields strung out in a wide valley that housed a meandering river.

'Look,' Bowman pointed up the edge of the village where three houses and some small barns lay as burnt-out husks.

'Lusignans?' Richard asked.

'Could be,' Bowman said, 'but I'd be putting on that second mail shirt if I were you.'

'When we next rest,' Richard replied, 'although knowing Brother Geoffrey, that will not be too long. I can hear him complaining again.'

Richard and Bowman halted at a fork in the road and waited for the cart and squires to catch them up.

Brother Geoffrey considered each fork. 'The right one, God favours the right,' he said.

Richard watched Nicola sigh within herself. 'The right fork turns south, and away from the village of Exoudun, which is where we are to make the exchange,' she said.

'You should never choose left,' Brother Geoffrey said.

Richard turned Solis to face the cart. 'Nicola arranged the meeting, so she knows the way. Have you ever been here before, monk?'

Brother Geoffrey closed his eyes. 'Choosing the path of evil will leave us short of divine support for our mission,' he said.

'Heaven, help us,' Nicola grumbled.

'Heaven's help is precisely what I'm trying to encourage,' the monk said.

Eva rode up to the cart and her horse sniffed Three Legs. 'What is all this fuss about? The old woman says the way is left, so clearly it is left that we should be going.'

'I'm not being ordered around by two women, of all things,' Brother Geoffrey tried to tug the reins from Nicola.

'Get off,' she slapped him away.

'I don't know who you are, old monk,' Eva said, 'but I am sure that I'm of a higher station than you. If anyone is in charge of this rag-tag party, it will be me.'

'Preposterous, you're not even English, let alone Norman,' Brother Geoffrey replied.

Richard turned Solis to the left fork and started to ride that way.

'Where are you going?' The monk shouted after him.

'The way you're going, you just have realised it yet,' he shouted back.

Bowman chuckled, tore his eyes from Eva, and took the same path.

'I'll have you all thrown into a donjon,' Brother Geoffrey shouted, 'the King put me in charge.'

Eva pushed her horse on too. 'I haven't yet found a man on this continent worthy of being in charge of me.'

Nicola laughed, coughed, then cracked the reins to steer Three Legs down the left fork.

'This will end in ruin,' the monk mumbled as the cart hit a bump in the road.

'Can we just push him off the cart and leave him?' Bowman asked

Solis's ears swivelled to the ditch by the road ahead. Richard rode by and wrinkled his nose up at a bundle of cloth covered in mud at the bottom. It smelt the same as Simon the Quiet had hanging from La Rochelle's walls.

'If we throw the monk out, he'll end up like whoever that was within two days,' Richard said.

'That was my point,' Bowman grinned at him.

'I heard that,' the monk shouted.

Richard asked Solis to walk on again as the cart caught them up.

'Are we sure we can trust the Lusignans at the exchange?' He asked.

'Of course not,' Nicola replied, 'that's why we've been sent, rather than anyone high ranking.'

'Who you call not-high-ranking?' Eva said loudly.

Nicola kept her face to Richard. 'If the Lusignans wish to make a business of ransoms, they need to deliver their hostages safely, otherwise people will stop paying for them,' she said.

'I hope you're right,' Richard said.

'So do I,' Nicola said.

Bowman coughed. 'I can't believe I'm saying this, but I'm with the monk on this. This is a bad idea,' he said.

'Keep it to yourself,' Richard said, 'we are doing it.'

'One thing that I've never understood,' Nicola said to Bowman, 'is why you follow this boy around like a dog?'

'Excuse me?' Bowman shot her a heavy look.

'What has he ever given you? You protect him, serve him even, but why?' She asked.

'I don't serve anyone,' Bowman replied.

Richard remembered what Bowman had told him in the forests of Nottinghamshire when he thought death was upon him.

'Don't ask him those things,' Richard said.

Eva caught up with them. 'I was curious of that myself, why do you serve a rude boy?'

'You'll have to pour wine or ale down my throat for hours before I speak on that,' Bowman sped up so his horse went quicker than the cart.

'You've put him in a mood now,' Richard said, 'thanks for that.'

Richard followed the road as it curled around some more low hills and the terrain flattened out. They joined a road that was wider and had been cut with some effort through a forest.

'This is the main road,' Nicola said after half a day's travel, 'it should be busy.'

'We've barely seen a soul,' Brother Geoffrey added.

'I don't think we've seen anyone at all,' Richard said.

Up ahead, Bowman stopped when the road reached a bridge over a gently flowing river. Richard heard the water before he saw it.

The cart and Richard caught up to Bowman and Richard considered the wooden bridge. 'Why have you stopped?' He asked.

Bowman turned his head to the left where a sprawling wood lay a short way off the road. Then he looked over the water. 'The forest is dense on the other side, see how the road curves right away. You can't see down it,' he said.

'We have been promised safe passage,' Nicola said.

Brother Geoffrey fidgeted on the cart's bench. 'I told you all this was the wrong way.'

'Quiet,' Eva joined them and scanned the woods, 'I agree with the blonde man. This is wrong.'

'That's what I told you,' the monk said.

Nicola sighed. 'If you can give me a good reason to turn around, I will gladly do so,' she said, 'there are always more roads to take.'

'I think I can give you a good reason,' Richard said.

'We should never have turned left,' Brother Geoffrey said, 'and it takes this long for you all to agree with me.'

'Everyone,' Richard shouted and the monk recoiled from his voice.

Richard pointed towards the bridge. 'How about that?'

Bowman's hand flew down to his sword.

'Them?' Eva said.

'Of course,' Richard said, 'who else would it be?'

A horseman cantered along the wooden bridge, his horse's hooves clattered loudly and his shield faced the group. It's pattern was red and yellow.

'Eustace,' Bowman hissed.

'We need to turn around,' Richard said as a small group of infantry emerged from the far back and started to cross the river behind the big Martel man.

'Is that all?' Brother Geoffrey asked, 'it's just one knight.'

'Turn the cart around,' Bowman shouted.

Eustace pulled his horse up before the end of the bridge. Richard could see his green eyes clearly, but they were locked on the cart rather than him.

Nicola made her horse turn and the cart bumped off the road and Brother Geoffrey nearly fell off it. The chests bashed into each other and their iron fixings rattled.

'The trees,' Bowman pointed to the woods on their left.

'Stop,' Richard shouted, 'everyone stop.'

Nicola halted Three Legs just as the mare had turned around.

'Why are we stopping?' The monk clutched the side of the cart with white knuckles.

'The crossbowmen along the treeline. There are twenty of them,' Richard said.

'They have clear shots,' Eva groaned.

And you all have no armour, Richard thought. The weight of his mail coat had been forgotten since he'd put it on, but he was the only one of the party who stood any chance at all against a volley of crossbow bolts. Their horses made big targets too.

'Do you want the good news?' Bowman asked.

'I hardly think there is any good news here,' Richard said.

'Your uncle isn't on his way to harm your sister.'

Richard spotted Luke's white tunic with the horizontal blue line. He stood in the middle of the crossbowmen.

Brother Geoffrey went to speak but Nicola elbowed him in the ribs. 'We know, this was a bad route,' she said.

Eustace rode over slowly, no weapon in his hand, and he smiled at Richard. 'Imagine our surprise when we heard about this,' he said.

'Imagine mine when you appeared,' Richard replied.

'The boy has grown some attitude,' the Martel laughed.

'I captured you once, I will do it again.'

'I think you overestimate your situation,' Eustace said, 'but I really, really, do not care about you. I want the cart.'

'The cart is mine,' Nicola said.

'Not the cart, I want the contents. We heard what it is, it's very hard to keep a secret on a campaign. Now, I'm going to be taking the ransom. The question is, will you and your squires keep your crossbows to yourselves and let me take it, or will you make us kill you all?'

'We'll take a few down with us,' Eva said.

'That is why I'm offering you the choice,' Eustace said, 'I lost too many men at Becherel.'

Bowman kept his eyes on Eustace and drew his sword.

'You might kill him,' Richard said to Bowman, 'but the rest of us will die.'

'Maybe that's a price worth paying,' Bowman muttered.

'Do I know you?' Eustace peered at Bowman.

Richard had a terrible feeling that his friend was about to get him killed.

'Of course not,' Richard rode forwards to get in front of Bowman.

'Give me the ransom. Your uncle wants you killed here,' Eustace said, 'but I know the Queen has a soft spot for you. I think she wishes to fill her court full of young men and it makes me sick. I don't want to kill you while we're in her domain because it might make our exit difficult.'

Richard backed Solis up and turned to Bowman. 'Get back, you need to take Eva away,' he said.

Bowman's eyes blinked and he nodded.

Richard's eyes met Nicola's and she nodded and winked back. Richard wondered what that meant as Nicola started to turn her cart back towards the bridge. Then he guessed.

'You can have the cart,' Richard said, 'if you allow the driver and her horse to go free once you've taken it to wherever you want it.'

'I knew you were smarter than your father,' Eustace said, 'he thought he had morals. A backbone. He was weak though, and could never admit it. At least you know when you're beaten.'

'I'm not beaten,' Richard said.

'You are, boy. Now run away with your tail between your legs,' Eustace grinned, 'and you better run fast, because there is nothing I can do if your uncle decides to shoot at you anyway.'

'What sort of a deal is this?' Richard kept backing Solis up.

'The sort that shows you the nature of power,' Eustace waved Nicola onto the bridge and the cart rolled onto it with a bump. Brother Geoffrey jumped off and ran over towards Richard. 'You can't let him take it,' he said.

'Quiet, monk,' Richard said, 'leave it to me.'

Brother Geoffrey ran over to Bowman with his hands raised. 'Let me up.'

Bowman swore and held a hand out for the monk so he could sit on the horse behind him.

'We'll meet again,' Eustace said.

'You can count on it,' Richard turned his horse and in the same movement broke into a canter, 'we need to clear their range.'

'Go,' Bowman shouted and the whole party changed direction as fast as it could.

Richard looked over towards his uncle just as he dropped his arm and shouted something. Richard put his horse into a gallop and Solis put his head down and accelerated. Bolts flashed through the air. Some hit the road, some went overhead. Two hit Eva's men, who without the support of saddles, were knocked straight off their horses.

Our shields are on the wrong side, Richard thought, this was a well-planned ambush. Eustace meant for him to turn around before they shot at them.

A bolt killed one of the Queen's men, and another's horse fell and spilled his rider.

Another Irishman fell from his horse too, but everyone else galloped out of range before the crossbowmen could reload.

Richard pulled up. 'Who is hurt?' He shouted.

Eva rode to a wounded countryman who had a cut on his arm. The man nodded back.

'I'm unhurt,' Brother Geoffrey said.

'Shut up,' Bowman said.

Two of the Queen's men had flesh wounds and some of the horses had grazes, but that was it.

'We need to go back for him,' Eva pointed to an Irishman who had been unhorsed. He sat on the ground rubbing his eyes.

'He's hit his head, I'm fetching him,' Eva turned her horse back around.

'No,' Bowman said, 'they've reloaded.'

The next volley was aimed solely at the dazed man. One bolt skidded off the road surface and sunk into his guts.

'No,' Eva shouted.

Bowman cut his horse in front of hers. 'He's gone,' he shouted.

A bolt hit the man in the shoulder and he twisted to the ground.

'We should go, they could still chase us,' Richard said.

Eva howled in her native tongue at Bowman's face, but turned her chestnut horse around.

'We can still make it to Exoudun,' Brother Geoffrey said, 'Nicola will go there when they free her. If they free her.'

'Yes, let's make our way there,' Richard said, 'and hurry.'

Exoudun sat on the bank of a river, although the treeline along the waterway was so thick that Bowman had to point it out to Richard. A small stone keep kept watch over the village from on top of a steep mound. Richard rode through green fields and a vineyard until he reached the keep. Villagers regarded their arrival through doorways, all disappearing before Richard could make eye contact.

'Surely not am ambush here?' Richard said.

'They're just frightened,' Bowman replied.

'Are you sure this is the right place, monk?' Richard asked.

Brother Geoffrey shrugged. 'God led us here, not I.'

'Dodging responsibility already,' Richard grumbled.

'I remember Earl Patrick saying he was no man of God,' Bowman said.

The monk slid off the back of his horse and rubbed his rear. 'I hate saddles,' he moaned, 'but no saddle is worse.'

The saddleless Eva shook her head at him.

The gate in the palisade swung open and a man in a blue tunic strode out. The tunic was embroidered with some sort of pattern in what Richard thought was gold thread. He knew the man's face.

'You?' Guy of Lusignan looked up at Richard, 'what are you doing here?'

'I came to get my friend back.'

'Oh, William was your friend?'

'Of a sort,' Bowman said.

'I have a mind to kill you now and forgo the ransom,' Guy said, 'you held the barricade and stopped me capturing the Queen. I had no wish to settle for your landless friend.'

Richard remembered Long Tom and his eyes hardened. Richard had quite liked Earl Patrick, too.

'What bothers me with this scene,' Guy put his hands on his hips as some of his retinue joined him, 'is that you have brought a host of squires.'

Guy walked forwards and peered at Eva. 'And some others, I don't even know what they are. But you seem to be lacking in no small way, the actual ransom. Unless you're each carrying a hoard of silver in your underclothes?'

'We had it,' Richard said.

'Oh, you had it,' Guy laughed, 'that's fine then, I'll just hand William over and you can all go home.'

'It was stolen,' Richard said.

'Of course it was. By you, no doubt. You arrive on my lands with armed men and no coin. That old woman with the near-dead horse isn't even here, so why am I to believe that you are anything to do with the deal the two of us made?'

'Nicola drove the cart with the ransom,' Richard said, 'when they release her, she shall ride here.'

'When they release her?' Guy chuckled, 'these thieves are most accommodating it seems. I know when I rob someone, I just kill them. It's simpler that way, and I'm a man of simplicity.'

Richard didn't doubt that for a moment.

'To my simple mind,' Guy was joined by more of his men, and these ones were armed, 'you are trespassing on my land. Either you're here to rob me, or you are the most incompetent rabble who have ever tried to deliver a ransom. Who gets robbed in these parts? Except by me of course.'

'May the Lord have mercy on us,' Brother Geoffrey made the sign of the cross.

'Let me explain,' Richard dismounted and motioned at Solis to stay.

'You like to wave your bravery around, don't you?' Guy's men chuckled with him.

Richard approached Guy.

'Don't bother trying to explain,' the young Lusignan said, 'because you look rag-poor, I won't even bother robbing you today. You can all just go.' He glanced along the group and his eyes settled on Eva. 'Although she is very welcome to stay.'

Eva half-choked. 'You have got to be joking. You're even ruder than him.'

Guy burst into a great laugh. 'I like her. Now, the rest of you can bugger off.'

'Well, that's us told,' Bowman turned his horse away.

Brother Geoffrey looked at Richard and shrugged.

'Really?' Richard said to both of them before walking closer to Guy.

'Boys, we've got a death-seeker,' Guy stepped forwards to meet him.

The Lusignan was half a hand taller than Richard, thinner and with a younger face. Richard felt danger from him too, even more so than he sensed from Eustace. There was something extra in his eyes, and it made Richard want to step back and leave.

Those eyes seemed to pulse. 'I play a game with boys like you,' Guy said, 'I call it Fingers or Freedom.'

'Come on, Richard,' Bowman said, 'no good can come of this.'

'I can explain what happened,' Richard said.

'In my game,' Guy continued, 'I take those who are arrogant and deserving into my castle. A week later, they are offered a choice.'

'Their fingers or their freedom,' Richard sighed, 'I get it, I really do. But can you just let me explain.'

'Fine, but if I don't like it, we're dragging you into my castle for a week,' Guy's eyes twinkled.

'You could try,' Richard said and immediately wished he hadn't. 'Look, we had the ransom in the cart, but my uncle and a thief from the Martel family ambushed us and stole it. They followed us all the way from Brittany just to do it. They agreed to let Nicola go, she'll come here and tell us where they are. You see where I'm going with this?'

'I do,' Guy grinned and Richard saw the grin missed a tooth, 'although I still think you're talking out of your rear-end. The ransom is doubled.'

'Doubled? What?'

'For my time that you're currently wasting,' Guy said, 'doubled.'

'You can't do that,' Richard said.

Guy looked around and his men shrugged or sniggered back. 'Looks like I just did.'

'When Nicola comes back, we can all go and recover your ransom,' Richard fought against himself to take a step forward so he was nose-to-nose with Guy, 'and if I were you, I would be raging at the disrespect of the men who not only stole your ransom, but did it in your lands. Are you going to let that go?'

Guy stared back.

Richard waited.

Guy clapped Richard hard on the shoulder and roared with laughter. 'I know you're trying to manipulate me, but you're right and I'm going to kill each of them for it. Slowly, too.'

Richard held his ground and gaze.

'If,' Guy lost his humour and frowned, 'if Nicola comes back. If she doesn't, do you know what I'm going to do to all of your little party?'

'Play your stupid game,' Richard replied.

'This one gets it,' Guy laughed again, 'I'll give the old woman five days. You had better hope her knackered old horse doesn't drop dead on the way back.'

'She'll be back,' Richard said, 'but I also need to see William to check he is actually still alive. And has all of his fingers.'

'Why would I take his fingers?' Guy said, 'when I already have his freedom.'

Richard groaned inside, this was going to be exhausting.

'I'll take you and a servant to see him, the rest of your band of idiots can stay here. Oh, the woman can come too,' Guy said.

'Where is William?' Richard asked.

'In a much better castle than this one,' Guy replied.

'For that reason only, I'll come with you,' Eva said.

'Why are you letting me take a servant?' Richard asked.

'So that you cannot accuse me of being an ungracious host, of course,' Guy grinned.

'Bowman,' Richard said, 'come with me.'

'Your servant?' Bowman said.

Richard shrugged. 'Do you want to sit in this village for days doing nothing, or come to see William?'

Bowman looked up at the small keep. 'Fine, but there had better be wine.'

There was wine. Castle Lusignan sprawled around a hill that looked down on a large village of same name.

'This is one of the most fortified places I've ever seen,' Bowman sat at a long table that evening, for Lusignan was only a short ride from Exoudun.

'The castle is a big as Dover, and even the village has walls,' Richard peered deeply into a silver cup.

'It's not poisoned,' Bowman burped, 'if it were, I'd be long dead.'

'I can't trust anyone who builds so many walls,' Richard said, 'people fear others to do what they themselves are most likely to do. A man who worries about being attacked by others is likely to be the one who attacks everyone else.'

'Keep your heavy thinking to yourself,' Bowman said.

Richard glanced around Guy's hall. His men drank and sang loudly as servants cleared away plates and bowls. The hall was as large as Tancarville's but more decorated. Whereas the Norman castle had reeked of martial conservatism, Guy's was festooned with tapestries and shiny trinkets that Richard suspected all had reluctant previous owners.

Eva turned her cup around in her hands opposite Bowman.

'You never seen wine before?' He asked.

'Of course, just not much,' she drained the cup, 'although I think I prefer decent Irish mead.'

'Stop staring,' Richard kicked Bowman under the table.

Guy walked over, his cheeks rosy and his eyes glazed. 'I think it's time for you to meet your friend,' he said.

Richard picked up the cup and drank from it.

Guy watched his hand. 'It looks like you already lost a finger,' he laughed, 'maybe you'll avoid my game after all.'

Richard slammed the cup down and stood up. 'Finally.'

He followed Guy down the staircase in the corner of the hall for a few floors, and felt an unexpected sense of nervousness about meeting Sir Wobble again. Mostly because they didn't have his ransom.

Guy reached the basement of the keep, dark, chilly, and with still air. The two guards stepped aside. Behind them a series of cells filled half the basement, barrels the rest.

Richard walked past two cells, one with a family huddled together at the back of it.

'Here we are,' Guy pointed at the last cell.

'You keep him in here?' Richard asked.

'Only at night,' Guy said, 'do you think me a monster?'

Richard raised his eyebrows.

The young Lusignan laughed. 'Someone open the door before I have to do it myself.'

A guard rushed over, fumbled with a set of iron keys, and opened the door.

Sir Wobble stood in the entranceway. 'I thought it sounded like you,' he looked at Richard.

'You look terrible,' Richard said.

Sir Wobble had managed to grow stubble and a thin unkempt beard shrouded his face. His hair had been cut and he was clean, but he was thin and his cheeks looked collapsed.

'Have they been feeding you?' Richard asked.

'See, I told you I was wasting away,' Sir Wobble said to Guy.

'We've been giving him the same amount of food as everyone else,' Guy said, 'and yet all he does is complain. I have to shut him up down here just to get some peace in the evenings.'

'He does eat more than a normal person,' Richard said.

'I told him that, but he never listens,' Sir Wobble pushed Richard aside and walked out of the cell, 'I know you'll have food going spare tonight, I'm going to get some.'

Guy didn't step aside and Sir Wobble bumped into him.

'He doesn't have the ransom,' Guy said.

Sir Wobble slowly turned his head to Richard. 'I don't need a visitor, I need my ransom,' he said.

'Eustace Martel stole it on the way,' Richard said, 'but we're going to get it back. I just wanted to check you are well.'

'Well?' Sir Wobble stepped back, 'he doesn't feed me, doesn't let me ride, and won't give me a weapon to practice with. He hasn't sent anyone at all to treat my thigh.'

'And yet you seem to keep finding nice clean bandages to dress it,' Guy said, 'despite the fact you're locked in here or under supervision.'

Sir Wobble pulled a face at Guy. 'I'm smarter than you,' he said.

'Shouldn't your thigh have healed by now?' Richard asked.

'It would have,' Guy said, 'if he hadn't insisted on showing off to my men.'

Richard sighed. 'I'm going to regret asking, but what did you do?'

'I showed them I'm better than they are,' Sir Wobble crossed his arms.

Guy laughed. 'It was a sight, I'll give him that,' he said.

'His men were throwing stones in the bailey,' Sir Wobble started.

'I know where this is going,' Richard said, 'you had to show them you could throw the stone furthest, and as you did, you ripped your wound open.'

Sir Wobbled grinned. 'Three feet further,' he beamed.

'You're an idiot,' Richard said.

Guy slapped Richard so hard on the back his semi-healed rib vibrated. 'We can agree on that,' he said.

Richard winced.

'I'm still going to kill you, though,' Guy smiled and walked away towards the staircase. 'Don't let the arrogant one out,' he said to the guards.

'Looks like he's keeping you down here, too,' Sir Wobble said to Richard.

'Are you serious?' Richard's eyes widened.

Sir Wobble looked blankly at him.

'He means you,' Richard said.

Sir Wobble sighed. 'Only because he hasn't got to know you yet.'

'You're not very grateful,' Richard said.

'You're not very helpful,' Sir Wobble walked back into his cell and sat down on the straw bed that lay on the dark stones at the back. 'What was the point turning up here without my ransom?'

Richard checked the guards were far away and stepped into the cell. 'We might not have a ransom, but we do have quite a few men,' he said.

Sir Wobble looked up at Richard with an open mouth. 'You are not breaking me out of here,' he said.

'Why not? Don't you want to be free?'

'Of course, but only with my honour intact,' Sir Wobble said.

'What honour?'

'I'm hoping to gain some by refusing your idea.'

'That's ridiculous,' Richard said, 'everyone will be so drunk half way through the night that all we'd need to do is kill those two guards.'

'No,' Sir Wobble reclined onto his bed and folded his arms behind his head.

'You're insufferable,' Richard said.

'You're late,' Sir Wobble said, 'it's been months.'

'I know, I'm sorry, a lot has got in the way.'

'My uncle saved us in England, remember? And things just got in the way of rescuing me and avenging him, did they?'

Richard sighed. 'Yes, a lot did,' he said, 'Long Tim died to earn your ransom.'

Sir Wobble's eyes moved to Richard. 'Really? He didn't care about me.'

'No, but he really did die to get us here quicker,' Richard said, 'I took a crossbow to the chest, and lost this,' he raised his hand with missing little finger.

'You should be more careful,' Sir Wobble said.

'More careful?'

'Or learn how to fight, you don't block an attack with your finger,' Sir Wobble said.

Richard felt heat rise within him. 'You're ungrateful, you know that?'

'I don't know why you bothered coming,' Sir Wobble said, 'being this late is worse than not coming at all.'

'If you knew what we'd been through to get here,' Richard clenched his fists.

'If you knew what I'd been through sitting in this cell, rotting away, wasting one of my best years,' Sir Wobble replied.

'Keep it down in there,' one of the guards shouted.

'Hell can take you,' Richard walked out of the cell, 'see if I care.'

'Don't come back,' Sir Wobble shouted after him.

Richard stormed back up to the hall and slammed himself down onto his chair.

'How is he?' Bowman asked.

'Still himself,' Richard found a jug and poured the contents into his cup without checking what it was.

'Not pleased to see you then?'

Richard emptied his cup. 'Not really. I don't know why we bothered.'

Bowman swayed a little on his chair as he reached for a jug and missed the handle.

'I think you boys are losing sight of why you are here,' Eva said.

Bowman looked at her. 'Can you pass me that wine, by any chance?'

Eva shook her head. 'You wouldn't last a moment in Ireland.'

'These southerners are not as bad as we'd thought,' Bowman said, 'they eat and drink and sing. This isn't such a bad place,'

'He will think differently in the morning,' Richard said to Eva, 'I wish he wouldn't drink.'

'Are you his nursemaid?' Eva asked.

Richard narrowed his eyes. 'Stay out of it, I just want to get drunk and fall asleep,' he said.

'You could be nicer to him,' Eva said, 'from what I've heard, you pay him neither coin nor respect.'

'You sound like my wife, or Nicola, or the other people who've said that,' Richard sighed.

'I don't need his respect,' Bowman stretched to drag the jug over himself.

A fight erupted on the far side of the hall and two men bundled to the floor to a chorus of cheers.

Bowman turned to watch and knocked the jug over. Light red liquid splashed over the table and narrowly missed Eva.

'Had that touched me, we'd be having a very different conversation,' she said, 'but tell me, how did the two of you meet?'

Richard didn't tell her.

Bowman held his hands up. 'I'm sorry, my lady, no harm was meant.' He sat back down. 'I met this one when he was a mere boy. I'd spent a decade fighting for anyone who'd pay me, or doing what I had to do so I wouldn't starve. My family had been torn apart when I was younger, the Martels saw to that, and my mother carried off to live with the head of their family. Which is where she remains, they even had a son who tried to kill me not so long ago.'

'That's quite a rush through a life story,' Eva said.

Bowman yawned. 'I'm tired.'

'So you met Richard, why stay with him?'

'Stop asking me questions,' Bowman said, 'he always means well, that's what it is. He tries to do the right thing, although he messes it up every single time. I never knew anyone who always tried so hard. If everyone thought like he does, the world would be a better place.'

Eva blinked. 'I was not expecting that.'

Richard looked at Bowman. 'I think he's about to be sick.'

'I'm fine,' Bowman stood up, 'but I know when I've drunk enough, so I'm going to bed.'

'Enough was a long time ago,' Richard said.

Bowman staggered away and Eva looked at Richard. 'Do you always try to do the right thing?' She asked.

Richard laughed. 'What is the right thing?'

Guy left his table and came over to sit at Bowman's empty place. 'What happened to my table?' he looked down at the wet red stain.

'Your hospitality,' Richard replied.

'The old woman just came back,' Guy said.

'Nicola? Already?'

'What other old woman do we both know? Yes,' Guy said, 'she has gone to her bed, but she has told me where my ransom is.'

'And?' Richard asked.

Guy smiled. 'Not far from here, along the river, is a castle. One that sits near some very favourable vineyards as it happens. Nicola said these Martels are celebrating in some style tonight, their success is overflowing.'

Richard straightened up. 'So tomorrow?'

'Tomorrow,' Guy said, 'they will still be as pissed rats who drowned in an ale barrel.'

'It looks to me,' Eva replied, 'that all of your men are currently well on their way to becoming similar rats.'

'They are Lusignan men, they can handle it,' Guy grinned, his missing tooth leaving a black hole in his smile.

'So what are we going to do?' Richard asked.

'We'll prepare and sail up the river as soon as possible. We'll be in disguise and slip into the castle. Apparently the ransom is in the keep, so we'll find our way in there while they sleep off their drink. Then smuggle it out.'

'As easy as that?' Richard said.

'As easy as that,' Guy said, 'what can go wrong?'

BROTHERS IN ARMS

The Lusignan knights and squires huddled down in the hold of the flat-bottomed barge looked utterly miserable.

'I wish this cursed barge wouldn't rock from side to side,' Bowman pulled his cloak more over his eyes.

'It's not rocking,' Richard replied, 'we're on a river, not the sea.'

One of the squires moved to the side of the barge and threw up over the side.

The bargeman shot the man a withering look. 'Better not have got any on my boat,' he said in a thick accent.

Guy and Eva were the only occupants of the barge who were as awake as Richard, and the three of them sat at the bow of the vessel as it made its final turn on their journey.

'That's the one. It's called The Pinnacle,' Guy said.

The castle had been built out into the river where a wooden jetty stuck out like pointing finger into the waterway. The castle walls rose up high and were studded with a number of tall, thin towers. The riverbank was lined with bushy green trees that partially obscured the green meadowland beyond.

Richard picked up the crossbow that had lain by his feet during their night-time voyage.

'Keep that hidden,' Eva said, an unstrung bow by her feet. She knelt down on the wooden bottom of the barge and started to string it.

Richard looked back at Guy's men. They might not be visible from the jetty, so the plan might at least get off to a good start.

Bowman sat with his back against the sides of their vessel and burped. He pushed himself up and looked ahead. 'I'd hoped we'd have another day before we got here,' he said.

'Shut up and string your bow,' Richard said, 'you didn't have to drink so much.'

'I didn't know we'd be embarking on a robbery this morning,' Bowman held the bow up to Eva.

She snatched it from him and started to string it for him. Two sheaves of arrows lay in bundles on the deck by their feet.

Richard turned his eyes to the meadow at the sound of horses and talking. Bowman squinted his eyes in the same direction. 'Two riders,' he said.

Richard saw them through the trees, flashes of colour between the trunks and branches.

'They've both got hawks,' Bowman said, 'it's your uncle.'

'Good, it's better if he's out,' Richard said.

'Those hawks on their hands,' Bowman said, 'you hunt with those on your own. Which is a shame, because it means they haven't taken any of their men out with them.'

'I can't see any birds,' Guy said.

'You're not looking hard enough,' Bowman chuckled.

'The other man will be Eustace,' Richard said.

'Good,' Bowman replied, 'I'd rather not face him until I'm a bit more awake.'

The bargeman turned and slowed his vessel as it approached the jetty. It glided up to dock in silence. Guy jumped over onto the wooden platform with the ship's rope and tied it in place. Wooden steps led up from the jetty to the stone castle wall, where a sturdy looking door was guarded by a solitary figure.

'He looks as bad as our lot,' Richard said.

The guard was asleep at the foot of the door and Richard could even hear him snore.

'This plan might actually work,' Richard got to his feet.

Guy walked up to the sentry, who woke up when the Lusignan's shadow fell over him. From the barge, Richard couldn't hear him, and they had a short conversation. The sentry stood up and walked past Guy towards the barge.

Behind him, Guy casually drew a knife, put one arm around the man and slit his throat. The look of surprise stayed on the guard's face as his last breath escaped him and Guy guided his body down quietly onto the wooden boards. Guy bent over and rummaged for a key, which he found. Richard picked up his crossbow and everyone started to leave the barge.

'We're in, boys,' Guy said as he fitted the key into the door and heard the lock disengage with a heavy clunk.

Richard felt the weight of his double-mail shirt as they walked up the steps behind Eva, who had been lent mail of her own. It was too large for her, but only fractionally, and was hidden beneath a faded old straw-coloured dress.

'Remember the plan,' Richard said, 'Eva goes first, scouts the castle and comes back. Everyone else is quiet and out of sight. We don't want to be noticed.'

Guy pushed the door open and peered up the dark tunnel that led somewhere into the castle. He turned back to Richard, licked his lips and grinned. 'Change of plan. I think I want to be noticed.'

Bowman groaned behind Richard.

Guy walked up into the tunnel and his men started to follow him.

'He's mad,' Richard said, 'he's going to get us killed.'

'I think so,' Bowman clapped him on the shoulder on his way in, 'but he's not boring.'

'Wait,' Richard said as he was left alone by the door, 'are you calling me boring?'

Bowman's laugh reverberated down the tunnel.

Fine, Richard thought and slid a bolt from the bag around his waist into place on the crossbow, 'if that's how he wants to do it, then so be it.'

Richard walked up the dark tunnel, which emerged into a storeroom that in turn led out into the bailey of the castle.

He stepped into the yard and into a scene of chaos. Guy and most of his men were running towards the keep where Nicola had said the ransom was, while the rest stood around loosing arrows and crossbow bolts up at the guards on the walls. The guards started to crumple but some shouted the alarm. Shouts and cries rose up from every corner of the castle.

Bowman and Eva waited for Richard, arrows on their bows.

'You are right, he is quite mad,' Eva said.

Bowman yawned. He raised his bow at a figure on the far castle wall who ran across the parapet. He loosed his arrow. It sailed up and clattered into the wall behind the Martel guard. 'It's too early for this,' Bowman grumbled.

Eva loosed her arrow next, which skidded onto the parapet at the man's feet. He half jumped to avoid it then disappeared into one of the tall towers.

'Mine was closer,' Eva said.

Martel men started to appear from a gallery of buildings built along the inside of the castle wall. Richard aimed his crossbow and shot his bolt. He had ten men to aim at, none in armour. The bolt embedded itself in the wooden roof above them.

Bowman coughed and Eva laughed. They loosed their arrows and both hit Martel men as they tried to scramble out and fight with Guy's.

A loose melee broke out in the yard, men appearing from all corners to fight the more heavily armed intruders. Bowman and Eva advanced and shot arrows at close quarters into whoever crossed their path. Richard reloaded his crossbow and followed. He glanced over to the keep, but Guy and his men had gone so Richard assumed they would be inside retrieving the ransom. He looked up at the walls where only a single target remained, a man aiming a crossbow. The guard shot it and the bolt hit a Lusignan squire in the shoulder, pushing him down onto one knee. Richard lifted his crossbow and squeezed the trigger. The bolt flew over the man's head and Richard swore. The crossbowman's next bolt hit a Lusignan knight in the leg and the man collapsed screaming with the bolt stuck in his calf. Richard's next shot hit the battlement behind the crossbowman, who turned his head and looked right at him.

Richard swore again and tried to reload as quickly as he could. He could see that his opponent was faster, so he looked for cover. Nicola's cart lay in the centre of the yard so Richard sprinted to it and threw himself down behind its wooden frame. A crossbow bolt smacked into it a hand's breadth from his head. He finished reloading and positioned to shot. He loosed the bolt and it flew up between his target's legs and snapped in half after it hit the wall again.

'Bowman,' Richard shouted as the enemy slid a new bolt into place.

Bowman looked over and Richard pointed up to the wall.

The blonde man raised his bow and loosed an arrow without thought before turning back to the main fight. His arrow hit the Martel man in the chest and he staggered backwards and leant onto the battlements.

Richard watched him for a moment as a single arrow rarely killed quickly, but the man sunk down and looked down at his wound instead of fighting on.

Bowman's half-brother, Nicholas Martel, rallied the men in the yard and started to move them towards a hall near the keep. Guy's men fought them on the move, reducing their number with each step they took.

Richard checked the walls were clear and moved to where Bowman and Eva tried to get around the melee to shoot into it from the side.

'Your half-brother's here,' Richard said to Bowman.

'I know, I saw the bastard.'

'Who?' Eva asked.

'A Martel bastard,' Bowman said, 'he nearly killed me.'

'Your brother is one of the enemy?' Eva loosed her last arrow which hit a man square in the face.

'I only met him once,' Bowman replied as Nicholas entered the hall and Martel men fought a rearguard on their way into it.

'But he tried to kill you?' Eva cast her eyes around for reusable arrows on the ground.

'I have started to wonder if it was just a misunderstanding,' Bowman said.

'You're getting soft,' Richard said.

Bowman drew his knife and walked over to the trail of bodies that marked the path of his half-brother's retreat. Bowman stabbed the knife down into a wounded Martel squire.

'He does not look so soft to me,' Eva said to Richard.

'Don't take his side.'

Guy emerged from the keep, followed by a string of his men carrying wooden chests.

'I don't know how this worked,' Richard said.

'It's quite simple really,' Eva shrugged, 'their men were hungover and wearing no armour.'

'I know,' Richard said as Guy arrived at the hall which his men had declined to enter.

'How many are in there?' Guy asked.

'Two dozen,' one of his knights answered.

'Well,' Guy said, 'the ransom is secured so we don't need to waste anyone by charging in there.' He walked up to the door which had been slammed shut. 'Who is in command?' he shouted.

Nicholas shouted back. 'I am. I'm a son of Geoffrey Martel.'

'Oh, so you think you're worth a ransom, do you?' Guy said.

'My father is rich.'

'I know who you father is,' Guy replied, 'but I do have to say, I'm sick of ransoms. I really don't want to go through all this again, however rich you are.'

Guy walked away from the hall back to his men. 'I'm bored. Fire it,' he said.

Two of his knights ran off into the keep, Richard assumed to find some fire.

'A son of the great Martel,' Guy laughed when he reached Richard.

'It's Bowman's half-brother.'

'Really?' Guy looked at Bowman who nodded back.

'I thought you were a bit of a country-fool, a good laugh but just a common soldier. So you're noble, are you?'

'I've been called many things,' Bowman yawned again, 'first time I've been called that.'

'You want your brother alive or dead?' Guy asked.

'I haven't decided,' Bowman said, 'although the rest of the Martel brood all need putting down.'

'Ah, you hate them, hatred is good,' Guy said, 'it focuses the mind.'

'I don't hate Nicholas, how can I? He's my blood.'

Richard knew how to, and he wondered how long his uncle would be gone hawking.

'I have a proposition for you,' Guy said, 'if you can be the one who fires the hall, or shoots your brother through a window, I'll give you this castle.'

'What?' Bowman said.

'What?' Richard echoed.

'I came here for the ransom,' Guy said, 'but it rather looks like I've accidentally taken the castle. The lands here are rich, so I'd be a fool to just walk away from it. But I expect the Martels will be keen to get it back, so it would suit me to install a castellan who is highly motivated to resist them. One who they can't bribe.'

Bowman looked at Richard and back to Guy. 'Right. I'm not sure how to answer that,' he said.

Guy laughed. 'I will turn those spurs from iron into gold. But you have to burn or shoot your brother.'

'Maybe he's just been brought up wrong,' Bowman said, 'maybe I just need to show him who I am, and we can be true brothers.'

Guy sighed. 'I'm not looking for sentimentality. I'm looking for ruthlessness and decisiveness. I'll make it easier for you, you shoot your brother, or you will never leave this castle alive.'

Richard threw down his crossbow and drew his sword.

'See,' Guy pointed at Richard, 'that is the decisiveness I'm after. Although it was more stupid than ruthless.'

'I see what you mean,' Eva said to Bowman, 'good intentions but completely messes it up.'

Guy laughed, and Richard relaxed his stance seeing as no one was taking him seriously.

The young Lusignan laughed harder at Richard. 'Your blonde friend told me that every time you use your sword, you tend to drop it.'

'Thanks a lot,' Richard said.

Bowman shrugged. 'He was giving me a lot of wine.'

The knights re-emerged from the keep with two flaming torches held aloft.

'Time's up,' Guy said, 'shoot your brother or I'll throw you into the hall before it burns.'

'Just do it, he'll burn it anyway,' Eva said.

Richard glanced at her. 'Really?'

Bowman grunted and placed his last arrow onto his bow. He looked over to Guy.

'You can try that,' the Lusignan said, 'but you'll need more than one arrow to kill me.'

Bowman sighed. He walked around to the side of the hall.

'Although it would have shown me the ruthlessness I was talking about,' Guy laughed.

Bowman stalked around the hall trying to look in through the windows.

'I haven't got all day,' Guy shouted.

Bowman raised his bow, took a careful aim, then shot. A cry rang out from inside the hall. 'There you are,' Bowman lowered his bow, 'happy now?'

Guy nodded. 'As long as you shot the right man, yes.'

Bowman's face was impassive.

'Burn it,' Guy shouted.

'Wait,' Bowman cried.

'Oh, you did shoot the wrong man did you? Trying to fool me? Sneaky bastard,' Guy said.

'Nicholas has an arrow in him, so don't fire the hall,' Bowman said, 'let them out.'

Guy shrugged. 'They can leave if they wish to, I'm not stopping them. Fire it.'

His knights held their torches up to the thatch that hung down to just above the windows. The flames licked the thatch which started to steam off the morning dew. Richard could hear shouts from within the hall as the fire started to take hold, quickly spreading up the roof.

He remembered Sir Wobble's story about his father and the lead roof, and wondered what it would be like to be standing inside the hall as the roof caught on fire.

He got part of an answer when the door flew open and coughing Martel men started to stream out. The fire spread further up the thatch and smoke started to seep out from the windows.

Guy's men ringed around the doorway and lowered weapons at the smoked-out garrison. The last man out of the hall was Nicholas Martel, clutching an arrow sticking out of his shoulder. 'We surrender,' he said, 'please spare the men.'

Guy laughed. 'I don't remember asking for your surrender.' He turned to Richard. 'Do you remember me asking for their surrender?'

'No,' Richard replied reluctantly.

The men coughed their lungs clear as the threat of Lusignan iron kept them in place. Richard thought there might be more Martel men than Lusignans.

'Grant us safe passage and we won't give you any trouble,' Nicholas used his other hand to try to stem the blood that started to stain his mustard-coloured tunic.

'Throw the weapons you still carry back into the hall, then I swear not to kill you,' Guy said.

Nicholas ordered his men to comply. They tossed some swords and spears back into the hall, which roared and sent a plume of black smoke up into the morning air.

Nicholas approached Guy. 'Thank you for acting with honour,' he said.

Guy chuckled. 'I swore not to kill you. I didn't say anything about my men. Kill the garrison.'

'No,' Richard shouted.

Bowmen stepped forwards to protest, but by then the volley of crossbow bolts had already withered the defenceless Martel soldiers. Before their bodies hit the ground, the Lusignans closed on them and in a flurry of swords and long knives butchered them in a moment.

'You gave your word,' Nicholas watched in horror as the last of his men who lay wounded on the ground were finished off.

'I did,' Guy said, 'and I feel like I'm repeating myself, but I swore not to kill anyone myself. And I actually did tell your half-brother to kill you or I'd kill him, so there's that matter to discuss, too.'

Bowman's fingers went white gripping his bow. 'You told me to stick an arrow in him,' he pointed the bow at his brother, 'and I have done that.'

Guy blinked twice then shrugged. 'I see you've played me at my own game, there,' he started to laugh.

Richard wondered if he did anything other than laugh or shout.

'You can finish him off, now,' Guy said, 'if you like. I'm quite impressed with you actually, no one has ever tried that on me before.'

'I'm not killing him,' Bowman said.

Nicholas's eyes widened. 'You? From the forest. What are you doing here?'

'Eustace never recognised me,' Bowman said, 'and your wound failed to kill me.'

'I can see that. Why are you trying to keep me alive?'

'Maybe I'm getting old,' Bowman said, 'but part of me wants to give you a chance.'

'Me a chance? You're the criminal,' Nicholas said.

'I'm bored,' Guy said, 'who wants the honour of killing this one?'

Four of Guy's knights walked towards the Martel Bastard.

'Don't do it,' Bowman shouted.

The knights rushed to get there first and Nicholas started to back away.

'Yield to me,' Richard shouted.

'What?' Nicholas looked at him and Richard saw the fear in his eyes.

'Yield to me, quickly,' Richard ran to him.

'No, no, no,' Guy shouted, 'gut him.'

Nicholas dropped to his knees and held his working hand up to Richard. 'I yield to you,' he said.

'I accept,' Richard looked up, 'he is now my prisoner and under my protection.'

The knights stopped and looked at Guy.

'Can he just do that?' Eva asked Bowman.

'Yes,' Bowman said, 'those are the rules of war. They're not always followed to the letter, but the whole idea of knighthood is built on taking prisoners with honour.'

Guy sighed. 'I'm never going to hear the end of this. The day Guy of Lusignan was bested by an English poacher and a knight with less land than my saddler.'

Nicholas let out a deep breath. 'Thank you so much,' he said to Richard.

'I honestly don't know why I did that,' Richard said, 'you would have hung us in England.'

'You poached on my family's land, that is the law.'

Bowman walked to them. 'Once that bolt is out of you and we're away from here, we will talk,' he said.

The Martel Bastard nodded.

'The ransom is on the barge, my men will clean this place up and garrison it for now,' Guy said, 'if you want to see your hungry friend, get on the boat.'

Richard wasn't sure that he did want to see Sir Wobble, but

they all made their way down the tunnel and onto the barge. Ransom safely in the hold, the bargeman pushed off from the jetty and they started to make their way back to Castle Lusignan.

'You should bind his hands,' Guy said to Richard.

Richard looked at Nicholas, whose face had lost some of its colour.

'I don't think he's going to swim for it,' he said.

'Suit yourself,' Guy went down to the chests and made himself comfortable in a pile of blankets. 'But if you wouldn't mind being quiet, I have God's own hangover to sleep off.'

The barge reached Lusignan just as the sun dipped below the hill to the west. An orange glow spread out from the hill's summit for a while but started to fade by the time Richard went back inside the castle's hall. He threw himself down on a chair and stretched his legs out.

The hall was mostly empty and quiet with only a few of the garrison drinking near the hearth. Bowman gathered two jugs of wine from empty tables and put them down on theirs.

'You want to drink again?' Richard asked, 'are you not still ill from last night?'

'That was last night, young lord,' Bowman grinned, 'this is a different night.'

'Normally, I'd agree with your young lord,' Eva said, 'but after today I'll have some of your southern wine.'

Guy entered the hall with a pair of spurs in his hand. He threw them on the table in front of Bowman with a clatter.

'Golden spurs?' Bowman asked.

'They're yours if you want them,' Guy said.

Bowman looked at the finely crafted rowel spurs which reflected the light of the hearth. They looked alive in the dimly lit hall.

'Who can make a knight?' Eva asked.

'Any other knight,' Richard said.

'So you could have done it yourself?'

Richard folded his arms. 'It's not as simple as that, normally it's done before battle, or when there is land to give the new knight.'

'And I have land to give him,' Guy said, 'all you have to do is pay homage to me as your lord, and that castle and all its land is yours.'

The gold of the spurs reflected in Bowman's eyes. They meant a new future for him, one of landed nobility.

'Think about it if you have to,' Guy said, 'just make your mind up before I fall asleep tonight.'

Richard looked away from the spurs. 'We need to talk about William's ransom.'

Guy smiled. 'It would be churlish of me to refuse his freedom after we got the ransom back, seeing as I came out of the day a whole castle richer,' he said.

'But?' Richard said.

'No buts this time,' Guy sighed, 'your friend, if I have to be honest, has been a royal pain in my backside. All he does is complain. He whinges about not having enough breakfast, he moans that he can't ride, he repeatedly asks for somewhere better to sleep. I am sick of him. I'm letting him go, on the condition that he is gone before midday tomorrow, and he never comes back to Poitou again.'

'I'm sure he can agree to that,' Richard said.

'You can tell him the good news,' Guy said, 'I don't want to.'

Richard got up, left Bowman looking at the spurs, and found his way back down to the cells. The guards let him in and he found Sir Wobble fast asleep on his straw bed. The cell smelt of damp and a trio of white mushrooms grew in one corner.

'Wake up,' he kicked the bed.

Sir Wobble's eyes half opened and he groaned. 'What do you want?'

'Do you know where we've been?'

'Yes, those of the garrison they left behind told me,' Sir Wobble said.

'You'll be pleased to know we brought your ransom back, and Guy has agreed to let you go,' Richard said, 'we'll leave in the morning.'

'Really?' Sir Wobble sat up, 'it's over?'

Richard nodded.

Sir Wobble stretched his arms and got to his feet. 'It should have been over long ago,' he stabbed a finger into Richard's chest, right on his painful rib, and stalked off out of the cell.

Richard sighed and followed him back to the hall.

'You look terrible,' Bowman said as Sir Wobble sat down and looked for something to eat.

'So do you.'

Richard joined them. 'The Queen offered you a job,' he said, 'well, she offered it to me first, but I turned it down.'

Sir Wobble glanced at him. 'What sort of job?'

'She wants you in her household.'

'Household?' Sir Wobble cracked a faint smile, 'that is a big step up from serving Lord Tancarville. I could really make a name for myself.'

'I was hoping you could come back with me to Yvetot instead,' Richard said, 'the Little Lord is on his way there and we need to stop him once and for all.'

'Why would I help you after you left me rotting in this prison?'

'Because Sophie and Sarjeant could be holed up in the castle with the King's squires, trying to hold out against the Little Lord. Who you don't like, either.'

'It isn't really much of a choice,' Sir Wobble said, 'protect some little castle no one has ever heard of, or go to a royal court with earls and dukes and the best knights in Christendom.'

'You're picking the Queen over your friends?'

'Friends?' Sir Wobble said louder than he'd intended, 'what have you ever done for me?'

'He's got you there,' Bowman laughed.

Richard frowned. 'Delivered your ransom here for one, not to mention fight my way across Brittany to earn it. I broke a rib, nearly lost an eye, and actually did lose a finger for you. What more do you want?'

'Do you know what it's like to be left in a cell at night?' Sir Wobbled asked, 'to not be allowed to leave one castle for months? To see the same river, same trees, same insignificant and talentless people every day?'

'I got here as quickly as I could,' Richard said.

'Well it wasn't quick enough,' Sir Wobble shouted, his cheeks red.

'I don't think I've ever seen him get angry,' Bowman said.

'I nearly died saving you at the nunnery,' Sir Wobble said, 'coming here balances that. You owe me a few months. I'm going to serve the Queen and make a name for myself, and in a few months I'll come and see if you need my help. Then we'll be even.'

'My wife could be dead by then,' Richard said.

'You should have thought of that while you had all the fun in Brittany,' Sir Wobble said.

Richard held his four-fingered hand up. 'It wasn't all that much fun,' he said.

'Also,' Sir Wobble said, 'you seem to have forgotten my uncle, who died at the treachery of that Lusignan, and you haven't even tried to take vengeance. Instead, you go on a raid with him, and have even more fun without me. I've had to look on the man who murdered my uncle every single day.'

'Is that what this is about?' Richard asked, 'you feel left out?'

'I don't care,' Sir Wobble said, 'I don't care about Yvetot, or you either.'

'Don't be like that,' Richard said, 'if you hadn't fallen asleep at Niort, the ambush might never have happened.'

Sir Wobble reached for a sword that wasn't there. 'You dare blame me for Patrick's death? How dare you, I'll slit your throat.'

'Calm down, boys,' Eva said.

'Who are you?' Sir Wobble asked.

'Someone who cares for a peaceful night,' she said.

Sir Wobble got up. 'I care that I'm starving, I'm going to the kitchen,' he said.

'That was intense,' Eva said once he was gone.

'He's just feeling emotional after being set free,' Richard said.

'Sounded pretty serious to me,' Bowman said.

'What about you?' Richard asked, 'are you going to leave me too? You haven't taken your eyes off those spurs.'

Guy came back. 'The day is catching up with me, so it's time to decide. What will it be?'

Bowman sighed. 'These are certainly a fine pair of spurs,' he said.

Richard swallowed.

'I am going to keep the spurs,' Bowman said.

'Very sensible choice,' Guy beamed, 'I know you'll enjoy your new castle.'

'You can't,' Richard said. The idea of a world without Bowman suddenly made him feel very lonely.

'But,' Bowman continued, 'you can keep your castle. You see, Richard here thinks the world is a romance. He is naive and foolish and a tad boring. But you, you're fun and unpredictable.'

'I don't understand,' Guy furrowed his brow, 'those are my best features, why are you rejecting me?'

'Because, respectfully, you're insane,' Bowman said.

Eva spat her mouthful of wine out over the table.

'Insane?' Guy said.

'You're mad,' Bowman said, 'truly mad. There is no doubt you would get me killed. Now Richard, while good at heart, will also certainly get me killed, but dying for him gives me the smallest chance of avoiding hell. Dying for you would put me at the burning centre of it.'

'That's quite a rejection,' Guy looked at Bowman.

Richard felt a tear in his eye and tried to wipe it away without anyone noticing.

'I'll help you, young lord, we'll go and fight to save Yvetot,' Bowman said, 'then we'll find that silver in the crypt and go and find out about your father.'

Richard sniffed. 'Thank you,' he said.

'While we're at it, we'll deal with that shit of a Tancarville once and for all,' Bowman said.

'I've never seen the like,' Guy said, 'the two of you are truly brothers in arms.'

HISTORICAL NOTE

My first book was the non fiction work 'The Rise and Fall of the Mounted Knight' which I created in part to dispel some of the myths surrounding the medieval knight. That desire to reflect their world as accurately as possible transferred over to this series of novels, including some of the characters. For example, Richard's father William Keynes did capture King Stephen at the Battle of Lincoln in 1141, the kind of deed that is not easily forgotten. Lord William Tancarville was the very real, and very famous, Chamberlain of Normandy, who did have an academy of aspiring knights training at Castle Tancarville. Tancarville was entitled to the silver basins used when he helped to wash the King's hands, and it is a fact that he did take advantage of that privilege to collect the King's silver basins as he did in Golden Spurs. Tancarville was a fiery character with a temper; he did murder another noble and was probably quite unpredictable to be around. He probably suffered from some very real anger issues, and as his life went on, some loyalty issues bubbled up as well, so leaving the King's Breton campaign in murky circumstances is very much in-character. Sir Roger de Cailly, who was really from England, and Sir John de la Londe, did both serve Lord Tancarville and both witnessed surviving charters he issued, although little is known of their characters and temperaments.

The attack of the Flemings and Count of Boulogne on Neufchâtel did happen in 1166, and Lord Tancarville rode there in response to their invasion. The Chamberlain led the defence with the soon-to-be Earl of Essex William Mandeville, who in general tried desperately hard to make up for his father's rebellions against Henry II. Mandeville was known as a dashing knight and is closer to the modern romantic image of that warrior class than Tancarville was.

Sir Wobble was a very real person too. He actually had a nickname close to Sir Gobble because he was noted for his tendency to both eat and sleep in large quantities. When he tried to charge into Tancarville's front rank at Neufchâtel and was rebuffed by his lord, those words from Lord Tancarville are quoted from Sir Wobble's biography commissioned in the early thirteenth century. Believe it or not, the skirmish around Castle Peacock happened, if that biography is trustworthy (and historians think it is), and Golden Spurs tried to be faithful to that account. When Sir Wobble was chided and mocked by Mandeville after the battle for failing to capture anyone, not even a bridle, Mandeville's words are again quoted from the historical record. In later life, Sir Wobble used the event as a cautionary tale for younger knights to avoid making the same mistake he did. That is, the business of a knight wasn't really even the defeat of the enemy so much as the personal capture of a few of them. This emphasise on looking out for oneself is at the heart of twelfth century knighthood, for the chivalry of later years did not yet exist. Sir Wobble is the ideal personification of the selfish but perhaps proto-chivalric ideals of knighthood of his time.

Sir Wobble was also the nephew of Earl Patrick of Salisbury, who was indeed killed by Guy of Lusignan in an ambush in Poitou whilst escorting Eleanor of Aquitaine. Sir Wobble charged the Lusignans by himself, in a rage, once his uncle had died, and really did receive a wound in his thigh from behind while backed up against a hedge. Even the story from his captivity where he tore his wound open while proving he could throw a stone further than anyone else is (quite probably) true. He even convinced someone to smuggle in fresh bandages to him in loaves of bread, which is hinted at in this book.

The arms and armour used in the twelfth century have also been reflected as best as I could in these books. Richard's use of two mail shirts is potentially accurate. The phrase 'double-mail' appears in medieval records, although we don't yet know if it meant two layers of mail, or twice as many rings used in a denser weave, or any other interpretation of the term. What we do know, is that it was considered to make the wearer pretty much invulnerable. In accounts of the Battle of Bouvines in 1214, the invulnerability of the knights is stressed by more than one source; indeed to kill them, you had to stab them through their vision-slits as even their leg armour was laced into their main hauberks. As well as almost every sword cut, mail armour did frequently keep out arrows as well. There are references to Christian infantry during the Third Crusade looking like hedgehogs due to the number of arrows hanging out of their iron mail. Twelfth century crossbows were not as powerful as their more advanced fifteenth century counterparts, so were not quite as lethal as we usually think of them. Modern tests have shown that mail made to a historical specification can keep out a crossbow of thirteenth century spec, so it is possible that Richard could survive a close range shot wearing two layers of it.

Arrows don't kill someone struck in the stomach instantly either, despite what Hollywood might show us. It would likely take many of them to stop an adrenaline-powered charging horse, and writing accurately on warhorses, as well as their care, was very important to me. I am lucky enough to ride two horses a day, including one veteran warhorse who I've jousted on for years. This has included open-field jousting, that is using a lance against an opponent with no barrier to keep us seperate, and sometimes not in a straight line. Occasionally not one-on-one either, and this attempt to re-create the thirteenth century tournament has given me a tiny insight into how Richard might have approached riding into battle on Solis. I've had my hearing ring when swords crash into my helmet, and had steel swords bite into my face. My nose still carries one scar. These visceral experiences, while they're happening, drag you back in time and open a small window to the knightly past.

Horse size is probably the main myth that drove the creation of The Rise and Fall of the Mount Knight, for almost everyone's default assumption is that knight's rode large horses to war. These assumptions have come from older books, film and TV, and sometimes even professors and teachers, so is an understandable one. However, archaeological remains from the medieval period paint a picture of twelve/thirteen hand horses, that grow from the 11th century up to fifteen hand horses at the end of the 15th. The Bayeux Tapestry shows us thin, finely built horses with small enough bodies that their Norman rider's legs swing far bellow their bellies. They can be no shire horses! The seal of the twelfth century knight Raymond le Gros shows him on a horse so slight it is a wonder he could be carried into battle on it. It took careful breeding to bring the size of horses up over centuries, but we don't just have a few skeletal remains or even artwork to go from. The very best, and irrefutable evidence comes from surviving horse armour and saddlery from the fifteenth century. Surviving wooden war saddles by their very nature show us exactly how wide horses were, and give us a clue to length, too. Of these saddles, I have never seen one wide enough to fit any modern well-fed horse. The full metal horse armours that survive tell us exactly how big the horses were in the late fifteenth century, and even then they are not likely larger than a modern Iberian horse at around fifteen hands. The evidence for this discussion continues, but the final piece that nails it for me is the simple practicality of mounting the horse. Knights were frequently unhorsed in battle, where they would be wearing their armour. To be unable to remount on their own, because their horse was tall, would make the whole concept of a mounted knight laughable. A horse of thirteen or fourteen hands could be remounted by any self-respecting knight, on his own, when his life depended on it. We can get onto our modern fifteen hand horses in full plate armour from the ground, but even then avoid doing so because of the strain it puts on their backs. A medieval battle lends to very different requirements for a warhorse than the sweeping charges of the Napoleonic era – good things can come in small packages.

The second horse I ride is in part the inspiration for Solis. Squire is a Palomino Iberian horse whose head is mostly vacant, but has the tendency to do things that you wouldn't expect. Whilst fighting with poleaxes in our riding-arena, with him loose so he could see and learn what we were doing, Squire, instead of being wary of full contact fighting, ran over and tried to catch a poleaxe in mid-air. The idea that he could have received a blow to his own face doesn't seem to have crossed his mind. He has also picked up sticks and chased around other horses with them in his mouth, flailing it at them like a whip. The list goes on, but however outlandish an action Solis might undertake in these books, you can be rest assured there is real-life inspiration behind it.

If you're interested further in the historical side of Richard's adventures, check out 'The Rise and Fall of the Mounted Knight' on Amazon.

Next up - Book Three in The Legend of Richard Keynes series:

Dogs of War

Sign up to the mailing list on the author's website below to be the first to hear when new books are released.

But if you can't wait, investigate the author's non-fiction work:

The Rise and Fall of the Mounted Knight

www.clivehart.net

Printed in Great Britain
by Amazon